BLIND MAN
AND THE QUEEN

by G. Dan Buford
978-0-9718191-4-6   Separate But Equal
978-0-9745310-5-2   My Baby's Father

by Guichard Cadet
0-9718191-2-2   The Canon of Loose Cannons
0-9718191-0-6   Bard From Par Taken
0-9647635-4-0   The Masks of Flipside
0-9647635-0-8   LoneWolf's Cry

Other La Caille Nous Titles

0-9718191-5-7   Pick-Up Lines
                       Michael T. Owens

0-9718191-3-0   Backfield in Motion
                       Undra E. Biggs

0-9647635-6-7   When You Look At Me
                       Undra E. Biggs

0-9647635-2-4   The A# Blu's
                       William Laurence Jones

BLIND MAN
AND THE QUEEN

a politics of Black love novel
volume 3

G. Dan BUFORD

LA CAILLE NOUS

Chapters 5 and 6 appeared, as a short story, under the title: Fists, Knives, Guns - in the anthology: Don't Hate the Game: Sports Fiction by Black Men by Michael T. Owens (2009)

ISBN-13: 978-0-9745310-3-8
LCCN: 2022940299
A.P.E.

This book is available in print and ebook formats.
La Caille Nous Publishing Company
New York, NY
www.lcnpublishing.com
www.thebufordnovels.com
Send all correspondence to: lcnpublishing@gmail.com

In memory of

Sterling Todd Ashby

Acknowledgments

This time around is even harder to acknowledge the many who inspired me to write this novel. I am reaching back nearly forty years to let all know how much I cherished the bonds we shared as children. At its core BLIND MAN AND THE QUEEN is about family, the one we are born into and the ones we form in our youth. The tween and teen years were a special time for me, in those Brooklyn streets where one simply went outside and knew there would be other kids playing or on the block passing time. Also, let's not forget, walking down the hall or up the block and ringing a friend's bell. Looking back, in writing BMQ, I think of how much we influenced each other, how much each of the teachings we received from our parents we passed on to each other. That is what made us family. So without any more delay and lest I forget anyone, I will use broad strokes in part to let you know I remember - like it was yesterday.

Earl, Tasha, Ethelena and their entire family (Reina, Lance, Adrian, and...); Donn, Peter and the Worgs family; Nat, Niche and the Stewart family; Ocean Avenue: 1199, 1245, 1249, 1261, 1271, 1291, 1280, 1290, and those who came from nearby and afar to bond; Ant Jeanty, Chin, Ernie Walker and family; Sharon, Sherrod and the entire family; Don Mo, Phil, Ralph, Malik, Kevin Jackson, Our Lady of Refuge (OLR) - The Baron Sisters; Kelly, Eric and the Mailbox Crew - RIP Kester and Gardner; Dre, Deron and the George family; Peter Bates, Deric, Angie and the McCants family, Erskine, Joe, 35th Street Crew, and Midwood High - Tyrone, Derrick, Lionel, Nicole Berry and so many others. My entire New Paltz family, with special note to AWA (African Women's Alliance), The Fahari, the BSU (Black Student Union) and my Kappa family (everyone), with special note to my prophytes from the Main Line, Final Four, Soul Survivors and Lone Star.

Though I could be a prolific writer and drop a new novel each twelve to eighteen months, I've opted not to but do plan to change that, as the years are piling up. When I'm not writing, I am reading, and in this past decade doing a lot of it online - articles and blogs. Still I find time to read books, specifically novels, and in turn form these little writing communities in my mind. Some of

these writers I hope to meet one day and the others though I know them, their books bring me closer. These writers' works inspire me so I take this moment to share them with you: Odessa Rose (In The Mirror), Ifeona Fulani (Seasons of Dust), Myriam J. A. Chancy (The Loneliness of Angels), Michael Thomas (Man Gone Down), Marlon James (A Brief History of Seven Killings), Stephen L. Carter (The

Emperor of Ocean Park), Colson Whitehead (The Intuitionist), Claude Brown (Manchild in the Promised Land), and Sam Greenlee (The Spook Who Sat by the Door), a book that continues to push me and challenge me to make the impact I want. Honorable mention to a few others: Tajuana Butler (Sorority Sisters), a positive portrayal of women and their bond; O. H. Bennett (Recognition); Gigi Ishmael: Publisher, The Ishmael Tree - thank you for keeping me plugged in to the industry; and Kip Jackson (Two Shot Productions) for always being a friend and brother.

In closing, I thank Kenya Daley for her editorial help. Thank you for a thorough reading at a time when I was ready to shy away from leaving this book with so many pages. To Randolph Morton who read the first three chapters of the earliest completed draft. To Monica L. Cook, the first to read the finished manuscript. It is always a joy to hear your feedback. Every writer should be as lucky to have you in their corner.

-

Artistic license: The State of New York did not have the Death Penalty for the period wherein an execution takes place in this novel. From the previous novel to this one, there's a slight adjustment to Ernest's age and the year he immigrated to America.

Music lyrics included in text under the Fair Use Act come from the following artists and songs: CD-3 (Get Tough); Dhar Braxton (Jump Back); Fonda Rae (Over Like A Fat Rat); Vaughan Mason & Crew (Bounce, Rock, Skate, Roll); Eric B. and Rakim (I Ain't No Joke); Public Enemy (Rebel Without A Pause); Cynda Williams (Harlem Blues); Pepsi & Shirley (Heartache); Bob Marley (Redemption Song); Prince (A Girl Called Nikki); Sade (Love Is Stronger Than Pride).

Dedicated to Charlton W. Davenport,
thank you for your leadership.

Part One

THE EVOLUTION OF A MAN

Chapter 1
NAKED AMBITION

The bus arrived at *The Deuce*, the perfect place to start. Whenever we met up during school breaks, no matter the agreed upon plan, he would detour us to Times Square – Forty-Second Street, The Deuce as he called it, from his teen years, the b-boy days. He would reminisce about bygone days as if the place were the ruins of an ancient city, where a civilization, a culture had been bombed by the rapid advancement of a foreign invader and now the slow rebuild had begun, homogenizing a milieu where kids once frequented arcades filled with pinball machines and video games. The Deuce served as a neutral zone for the ones deemed DBL, down by law; a place where inexpensive greasy pizza slices coupled with large soft drinks in ice-filled paper cups with a soda brand's logo was all one needed for nourishment. That, and a triple header of karate flicks, where if we arrived by eleven o'clock, we could stay in the theater until four in the morning. Even then some theaters never closed. They ran all-nighters and homeless folks would come with their wine and other means of assistance, not so much to watch the movie but to participate with impromptu dialogue, demonstrating they too had been warriors for a cause.

Our – when I say 'our', I mean the four of us. For it was rarely only Attitude and me, and even when it was, he would walk the edge of our aloneness like we were being chaperoned or he was a monk who had taken a vow, the way the monks, in our favorite karate flicks, had. We loved discussions centered on faith, celibacy and upholding other ideals way bigger than us. Still it made me question, how Manny had moved through street life and campus life, never seemingly holding on to any allegiance long enough to marry it, meaning to come out with a woman he loved, a partner.

No previous phone number worked for him. I called back to campus and not even Ken and Barbara knew how to reach him. I didn't tell anyone the specific reason I needed to find him. I did my best not to give any clue something was amiss. But the clock was ticking.

This time, the fire had burned and they had a suspect, a terrorist they labeled him. They even had a name, his code name, though they misconstrued it as 'Ah-man' and not 'A Man'.

He had many names. I met him as Attitude. Some students called him The Big Man.

Days before the fire, they spied Manny with me, in front of the library. They had been waiting for 'Aman' to surface yet did not realize he was one of their feted campus icons, conveniently ignoring Manny's term as president of the Radical Students Association.

His hair grown out, a full beard and wearing a hoodie, he had morphed into someone they dared not approach in broad daylight.

No coercion, they left the judgment up to me, to decide whether Aman should be killed.

After the meeting, I left campus and boarded the first bus to Manhattan. I used one of my two backpacks as a pillow; the bag with two jeans, three tops, a week of underwear and my toiletries. The other had my notebooks, Walkman, camera and the gun they gifted to me, in case I personally had to kill him.

With a little over two hundred dollars, food and a place to sleep would not be an issue for a few days though I intended to find Attitude within a day so we could clear the air.

I checked everywhere and asked everyone who hung out at the various places we'd frequented. As the days ran longer and the nights lost their chill, I wondered why, with all the art he had done and coming of age during tagging's heydays, no graffiti murals bore his name. For all I knew and learned of him, he had no tag.

A man with so many names: Manny, The Big Man, Attitude, A Man - his code name; and he had no tag?

He seemed to be always flowing, always going with the wind.

Days skipped by and I took to asking strangers for help because my money began to run out. Being in the Society taught us strangers were not strangers if you believed in their kindness. All one had to do was find a library on a college campus and just sit out front. Your questions would be answered, your belly filled and you'd get a warm bed to sleep. All this and with the stranger not prying into your affairs, but the question you asked, to make a stranger a friend, did expose you.

On the seventh day, as I left the young woman who had let me share her dorm room for a night, I asked, "Where would you go if you were looking for love?"

The sister smiled and said, "Well since you're nearly out of money, you have to look for the free kind. Walk down Broadway and accept all flyers extended to you."

"Thank you. And, don't forget to drop my name whenever."

"Yes, I know. Tell them Hope Kendall was here."

We both laughed and nodded.

<0>

I collected my first flyer on Broadway and 110th Street. By the time I reached Forty-Second Street, I had twenty interesting venues to choose from. I planned to keep walking at least to Eighth Street but I was hungry and also did not like the way I smelled. Even though I showered this morning and a little sweat never hurt, I had this smell to me, too clear, lacking some spice. I walked east toward Fifth Avenue to find an older, not old, a classy gentleman, preferably married who looked to be out of practice so he would not try to do a marathon. The little adventure would be good for laughs with my tightest. The little adventure would ensure I didn't come off as needing some, or attract the needy.

I saw him, about twenty feet away. He was wearing a navy blue blazer, beige wool slacks and burgundy loafers. Our eyes met and I took a deep breath so he could see my fullness. I walked toward him with a simple, straight-forward gait. "Excuse me, are you taking a long lunch?"

His eyes went from blank to apprehensive. His mustache, dark but thin. The faint smell of Drakkar Noir. "How old are you?"

I barely opened my mouth as to give off a sultry sound. "Twenty, turning twenty-one in late fall."

He quickly circled the thoughts around his eyes. "Are you expecting me to pay you?"

"No, just a decent hotel, some food and drinks and a new outfit."

"That sounds like pay to me."

"I don't want any payout. You simply keep it classy and afterward buy me an outfit."

He sipped soda through a straw. "It all sounds a little expensive. I can just buy me some head for twenty dollars."

My laughter bubbled at his audacity. "I'm not giving you head."

He returned my laugh and walked away.

I had seventeen dollars and change so I bought a quick lunch. By the time I meandered down to Eighth Street, it was four o'clock. I turned toward Washington Square Park for some shade and relaxation, to watch performers and take in the vibe of the Village's bohemian culture. Attitude loved this park. He would sit here for hours, doing sketches of life and scenery and abstracting them. He said he most loved the park for its circular design, the various paths, the many exits. People separated themselves based on need - those with baby strollers, those looking to feed the pigeons, students passing time between classes, workers on breaks and the lurkers, park-goers who just spent time, passed a joint or a bottle on the low. For the most part, Washington Square Park was heavily policed because it attracted such a diverse base including tourists who loved to stop by the fountain to marvel at the performers - dancers, acrobats, musicians and, near the southwestern exit, chess matches. On two previous days, I had taken the subway down to the Village and walked from Hudson to Bowery, and saw no signs of him.

So many days in Manhattan and to not run into anyone who knew him made me wonder whether he only had juice and influence in small circles. To be so conspicuous and carefree, have various monikers but still be invisible confirmed he was in hiding. Days had passed yet with the sting of the flames of the bonfire, the sight of a burning campus administration building, where even though many groups and individuals stood to watch, lament or cheer, the final finger pointed at me. He, A Man, had become my responsibility.

I leafed through the various flyers I collected during my walk and discarded those for commerce of wares, except for flea markets. I also tossed out the ones for pay parties where the indicated style did not convey dress as you are. I wanted to find him by ten o'clock, and if not, I'd take the last Metro-North train home. I wasn't sure whether eleven o'clock or midnight would be the deadline for a train stopping at my destination.

I had five spots to check out. All were free events. Two flyers had black and white designs, in very different styles. The other three were full-color jobs. One stood out because of its abstract nature, address with no other information. I was somewhat familiar with Attitude's art and though I knew this would not be something he would draw, I could see him appreciating it. I started with that event since it was closest to the park.

It was a no-go because there were no spirits. I chatted with a couple of the attendees and headed to the second place, the black and white flyer with the understated image, conjuring a film noir, the address on Broadway, not far across Houston Street. I showed the flyer to a guy at the door. He was security but he wasn't forceful, at least not with me. I handed him the postcard size flyer and he asked, "Print or Purchase?" I went with Purchase since it was the second option. To which he said, "Ten dollars."

"The flyer said this was a free event." I only had eight dollars left in my pocket and needed it for subway and Metro-North. The security guard without uniform did not offer another word, indicating I did not have the proper access. "How much is it for Print?"

He had a yellowish haze to his eyes, a bright smile and full lips. "Print is free."

"OK, I will do that."

His shaved head and raised angular shoulders fortified the calm of his demeanor. "Which artist?"

This was when someone having too many monikers became a hurdle. I went with the one given to me, using their mispronunciation, when I was assigned the task of finding Manny. "Aman."

"He doesn't have studio space here."

By now a line had formed. I didn't want to be a hindrance or wear out his patience so I stepped out of the way and eavesdropped as others handed him flyers. Each person chose between print and purchase, but each said something different. For purchase, no money exchanged hands even after he said, "Ten dollars."

A woman motioned me toward her. She was behind the fourth person. I got next to her on the line. When we reached the security guard, she said, "Purchase".

He answered, "Ten dollars."

She told me, "Tell him your name."

"Hope Kendall."

His head moved back a little as if my name had knocked some sense into him. His eyes remained steady, his voice calm. "I will need to see ID."

"I didn't see you ask anyone else for ID."

"I know most of them or they knew what to say." He did not smile.

I showed him my ID and the woman hugged him. I followed her into the building. She pressed for the elevator as people walked past us and down the hall toward the back of the lobby. They lined up behind others who were picking up prints from a station, a booth. She pressed for the fifth floor. We were the only two in the elevator. I waited for her to say her name since she knew not only my name but what I look like. "We were beginning to think Davenport was lying when he said you had bought in."

I didn't want to say the wrong thing yet was curious as to what Manny said I bought into. "I never got your name."

"You don't know who I am?" She smiled to hide the slight frown that formed near her mouth. "Cindy…"

She stopped short of her last name but I sensed she wanted to say more. I needed to ask one more question before the elevator doors opened. I had the words, Are you Manny's woman, in my mouth. Instead of letting them out, I allowed them to bunch up and swell. I swallowed the breath instead of pushing out the sigh. I thought of simply returning back downstairs but wasn't sure what this would mean for Manny. Or, could my walking in sabotage whatever he had going on?

The elevator reached the fifth floor and stopped. Cindy pressed three numbers on the panel. The elevator door parted, giving access to a long hall. There were only two doors, one to the right at the back of the hall, similarly situated as the first floor booth. She opened the door across the elevator. Cindy veered left in a casual manner yet clearly distanced herself from me. All eyes facing the entrance stared at me, as if in disbelief. One man approached but remained more than two real arms' length away. I glanced to my left and saw Manny look at him and over the man's right shoulder, at an empty space. There were twenty-five or so people in the room and by now they were all looking at me. "She's real." The man took two small steps forward and stopped. I sized up his six-two slim build, scruffy beard, reddish brown hair strewn about, as if trying to hide his family's wealth. His shoulders were not broad but under his brown shirt I detected firmness, one he tried to hide. "Before anyone says anything, answer this: Are you Davenport's woman?"

"No," I said, already forming the return to yes, in case I had misspoken.

He turned toward Manny and said, "Pay up, motherfucker! Told y'all there was no way Hope Kendall could be his woman."

I didn't look at Manny. "I'm Attitude's woman. I can't be Davenport's woman because he never lets me get close to his art."

"Come here!" He ordered like he was in charge of this operation. I pondered a power struggle, one he could not win because Manny Davenport was one of the baddest, move-in-silence dudes, when the role called for it. So, I went to him and he bent his head as if preparing to kiss me. I closed my eyes and slightly parted my lips to receive his kiss. Nothing happened. Everyone in the room laughed. I opened my eyes. He stared at me ever so briefly and extended his right hand. "Hi. I'm Edwin."

We exchanged a light grip and I pulled him to me with my left arm, tippy-toeing to kiss him on his cheek. "Nice to meet you!"

"Let me take your bags for you."

I handed him my bags and he walked to the loft's northeast corner, into a room. Everyone probably expected me to walk over to Davenport. I turned right toward the open kitchen, to where I saw a guy playing bartender. Drinks and smokes flowed. Raucous laughter filled the loft. The place was posh not only in what furniture brought to it but by the artwork on the wall. I participated in conversation, turning down offers for heavy drugs and other propositions. The music played and people danced solo, with a partner or many partners. The dancing was not the focus. Nothing was the focus except the ability to be yourself.

Attitude - Manny Davenport, had told them I bought into this, but I could not tell what this was.

People came in and out of the loft throughout the night. I counted a core group of ten people who had been there since I arrived. There were four bedroom compartments and in three of them people entered. Some stayed only a few minutes while others lingered. I studied the movements around the loft without being too obvious because I knew I was being watched. Their gaze was for the moment I would talk to Davenport.

Cindy stayed on opposite sides of the room from me. Whenever I moved closer, she found a reason to not be stationary. At first I cared but after a couple hours of seeing the freedom people were taking with each other, how easily tongues met and touches turned into gropes, I decided the best course was to not linger with any person or group. I thought I had the coupling figured out, until one of the women grabbed two of the four constant men. Earlier one of those men had grabbed another man.

I looked for and spotted Edwin standing in the doorway of the bedroom not situated on the eastern wall. He looked at me as if inviting me to walk over. I sensed to go over there even for small talk would be the worst move to make. I shot him a quizzical look, to convey the words: you had your chance. I had walked over, readied for your kiss and you flaked. So, please stop testing me.

He broke eye contact and walked into his room. With that settled, I walked to where Manny stood with a few folks. I made sure not to stand next to him as I knew our first hug had to be how he needed it to be played. I joined their chat, a free-flowing affair with topics switching from painting to music to sports. After nearly twenty minutes, with a slight shift of his head, he motioned me to a side conversation. He hugged me so he could cradle my neck with his left arm to whisper in my right ear. "Don't say a word! What are you doing here? Are you trying to get yourself killed?"

Two of his thick dreadlocks brushed against my right cheek. As I held on to him, I processed what he asked the only way I could. He told them I was his woman to counter the fact I took on a mission with aim to kill him.

But, why could I not have been his woman before? We had this thing, this love, a mutual infatuation hanging over our heads. For two years, since my freshman year, we alternated on which of us carried the torch. It spiraled out of control because neither of us ever stood still long enough for the other to act. Each time one of us made a move something else took priority. "I'll wait for you in your room."

I opened the door where Edwin had placed my bags and sat on the bed. I listened to the various motions and noises outside the room. It was barely ten o'clock so I didn't know how long I would need to wait.

Around midnight, I felt sleep overtaking me so I undressed and got under the covers. The room was small, about ten by ten, with exposed brick on the northern wall where two lithograph prints clashed with the loft's overall sensibilities of original paintings. This was one of three bedrooms on the eastern wall. The fourth bedroom was Edwin's, and its door faced the loft's entrance.

By the time Manny came in, I had dozed off. He slid under the covers and I felt the side of his naked body against mine. I got closer to let him know I was ready and willing. I rubbed his back with my right palm and started to reach around. He snatched my hand, turned and put his left index finger in front of his lips. The reflection from the moon and the street's lights penetrated the bare window. My eyes communicated I wanted him now, just for him to be in me, this very first time. It did not have to be his best, great; just him in me.

When he made to lie back down and close his eyes, I aimed to show him I was serious by opening my mouth and sliding my left cheek downward, from his stomach. He grabbed my throat and said, "Stop! I will fill you in in the morning."

His grasp was not one I could not easily break and punch the shit out of him but I saw his eyes and there was fear, trepidation. He released his hold and it was then I heard a noise, various noises, but this one in particular concerned me. "Is there someone outside the door?" He seemed exasperated by my question. I rushed off the bed and pulled open the door. She was sitting on the floor, her back against the large living space's exposed brick. She was naked and so was I. She stood up and we each sized up the other. She was a bit taller, proportioned; longer limbs, a slight outward slope to her back; wider hips with a downward curve. "Would you like to come in?"

With no hesitation, she said, "Not tonight!" Her voice expressed no sadness, as if relieved to have gotten the answer she needed, why she had exposed her insecurities not from sitting outside Manny's bedroom door but by letting me past the security guard.

I shut the door and got in the bed. My eyes asked for his forgiveness. I never knew love like this. As much as I always felt love didn't have to include sex, I knew I had a yearning. Cindy had a yearning and after she entered the room next door to make a trio, what had been silent creaking between two people became continuous hard bounces; the silent whispers metamorphosed into lustful moans. Throughout the loft, not solely on its eastern side, there was a competition as to which room could out-croon and outlast the other, but not us. I covered Manny's back with my arm and found a place to burrow my nose on the edge of his pillow.

<0>

The next morning, Manny shook me and told me to go shower. The sun peeked around the neighboring buildings. He handed me a towel from his closet. Adjacent the room's exit, the closet's width barely six feet wide, its upper portion had four shelves, two of them subdivided. I noticed the orderly manner he organized his affairs. I wrapped the towel around my body and asked which bathroom to use. The loft had two full bathrooms and there was a communal bathroom in the hall with three showers, not separated, more along the locker room variety. I chose the bathroom at the far end of the loft, to the right of the kitchen, directly across his room. I made mental notes, counting a length of about another twenty-eight feet. I noted Manny never mentioned money when we hung out. I had presumed his family's financial standing to be below mine. I did the math, estimating as a soon-to-be college graduate rooming with three others, he could afford to live in a twenty-four hundred square foot space in the edge of SoHo. Still this was not a grunge space, the polished hardwood floors, the ceiling beams accentuating the industrial feel, the post-modern furniture, the walls lined with modern art likely created by them. An operation downstairs where people came to pick up what they had paid for.

Last night reminded me of an off-campus college mixer but a step above, like the ones affluent students hosted. I saw no exchanges of cash while drinks and drugs flowed at a rapid pace. Conversations led to sex in bedrooms and bathrooms or people headed out the loft for interludes. Everything had a light feel to it yet Manny warned me danger abounded. I stepped out of the bathroom to find the sun higher in the sky. Still, the late May chill fought off the radiance, seeping through the window panes. I reached the furnished, sitting portion of the living room, where two matching sofas faced; they lacked the fluffiness of a grandmother's furniture. Their sleek design allowed them to be surrounded by high chairs, metallic frames supporting leather seats; several chaises placed haphazardly, as were a few small tables. Two people came out of the middle room. Under the morning sun, their bodies shone, one a porcelain pink, and the other a metallic bronze earned under hours of tanning. They said hello in a casualness indicating that I, wrapped in a towel, was the odd one.

I went into Manny's room and closed the door. I shook my jeans - glad I had done laundry yesterday. Manny got out of bed and I checked out his body, lithe but in a boxy frame. He had a permanent scar, a bruise, a slight disfigurement protruding from a rib. I had felt it when my arm crossed his back. He had been a vegetarian ever since I met him and, truth be told, I rarely saw him eat. Even when we hung out as a group, he'd consume morsels of his purchase and the most natural drink he could find. For a man who espoused no religious or even cultural ties and beliefs, he relegated himself to the barest of liberties. He draped a towel over his shoulders and offered no words. His slight glance and erection letting me know we would talk later and, yes, my nude body was indeed temptation.

We were not the first to leave nor the last out of the loft.

Downstairs, out of the elevator, Manny turned right and I followed. The man at the station greeted him with, "Good morning, Mr. Davenport!" and Manny returned it with the same inflection and the man's name. The booth in the back was the entrance to a large storage, a duplex with hundreds of lithograph reproductions and some original paintings.

The man bent down and handed him a box, from which Manny took out its contents and placed most of the postcard size flyers into his backpack.

The rest he held in his hands. We made a left out of the building and a right when we got to Houston Street. I asked, "Is it safe to talk now?"

"Yes."

My words flew out of my mouth, exposing my excitement to be part of his world. "What are you into? Why did Cindy think I bought in? Is she your woman?"

"No, you're my woman, at least to them. I knew you'd eventually find me so I had to provide you a cover."

"Why do they want me dead?"

"Not them personally but there's a reward out on your head."

We walked Houston, heading east.

"Why? I had nothing to do with what happened on the campus." He slowed to stare at me. I continued, "I asked for your help in one thing and next thing I know a building is burning."

We reached Second Avenue and a rush of people moved across us in all directions. Manny didn't address what I said. "You showing up almost messed up this operation. But you and Edwin played it well." He half-handed a flyer to a young man who stopped. "If you want a print of this, it's ten dollars. Take this flyer to the address listed."

The young man said, "No thank you." Manny gave him the flyer and we continued walking.

"What exactly is the operation? Is it dangerous?"

"Yes, very. Now that you've covered this part of my story, I need you to stay away unless I call you."

"What? Why?"

"What did you see last night?"

"Drugs. Orgies."

He cut in. "Yes and that's not your scene. You sleep with one you must sleep with one more to be accepted. From there you can stay in that box or try to get deeper. The only way to do so is to sleep with many more..."

"How deep are you in?"

"This is my third year in."

"I want in."

"Aren't you a virgin?"

"I'm not a virgin." I punched him on his right arm. He laughed and stopped to go into his sales pitch. The woman gave him the ten dollars. He thanked her, signed the flyer and gave it to her. "Is this what you do all day?"

"Is something wrong with it?"

"No. I just never knew this side of your life. What percentage of sales do you get?"

He slowed to stare at me again and handed me a flyer. I looked at the postcard flyer and still did not make the connection. "This is my art. Each week I try to finish a new piece. I walk around and try to sell one hundred copies of it a day."

"One hundred?"

"Yes, and I get one hundred percent. The four of us bought the building together, and whoever raises the capital, only through sales of their own work, can buy the others out."

"Doesn't that type of competition breed jealousy, animosity?"

"Not if you buy in." He paused and waited for me to question. "Plus, we have been buying property together for years. There are hundreds of us."

"One thousand dollars a day?"

"I take a day off here and there, and don't always get to one hundred sales each day."

"When do you get a chance to paint?"

"After I sell at least one hundred copies, I end my day and work if I want. If I can't sell five hundred copies of a piece a week, why go on to work on the next piece?"

I had never looked into his eyes this much. I saw an innocence I had never. I loved the way he had slowly built his hair like a crown, a fortress of spikes dangling around his face. "Am I your woman? Am I supposed to sleep with your friends?"

"No. You were not supposed to go to Edwin. When did you become so compliant?" Amidst a short laugh, he put his arm behind my neck, across my shoulders. "Go home when we reach 42nd. You've covered me enough. I appreciate it."

"What, I'm the jealous woman?"

"It's the best story in the world. You came looking for me and you didn't like what you saw." He laughed again, removing his arm as he made another sale.

"As long as you're honest with me, I have no reason to be jealous. Is Cindy your woman?"

"She wants to be but I only met her a few weeks ago."

"Semester is just ending. How long have you been in this loft?"

"For almost a year. This school year, my classes were mainly studio, and didn't require attendance."

"No wonder I couldn't find you on campus. Are you going up for your graduation?"

"No."

"Is Cindy your woman?"

He laughed. "Do you mean if I've had sex with her?" I didn't answer. "I told you what the operation is. You're my woman but this is not the place for you, if you can't flow. And, I'd prefer you not to."

"Why? You're jealous?"

"No. It's just that this is not an operation where you can jump in and jump out. People will get suspicious, and feel their identities have been compromised. There will be consequences."

"Is Cindy your woman?"

"No."

"OK, after we sell a hundred copies. Take the Metro-North home with me. I want you to meet my parents."

His loud laugh shielded him from the incredulous notion. "We're back to this again! Your family will not approve of me. That's why I have never gone to meet them. Have you even told them about me?"

My silence must have made him think I agreed with his assessment. I calculated a counter. "Have you told your family about me?"

"Yes, right after I met you your freshman year." My silence meant my mind went into the future, of our life together, and he read it perfectly. He said, "This thing between us, it's not just you who feels this way. But I know what my life is like."

We didn't talk much the rest of the way. He sold five prints by the time we reached East 42nd Street. "I'm going to turn here and head to Grand Central." I paused so he could say something, ask me to stay, or express an emotion. But he was the master of the stoic demeanor. "Give me a flyer so I can get in tonight."

"Ten dollars."

"What?"

"I don't give credit." I fake stepped toward him like I would pop him one. He laughed, signed a flyer and handed it to me. "I really don't give credit."

"I don't either but you owe me."

He pulled me to him and said, "You gotta kiss me to make it look good. Chances are we're being watched." We had slow-kissed before but never this out in the open, under the sunlight, on a crowded street. We kissed, the way people do when they were about to cry. As it ended, we hugged and he whispered, "Don't come back to the loft!"

Chapter 2
THE FALL AFTER THE UPRISING

They used the loft as their residence, strictly for entertaining and sleeping. The building's first two floors were commerce, a gallery and storage. Floors three and four were studios and offices rented by artists participating in the co-operative; space to work and meet with clients.

Each of the loft's inhabitants had different ways to attract buyers. They invited loyal customers to the mixers and sold them on the lifestyle. From there, the referrals rolled. Manny strictly sold lithograph prints via postcards and never invited people upstairs.

He walked one avenue per day, either Second Avenue up to 125th Street and back, or Ninth Avenue up to 110th and back. He handed flyers or sold to certain people, those who made eye contact as they approached. Regardless of the emotion conveyed, he went into his sales pitch.

I loved walking the streets selling his art. In the early weeks, he did not let me venture to sell on my own, even on days when he rested or went to his work studio to paint. The first week of July, he finally let me. My first solo day, I walked Second Avenue and sold twenty prints. He tackled Ninth Avenue and sold one hundred and thirty. He said I had done well for my first solo day.

I loved being at the loft. Everything was going smoothly. I developed a pattern to be in his room, with the doors closed, way before bedtime even on nights when there was no mixer, when just the inner circle lounged in the living room.

One night things got strange. Somewhat early in the night, about ten o'clock, quiet for a Thursday night, light-hearted talks, drinking from goblets and ceramics, skinny joints, roach clips, a bong, cocaine on a glass tray and only a few visitors remaining. People had already taken off their clothes. One of Manny's roommates, the one in the corner room, offered me his bed, and he didn't mean for me to have it alone. I smiled and said no thanks.

Whenever I spent the night, I would be in Attitude's bedroom before the undressing started. That night I lingered because he had taken a seat in one of the leather chairs and Cindy had squeezed in with him. That gave hint I would be privy to the conversations held in my absence.

People spoke about random things until Edwin said, "So, Manny or should I say Attitude, or better yet Davenport? This love thing you've got going on, is it just between you and Hope?"

Attitude took a pull from the joint and blew the smoke into Cindy's mouth, a shotgun. He simply said, "Love is free."

Edwin continued, "Is freedom love?" Manny didn't say anything. "I mean if there is freedom in love, then I surmise love is power. Wouldn't you agree, Hope?"

They smoked, snorted and drank. I had finished my drink and was the only one without an item in my hand, the only one with my clothes on. "Sometimes love can be powerless."

One of the women, the one who only went into the middle room, turned to look over her left shoulder. "Which would you choose, love or power?"

She slyly implied I had overstayed my welcome unless I truly bought in.

"I choose love because power cannot bring love, at least not true love." I took off my t-shirt and removed my bra. In the right corner of my eye, I noticed a hard twitch in Manny's left eye, followed by a blink, a signal for me to be cautious.

"So you would choose Black Love over Black Power?" She walked me into an ambush.

Before anyone could think her question stumped me, I fired back without raising my voice. "Love is always Black, whereas power can be anyone's who is willing to grab for it."

The room fell quiet. Nothing moved. I stood and took off my pants and underwear. Cindy walked to another seat. I sat where she had been sitting. No one said a word. Most people who didn't live there simply got dressed and left. The questioner and the other roommates along with those who frequently spent the night went into their respective rooms.

Only the three of us remained. Less than thirty seconds passed. Cindy got up to let me get a good look at her face, body, beauty. I hesitated because I had never been with a woman. I knew even though my words put me on top of the pecking order, my nervousness in bed would chip away at my standing. I stared at her, sending out signals not of rejection nor disapproval. She got the hint and went into the corner room.

Manny grabbed his face with both hands and walked away. I rushed into his bedroom after him. For weeks, we had been getting away with talking in low tones, sort of a secret language of half-words through groans that could fool ears into thinking we were having sex, the type married couples had when visiting the in-laws.

"So what exactly are we doing?"

"Let's not have this conversation. I am involved in things that leave too much room for interpretation, and I am trying to protect you."

"Davenport, you are an artist for God's sake."

"Davenport? You don't know Davenport. You know Attitude. You know Manny."

"Well I want to know Davenport!"

"Go to the library and look up the name Derek Davenport." He rolled on to his stomach. "Now go to sleep!"

I had a choice to make, so I got dressed and left.

<0>

I stayed in the city at a good hotel because working for Manny, the pay was good, quite generous. My family did not understand my job when I tried to explain it. They did not understand my plan to leave school and live in, what they termed, a hippie commune. But when I mentioned his full name, I realized the name Davenport meant something to them, for Manny's father was of their generation.

In the Society's historical record, pretty much everything with his father or mother had been redacted. The regular press had much to say about Derek Davenport. I read the clippings, court proceedings and matched them with the Society's historical record, the parts not covered up. There was no mention of Manny. For the Society did not believe an act done by the father should stay with the son, unless the son's mission was to repeat it.

And, here was Manny Davenport trying to revive the Black Love underground movement.

I felt like throwing up.

The main story: In 1972, Derek Davenport and two other men opened fire in a party, a crowded room. The police arrived as they fled the scene. There was a car chase, a fiery crash.

Davenport opened fire, shot and killed two police officers.

The police returned fire, wounded him and captured him.

The mainstream publications never mentioned two other policemen. The Society's historical record said he acted alone, killed two undercover policemen inside the party and two regular policemen after the chase. This meant Derek Davenport was a traitor. He double-crossed his partners, two members of the Society. Their names were redacted in the Society's historical record.

The mainstream press made no mention of any deaths inside the party, if any, how many. Why would Manny's father go against an operation the Society was running? What was the operation's aim?

I read everything in the library's microfiche records that contained the words 'black love' and none of it correlated to Derek Davenport or the Society.

After nearly two weeks of research and even with all I pieced together about Derek Davenport, I never got any closer to what really happened inside the party and to the other two dead men.

Being out of the mix for weeks, I could not simply walk back into the loft, without a valid reason for my absence. I needed to show I had fully bought in especially if I had harmed the operation in any fashion.

He needed to see my total allegiance so I created a design with the tag line "The Sum of their Fears exists due to an inability to accept…" At the bottom left hand corner, in a circle, the words "Black Love".

I got to the loft at eleven o'clock, expecting him to be there, thinking the mixer would be in full swing. I opened the door to a somber mood, of the residents and the everyday guests. They were all dressed. Manny was not there.

Cindy stood. She did not come to me yet I felt her presence near me, a strong connection. "Davenport's not here. They killed Barbara's brother, Lincoln."

I heard her words, the pronoun 'they'. I would have to process all her words at a later time. "OK, I have to go to her. For now, I need you all to pass out these flyers."

I placed the box on the table and the woman from the middle bedroom pulled a flyer to read, immediately recognizing the reference. "Churchill? I see."

Edwin balked. "No, that's not happening here. How would you feel if we threw a white power party?"

"Power is not love!"

"Neither is love when it is not free, when it's not blind." He waited for me to back down. "You throw this party and someone will likely end up dead."

"You don't have to be involved." Edwin grabbed a bag and left the loft. The others acquiesced in a sheepish manner, as if Manny taking flight because of Barbara's loss made them realize the gravity of the Society's war, that it took precedence over this operation. I asked, "Did y'all really buy in or was it just some cute shit to say?" I grabbed a handful of the two-thousand flyers and left the balance for them to figure out.

Chapter 3
BLACK LOVE PARTY

The party started before they walked in. Hours before, at noon, when we opened the building's doors, to what felt like but was not a rush, hundreds spilled into the lobby. Most took the stairs instead of waiting for the elevators since each of the two cars held at most ten riders.

They had not been part of the early rush when the first dee-jay set it off, to kick off the twenty-four hour party. Most attendees would stay just a few hours. The early comers were interested in seeing the actual loft. They were the customers who picked up their purchases at the back of the lobby. Today was a treat, as most of the loft's other parties were small private gatherings, for the inner circle or well-connected.

The loft had been emptied of furniture, supplies, shelves and canvases. The walls – free of canvases and other pieces still expressed a luxe sentiment from the mixture of paint, abstract drawings and graffiti - held nothing except them.

Wallflowers never concerned me until I saw them. They held up the walls like permanent fixtures and would likely be the last to leave the party. They were not the shy, awkward wallflowers, those who could not dance. Their fashion, chunk jewelry and gold ropes were those of the ultra-cool kids, the ones a level beyond the fishbowl of mainstream acceptance and popularity. They entered in scattered groups. They tried to blend with the room, moving in the plane of the various partygoers and strobe lights that had yet to affect the vibe because of the outside sunlight. I noticed them as soon as the first group entered. I did not recognize any of them but I kept a count. They came in roughly twenty minute intervals and thinned themselves into the party atmosphere.

The second of the scheduled six dee-jays moved from a blend of seventies funk and disco to a freestyle instrumental dance mix.

Near the kitchen an animated conversation competed with the music.

Another group entered: two girls and six boys. They were now forty deep. I recognized two of them. Our eyes met. They pretended not to see me or perhaps they did not remember me. I shadowed their hurried strides as they split from the others who went to different points of the room to whisper to the other wallflowers. Young men carrying bags, of any kind, even sophisticated small handbags with designer logos meant the heat had come. In fact, except for an eclectic group of artists and a select few partygoers, this Black Love party had not attracted the full energy and specific people I targeted when I planned and designed the flyer.

The sun set behind Broadway. Its descent landed in filmy shadows across the western-most windows. Thirty-foot ceilings, industrial feel, of iron work, air ducts and exposed brick. Plastic cups, the smell of reefer, open windows allowing in the outside heat, the music dived into hip hop and the scene became chaotic. Nearly a thousand people jammed the dance floor. With drinks flowing, all kind of flavors in the air, nationalities and ethnicities blended on the dance floor, except them. They spread out, separating into duos or lone wolves, pacing the room, the outskirts, through the crowd, trying to appear as nonthreatening as possible. Their disguise, their resistance, the facade broke when the third dee-jay of the night scratched the mix so badly the entire room froze. From my position in the room, I could not see his face but knew the culprit, his notorious intro whenever he jumped on the turntables. He played a song I'd heard on the radio but never really partied to. The song unlocked time and as all dancers grooved, they, the wallflowers were drawn to the center of the dancefloor. They rapped to themselves, along with the record, as if at attention to their nation's anthem. One of the record's MCs harmonized words that seemed to personify their existence:

> *I used to be a kid that liked to steal*
> *but my mother said son take this for real*
> *life is funny life plays tricks*
> *you better listen up or catch the wrong licks*

The dee-jay started the call and response, "Flatbush! Flatbush!"

The wallflowers responded, "Flatbush! Flatbush!"

Ernest had been playing the back, standing near the kitchen, and must have assumed perhaps one of theirs, one of the wallflowers had bogarted the turntables. He moved through the crowd, using his forearm to nudge people out of the way. He came to a spot where he could see the dee-jay booth – a long folding table propped up on top of three sound system speakers. I sensed Ernest's surprise when he saw none other than The Big Man looping the sound. The entire room now seemed to know the chorus:

> *We know the world is rough so GET TOUGH*
> *We know the world is rough so GET TOUGH*

This went on for about two minutes until some white guy ran out and grabbed the mic and shouted out his hood, then an Asian dude, then a white girl. Everybody felt comfortable representing their town but the kicker came when this white kid grabbed the mic and shouted, "Sandusky, Ohio! Are you with me?"

The shout-out did get a major laugh. The Big Man did an exaggerated scratch in order to change the tempo and pass the turntables to a new dee-jay, foregoing his full rotation on the turntables. The music stayed on hip hop as Manny came to the floor to exchange hugs and reminisce with the wallflowers. I had not seen him in weeks, not even when I went to be with Barbara and expected him to be at her house.

Girard made to approach Manny but Ernest grabbed him by the arm. Ernest whispered something in his ear. They blended into the crowd and headed out of the loft.

I followed them to the hallway. "Hey, Ernest! Girard!"

People loitered in the hall. Groups of four or less were trying to cool off from the loft's heat or making plans to go elsewhere.

They faked like they needed a few seconds to recall my name. Girard said, "Hope? How's everything?"

"Have y'all had a chance to talk to Attitude?"

"It's mad crowded!"

I gave him a quizzical look, a plea for them to drop the charade.

Ernest tried another angle. "What's your word like?"

"Meaning?"

"Is your word your bond?" After I nodded, he said, "What is Manny into? That day a few months back on your campus! What was that all about? With the fire, the gun play?"

I looked at Girard. "He doesn't know?"

Girard looked me dead in the eye. "When we met you, before you knew who we were, you asked Ernest to kill Manny, and Barbara asked me to kill Ken."

I choked up to hold back the rawness of my emotions. "Yes, I had my reason but days later someone else asked me to kill him. That made me suspicious."

They stepped toward me. "Who?"

I didn't answer that question. I had to throw them a curve. "But I found out why Attitude burned the building. He freed us. We're free. All of us."

Ernest tried another track. "So you think you're free 'cause you're styling and dressing like Denise Huxtable?"

"You and your crew came to this party thinking?"

"Yes, because Love is dead but then we saw this flyer." Girard left out the major word of the sentence.

"Wait! How do you even know about Black Love?"

They looked at each other and together asked, "How do you know about it?"

"This is my party. My name on the flyer, my tag on the bottom right corner." I needed to know what they knew about Love. "And, since when do people come to a Black Love party to murder someone?"

Ernest asked, "The people who put a hit on Manny? These are the same people who killed my brother, right?"

I noticed a reflexive movement, the lump in Girard's throat. I answered too slowly. "No, well I'm not sure...No, I mean I don't know anything about your brother."

Girard said, "I'm going back to the party. You two work it out. I will cover Manny until noon."

I sensed the mistrust in Ernest's eyes. He expected me to say something. When I didn't, he went back inside. I followed and stood next to him, tracking his eyes as best as I could. He observed the party. His eyes avoided Manny's direction and I danced in place to dismiss the quiet between us. We maintained this offhand, offshoot posture through a few songs until I heard-

Had my love but you lost my love

"Do you wanna dance?"

"Dance?"

"Do you know how to dance?"

He said, "Yes of course." He looked around the room at the various people dancing, but mostly at the ultra-cool ones, the wallflowers who finally joined the party. I grabbed his hand and it felt cold even though the loft was a sweatbox. The club, dance mix of *Jump Back* amped the loft to another level - soul clap, spins, screaming; the party in a total frenzy. Not burdened by his height and muscular frame, Ernest showed off nimble feet, the synchronization of shoulder dips, knee bends and occasional spins – half and full. The song's quickened pace carried me back to the sexual energy of when I first met him, freeing me from the tension I feared from the presence of him and his crew, whether they would shoot up the party, to disguise a hit on one person.

JUMP BACK Get your act together

'cause there's nothing wrong with me

JUMP BACK Nothing lasts forever
now it's time to set me free

I was deep into the groove, in a trance, only responding to the JUMP of the song. Sweat dripped from my forehead and chin to my torso and the floor. Soaking through my loose gray tank top, bra and Benetton boxer shorts over cotton T-back panties and bare feet, I spun halfway to bump my left shoulder into Ernest. I slid my body down his leg, completing the spin. I wanted to be close to him for the next line, to sing along and to back up into him. I wanted to feel him but the lyrics-

Love is a two-way street
a place where we'd never meet

-caused him to ask, "What?" and he froze on the dance floor. I got closer to hear what he was saying. "I never knew." I backed away to keep dancing, maintain my vibe but he walked up to me and said, "Had I known that Love is a two-way street, Lionel wouldn't have killed Benny."

I heard him over the music but said, "I can't really hear you."

He shouted near my right ear. "Deirdre. You're Deirdre."

"No, Hope. My name is Hope."

He surveyed the room and repeated the words, "Love is a two-way street a place where we'd never meet." He stood there as if frozen in time, analyzing the meaning, the party lights rotating around him, the strobe lights' hallucinating effects swirling the people's movements around him.

I squeezed his left hand. "Are you OK?"

"Now I see why we're not supposed to be here. What year is this?"

He had me out of sorts. "Summer of '87."

"But for some reason, it feels like I'm back in 1983." He looked over to where Girard stood. When they made eye contact, Ernest shook his head from side to side and looked at a few of the people from their crew. Again,

Ernest shook his head from side to side. Girard replied by shaking his head up and down, as if not agreeing with what Ernest had communicated. Ernest repeated the motions to another guy who seemed a bit older and was standing a few feet near the dee-jay booth.

The guy nodded.

Ernest repeated the motion to Girard and did not wait for a reply.

Ernest bent to whisper in my ear. "Come. Leave with me. I gotta tell you something that will help you in taking the hit off Manny."

When I met Ernest and Girard back in early May, they seemed to be ahead of their time from a knowledge standpoint. Ernest's head movements just confirmed it. I said, "I have to go get my stuff." I walked to Manny's room, left of the dee-jay booth. I threw on baggy jeans, sneakers, denim shirt and a baseball cap. I returned to find Ernest standing exactly where I left him on the dance floor. "Ready?"

He sized me up. "Backpack with supplies and you're strapped. I like that."

How he could tell I had a gun I did not know but I liked his awareness, his eyes. "Is this some elaborate ploy to get me to – bed?"

"Nah, you're Girard's."

"How do you figure that?"

"He likes ultra-smart chicks."

"That's not all it takes. I get to choose."

"Plus, you're a little too free for me."

"Yes, I am but Love is not about freedom. At least I never saw it that way." We used the stairs because the line to board the elevator was too long. We moved swiftly down the five flights. "How did your brother die?"

"That Society, Manny, you and the other people on campus are in."

We hit Broadway, the heat, traffic and noise.

I cut him off. "OK, no matter what you tell me, I cannot share anything about the Society. Information flows upward, not downward."

"And, you're up top from me?"

"Yes." I waited for him to agree. "All I can do is promise, if what you tell me helps to make sense of what Manny is up to, enough that I put my name on the line for him, I will offer you my protection."

He nodded. "Come. We gotta head to Brooklyn."

"Subway is this way."

"We gotta walk. Too much noise on the subway and ears that stay with you for long periods of time."

We walked Broadway, toward the Brooklyn Bridge.

Third Saturday in August, the sun long set, headlights, streetlights and the moon coupled with the noise from voices and cars created a mood, a rhythm. I wanted him to hold my hand so I could feel his pulse, where the story, he would tell, hurt him. "Can I hold your hand?"

"No, that would indicate an alliance and I'm not ready to offer that. But if you can walk from here to the heart of Brooklyn with me and no one stops to question you or us being together, and are able to ride back here to meet up with Girard or go to your home, then yes, then you can hold my hand. I and..." He looked at the other three corners of the crosswalk of Broadway and Spring Street, and at the many eyes looking our way. "...we will protect you at all costs to ourselves."

There were people, conceivably from his and other crews, who had come to the party but not upstairs. We crossed the street and though anyone I saw could pose a threat, I felt safe with Ernest even though deep down I knew I was captured and couldn't leave his side unless he gave me clearance.

I had heard about the other side, the dark side of the Society. To hear about it, even read about it in the historical record left me fascinated. Living it felt different, brought trepidation because now I had to make quick decisions while suppressing all fears.

Ernest began telling his story, their story, A Man's story:

"On Christmas 1980, while my family attended Midnight Mass, we heard the sirens of fire trucks, ambulances, and the voices of people running past the church. A hysterical neighbor flung open the church's large castle-like doors and she screamed, "The house. The house is on fire...""

My mother led the way out of the church. We ran behind her and arrived to thirty firemen and neighbors from our block and the surrounding ones standing across the street. The flame raged as my mother began to sob. The firemen looked at each other and one said mockingly, "We don't need no water. Let the motherfucker burn!"

Chapter 4

Mother Father Sister Brother. We had that, that kind of love where the message was clear as the song of the times: MFSB's *Love is the Message*. I had heard it in passing, but in this new neighborhood, the song was a theme transported in the cassettes of boom boxes carried on shoulders or dangled in hands like pocketbooks. The transporters, youths, all with nicknames and forced baritones with exaggerated tempos, would make up lyrics. They sang of love, loyalty, leading a righteous life.

We also had love, the nine of us. MFSB - Mother. Father. Four Sisters. Three Brothers.

I was the youngest boy, fifth child. Before we moved to this new neighborhood, to Brooklyn, Eric took me everywhere with him. He was my idol, my teacher, sparring partner and gatekeeper to any folly I contemplated, to stray off the path my parents set. Suddenly, from the first day after my mother settled us in and gave us boys the freedom to roam, Eric didn't take me anywhere with him. I thought it was because he recently turned sixteen and I had yet to turn thirteen.

He simply told me to stay in the house or go outside to make my own friends.

The first weeks after the fire, we'd managed as best we could. On the first night, heading into Christmas, we split ourselves amongst cousins. Two days later, we moved into a week-to-week furnished three bedroom apartment my mother's friend recommended. We sat in the living room to watch the ball drop, welcoming New Year 1981. Being uprooted had softened my mother's strict bedtime routine for me and the twins.

Toward the end of the second week, my father got permission from the fire department for us to go retrieve anything worth salvaging. My father took all the boys and my mother took the girls shopping. Even though I had lived in the house for years, I did not miss living there. The bedrooms were small. The halls narrow and the sunlight came in at odd angles, even in the early morning when it should have lit up and warmed the house.

The basement had suffered the least damage so we gathered keepsakes, records, books and albums.

When we arrived to see our home burning to the ground, we all had emotional reactions. My mother cried, out loud at first, "Why? Why". My father arrived later, simply shook his head and started devising where we would stay until he was able to find us a place. My mother, she had a plan and looked at my father and ordered, "Brooklyn!" So, we moved to Brooklyn. Deep in the heart of it, Flatbush section.

We lived on a side street off the main avenue, a river whose currents carried trouble around the corner, past or into our house. We lived in the second house on the northern side. Compared to our house and block in Queens, this neighborhood was crowded. The main avenue only had tall buildings. I could hear cars all the time. The heavy traffic started right after sun-up and ended around nine o'clock at night. Even in the late night, cars flew by. In the morning, people turned the corner to get to the subway. They had to walk by our house for the subway.

Our side street had less car traffic than pedestrians. Unlike the adults whose traveling pattern mimicked the cars' hours, the kids stayed out all night. From upstairs, in my bedroom window, I observed them. Some were my age but a few were Eric's age or a bit older. They walked, ran and loitered. These kids were into music or snatching pocketbooks and doing stick-ups. Eric hadn't done any of those things in our old neighborhood. He also did not know Manny. That name stayed on everybody's tongue. As people passed by our house, I would hear Manny this, Manny that. Then one day, I heard Eric's voice. I could not see him. Eric's voice sounded far, perhaps around the corner. "Get him Manny!"

When I made out "the get", I knew why Eric had not turned the corner. One house past ours, heading toward the subway, three boys surrounded the victim, who cowered against the tree, remaining still as Manny pressed the knife to his neck. The other two boys went through his pockets. They ordered him to take off his coat, the kind my mother refused to buy me, the current fad, a bubble goose. They also took his Puma sneakers. As they walked away from him, they did not even bother to threaten him to keep quiet.

I was not sure if Manny knew where Eric lived but he looked up and our eyes met. My first instinct was to slide over and hide behind the curtain, but he did not do as I expected. He just turned his head without telling the other boys to look up.

This neighborhood was different. I knew I could not simply hang out with Eric and think everything would be alright. But I also could not stay to myself and hide in the house, especially since school had started after winter recess.

My parents had finalized all of our schools, except mine. My sisters got first priority. Early mornings they would leave for school, catching the bus on the main avenue, two blocks south. My brothers had no choice but to attend the public high school in our zone. My mother did not want me to go to the P.S., the elementary public school closest to our house. She said her friends who knew Brooklyn said it was filled with *vagabonds*. My father did not agree that I should go to Catholic school with my sisters. He felt I needed to be tough, to understand my older brothers' ages meant I will have to navigate the streets by myself. My mother held out, trying to use her connections to get me into a different public school in a better neighborhood.

With two older brothers, not being tough was barely an option. Dealing with two older sisters and two younger ones proved a bit trickier. My sisters never came out and said what they wanted. They expected things to be done, yet they pampered me. My brothers were dictatorial yet hands-off, except for the few times I would fight with Eric. This was more roughhousing, his way of toughening me up.

I hated winter yet was glad I didn't have to wait three months to go to school to see who was who in my age group. Not that I would have stayed home all summer, but school would make it easier to learn names and reputations, a much better structure than showing up at the playground and trying to fit in. Since I was big for my age, I normally faced either of two situations in new environments. Someone would pick a fight with me. Most times I worked hard to avoid the fight, to give the person time to learn I have two older brothers and four sisters who like to push people around.

In light of my family dynamics, my standard response to any threat, "Picture me being soft!"

The only difference with school this time around: I did not have Eric to lead the way. Lionel was a senior at the high school and Eric a sophomore. Not only would I have to finish the last part of sixth grade alone, junior high and high school would be the same.

My mother had no luck in changing my designated school. She asked if I wanted her to walk me to school for my first day. My older sisters laughed. She cut them a look. She then saw the confident look on my face. She caressed it with both palms and planted a soft kiss on my forehead. She left for work.

My brothers had left without saying anything. They were entrenched in the neighborhood's rhythm. I saw it mainly in their walk. In my sisters, it showed itself in the way their smirks froze on their faces, indicating a softness that had been erased. We left the house at the same time. They walked south to the bus, and I crossed the main avenue and headed east.

These past two weeks, since I had been the only one home, my mother would send me to run errands. I'd avoided the main avenue and the streets on the other side. I always went the stores on our side, even when she said prices were less on the other side. Though I had my concerns, I liked the feel of the neighborhood, especially the walking access to a subway line.

For school, I had a simple plan. I needed one hard kid to partner with, not a troublemaker, someone who would get me into nonsense. I needed someone like Eric had been, before we moved to this neighborhood. Perhaps it was not the neighborhood but an age thing. I say this because Lionel had been getting into trouble for years. If this was the case, then I had about four years to learn to avoid trouble.

Easier said than done when *love is the message* yet you are growing up in the early 1980s, Brooklyn's stick-up era.

I walked slowly and listened in on the various conversations from kids passing by. I got to school but didn't go into the schoolyard. I sat on the side street, diagonally to the yard, in front of a small building, on a short black metal guard rail protecting a small lawn. I just sat there in the late January cold, a day with not much wind. I scoped the scene, checking out how the kids interacted in the schoolyard, the division and cooperation, how close to a hundred kids occupied a fenced-in playpen. Some played basketball on two hoops bolted against the same wall; baseball diamond, on concrete, angled toward the wall; against that same wall, far left of a basketball rim, a painted strike zone where a pitcher threw a small blew racquetball toward a stickball batter; in the wide empty space behind the shortstop position, a group jumped double-dutch; through it all, other kids played tag, while near the swings and slides twenty or so boys and girls chilled in conversation.

Ten minutes after the bell, I went into the main office to get my class assignment. All eyes were on me. Before the teacher got a chance to introduce me to the class, a boy, Girard, motioned for me to sit, at a desk one row up and one seat to the left from him. The teacher told me the routine. The first three subjects were taught in this room. Afterward, we'd go to the cafeteria for lunch, outside for recess followed by gym. Our last three classes, we would switch rooms before returning to this classroom - our homeroom - before dismissal. She filed my papers into her binder and pointed me to take the seat Girard had indicated. She introduced me to the class. "Everyone, this is Ernest LeGagneur. He's new to the school."

Right after I sat down, I heard, "HBO, HBO" and various people giggling. I'd assumed things would not get interesting until recess, or maybe even a few days later. I didn't bother to turn my head because I had seen this scene play out at my previous school, with other students. *Haitian Body Odor.* First time I heard this HBO taunt was last year in the playground. This boy had been teasing this new girl. Eric took it really personal and without so much a warning, Eric popped him. The boy hesitated because he knew Eric and they never had any conflict.

If Eric fought, I fought. The way my father taught us, you do not wait until your brother is losing or even winning. First chance you get, jump in to finish off the initial problem. Most times other people will just mind their own business but there will be instances where they'll jump against you.

HBO. I ignored the voice because it was not true - *morning shower, underarm deodorant, fresh clothes.*

HBO. The third letter had barely slipped his lips when I heard a thud, of a punch thrown hard and connecting against the flesh, right on a bone. I turned to see Girard pounding on the kid seated two desks behind me. No one moved to jump in or stop it. Part of me thought of joining on beating the kid down, but the teacher moved quickly down the aisle. As she pulled Girard off, she said, "I am tired of you getting into fights in class. This time I am sending you to the principal's office."

"He was saying mean things to Ernest." I read his switch, quickly, the way my twin sisters shifted into an innocent pitch.

The teacher's tone meant she had control of the classroom. Not only from her voice but the fact no one had moved. "That still is no excuse to be fighting. If Ernest is the one he's bothering, how come you don't see Ernest fighting?"

I had found my running partner so I could not let him take all the blame. "I was actually going to wait until recess and break one of his legs."

The entire class laughed. I had exaggerated but I did want to send the message I played for keeps and any silly little games other students had in mind would cost.

The teacher stared at me and I lowered my gaze. She scolded Girard and told him to return to his seat.

An hour later when the bell rang for recess, I let everyone leave the room, staying to introduce myself. Girard didn't even wait for the introductions before showing his excitement. "Man, where you been? It's almost a month since y'all moved here. Eric and Lionel said you'd be coming to this school."

I interrupted him. "You know my brothers?"

"Yeah, of course! We are all in Love."

"In what?"

We walked toward the schoolyard. "The Love Connection. We run things around here. We're Fists. Eric and Manny are Knives. Lionel is Gun."

"What?"

"You'll learn."

And that I would. During recess, Girard introduced those in Love and pointed out those who never will be. Even if you were not in Love, no one messed with you unless you stepped out of line, like the kid in class.

By day's end, I learned the crew was organized in clusters. Three groups of two people made up a cluster: Fist, Knife and Gun. Clusters were arranged by age groups but not always.

"Come. Let's go give our books to the girls." By now I had stopped asking questions. Throughout the day Girard seemed to have a planned format to indoctrinate me, to catch up for the weeks I missed. The girls were also in the sixth grade but in one of the other two homerooms. They were waiting for us near the lockers. "This is Cherise, my girl. That's Deirdre."

Though Girard stopped short, based on Love's structure, I knew Deirdre was my girl. Cherise was about five-two. Her hair hung down to her jaw line, bracketing cute puffy cheeks and dimples, small hoop earrings and stately round eyes. Deirdre had broader shoulders, a slender build and a more developed body. She stood confidently knowing eyes either bulged at her appearance or fell demurely to the floor. She gave a half-smile that wanted to open but only if my reaction to her merited it. She had a way with colors. Her lavender blouse contrasted with her metallic blue bubble goose coat. Her lip gloss sparkled, a welcoming trance.

When we failed to say a word to one another, Cherise asked, "What time are you coming by?"

"We're heading to the park and should be by you at five." Girard took a step toward her and planted a soft kiss on her lips.

"OK."

I did my best to not bust out laughing at the cute little scene between this little tough guy and his adorable girlfriend. As we walked away, I simply waved to Deidre and Cherise. They waved back.

We walked east, heading further away from my house and closer to the high school. I figured it was time to get certain things clear before Girard thought I was there to follow his orders. "I do my own homework."

"Me too. They just take our books home so it's easier to hang out in the park. Plus, I help them with their homework." He laughed, as if I'd said something funny or a thought crossed his mind. "Cherise's mom is overprotective. She wants her home as soon as school lets out. If not for that, they would be coming with us."

Chapter 5

It was a playground, not a park, in the traditional sense of grass, kiddie swings and benches. A concrete ballfield, with tennis courts, softball diamond, handball and basketball court, two *rims with no net*. Crowded with twelve year-olds and older, close to one hundred people, mainly boys, but the place packed enough girls to turn one's head a few times. We entered through the gate near the basketball court. The words were, "G, what's up!"

"Love is in the air, baby!" It took some restraint not to bust out laughing even though Girard had primed me on why they called their crew *"The Love Connection"*. From the little I'd seen these past few weeks of living around here, their antics bordered more on hate stuff. I saw how they ran around the corner, to and from the main avenue. Not all of them, but many of their faces brought memories of stick-ups, fights, snatched pocketbook or just plain rowdiness.

We walked near the basketball court, edging the out-of-bounds line, and headed to the other side where a metal backboard posted with no rim, only four gaping holes, where bolts had been stripped and pulled through, the rim now gone. A person behind me shouted, "Yo! Look up!" I turned to find he had thrown the ball hard, a bee-line toward my face. My reflexes allowed me to catch it with ease. After two quick dribbles with my left before taking a step, I switched to my right and made my way to the basket. Though one more step would have let me lay it against the backboard, I spun and threw a bullet pass back to him. A simple catch for him, he nodded. "Ernest, right?

They call me Slick 'cause my game is pure and smooth."

He dressed the opposite of someone fronting to exaggerate his ball skills – a simple long sleeve thermal, loose gray sweats and white leather Pony sneakers with the logo in black. His movements were fluid; shoulders tilted from side to side, giving his medium build the look of a scarecrow being blown by a gust of wind. Slick stood in one spot, dribbling the ball back and forth behind his back, while our eyes and head nods confirmed what we each felt – on the court we were *the real deal*. I could tell for him that basketball was his real love, and whatever *love connection* these other kids were claiming came second, if at all.

I broke our silent communication by walking away, toward where Girard had stopped. As my shoulders passed Slick's, he shot the ball from about thirty feet out. No need to turn around because I knew it went in before the others reacted with sounds of wonder.

By the time we made our way to the benches and short fence by the handball courts, Girard told me so many names. With each name, he uttered a person's rank in *The Love Connection - fist, knife or gun* - and whether the person was cool. Years would pass before I learned, to Girard, everyone was cool. It took a major trespass for someone not to be cool. My older brothers, Lionel and Eric were in the group we joined. There were about fifteen guys, and everyone pretty much said the same thing, *what's up Love*, except for Manny. "Yo E, that's your little brother? Man, I saw him looking out the window last week. He's SOFT."

His exaggeration of the word coupled with a fake little twang, pronouncing it "sawft" confirmed everyone would laugh. Before I had the chance to spit some words back at him, Manny reached out and slapped me. He did not do it with a lot of force, but it was clear we were about to get into a slap box match. Slap boxing was part play, while also serving as a means to establish the alpha males in youth crews. Open hand, no closed fists. Most times the boxing match was a quick pace swing-fest with little technique – an arbiter to test reflexes or toughness. The key to winning was to not duck nor shift your feet. Use your reach; move your head to either side or back, push with one shoulder, swing with the other arm.

My customary reflexes had abandoned me, leaving me there to process what just happened. No more than two seconds ticked before Girard's left hand slapped Manny. Manny's first swing missed because Girard stepped back. Since it was an error that gave Manny an advantage where he could plant his strong foot, I did not give Manny a chance to complete his second swing. I grabbed him and tossed him into the fence. That shorter fence reached only a few inches above his waist; he nearly fell over.

Again, reflexes.

Of knives being drawn.

Switchblades. Double-O Sevens. Even Eric had his drawn. Then I felt a second wave from behind me, coming from the basketball courts. The *fists* were with me. Then Lionel's voice boomed, "Everybody chill. It's all love."

Manny had balanced himself by grasping the fence, in the middle with his right hand, the fingers clutching the open circles while his left hand held on to the top bar. His steady steps toward me indicated no intention to retaliate. His extended right hand confirmed this, but the upside-down smile told of a calculation being done. The precise nature escaped me because his face gave way to no plot. Manny's smooth brow aligned flawlessly with his dark Caesar haircut. Topped with three-sixty waves, the haircut had the flash and symbols of our times: two parts - a crescent on the left and a dollar sign on the right. I responded to his reach by giving him a pound. The low, reassuring sound of his voice uttered, "It's all love. OK?"

"Okay!" My word came too quickly, indicating eagerness not to be Manny's adversary. It hinted at my confusion and drew me back to thoughts of my lagging reflexes.

Everything went back to normal. Small talk continued. Minutes later everyone agreed to meet later that night at *The Center*. The Love Connection split into small cells of two or three. I looked at Eric, to his eyes to see why he pulled out his knife; they said, "No he was not going to hurt me, but yes, he's got Manny's back."

I walked away with Girard, thinking of how he had covered my back twice in one day, once in class and now in front of his whole crew. "What's up with that kid Manny?"

"Oh, he's cool! That's my brother."

"I thought you were an only child?"

"He's my brother because we want to be brothers, not because we have the same parents."

"Am I your brother?" I was goofing on him because as hard as Girard tried to maintain an innocent-boy persona, the swagger in his walk, his predilection for peace, and the way he enunciated his words foretold of a boy who had been trained to make the hard call, much like my father had trained Lionel, Eric and me.

"Time will tell. Time will tell." Girard's words implied a deviation from early this morning when we first met. I considered whether he and others had picked up on my aversion to not just Manny but *The Love Connection.*

Chapter 6

Walking back to the neighborhood, we didn't say much, both probably contemplating if we would become as tight as Eric and Manny had gotten. The playground seemed much further from our school than the distance we walked earlier to meet the others. Using our school as the marker, everything on this side of the main avenue seemed to be someone's idea of progress. Few trees, concrete pavement, brick facades, parking lot for each of the two schools, six-story buildings towering in the background, overlooking colonial homes with fading paint and little evidence of human use. After a pattern of two corners with STOP signs and then a signal light, we hit the main avenue.

Traffic was heavy, much like the daily view from my window. Evening rush hour had started. Darkness approached, blurring the lines between the youths' daily activities and what parents reminisced of. Girard lived in the middle of the main avenue. Judging solely on the façade, his was the block's nicest building. The lobby had sitting benches, a desk and chair for a doorman who was not present, and a fountain with a nude statue. We took the left bank's elevator to the third floor but didn't stay long, just enough time for Girard to grab two juices out of the fridge. He handed me one.

We walked up the stairs to two floors above.

Cherise lived on the same apartment line, above Girard. The apartment had the same exact specifications, but her furniture struck me as something one would find in an octogenarian's home. The girls had started doing their homework and decided to join in on our plan. "No you can't come to The Center tonight because it means I will have to leave early to get you back here for your curfew."

"So?" Cherise's tone indicated Girard had come to expect her to do as he instructed, so when she balked at any of his suggestions, it was best for him not to argue. "Plus, my mom said it was OK for me stay out late as long as I finished my homework before leaving."

"Here, Ernest. Here's your notebook. I started your math homework…"

I interrupted Deirdre. "I do my own homework!"

Deirdre had the look of a girl who had never been put in check. Her voice rose, indicating she was about to tell me what I knew and how I learned it. "I was just…"

I cut her off. "I do my own homework." She rolled her eyes at me, picked her books off the dining room table and went to sit on the sofa in the living room. I looked up to find Cherise suppressing a smile, and Girard trying to hide a frown. The other parts of the day and *the love connection* I could accept. The Deirdre connection did not make sense. She did not look like the type of girl who needed her best friend to help her attract boys. Her demeanor bolstered a spoiled, lip gloss, bubble-gum chewing younger version of the woman in movies who got some fool to kill her husband. I considered myself a kid, and had never had a girlfriend, not even the cute little stuff kids did in third grade. I really did not want one. But there she was planning to go to *The Center* with us. It's like Deirdre assumed since Girard and I would be hanging out, and she and Cherise hung out, then we would be *in love* together.

After about two hours of homework, we exacted our plan of Girard coming with me to my house, posing as my reason to leave for the night. We turned the corner off the main avenue and the girls lagged until we went into the house. They would pass and wait down the block, toward the train station. To bring the girls in the house would have complicated my explaining going out on a school night when I had just gotten home. I knew my mother would give in and let me go. She went through the same battle with Eric three years ago.

My two older sisters did not care whether I went out - only unhappy they still had to follow a strict after-school curfew. Them and my brothers were all one grade behind because the school system felt it had to account for them not knowing English when we came to the country in 1972. Ghyslaine, the eldest girl, about to turn eighteen, a high school junior; Marlene turned fourteen in November. The twins were eight years-old and only curious about Girard, sizing him up as a potential new playmate. I left him with them in the family room while I went upstairs for a t-shirt and shorts. Minutes later I came back to find him really into it, debating with them about dolls and pushing trucks and race cars to the other side of the large room. "Yo, G! You're ready?"

Girard showed no embarrassment I caught him playing with dolls, and he even consoled the twins who felt jilted. "We'll play some more next time I come by." They gave their OK. We headed towards the exit. "Bye Mrs. LeGagneur."

"Bye-bye Girard. Nice to meet you."

We waved to my older sisters, but they simply rolled their eyes at us. We ran out the door, down the porch steps and toward the train station. "Man, your big sisters are tough."

"Yeah, but they're cool once you get to know them. They're cool."

"At least the little ones are sweet." I laughed knowing he had yet to witness their mean side. His interaction with the twins solidified my view that Girard yearned for familial bonds. Even his dealings with Cherise bordered more on a kinship than the preteen coupling of youngsters rushing to play adult sexual roles. I thought, OK, I could see treating Deirdre that way, as long as she behaved.

That became my mindset as we met up with the girls at the next corner and walked to the subway station. I smiled at Deirdre and the surprise registered on her face. We had not exchanged words nor gaze for hours. We had only stolen quick glances to measure the other's curiosity. Girard and

Cherise held hands while we walked behind them, a yardstick separating our shoulders from theirs. On this side of the main avenue, each block comprised of at least three trees, with none younger than thirty years old. No more than four homes on each side of the short east-west blocks; with about eight homes on each side of the north-south streets that ran parallel to the main avenue. The homes were Victorians built either in the late nineteenth or early twentieth century. Yards now paved for barbecue grills or manicured by self-professed landscape artists, amateur weekend gardeners. The porches bordered by lawns. White flight had made for a more diverse neighborhood on the main avenue and the blocks nearer to the schools and playground. On this side, most of the homes were still occupied by descendants of the original owners or being rented by transplants like my family.

Entering the subway station woke me to the stark reality of the times we lived. January 1981, Brooklyn, New York. The Stick-up Era. Graffiti on the walls. Everyone tagged the walls, with either or both insignias – the crew's and his name. The station looked dirty but smelled clean. The clerk in the token booth glanced down, back to his newspaper, as if resigned to the fact we would not pay, or complicit in that we should not, for we were students who probably had transit passes, even if they only permitted us to ride for free until 7p.m. We hopped the turnstile, while the girls walked through the gate.

I had never been to *The Center*, but hearing the three of them speak of its reopening after the winter recess, I could tell it existed as more than the nighttime distraction the adults envisioned to keep teenagers out of trouble. The Center had become a place where *Love* met. It was there, two years ago, youths who lived primarily in a zone occupied by four major Flatbush high schools decided to put aside the petty squabbling and rivalries that predated most of the various neighborhoods having black folks. Some beefs dated back to the 1950s.

The Center opened from Tuesdays to Thursdays at the three largest high schools, with each school rotating the programming. At this high school,

Wednesday's programs focused on sixth to twelfth graders. Other nights were dedicated to senior citizens, and parents with young children. This school was the main rival to our zone high school. The place had security but they were positioned far from the entrance, way down the hall near the staircase, to block people from entering the other sections. I spotted the boys' bathroom and went to change into gym clothes. Girard and the girls did not change. They waited for me near the entrance to the main gym. I glanced at the various games being played, but my focus was basketball. Since I always played with my older brothers, I looked for a way to join the game featuring the older dudes. The layout dictated the pecking order. A sliding wall divider split two gyms. On the right, two games on half-sized full courts, with observers sprinkled on the sides. G went to the right side, to hang out and talk with the other boys who weren't really there for sports, but mainly for girls or to be seen. That gym had the most people, about three hundred. The girls went to a group of girls in that same room. They chatted while waiting for their turn to jump double-dutch.

The gym to the left looked organized and competitive as any boys' varsity game I'd ever attended. Bright lights. Polished floors. Bleachers halfway packed, about two hundred people, on the side near the entrance. The actual scoreboard kept time and score. Two older men served as referees, and everyone else stood near the court, on the other side, next to the folded bleachers.

Slick was on the court, holding his own. He played offense at a measured methodical pace but on defense he moved frantically, arms stirring and reaching for the ball, or dishing light shoves to the guy he guarded. On the next side out of bound play, he reached his hand out for me to give him a pound. "What's up Love? You running?"

"Who's got next?"

"Get in for me!" He pointed to the other players. "Yo, Ernest is taking my place."

I removed my tank top and t-shirt to fit in with my teammates, and scoped the players and all the other on-lookers. Though all eyes were on me,

I only recalled three - my two brothers and her. To this day her name escapes me. For simplicity's sake, just call her Trouble.

Consider this moment the starting point. Everything else that day had been manageable.

I got on the court; *Skins*, my team was down by twelve. The games ran for eight minute quarters, with a running clock, except for foul shots and injuries, and a thirty-second shot clock. The game I joined was in the last quarter with 6:32 to go. For the rest of the night and the countless games we played, only my next two plays would matter.

The first: I got the ball in the half-court set, took two quick dribbles and went hard down the middle. The hit was not a cheap shot, just a hard blow across my forearms. Thrown off-balance. Fell. Before my butt hit the ground, my left foot planted, slipped, staggered to cushion the bump. The referee blew the whistle and I made both foul shots.

I was twelve years-old and considered big for my age. All the other players on the court were fourteen to eighteen. That made me *middle of the pack*, in height, weight and strength. Shirts shot after a couple of passes, got their own rebound and scored on a put-back lay-up. My team's defense did not concern me. I felt we needed to score, and I took up the challenge.

Since Slick had been running the point, I clapped twice for the ball.

The second play was what I called my speed game. The ball reached my hand twenty feet before half-court. A few quick dribbles then I made a lay-up. Only four others had passed half-court.

OK! All nine players were looking at me and had a choice to make. After a couple of rushed shots and with my team rebounding and running into a speed game, Shirts tried to slow the game down, by keeping at least two players back to defend our lay-ups. It worked for one play because the guy I passed the ball missed an easy fifteen foot jumper. He was wide open so I cut him a look that translated to I categorized him a scrub. Other Skins laughed and he joined in. By now, our confidence in each other as players had grown. We were picking up on defense much earlier. We didn't get a steal but a rushed shot. Rebound ours.

22 seconds to go. I took three dribbles and crossed half-court. Jumper. Swish. Nothing but net. Tied game.

With the court my sole focus, I had forgotten to glance at the only three spectators who mattered. Unlike the other spectators who cheered loudly and with lots of movement, they simply nodded their heads. The other players on my team talked trash to the other team – something I never did on the court or in life. I expected to perform this well, and I wanted to get to the point where others expected it of me. So silence served as my main weapon!

17 seconds to go. Tied game. "Press them!" When I did talk, I talked strategy. My voice surprised the others, especially the guy assigned to me. Throughout the game, I barely guarded him to give him enough room to maneuver so I could do a quick study of his game. My handle was average but I had no set pattern to my motion. Kid had a wicked handle, but quite predictable, in that he never dribbled only once with either hand. Most times he dribbled with one hand three times. His pattern lied more on two down dribbles before crossing over, a pass or a shot.

9 seconds to go. I gave enough space for his teammate to see he was open. His eyes showed he didn't want the ball. Ball got to him at the top of the key. To make sure he did not pass the ball to someone else, I didn't go belly up on him. He dropped the ball with his right hand. OneTwo. Crossed to his left. One...*rip*...

I stole the ball with my right, threw it around my back. Two quick dribbles with my left. I repeated the shot I used to tie the game. The buzzer-beater effect, for the win, magnetized a bunch of people, and they spilled on to the floor to join the celebration. All nine other players stared dead at me. I simply pumped my right fist.

The guy I had been guarding approached me first. "Good game, son! What's your name?"

"Ernest."

Slick ran over to my side, grabbed my shoulder and started shouting, "Yo! This kid is money! Yeah boy! This is Ern-Money. What's his name?

A whole lot of people replied, "Ern-Money!"

Slick guided me away from the court to the side. His breath pulsed as if he had been on the court running with us. "What grade you in?"

"Six!"

"OK, check this! Do junior high only until the eighth grade then transfer to our high school. We're gonna win the city championship my senior year. Cool?"

"Yeah!"

"Seriously, Du! I am in the ninth grade. So when I'm a senior, you be there, and we can run shit!" Slick kept nodding his head over and over, looking around the room, at the other kids from the rival schools. "I'm in this game. Who's out?" He said it like a command and it became clear Slick had juice.

One of the other Skins players gave up his spot. Before the next game started, Lionel, my eldest brother, came over and grabbed me in a friendly headlock. Lionel was an emotional dude but never showed affection. He whispered so no one could hear him. "I'm proud of you, son. I'm breaking out, heading back around the way. Don't lose a game tonight! Each game I got a cover of a yard per player on our side. Pretty much everyone in this gym got loot on these games. So, run shit!"

That's what we did. I lived up to my new on-court nickname, adding layers to myself, going from simply Ernest to Ern-Money. We all contributed heavily to winning the night's remaining four games, but Slick had this pure game. His full moniker was Slick-Money because he was smooth, slippery even. Slick was pure; on the dribble, the ball seemed to never leave his hand. Not only was his handle quick and unpredictable, he kept his body low with his shoulders in front and his eyes looking down court. The passes he threw on the break were precise. His effortless jumper netted murmurs from the crowd and 'good shot' from opponents. Slick possessed the courage to go down the lane, and enough respect for the game to know: No harm!! No foul!!

Purposely rooted in fundamentals and athleticism I played a very basic game. I attacked two ways, with the speed game being my secondary option.

The speed game consisted of the team moving vertically as fast as possible, settling only for jumpers only if the other team did not come out to defend. The speed game's effectiveness rested on the simple premise, most people cannot or refuse to move at their highest speed for a prolonged period, even while performing a simple function such as making baskets.

For my primary game, I positioned myself on the low block, either lay-ups, step-back or fade-away jumpers.

11p.m. One of the refs, the one who served as The Center's director called for the ball. I gave Slick a pound and looked him in the eyes and nodded. He acknowledged the gesture as my way of thanking him for letting me in. Eric came toward us. "Yo Eric, what's up, son! You weren't kidding. Ernest got NBA skills!"

"Why would I B.S. you? We're in Love, son!"

"Ern-Money, stay out of trouble! I am deep in Love. Made Gun at 14, two weeks ago. So if you ever need help with something, simply tell me. Don't get involved with any stupid shit!"

"OK!" At that, Slick walked away. I turned to Eric. "You like what you see?"

"Nah, that girl is trouble. We're heading out." Eric and I weren't twins but that sense he had of cutting right to my mind's hiding place always gave me pause. Physically we could pass for fraternal twins because he got his genes from our father's side of the family: thick limbs on medium frames, of people who grew quickly and stopped early. The previous summer I had a growth spurt and at twelve years-old, I stood five-foot nine-inches, and nearing one hundred and eighty pounds. My genes and build came more from my mother's side and in a few years I would likely end up similar in size to Lionel.

Only about fifty people remained in the gym. Of them, I recognized very few from earlier at the ballfield. Trouble still sat in the same spot. Throughout the night, I glanced to see who came by her and how long they stayed. Trouble looked sweet, in a *'Now & Later'* candy way. Juicy lips, wearing a pink top and dark Lee denims. White leather bubble goose coat and a sneer with slightly parted lips, as if nothing moved her.

Manny came to stand near us. Though neither said anything, it was obvious by my gaze where my mind was. Eric said, "Ernest, let's roll!"

"I'll catch up. Speed game! I'm gonna get her number and be with y'all by the time the train comes."

"What about Deirdre?" Girard had snuck up behind me. He was right and wrong at the same time.

"Take her and Cherise with you. I'll catch up."

He gave no more than a quizzical look before turning around. Eric motioned to two girls sitting on top of the bleachers, close to the gym's main entrance. His and Manny's girls.

Manny whispered to Eric, "Yo, I will wait with him. Tell the girls, we got static that needs squashing before it gets out of hand." Eric turned and went out of the gym with Girard and the four girls. Manny walked to the bleachers and sat on the lowest row. I wiped with my towel and put on my clean top, took off my sneakers, put on the sweat pants, over my gym shorts, and stepped back into my sneakers. By now, no one from our neighborhood was in the gym. The few people who remained were some of the boys I had played against, and a couple of girls.

Step by step up the bleachers, I saw this welcoming look in her eyes. We exchanged simple sentences. Two years her junior. Unless one of us defied tradition, geography made us rivals. And, even with Love, ours was a gulf few dared cross. No more than two minutes into the conversation, Trouble turned me down when I asked her number. Her reason, she would see me again. True, and though good enough for me, I did tell her, "No guarantee I'll want your number after tonight."

She laughed. And, I'm certain that's what did it.

People who knew Trouble must have known no one, nothing, moved her, at least by what could be deemed easily. Next thing I knew, the dude I had guarded during the first game was standing in front of the bleachers screaming something at me. At first it didn't register because I was so enamored by Trouble's lair. I heard Manny say, "Ayo Love, he's with me!"

"I don't give a fuck who he's with."

Manny didn't move from his seat. "Ern-Money, let's roll!"

Not the words I expected from Manny, but I was new to this Love thing, so I simply followed him by telling Trouble, "Take care. I'll see you."

I barely reached the bottom of the bleachers, when she yelled out. "Man, you're SOFT. You come up here like you want something, but scared to take it."

My first instinct, a reflex, to turn and look at her but it hit me where I was at, so I simply said to the guy I had guarded, "Sorry about that!"

And he said, "No harm! No foul!"

Love was a good thing, I thought to myself, making my way toward Manny and the gym's exit.

"Y'all both soft!"

"I ain't soft. That punk don't want nothing." The words did not faze me because Trouble obviously had a wicked handle on his emotions.

Manny kept quiet. He, like Trouble, sported a heavier leather version of the bubble goose coat most of the kids wore. His look was expensive, b-boy and hard. Cazal glasses. Black leather goose. Charcoal gray Chinese Mock Neck. Calvin Klein Jeans and blue suede Puma sneakers. Manny stood a half-inch taller than me, but he had a frail look to him though I would not tag him as skinny.

We walked on the same strides, out of The Center even after we heard the words, "Yo, did I say you can leave?"

Outside. Still a clear night. Quiet except for a car every thirty seconds or so. Cold, probably heading down toward twenty degrees. Manny's motion caused his blade to slide down from his coat's right sleeve to the edge of his palm. We turned slowly, with Manny folding his right arm on top of the left one, to hide the blade. There were about thirty of them, and no more than six girls. There were three distinct poses.

Hands in side coat pockets. *guns*

Arms folded, like Manny's. *knives*

Fists clenched. *fists*

Trouble's hands were in her pockets. Not absolutely certain how to pose because I connected to Love only this afternoon. Manny was calm, almost joking with the guy, but there was this undertone, an anger to belie he had stayed as my back to take a short. "Yo, I thought we squashed that?" When no one answered, he added, "Ron, what's the word?"

Another voice in the crowd spoke but I could not tell whose. "It's not my call, but I will shoot him if need be."

"Nah, no need for all that." Manny turned to the side, so only I could hear him. "Dude that's beefing with you is Fist, just like you. You think you can beat him?"

"Easily!" Partly insulted he even had to ask, the word jumped out my mouth, at the exact moment I questioned myself as to Manny's true loyalties. I asked him, "How do we know they won't jump us?"

"Ron is my man from way back and he's Gun." Manny maneuvered his right arm, to slide the blade back from where it had slid down. *All other arms unfolded.*

Hands out of pockets.

Fists unclenched.

Manny reached in his pants' right pocket and pulled out a wad of money. "Fight to the death. Fifty minimum. If you are in, stay up. If not, step back."

Twelve people stayed up, including Trouble and the guy who wanted to fight. The others stepped back.

"I got fitty on Ern-Money." Her voice had a rhythm, a young hustler's vibraphone. It chilled me to a sudden stop, pondering why I had been drawn to her, of all the other pretty girls in The Center. "Ain't you gonna bet on yourself?"

Manny knew her rhythm, countering it with, "Of course! I got his right here! So that's Five-Fitty, split three ways: 180, 180, 190 to Ern-Money when we win!"

Until that night I had never been in a fair fight, one-on-one against a stranger. Got jumped once. Fought my brothers and sisters, but never one-on-one against a stranger. I never had reason to, and right then I realized why I hated being in Love. Dude swung two, three times, and I evaded his punches without moving my feet. He had a predictable pattern much like how he dribbled the basketball. And, what worked against him on the court could work here, to rip him…apart. I connected with my right palm. The noise and sting froze him. Slapped him again with the right because he was expecting the left. This last one, I had a chance to wind up and threw it overhand. He swung his left. I moved back a little and as his hand passed, I connected with my left. If we had been using closed fists, his jaw would have broke. Since I knew he had nothing for me, I felt no need to further humiliate him in front of his entire crew. I jumped on him, crashing him to the ground. I put him in the yoke, blocking his air supply, until I heard Manny say, "Yo, Ernest, chill!"

I stood up and the guy who collected the money from their side handed it over to Manny, who divided the money, handing Trouble and me our cut. The kid I fought was just getting to his feet, so I helped him. "Are you all right?" He nodded. "Sorry about that!"

"No problem! It's all Love!"

The others shook their heads and they made to turn to go in the opposite direction, to walk home. Manny and I turned for the subway station. For some reason, she made to go with us. I asked, "Where're you going?"

"I figured I'd walk with y'all then circle back toward home."

"Ayo!" I called out. The other group stopped and turned. "You forgot someone."

"We don't want her. She's trouble." Though I am sure all of them didn't speak, it sure sounded that way. Trouble looked at us for a brief moment and walked ahead toward the subway station. As if of the same mindset, the way Eric and I flowed, Manny suggested we make a right and walk home, instead of heading down the dark street Trouble had taken. We talked like brothers, joking most of the time and with him imparting knowledge every now and then. Though he came off a bit preachy, Manny pointed out where I had gone wrong: Always go home with the girl you came. Never fight another man for his woman unless you are absolutely sure you want her. And the one I already knew, never kill a man.

I went straight home but Manny went to meet up with the others. By the time, my brothers came in the house, I was already asleep. The next morning, neither Lionel nor Eric spoke to me until I forced the issue and told them what happened after Eric left. They already knew and their silence verified what I felt. On technically my first day outside in this new neighborhood, I did not do well. No one cared I did not want to be in Love. Too many rules. Too many subtle messages. I spelled it out for them, "I am not cut out to being in Love."

They ignored my plea and told me to go to school.

Girard was waiting on the avenue, on the corner nearest my house. He cut right to the point. "I heard what happened. And, by now I'm sure Deirdre heard. So she's going to be mad at you, but…"

"Fuck Deirdre!"

"Son, that's like saying fuck Love!" He left it as an opening but I saw it as more of a hole, a grave I had to be careful not to dig further and make my own. Everyone, who was anybody, was in Love. Who was I to want otherwise? What else was there? I waited to let him continue. "Ern, you can't take all this so seriously! Love is a show, a gamble. It is what keeps the peace. Without Love, someone would have died last night. Maybe a few people."

"OK!" With that, I agreed to be part of the show. That is what it was. This connection we feel and claim. This Love, of fists, knives, guns.

Chapter 7

For a little over two years, I navigated Love using music as my guide. Although basketball opened doors for me and gave me instant credibility wherever I went, the music helped me relate to kids who knew Love differently. No matter the sound, the style, the country of origin, my ears picked up the essence being communicated. One moment I would be with b-boys, break dancers who carried cardboard boxes and a boom box, looking to battle other dance crews for money or bragging rights. The next, I would be on the benches behind a fenced-in basketball court listening to latest rockers from Jamaica.

In junior high school, through teammates, I gained some appreciation for rock, punk and heavy metal. The school bordered the next south Brooklyn frontier black families had come to inhabit. The clash was racial, filled with slurs, flying bottles, baseball bats, being chased and countering whatever trespass came toward us or anyone who looked like us. Black kids quickly learned to put aside any cultural and nationalist divide and embrace any black person willing to stand and fight. After school and ball practice, I would chill with them whether they roamed various avenues, chilled on their own blocks to listen to music or shoot dice. C-Lo was the game. I mostly watched, learning without losing money and getting into any riffs. The roll of the dice could not be avoided, as they were fanatical about all sorts of board games – Monopoly, Life, and Risk, a war game, a favorite that led to many arguments and debts.

We played Risk in front of the buildings where the supers or tenants did not fuss at our presence. But, the ballfield was our favorite place to be, on the dimly lit side of the handball courts. Dice flung against the wall for C-Lo and Craps, while near the back fence, a Risk game board splayed atop a stone column, surrounded by youths bent on world domination. On an average night, about one hundred of us, from the three neighborhoods closest to our zone high school, would click with those who were of like mind. The music would be on but low enough as to not disturb the few houses on the western side of our hangout. Those days could be seen as a battle between the upbeat jams some called Uptown music, Reggae and Hip Hop. Kids carried spray paint, markers and cardboard boxes to battle. For the most part, especially within Love, a real fight was rare. Still there existed a dark element to Love, where we diverged on the reason why Sweet G's "Games People Play" became a major hit. To some the song served as a warning and to others, a blueprint. People in Love stayed flush with cash. I never asked how they made their money. Pretty much everyone had bank. Some, like me, got it from their older siblings. Others like Girard had little on-the-level jobs. With him, it was hard to tell because G moved like a hustler but you never really saw him involved in anything nefarious. At most, he rolled dice or held a quart or a joint. Yet he talked of crime as a necessity for some while being something to avoid.

Life around the way seemed unstructured, at least on the surface to outside, peering eyes. Adults would whisper about kids with no direction. They could not be blamed for not being able to distinguish someone like Girard was more into figuring things out or coming to the house to be with my family. Whenever he came, I used it as an excuse to go roam. Even though I played sports throughout the year, my mother expected me to be home when I didn't have a planned activity. My favorite sport was football. Girard wanted no parts of it. He swore he didn't mind getting hit. That I believed because he was quick to slap box or wrestle someone, but there was also a side of him who enjoyed coming to the house and engaging my mother and sisters in the conversation of their liking for hours. I could tell he didn't like getting sweaty and dirty from the first night at *The Center*.

I convinced him to play football in this outside league since our junior high school didn't have a team. I told him to play defense but he preferred the idea of learning offensive strategies. My speed and strength made me a natural at defensive end and outside linebacker. Girard played half-back, mostly on options and some plays at wide receiver. I think he made the team because we came together to the tryout.

There were times Girard would disappear for hours after school or on weekends. When I needed to reach him, I would check with Cherise. She usually knew his whereabouts. They had bonded the way elderly married couples talked of meeting as teenagers before the war and having spent their entire lives together. Their openness with public hand-holding and kissing eventually led to an early maturity where they would go into his bedroom and pop in a cassette of love songs.

This bothered Deirdre. She wanted to bask in that type of showy affection. Though I spent lots of time with her and people considered her my girlfriend, we never clicked like that. She didn't say much, especially when something bothered her. She bottled her emotions as if expecting me to shake her with words or deeds. A part of me admired that about her, the knowing that both of us were in high demand by others. Deirdre needed me to flaunt her and I couldn't blame her. The years of hormones and expectations to make lifetime memories, our second Valentine's Day together, we had only really kissed, with tongue, just once before. She pushed herself into me. The volume of her breasts masked by her bra and the winter sweater, the heat of her body exploding through her clothes, she unbuckled my belt in the hall near the bedrooms, close to the bathroom. She grabbed it in her hand and looked at me. I turned to survey the place and we closed Girard's bedroom door for at least a solid hour. We played music to mask the noise. Deirdre blew my mind. Unlike when Girard and Cherise went to either of their bedrooms, our connection was not an easily muffled sound. Deirdre and I knew, whatever had brought us together, for it to work, our honesty had to erect a barrier between us.

We were older than them by months. We were taller. We held our passion behind steely looks and mannerisms. She confessed to having started the pill the week we met. She had no plans of getting pregnant before or during high school. We coursed through the end of seventh and eighth grade like little love soldiers, wound up dolls, who took pictures with big smiles, exchanged belt buckles and chain pendants. We passed time together and occasionally, when I failed to express the desire to be with her the way Girard did with Cherise, Deirdre would call my bluff, ask whether I thought there was a better looking girl around the way. I explained to her it was not that, and I could see many of the neighborhood guys being a better fit for her. That confused her and brought a silence between us, a chill.

The cold snowy winter dragged into the spring. We spent a lot of time indoors with the girls. May was a much needed reprieve and we started going to the ballfield. The place had begun to lose some of its lure. As older dudes graduated high school or to bigger antics, fewer younger ones took their place. First came Atari 2600 and with new competitors like ColecoVision, kids started huddling around the television. Before then, some had already gravitated toward the large arcade. I rarely stayed at the arcade for long periods of time but it was a good first option to catch up to Eric, Manny or Lionel. I hadn't seen Lionel for a few days. Lionel was a man of few words, who turned himself into a lefty because in a fight, the opponent did not expect it, especially if you carried yourself like a right-hander. Lionel had a heavy left hand, a quick one. As the eldest, he had found moving from Haiti to New York more of a challenge. For me, my biggest obstacle was calling football soccer. Lionel never really enjoyed sports as one would think someone of his size would. Football-soccer and handball were his lone interests, minor ones at that. A couple of months ago, Lionel turned twenty-one and with it came an uneasiness to do something with his life. He never stated what or where the pressure was coming from. I asked him if it was our father and he said no. Physically, I could see why he was uncomfortable. He had finished growing. In his BVD nylon tank top, he looked like an action hero, complete with the ripped muscles garnered strictly from pushups and running. He wore a tank top, even though the temperature was in the low sixties. His custom belt buckle with the word LOVE dangled off his jeans' belt loop; pants worn loose to hang off his waist to flaunt his matching BVD nylon briefs. Lionel was a man, not prone to trends, he still sported an Afro he rarely picked or opened up to only flatten into a perfect sphere. I always saw him as a grown man even in my first recalled memory, likely at age three. Full of wisdom but mixed with impulse, Lionel lived on a side of Love he treated as his calling. He once explained why I needed to get to the point where I could do three sets of one hundred pushups. He ran everywhere, throughout the day. He explained people, especially police, got used to seeing him running. The police used to stop him but he never had a weapon, drugs or stolen goods. On days when he actually did something wrong those same people would not think twice about his running. Lionel spent most nights out either sleeping at some grown woman's apartment or the pad he chipped in with some of the older dudes in Love. Lionel never had a job. He lived on the dark side of Love, the brutal and criminal element. Never a stick-up kid, he enforced the rules, collected from those who did not pay gambling and other debts, and pulled women as they stood with their boyfriends. I was not privy to what he, Eric and Manny talked about. Whenever Girard and I hung around them, they went silent. The only inkling I had as to how deep in Love they were came the time when I realized Lionel had no counterpart in Love, like I had in G, and Eric had in Manny.

A few months after we moved to the neighborhood, Lionel's counterpart was killed during an armed robbery, for his trail bike and gold chains. I didn't know we were going to a wake until we got there. Lionel didn't want our parents and sisters to know. It was not clear to me until Girard pointed it out. Deirdre's oldest brother wanted to be Lionel's new counterpart. Lionel always shrugged him off.

No guy openly asked another to hang out like they're dating or something.

So Benny always provoked Lionel, as if to show he was that tough. I always felt knife was tougher than gun, and fist tougher than knife. For me, it was the amount of time it would take to kill a person using a particular weapon. Still, gun was a higher level because it required more patience and cool.

And, Benny was not cool. On the surface, Benny had the rugged exterior, complete with a permanent bruise on his right cheek. He stood at six-two, my height, two inches shorter than Lionel, who had Benny by about thirty pounds.

Benny's weakness manifested itself in his jumpiness. His feet never seemed planted on the ground; they mirrored his speech pattern. He was showing his lack of cool, by arguing every call and trash-talking. Mind you we were playing handball using the Spalding balls with the extra air that made the balls bounce higher and move quicker. Lionel was on my team, and Benny partnered with some kid I had seen but who was not in Love. We were serving them, something like 11 to 4, with game 21. Benny was clearly the weak link. He may have been drunk or high on something, or simply jumpy. Lionel had dark irises but I noticed a yellowish brown tinge in his pupils like he had stayed up late last night or had something heavy on his mind. The game was so lopsided we used it as a time to talk, to catch up. Benny kept breaking in, arguing every call, constantly asking the score and just being a general nuisance, not only to us but to the people on the neighboring court. In total, there were about fifteen people inside the grid that housed the four handball courts, and probably another fifty in the ballfield, equally divided between the basketball court and the concrete baseball field. "L, can you give me some money for sneakers? I don't want to ask Ma."

"Ask Eric or Manny! I'm saving money for something big."

Benny interrupted us. "Man, stop talking and serve the damn ball!"

Lionel looked at me and shook his head. We both laughed. Lionel served the ball, and Benny called it out. It really was in. "That was in." Benny held on to the ball and made to walk up to the service line. His partner didn't budge to come forward. Lionel repeated it with force. "That was in."

"Man suck my thumb! That ball was out!" Four words, split two ways after the second word of each sentence. Benny said them, like he had a heavy tongue, developed from trying to not stutter.

By now he was in my brother's face. My brother took a few steps back and laughed. He talked loud but in Kreyol. "M'ap tiye neg sa! Pa kouri!" He then agreed with Benny. "OK, your serve!"

Benny's serve was out, yet he tried to count it as a point. When Lionel corrected him, he said it again, "Man suck my thumb!"

"OK, bring your thumb here and I'll suck it." All this time, I'm not really processing where this would head. I had taken Love for granted. That everything would be peaceful, and everyone in Love felt the same thing for each other. But there was this thought in my mind, not from the song of the day about the games people play. The words were ones that placed Deirdre and I on different planes, just like Lionel and Benny were on different planes.

For me and Deirdre, for them that day, even though I did not have the words, I knew: *Love is a two-way street, a place we'd never meet.*

And, Benny and Lionel, though they were together on the handball court, they were having two different conversations. Benny was asking for acceptance. He wanted to be a Gun, especially since Lionel, who had moved into his neighborhood, never had to be anything less. And, I was dating his little sister but not really giving her standing. And, Lionel wanted out of Love. His eyes said so. I knew how he felt, so I was willing to see how this would play out.

Benny moved fast, knowing his dare had been met, wanting to see the consequence. They had not been talking that loudly but everyone had zeroed in. Some had even taken steps forward to get a closer look. But as soon as they walked forward, they ran away. It happened fast. Benny stuck out his right thumb. Lionel sucked it down and up twice then bit into it on the third down. As he bit, he clapped open a Double-O-Seven knife and gutted Benny. Lionel pulled the knife from the left hand pocket of his black denim jeans, flicked it open with a bend and pop, a flick of his wrist. I had seen my mother gut fish with less hesitation. Benny's left hand grabbed Lionel's shoulder. The pain was such that he couldn't project his scream. Because of his thumb, held by Lionel's teeth, he couldn't fight back the thrust and slashing motion of the knife. When Lionel took out the knife, there was no way a lawyer could argue it was not premeditated. The cut was precise and formed a letter, a capital L.

Lionel was gun, so why did he use a knife? That was my first thought.

I didn't run because he had told me in Kreyol, he was *going to kill this negre; don't run!* I didn't run because he was my blood brother. I didn't run because he told me to serve the ball. Everyone in the ballfield had run. Everyone, except Girard and Manny. I didn't know why they were still here. Lionel even told them to run. Manny defied him. "No we're brothers. We stand together."

I envisioned the ball bouncing millimeters past the service line. It would cut sharp right across and over Benny's wishbone, an inch or so above the tip of the capital L.

Girard said, "He asked you to put him out of his misery."

Though I didn't serve the ball, I was going to stand with my brother. We leaned against the short fence waiting for the police and ambulance. We thought they would come quickly, but no one who ran called them.

They came because someone had run into Eric and told him.

Love had rules and even in a moment like this, they were people willing to follow them. When Eric showed up, he was frantic. "Why are y'all still here? I called the ambulance thinking y'all had bounced." I had never seen him so ruffled. He asked Lionel, "Why? What have you done?" Then he turned to me, turned on me. "You let him do this? What's wrong with you?"

I peeped something a while back but never asked. When Eric stepped back to assess the situation, it confirmed he was the leader of our cluster. When we had a decision to make, even though he wasn't the oldest, his reasoning and voice was final.

Lionel was quiet and pensive. The sirens were nearing us, alternating between the ambulance and the police. Lionel's final words to us, "Listen! We gotta stay in Love but leave the criminal shit behind." He handed Eric his gun. "You and Manny, when I call home, you two come to the jail. Ern and Girard, I never want to see y'all again. Don't come visit me! Don't call me! I don't exist to y'all."

Girard started crying. Until his sobs, I hadn't taken Lionel's words literally. The grave look in Lionel's eyes finalized it. He pointed to the hole in the fence where people snuck into the ballfield, after dark, when the gates were locked. We slid through the hole and moved along the side of the building. This side of the building had no windows. We descended the steps to where the superintendent placed the garbage cans. We accessed the basement door and waited until the cops cuffed Lionel and the ambulance carried Benny's body away. Tears were running down Girard's eyes, while the three of us held back our tears.

We walked up to the lobby and out the front entrance.

Chapter 8

Word traveled fast and through channels I couldn't have imagine existed. As soon as we opened the door, my mother smacked Eric. He took the hit and kept walking with the same focus used as we circled back to the house. The three of us hesitated in walking up to and past her. Her stare, nearly eye level to mine, asked the question even though she probably knew the story inside out, that I was the one there, the one who had not stopped Lionel. We slid by her and joined Eric in the living room. She stood while her eyes shifted to each of us. The four of us hung our heads low in shame while she called us every name in the book. My mother worked with old people. She told me she preferred their company. She loved to hear their version of history, to make up for the formal education that had eluded her. The eldest of three children, she ran away from her small town at fourteen when she saw what life had planned. She ended up in the home of an older man. He said she was big for her age – tall and robust, dark, gorgeous, regal, like a wooden statue carved with its arms undifferentiated from its sides. The older man had a wife and a son. The wife was sickly, unable to care for the house. The son had ambition. Neither father nor son knew of the other. She slept in a shack not far from the main house, in the back of the yard, next to the rooster, the three hens and the goat. She endured; in fact, she thrived, as the ear, the journal of an old woman who had seen so much the skin on her face had wrinkled hard, in scales like drawn lines mapping out the struggle of her ancestry.

My mother was hurt because she had in essence lost her eldest child, even though she had warned all her children the terrain of life fired shots from above, randomly. She had preached to us in an ecclesiastical cadence from the sliver of space she'd made room for belief in her life. The elderly, with their faces scrawled upon like pages of old notebooks, their frailty had shown her the circle of life lacked order and one's best bet was to stay low while moving forward. She yelled until her voice began to hoarse before dismissing us with the proverbial words, "Wait until your father gets home!"

We went into the bedroom I shared with Eric. Two sat, each on the bottom edge of the two beds. By now we were all crying, not sobbing, just tears. Our sisters followed us into the room. They had been in the next bedroom, the smaller one where the twins slept. Ghyslaine recounted the story and asked me to fill in the blanks. Ghyslaine, the eldest daughter, looked as my mother did throughout her young life. In the albums we would joke she was my mother's do-over. As such, my mother smothered her and filled her with life lessons she was not prepared for.

After I finished explaining how the entire scene unraveled, Ghyslaine hugged me. Each sister hugged one of us, as if this act by Lionel had formally bonded Manny and Girard into our family. My sisters' love for us had never been so visible, so needed. Their eyes confirmed what we felt – life, as we hoped and imagined, was over.

My father stormed into the room as if ready to tear us to pieces, but the scene of love startled him, froze him as he clutched a rolled up newspaper in one hand and his hat in the other. Without his hat, and the sweat sticking to his shirt showing the outline of his sleeveless undershirt, I could see Eric, how he would age. His hair would recede like an upside down vowel until it reached the sideburns. From there it would push a bit above the ears. The skin would be taut, the color of roasted nuts, leading to a downward slope, a roundness to the shoulders indicating a strength that had not come from the current ways he made money. My father once told us boys he only worked to get out of the house, the same reason as he had done since before becoming a teenager. He got up each day and joined the new legion of people who had decided to take a piece of the MTA's action. They congregated at Church Avenue. He drove an old Buick up and down Church Avenue, picking up fares, from people who had lost faith on the B35 coming on time to take them from the subway to their homes or from home to the subway. While doing that, hidden in his newspaper, he carried scraps of paper for people, numbers for the *bollette*. Other than that, my father never talked about what took him out at six in the morning and brought him home no earlier than midnight. My mother left at seven and got home by five. Yet unlike the conventional bickering one hears about marriages, my father always backed whatever my mother said when it came to how the house would operate.

My mother stood behind his right shoulder, an edge to her face, as if waiting for him to explode, perhaps the way she had done when she finally reached him by phone. He had this new look on his face. The eight of us united in forgiveness and love had dissolved his anger, obliterated the look from when he first opened the door.

I had to recount the story again. My father shook his head and said, "OK!"

My father had met Girard and Manny only in passing, at the house, exchanging simple greetings. Unlike the scared type of parents, from our extended family and friends, who would call their neighbors' children *sans-avez, vagabonds* and worse, my father had no fear of what we would learn outside the house. He taught us life as he knew it because he knew we were no angels; he knew how he was raised. He had given the lessons to Lionel, who passed the information down to Eric who forwarded them to me. My father was not a vocal or emotional person. All he asked them, "How come you two didn't run?" They gave the answer they gave earlier. My father pointed to the six of us. "OK! You see these two. Even though you lost one brother today, you have gained two new ones. Love them as you do your own!"

"We do!" There was no need to cue us in. We all said it at the same time.

"I have to make a few phone calls. Ghyslaine, I need you to take the twins upstairs to your room. After I'm finished, Eric, only you answer the phone. If anyone asks, no one is here but you and Ernest."

The call my father anticipated didn't come until nine o'clock, seven hours after we left Lionel. We had been on edge for the past four hours, pacing the room or going up and down the stairs. By that time my mother had come to her own decision. She would take my sisters and go stay with family for the night. She kept saying there would be some sort of retaliation from Benny's family, or the police would come to the house. My father kept reassuring her Lionel did not have identification on him and he would not tell them his family's name. That, my father was sure of.

Though Eric placed the 911 call from a pay phone, my father still felt he had been careless and brought the family more danger. My father's life, in Haiti under various presidents, the US Occupation and rise of Duvalier, made him weary of involving police in private affairs. To him, this was a war between families. At no time, did he say what Lionel did was wrong. He waited to hear the reason. This side of my father was foreign to me. He had never talked to me alone. As a group, he treated all of us children well, but he only spoke to the three eldest. Of all the children, he looked most like Eric. Eric in turn was a replica of his voice and personality. They had a bond that was hard to explain. I picked up on it in how my mother dealt with Eric, with him being the one she always sent to interrupt my father when she needed something.

My mother left without hugging anyone. The taxi only had to honk once. My sisters sported worried looks and held us tight with their farewell hugs.

With the women gone, the five of us sat in the living room. Our silence finally broken by the telephone's ring, my father put a finger in front of his lips and pointed at Eric. The phone conversation between Lionel and Eric was brief. Eric rarely spoke. His only replies were to agree. When he got off the phone he communicated what Lionel wanted him to do. We followed him to the attic, an open space reconfigured into one large bedroom for my older sisters and a smaller bedroom for Lionel. Using a milk crate as a step ladder, Eric reached and brought down two shoe boxes from Lionel's closet. We followed him back to our bedroom. In our room, he did the same thing but only brought down one box. "Manny, we need to stop by your apartment to make up the balance. G, count the cash."

My father never once asked how Eric and Lionel had gotten their hands on so much money, and why each box contained a handgun. My father wanted different answers. "What did Lionel say?"

"His lawyer will contact us. For now, he wants me and Manny to bring one hundred thousand dollars and two guns to a man named Doppler."

Before Eric was able to finish, Girard spoke the words that turned everyone's eyes to him. "Doppler? That's my father! How does Lionel know my father?"

"I don't know. Lionel's been working with some guys and put me and Manny down on some moves. I've never met this Doppler." My father didn't ask Eric what kind of jobs and neither did Girard. So, I did. Eric stared at me and turned his attention back to my father. "He said it was important to keep everyone away."

"If there is another adult involved, then I must go with you."

Girard spoke up. "No. I will go. Whatever the situation, seeing me will make sure Lionel and everyone gets a fair shot."

Manny seemed more puzzled than I was. Again, I asked the unspoken question, "I thought your father was dead?"

"That is what my mother told me. I had seen him only a few times. The last time I was four. After that my mother told me he had been killed. And since, I never heard from him again, I figured he was dead."

Everyone stared at Girard. I studied him, looking for a hint he was lying. My father took two steps away and rubbed his brow with his right palm. "OK! I understand the situation. This is not a war between two families. This is bigger than that. You are his son, his legacy. He is calling out to you. You don't have to go. Your mother took you away for a reason. Earlier, I said you are my son and I stand by that. No one goes anywhere!"

Eric defied him. "What about Lionel?"

My father didn't seem bothered by his tone. "No, that phone call. His lawyer was supposed to call. Lionel would have never called the house from the jail. They got to him. They must have gotten to him way before, not sure through who."

"So, we can't just leave him!"

My father's voice dropped to a remorseful tone. "He was warning you but he could not tell you the real situation. He is my son. He made his choice. He chose death."

"No!" Eric, Manny and Girard said.

Though I felt guilty for not siding with them, I could not go against my father. Until that moment, I never thought Eric could.

That night Eric made a choice. My father did not try to stop him when he grabbed the boxes.

Manny followed him. As Manny left the room, he turned one last time to let his eyes find my father's eyes, to show he meant no disrespect.

Girard had one foot heading out and one standing still. I felt he would only budge if I moved. My father had spoken. I was not leaving.

I heard the front door slam.

Girard sat on the bed and as if a force propelled him, he got up to run out of the room. My father called out to him. "Girard, come here!" My father met him halfway. "Do you trust Ernest with your life?"

"Yes."

Without looking at me, he asked, "Ernest, do you trust Girard with your life?"

"Yes." I only answered that way because I was expected to, and I guess the same could be said for Girard.

My father said, "You go in with your eyes open. Ernest will later go in with his eyes closed. But you never lead, unless it is time for Ernest to get out."

"OK!" At that Girard smiled for the blessing my father had given him. "I will do the same for Lionel and…"

My father stopped him mid-sentence. "Lionel is dead, and you must accept this. Lionel is dead."

Girard didn't say anything else before leaving to go catch up to Eric and Manny.

Chapter 9

My father led me to his bedroom. The room had a king-size bed, a sitting chair by the window, dressers - one with a small bench in front of its mirror, and two double closets. One closet's door was open, most of its contents emptied out. Whereas Eric had stepped on a milk crate, my father opened the other closet and bent down to unearth his past. The old box's flaps were folded into each other, jammed to indicate someone had locked it but based on an honor system, if found no one should pry. He had hidden it under a pile of clothes from a time where he was probably in step with that era's idea of cool, a *flanneur*. Inside the box, a slightly smaller one was wrapped, sealed with masking tape, its color faded, a caked-on layer of dust, indicating the number of years the box had been sealed. There was not nearly as much cash as the boxes Eric had exposed, but there was a gun that seemed to have lived several lives. From under the money and gun, he pulled up two albums for me to look at.

He left the room to go downstairs.

An hour later, he returned with the family album I knew. He sat next to me on the bed. "Ernest, I am an old man and I am tired of running."

"How old are you?"

"I turn 69 in August." I knew the month and day but not the year and the other stuff the hidden albums had shown. The first two families, he started in his early twenties and thirties. Altogether he had sixteen children: six from the first marriage, three from the second, and the seven of us in this new album. When he said marriage, he did not mean church and state being united. He laughed when I asked if my mother knew about the others. He said, "There are no secrets between us. OK, there are some, but she knows the important stuff. She chose me and that choice got our home burned. That man blames me for his father's death."

"Are all of us your kids? Is that why you don't want to go visit Lionel?"

"Of course you are all my children! She left that man twenty-three years ago, and sure enough he came back for his revenge. I was just passing through town. I am not sure what she saw in me, such a beautiful tall woman." His eyes seemed to travel back but he still could not picture how exactly it happened. "By then I was forty-six. I guess I was the middle between that old man and his son. She ran out with a small bag. The old man was cursing, running after her, saying you promised her you would take care of us. As she jumped inside my pickup, telling me to hurry, he grabbed his chest and fell face first into the mud. She told me how she had waited a decade for me, had dreamt me and knew exactly what to expect."

My father repeated he was an old man, tired of running. I could see the years coming across his eyes and washing over his face.

"What do you need me to do?"

He still had not returned. "Lionel. Oh Lionel, what have you done? I never lost a child in the war. I was a soldier. A good soldier." He turned to a page in the first album. I had seen it and thought he looked young and strong, nothing more. He turned to a page in the second album. In this page he looked mean, angry and determined. I saw myself. "All of my other kids are regular people because I paid the price for all of my children, including the seven of you. When I wasn't working to put food on the table, I killed people in whatever army had the people's best interest at heart. I paid the price and owe nothing to anyone. Now this? I don't understand this. How did they get to Lionel, to us?"

At that my father grew quiet and the tears continued to trail from his eyes. Again I asked, "What do you need me to do?"

"Follow the rules, and when there are none, accept only two things. My uncle told me this the day I left for the army. Accept only two things in life: food and pussy. Those are the only things a person cannot ask you to return. And, only cowards poison those means of sustenance!"

"What happens when they come back?"

"They are your brothers and you trust them with your life. You protect yourself first. But remember, they are some ties that are knotted stronger than blood ties."

"Love."

He smiled. "Yes, a woman's love."

He put the two albums and everything else back in the small box and into the bigger box. He went back to the closet and buried it where it belonged. I needed more information than he planned on giving me. Yes, all the other children loved him as much as the seven of us did. My father had planned his life, so that he got to see all the kids to their teens. Afterward they knew how to reach him, but I wondered if they really knew him. Not only did I learn I had family tucked away in a closet, he said I could call and they would help me because I was one of them. He said I had nothing to worry about.

To ease my concerns, he offered me a drink. Barbancout Rum on the rocks. He told me to let the ice melt into the liquor, water down the strength, until such day I could handle the liquor served straight up. He drank his without ice. We sat and listened to music. My father always started his jam sessions with Coupe Cloué. He called him *his main man*.

Under dimmed lights, I felt bonded to the rhythm of his heart, where joy had overtaken the pain he had suffered and endured.

After the second drink, I dozed off. I had gotten boisterous before falling asleep. I woke with my head on the right edge of the sofa. I woke not 'cause of the brightness the sun had brought into the room but because I heard the start of a conversation. My father sat on the loveseat he designated as his when the furniture first arrived.

After the fire, when we arrived to this Brooklyn house, my father used keys to enter, stating the insurance company had made good. My mother and sisters had organized the kitchen, shades or curtains for all windows, and the bedroom closets. Our clothes and everything else was new, sort of like Christmas coming weeks later.

Furniture came over the next few days.

This house was more spacious than our previous home. The first floor's front doors opened up to a foyer with shelves, a coat closet and two sitting benches. On the left side, large doors opened into a parlor room filled with book shelves, tall windows and the feel of being surrounded by wood, the way houses in black and white horror movies looked. Interior pocket doors led into the living room. The parlor room eventually became the playroom and got filled with board games, playing cards, toy cars and dolls. The living room seemed off-limits, even though it had the television and stereo. The new sofa set formed an arc around the television.

The kitchen took up most of the back of the house and it had a small bedroom next to it. Connected to that bedroom were a bathroom and a chamber that circled toward the dining room. Off the chamber, there was a door to get to the driveway and backyard and the basement. In the main hall, feet after the foyer's door, a staircase led to the three bedrooms on the second floor, and the stairs to the attic.

We had more space than the previous house, yet I still shared a room with Eric. Whereas we owned our last home, in this one we were renters.

I looked at the clock against the wall. They had been gone thirteen hours. They did not seem anxious to tell us where they had been and what happened. Since my father asked no questions, I just simply returned their 'what ups' and left it at that.

Manny and Girard had an uneasiness to their stance: their legs slightly ajar, their feet not firmly planted on the rug. Whereas Eric immediately took a seat, they stood until my father pointed at the sofa. They sat next to me but never looked my way. My father offered them a drink and they accepted. Eric poured his own drink though my father had not offered him one. "Since when you let Ernest drink?"

My father smiled. "What do you want to be when you grow up?"

There was a lull until Manny spoke. "An artist, a painter."

My father spoke in a calm tone. "Draw something for me."

Eric spoke next. "I want to be a musician."

"Play something for me." Eric went to the piano and started playing. I was not impressed because he started lessons at seven and continued lessons until junior high school.

Girard shot high. "I want to be president."

"President of what?"

"The United States."

"Come here!" Girard got up and stood in front of my father. Manny kept drawing. Eric kept playing. I just kept listening. "How do you plan to do that?"

"m kapab pale cinq lang. m pense si…" Girard's spoke a communicative Kreyol that lilted more on the French language side because of the way he accentuated the words.

Eric stopped playing and walked over. Manny looked up and tried to feign surprise but I could tell by his eyes he already knew Girard spoke Kreyol. My father asked, "Who taught you?"

"I learned by taking French in school and listening to your wife and daughters speak. These two here never speak it unless they're up to something, usually something bad."

Eric and I chuckled.

My father was impressed. "In two years you're that fluent? Language is important but it divides as much as it unites." My father said, "I taught my children to limit the use of our native tongue in public. That is how it remains a code." Girard nodded. "OK, tell me more. What other languages do you speak?"

"German and Spanish. I just started Russian and Japanese."

"Why those?"

"German because they are always opposite the U.S. in major wars. Spanish because there a lot of Puerto Ricans moving in around here."

My father stopped him by putting up his right hand. "What is your plan?"

"I want to bring people together and form a strong coalition…"

"Wrong! It is not wise to bring people together because they eventually turn against you." Girard was stumped. We were all looking at him. My father asked again, "What is your plan?"

When he did not offer an answer, I aided him, "You keep everybody separate but you treat them as your equal."

My father nodded and asked, "Ernest, what do you want to be when you grow up?"

"A father to my children."

"Manny, let me see what you drew."

We all looked at the image. Our confusion in seeing he had not drawn a solid object but lines moving in different directions. Manny's drawing explicitly told us we were surrounded, and we had to fight our way out. The lines' length, thickness, directions and proximity to each other had no set pattern. Girard made to speak, "The outer…"

My father shot him a look and he quickly stopped talking. My father looked at them and pointed at me. "Follow him. He's like the monkey who sees, hears and says nothing."

Eric said something that shocked even my father. "I leave for college in a few months. How are we to follow Ernest?"

"Leaving? The war is here. They've brought it to your doorstep."

Manny answered, "We're going after them."

I interrupted. "Am I seeing this wrong?" The three of them had a question in their eyes. They had seen or experienced something they felt gave them insight as to what they were up against. They didn't know during their time away my father had given me a legacy, a lifetime of experience, wisdom to analyze a situation for what it is and not what I wished it to be. I could feel their doubt, that somehow I was lesser.

I needed my father's permission to continue speaking so I stopped until he asked, "Ernest, what do you see?"

"A city that is not built on a grid, making it hard to penetrate. It's in a valley and the mountains serve as its protection."

My father waited for them to speak and it was clear they could not talk what they knew, at least not in the open. My father said, "Like I told Ernest, I'm an old man. I raised my children to know there's a war but I taught them how to avoid it. Girard, your mother did the same for you. But Manny, your father no matter how much he has tried to deter you, you have revenge in your eyes and heart."

Manny did not say anything.

We spent the day eating and drinking as a family, a circle of grown men.

Chapter 10

The days after Benny's death, the house felt like a dungeon masquerading as a fortress. The first week, even though he made us go to school, my father stayed at home from work that Monday. Manny and Girard only went home to show face and sleep. When we weren't in school, we stayed home unless something specific was happening. As more days passed and we got comfortable with the idea there'd be no retaliation, the house became more like a clubhouse. With less people, the house did not seem as big because we rarely went to the attic or basement. At first it felt lonely without my mother and sisters. I lost that feeling during my first visit to their new home. They moved back to Queens and rented a house not far from where we had lived. The twins still had to share a bedroom. There were no pictures of my father or any of us brothers. No one mentioned Lionel.

In fact, in our house, Lionel was also an afterthought. None of them mentioned him, at least not in front of me, knowing full well thoughts of Lionel invaded our every move when we stepped outside. He had pleaded guilty and got sentenced to twenty-five to life. The plea was to avoid the risk of what might come to light about Love during a trial. My father went to see him before he was sent upstate. I asked if I could go with him. He repeated Lionel was dead to me.

<0>

The streets were different without Love. No one mentioned it but love had not completely disappeared. It existed beneath the surface, sort of like in families who don't show affection. I kept waiting for some sort of retaliation for Benny, but nothing came. Deirdre, her mother and other brother scrambled out of town. In a way that explained the money Eric collected for Lionel, but it really did not. I was not sure whether the money was a payoff to her family, or a hit put out on her family.

Cherise's mother forbade her to talk to Girard or any of us. Though he never really discussed her, even after she moved out of town as soon as the school year ended, I could tell Girard had already pictured himself spending his life with Cherise.

The streets still had the bounce, the feel of love. The fashion moved from the layered clashing colors favored by pimps and hustlers, a machismo that embraced tight-fit, plaid pants, sharkskin slacks and bell bottom jeans. In moved solid bold colors and reliance on brand names from Lee denims, Wrangler, Devils and the early onslaught of expensive designer jeans – *is that your ass or the Jordache*; *Sasoon to be mine* – bringing notice how young girls had blossomed. Form-fitting jeans left an impression and mini-skirts had pull, a magnetic aura to match the boys' transition to silk shirts and polo tops away from mock necks or rayon and polyester shirts. Sneakers – Pumas, shell-toe Adidas and track Nike – knocked out Playboys and British Walkers and Converse and Pro-Keds.

Still, the streets had cliques and crews that quickly merged into a posse, where upon entry into dark basement parties or movie theaters, people announced themselves, and even when the refrain was 'Peace God', anything could still spark a gun battle. With all these changes going on around them, Eric and Manny stood solid, to a plan they had before Lionel killed Benny. By late July, all they talked about was going away to college. I had never heard of such a thing. I knew people went away to prison, but few who went to college, especially away from home, except the people who played sports.

Eric and Manny had a plan. They called it their farewell tour. They were both eighteen and could buy liquor. We drank quarts of Malt Duck, Boone's Farm and Ole English 800. We sneakily crashed parties and blended in under blue lights. I looked for signs but they definitely had stopped being stick-up kids and boosters. So, it's like they needed a new challenge. They operated like bank robbers but with two different styles. Eric was bold in how he approached girls. He simply told them we had a house all to ourselves and asked whether they wanted to come over for sex. Most girls ignored him or just laughed at him. Eric was brilliant in many ways but he never showed it. He felt he didn't need to because he had a compact build and a thick neck. He lifted weights and benched three hundred, one of those guys quick to take off his shirt in public – while playing sports, while dancing, while talking shit. When he spoke, his hands moved, rapidly as if he might just let off. People stayed out of his arms' reach unless they really knew him. He was quick to put his arm around your shoulder. His charismatic nature made people feel protected, an attribute that appealed to the ultra-attractive girls who hung on the scene.

So, Eric, even though his game sounded a bit out of bounds, he scored.

Girard and I moved more like amateur pickpockets on a crowded subway. Our subtle approach rarely worked. Even after managing to convince girls to come over, they would flake, talking about they didn't come for all of that.

All that changed one night as I studied how Manny operated. Manny was a guy, who at first sight, most people underestimated. Even though he was the same height as Eric, Manny didn't play sports, lift weights or eat a whole lot. He was not skinny but gave off a frail vibe. His rep was in his voice, the precise way he uttered his words, the intonation that made you search for an accent, even though it was just the Brooklyn one. His low pitch coupled with a nasal twang and those other elements made one get closer to hear him. But, to really see him, you had to step back a few feet or else you would overstep your bounds and think of him as small.

We had gotten to calling Manny, The Big Man, because he was a homerun hitter like Hank Aaron. He could walk into a party, speak only to guys and walk out with the finest girl in the place.

We were at a block party. I posted behind him, far away from the speakers. There was this one girl we knew of, but never formally met. She was sixteen, to my fourteen. That night she was the prettiest. Wearing a mini-skirt and doing the Smurf, she thought she was IT. Guys were stepping up and taking their best shot. I observed The Big Man's long range game.

Eric was talking to a few girls because that's how he rolled. He attacked a group, and technically, I guess the weakest one was the one he took home. Eric's girls were beautiful but they didn't have much substance. To get them to bake, all one needed was dough and sugar, or at least the appearance of having cake, basically controlling property, props and loot.

I never asked but none of us had jobs. Eric and Manny always had money, enough to give Girard and me. We all stayed fly in the latest gear, including the latest eyewear: Cazals, YSLs or Foster Grant frames.

"The Big Man, what's up, baby!" The streets were different. When we had love, there was stability. Men didn't travel solo only to morph into packs, forming alliances with whoever could get them the most immediate result. "I haven't seen you in a few days. I have five hundred on this weekend's games. What do you have?"

Manny didn't say anything to him, only nodded. He never turned to acknowledge I was a few feet away looking over his shoulder, studying the focus of his eyes and his hand motions. Eric had struck out with the group of girls.

I kept a count. Six guys had gone down swinging. Mini-skirt girl would give half a dance, a little talk and move away enough to show she had no interest.

Some girl, probably my age, with itty-bitty titties, came up talking about nonsense, that I was really big for my age, of how she saw me playing football last year and basketball and... "Get away from me!" She was shocked. Ego deflated, she rolled her eyes and walked away.

I needed to focus on The Big Man's moves.

Some next dude came up to Manny. This one whispered something in his right ear, patted him on the back, slightly below the left shoulder and walked away. For about two hours, it was pretty much the same thing: The Big Man standing still or dancing in place, and some dude coming by to say what up.

Girard was doing what he did best - working the room. He had the gift of gab and could bag a chick with a brain. Dumb chicks gave him problems. Since he was not one to accept failure, he was forever trying to understand how to reach dumb ones. He spotted me and motioned for me to come over, to probably introduce me to someone. I shook my head. I knew who those people were and I wanted no parts of them. They were the ones who fancied themselves as popular because of their gear and their little clique. Their power came in who wanted to be associated with them.

> *You are warm and the storm is still in my heart*
> *We will never part, hold on*
> *And we'll take this love to the stars.*

Then it hit me, on the kind of girls Manny got, better yet how he got them. Everyone was steady approaching mini-skirt. If I didn't know any better, I would say Manny's power came the same way, by those who wanted to be associated. But I vouch that Manny's more than a pretentious poseur because, not only had he been in Love with us, we had become family.

It was a mixed blessing that love no longer roamed the streets. The drawback was a girl wearing a mini-skirt could not stand alone. When it came to kids with no game, no power, they could approach her with no hesitation.

Yet, without love, she could resist the pull because even when people rolled in a posse, one could spot the gaps in their united front. But, she responded as the four of us walked by, admitting we had no one for the night, and hearing The Big Man say, "Nah, I got her!"

We'll get over like a fat rat.

She moved her arm away from his attempt to pull her, but it was only to see his next move.

Night was falling over Brooklyn, dying a natural death unlike the many parties where gunshots would ring out whether the party was in the street, park or in a schoolyard. This one held together because, in the August heat signaling the last days of summer vacation, there were many parties so this one mainly had people from the surrounding area. Everyone had accepted Lionel's actions, for they saw how we carried ourselves, above no one and below the radar. They had known the peace Love had established as well as the fault lines, the many of us who had been found guilty and were now doing years.

It was obvious the four of us had juice. She seemed to know more about us than we knew of her. She never walked with us, like she didn't want to be seen with us. She lagged yards behind, didn't cross streets immediately when we crossed diagonally. She waited to cross at the corners, maintaining her distance. Our house was a fifteen minute walk. My father would not be home for at least five more hours. She rang the doorbell and Eric called out the door was open. She followed the sound of our chatter and came into the living room, sat for a while and listened to us talk of nothing in particular.

She taught us about freedom, that love had sides but only if you divided it. When left whole, love could take you in and shelter you, make you comfortable in sharing, let you know how best to keep secrets. After that night, we would see her and she would offer a smile, perhaps some small talk. Knowing her and having others see her approach us brought about a curiosity. She always had the first option to come with any or all of us. Most times, she would giggle and say maybe. Other girls would come by the house and we would let them lead. That became our new M.O., to not grab love, to let love come naturally.

Part Two

OPEN SEASON, CLOSED COURT

Chapter 11
PARENTAL ADVISORY

Naked bodies rose off the floor. Talcum powder had mixed with sweat and the dirt from the soles of footwear, spilled food and drinks. The music played sultry grooves from cassette decks. The dee-jays were nowhere in sight. At some point, the Black Love party had devolved into the orgies of the loft's mixers. The mixers had a level of discretion to them. Nothing took place out in the open. At most, a sloppy kiss, a prolonged hug; but this was different. There were over a hundred naked people in the loft's open space. It was nearing noon and the room had a glare, sunlight beaming off naked walls and polished floors. The people's movements were raw, some to the beat, some so far off, the partakers looked like they were having spasms, convulsing from volcanic ash raining down on them.

I had a choice but I really didn't. This was my party and even though most were coupled up, tripled up, grouped up, I sensed the hard glances asking why I was the only one not naked. Had I not bought in? I quickly removed my clothes. As I bunched my clothes into my knapsack, I saw him in the corner, huddled up with a buxom redhead.

Girard looked at my nude body and I looked at his and gazed lower for longer than he had done to mine. He was limp not shrunken, fully circumcised. When I looked back up and saw his eyes, I quickly picked up the signals he was communicating. He urged me to leave, no questions asked. I turned my head, toward Manny's door. If I didn't go in there, it would remain closed to me forever. Opening it might mean his immediate death. Keeping it closed, Manny had a chance to get himself out of the predicament he'd placed himself.

The music stopped and a clock's alarm sounded. High noon. The noise, a persistent beep came from the middle bedroom. She opened the door and stood at the threshold. The people scrambled to grab their clothes. They dressed in silence. I sensed a satisfaction from her and the few who looked in my direction. In her eyes, I had proven myself. I grabbed my backpack to dress along with them. I would leave with the others. I felt my gun in the bag's small front pouch. My back was now to Girard and the woman in the middle room. I replayed everything she had done and said during my time at the loft. I had no name for her, not even a first name.

I held my backpack in my left hand and still had easy access to my gun. I could turn and open fire. First Girard and then her. I was a decent enough shot and would need only four shots total. Girard was nearly a point blank hit. She was about fifteen feet away, a straight line, diagonally. She stood there so sure of herself, her shape, a pear with only its bottom left uneaten.

The redhead with Girard had vanished. People filed out of the loft. I noticed none of them looked like the people who came with Ernest and Girard. I kept my eyes off her and more toward Girard. As he pulled up his pants, the weight of his gun made him look at me. He didn't deserve to die. He had kept his word.

Instead, I could put two shots to her chest and storm into Attitude's room and put four into him. Somebody had to die for this betrayal.

But what about Cindy? She didn't deserve to die but there could be no witnesses.

I needed Girard's eyes to tell me something but they looked through me, to a spot on the wall. I needed to know how many were in the middle room and whether the other two bedrooms were empty. All the other partygoers had left. I finally looked at her face. She looked at me and made no motion, as if she dared me. Her dark hair hung down to her right shoulder. On the other side, her hair stopped at her left ear lobe. Her gaunt shoulders; her chin pointy, bracketed by a flat forehead, forming an angular face with small dark eyes, button nose, pouty mouth, naturally red lips; with a slim build, her B-cups hung a bit, suggesting a woman approaching thirty. I needed her eyes to tell me something.

Girard walked to her, directly through my sight line, his sternest way of ordering me to stand down. He placed a soft kiss to her mouth. I turned my back as he hugged and thanked her for a great time. We exited the loft as the elevator arrived. We rode down in silence, as if we were lovers who had betrayed one another.

Outside, on Broadway, as shoppers rushed by us, he apologized and this took me by surprise. "I'm sorry. I don't know who you are but you clearly are not who you think you are."

Through the noise and my silence, I took in his handsome, boyish face. Through all he had been through in his life and these past hours, praying for me not to return, I sensed something about him I needed to test.

So, I gave him a peek into the Society.

During the Fall 1986 semester while we were pledging our way into the Society, we ran an operation. We being Miranda, Barbara and me; collectively known as The Conscious Daughters.

It started as a simple operation. We would do our homework and pass the answers to various people in our classes. We did the same for take-home exams. We recruited more Society sisters and other Black and Latina women to join us. We gave our answers to people of different ethnicities. We didn't think it would be that easy to prove the grading bias the professors had. Only this core group of women knew, not even our brothers in the Society knew.

The scoring disparity was too great so I told the brothers. They were angry at the discrimination and also at us, for what we were asking: for them to expose themselves in a cheating scandal.

They balked.

I made a decision with no one else's input. I asked Attitude's help. Attitude had been the head of the RSA – Radical Students Association – the previous year. The RSA's past successes meant they could get quick meetings with the administration. Since he could not show the school's administration how he came about his findings, the academic deans refused to have a meeting. He tried several different methods. This carried well into the next semester, the spring of 1987. We met and I told him to do whatever it took to get me a meeting with the Board of Trustees.

Finally, as finals week and graduation neared, when nothing else worked, Manny's faction in the Society, the Max boys came out firing. Gunshots in the middle of the quad. A few of us other Society members were in the cafeteria and didn't know what the hell was going on.

We came out and saw the fire, the burning building, hundreds of students throwing debris, a bonfire. Miranda cautioned us not to go toward the fire and most followed her. I didn't and a few followed me.

That's when I spotted you and Ernest.

The following Monday I got called into the meeting with the head of the Trustees.

Though no one had taken responsibility for the fire, I got called in. Someone had to have given my name. The campus administration made many concessions that various left-leaning student organizations had wanted for years. At the meeting, I learned something I never suspected and was tasked to kill the person they believed to be behind the fire, a terrorist named Aman. They didn't know his true identity, not even how to pronounce his code name. All they had was a name. My take was, how can you convict someone based on a name, one you cannot even pronounce?

I had to hear Manny's side of the story - warn him or kill him. I came to Manhattan and found Manny and learned he had told these people - the ones upstairs in the loft - I had bought in to be a part of their group.

Girard interrupted me. "If the meeting didn't happen until Monday, how come you told Ernest there was a hit on Manny that Friday of the fire, when we met you?"

"When you know the Society's history, you know what the next step will be of an event as big as the campus fire. I needed to clear my name, of being labeled a traitor so I said that to Ernest in front of witnesses, only to get it into the historical record."

My answer surprised him but he quickly hit me with another question. "When you and Ernest walked away, Barbara asked me to kill Ken. Wasn't your move to take Ernest to the cafeteria just a diversion to get Ken to follow you so she could ask me?"

I didn't answer. Ernest had told me so much about Girard I knew the question he asked was to get the answer for something else. So I shocked him and gave him the something else, the knowledge I could not give Ernest because he had not gone with them that day. "Hearing Ernest's story has put Manny's actions into context but it also leaves so many unanswered questions. I made a crucial error this past May when I saw you two on the TGI campus. I assumed you were college students visiting and already part of the Society. Your look and the way you were standing, especially yours, was straight out of a SBD playbook."

It was his turn to speak but he didn't volunteer anything. "What exactly did Ernest tell you?"

I ignored his question because he was really asking why I came back to the loft. "I don't know who, on our side of the Society, would have dared run a Stay Black and Die operation that uses children as the soldiers. Only one person would have reason to do that and all roads lead to Manny's father."

I grew up in the Society but I was only exposed to the rewards and the benefits. Even when told of the downside of our history, only the big events, the surface of things got relayed to me. No one spoke of the day-to-day life of the children who had become casualties, the misappropriated line items, because their parents got sacrificed.

I took a step closer to him, not as a false act in case we were being watched, but because I wanted to let him know I would be there for him, he had my loyalty. I said, "My name is Hope Kendall. Do you know what that means?"

He made no attempt to kiss me. "Yes, I know and I'm Girard."

He added no last name and that hurt me as much or more than it did him.

It felt like a sniper had taken us both out with one bullet, through the back of his head, the trajectory changing downward a little, shattering the bridge of my nose.

Girard and I went our separate ways, knowing our family's historical ties had bound us to one another.

<0>

My father cut me an unpleasant look when I opened the door. Instead of asking a question or saying something, he just took another bite of his French toast. My stepmother smiled before she spoke, sort of her way of letting my father know she was not taking sides. I felt bad because I did not want her to think my love or respect for her would diminish if she told me the truth, of what she felt. Last time, a couple of months ago, we had a conversation, I told them about Manny, that I was staying at his apartment, working for him and would likely leave TGI and finish college in the city.

Now, walking in as they finished brunch, the table setting having gone from magazine spread Better Homes and Garden style to crumpled cloth napkins, empty juice glasses and used silverware, with my place setting untouched, I could sense they saw the culmination of my vagabond ways, my summer of acting out. In grade school, I skipped the teen rebellion stage, with its predictable boy-crazy antics, so for the most part, because of that, my father had overlooked these past few months, until this moment when I opened the door looking for shelter, an escape, not from just the most embarrassing moment of my life, but the dreadful feeling of having made a vital miscalculation, that I was indeed sleeping with the enemy.

Chapter 12

"You told her about me? My last name?" He didn't say her name, specify who, as if he had not floated her name as bait to locate Manny. Girard came back to the house within the time frame I had estimated. The scenario unfolded the way I'd calculated. Hope would arrive and they would talk briefly and go their separate ways.

I said, "Yes, I told her about everything from the moment I moved to Brooklyn up to this past May." The two of them knew the Society, something they could not tell me about. She knew more than Girard, who knew less about how it operated, but through his research had learned about its deeds.

I told Hope about our childhood so her next moves would fall into the prescribed patterns I mapped out.

He asked, "Everything?"

We exited through the garden level. We needed privacy to talk freely. "I wasn't explicit but pretty much. And, she never flinched. I knew she would go back to the party for you and Manny."

"I knew she would come back. That's why I stayed." I shot him a questioning look. "She thought she was coming to save Manny's life?"

"She loves Manny but I don't get the sense they're fucking."

"They're not." The force he used to push it into the conversation told me another thing. His defensive reflexes made him want to elaborate.

I was not a gambler. I took risks but only after I had exacted the outcomes to two extremes. In this scenario, my straight shot of telling Hope who we were was because we wanted to change. I did not tell her what form that change should take. Our long walk told me about her stamina, her confidence. I wagered she would return to the loft party, doubting, not my capsulation of Manny's teen years but, what she had learned of Girard.

She faced me only once during our time together, at the end when it was time to part. Other times she cut cursory glances, brushed her forearms against me, not realizing I had only one speed, one way out of this. Girard had many plays, various entrances and exits like a furry animal that lived life planning for crises. She would go to save not one but both of them; thereby implicating herself in the other extreme, the other outcome.

The contract on Manny was in her name and she never refuted it, showed no fear during our walk, and never said who sent her. When she put together the flyer, she didn't realize what a Black Love party meant. She only knew the sanitized version of what she'd read in some historical digest. I had never heard of Black Love, only Love. Then, one day, one of the teeny-boppers connected to this new crew we ran with came home from school. He attended a specialized school in Manhattan and said some white dude was handing them out, not too far from the school.

Heads turned to each other with the swiftness. Dollar signs lit up in people's eyes and even then I didn't make the connection to Manny. We rolled deep – BMQ style, meaning Manhattan was the center of it all. Brooklyn-Manhattan-Queens, and Bronx-Manhattan-Queens. Crews from Staten Island teamed with Brooklyn, Westchester with The Bronx and Long Island rolled with Queens.

We only had two days of lead time to map out a strategy and get everyone to man their position. We occupied corners, clubs, restaurants and whatever venue allowed us to blend in, even though groups of Black and Latino youths couldn't really blend into most places in trendy, mainstream Manhattan.

Girard and I would be the point men. Forty of us went into the party. Each major crew sent a representative to make sure the loot would be equally distributed. As soon as we walked in, we saw Hope. We pretended we didn't see her, hoping she'd get the hint and leave before the action started. She couldn't be in the middle of it. She said it was a false alarm, that we had a misunderstanding what Black Love was and who invented it.

Girard had no doubts about the true history.

She told me she could not tell me about the Society.

Still, I sided with her, to give her a last chance to right a major false step she had taken. We left and I talked. I told her about Manny and she said she understood ambition.

I sensed something they could not admit. I could predict Manny's moves better than she and Girard.

G and I walked in silence until we hit the roundabout at Grand Army Plaza. I needed G to level with me and ignore any order requiring his secrecy. "Man, I don't know, man. I don't know. The things I saw at that party. I needed to see if she would come back to that and why." He took a hard pause and asked, "You told her my last name?"

I had not attached any extra value to not revealing G's last name? "I figured she knew through Manny."

"Nah, she's just learning who he is and about his father." Girard finally decided to open up. "I don't know if you recall seeing her. There was this woman with a weird hairstyle, a short bob on one side, and long on the right. Real dark hair, like she colored it jet black. Heavy make-up, that vampire look they call Goth. She kept staring at me like she had something to tell me. I couldn't go to her because I had to hold my position so we didn't come off as suspicious while others were doing rotations. An hour later, it's my turn to roam so I go to the back to the kitchen for a beer. By then, I'm zooted. I'd done smoked mad weed and drank 'nough LQ. So I'm tripping, having a good time, bobbing to some house music. Suddenly I realize we're losing soldiers, both men and women. I panic and rush back to my position and no one is holding it down. I look at her and she's looking at me like I need to hurry up. She's standing by the middle room. I go to her. It's her bedroom. Bust this, with no convo, she takes off her clothes and we get busy. Straight up the rawest ever, blew me, straight did me and of course, she expects me to return the favor. So, I go down and lick her a little. Then we bang some more. By now, it's almost like two in the morning and I'm like half-asleep and there's a knock at the door. Check this, she said come in. But the door was locked. I'm like, who is that? She asked me, who am I?"

G stopped talking. I could sense he had hit the brick wall of secrecy. I didn't hesitate to ask, "What happened next?"

"I know I'm not supposed to tell you certain things but this….haunts me, plays in my mind. She opened the door and a naked dude walked in. He looked at her and me, and got on his knees. I grabbed my clothes and headed out the door. And yo, when I step into the living room, the entire loft is full of naked people, just straight fucking each other, even what's left of our soldiers are in the mix fucking anyone who moves. I'm thinking I need to put my clothes on and bounce but I can't because I turn around and the Goth chick is standing in front of the middle room, looking at me while two dudes are all over each other and her. I head back to my position against the wall and grab the first woman who walked by me and held on to her, for dear life, until Hope returned. I held on to that woman for close to ten hours, like she was a raft in the middle of an ocean."

I laughed so hard people looked in our direction and cut us dirty looks. "Man, as many hookie parties we been through and you got spooked by that."

"No man, don't you get it?" Girard stopped himself. There was something critical, something he couldn't tell me that involved the Society. "Anyway Hope came running in right before noon, about eleven-forty-five. I looked hard at her to let her know she'd misread the ranking order. She made like she was about to go to Manny's room. I locked eyes with her, blinked and winked left. She understood the signal even though she never ran the streets, never knew position…do you know Hope didn't realize the Goth chick lived in the middle bedroom?"

"So, what happened?"

"When she ran into the loft, she undressed. So, we're both standing there naked. People looking at us like who's going to bow down. I blinked and moved my eyes downward to give her the cue to get on her knees. I could feel the Goth chick staring at us. I thought of getting on my knees to go along and pretend Hope was the queen. But then it hit me what Manny had done."

"The queen?"

Girard's eyes were misty. "He told people Hope was one of us, in Love. That was the only way he could protect her once word got out she put a hit on him." Girard's eyes moved and showed he sensed something he still refused to admit, that I could predict Manny's moves better than he could. We stopped walking. "You knew?"

"I read it the minute she said it was her party and she made the flyer. Why didn't you let her go to Manny's room?"

"He left way early in the night. Her name got cleared the minute she left with you. What would be the point?"

"To prove how much Manny loves her."

"She can't help him outside the Society. Plus it takes four generations - eighty years of inactivity for a family to sever ties with the Society."

We circled back toward the house. "Is the Goth chick the queen?"

"No, but this was her operation. She's a ghost, just like my father."

Girard's encounter with Hope had accomplished what the recent years could not. My comfort level with G was back, to what it was on day one.

Chapter 13

The four of us sat on the rooftop of one of the block's shorter buildings. The three shorter buildings were connected identical structures. On the southern side, after the third building, there was a gap, a small parking lot. We sat on the cement divider between the second and first building, the one connected to a row of taller buildings that filled the rest of the main avenue's eastern side. We'd always been leery of the corner buildings, especially since hearing the oft-repeated tales of people who had run off the tall building, forgetting the two-floor drop to the next. And, also those who'd done the same off the third short building, to fall four stories down into the parking lot.

We sat, pulling on joints and swigging off our individual quart bottles. We weren't sentimental about the change because we had celebrated all summer.

<0>

Manny and Eric left for college on successive days without much fanfare. Eric packed two heavy bags and headed for Philadelphia to study music. I rode with him to Penn Station where he would catch the train to Philadelphia. The Big Man went upstate New York on a mixture of scholarship and financial aid for Fine Arts. He had more to carry so Girard and I rode with him to Port Authority.

They left before the weekend and the upcoming West Indian Day Parade.

Now it was just Girard and me. We joined with a group of people from the block and walked to Eastern Parkway on Monday. I snapped photos using my Kodak 110 camera. We had one week left for summer vacation. I thought Girard and I would have hung out all the time. I can't say for sure which of us put distance between us so I will take most of the blame. Once school started Girard stayed involved in all things, from school politics to whatever club gave him a reason to befriend strangers with whom he had little in common. When those activities were done, he roamed the streets and hung on the avenues, shooting dice, drinking brew or just kicking it with anyone who was around. He had a way of being a friend to everyone but I really could not say he had many friends. This is not to say the people he hung with did not like him or would openly betray him. It's just when he was with the Chess club, he was one of the better players but he never delved deeper into the other things they wanted to do, so when practice was over, he moved on to the next group.

The same was true with the hard core street cats who liked to play hookie, get zooted and shoot dice. He would do most of what they did, except play hookie or criminal things. He was one of the rare people who got a pass for not following them in their criminal ways. He had the fashion, the lingo, the walk, the hard bop with the exaggerated shoulder dip, and the love of music. In music, he was an isolationist. For a dude who loved other cultures and interacting with people from other places, he only liked rap. I found that odd because hip hop wasn't the music I grew up on and was part of the ways I stretched myself was through music.

Freshman year, we took Band class and though I only knew the basics, I managed to make it as an alternate Guitarist. I passed the class but never got to perform on stage. Having taken piano lessons as a child for many years, Girard had a chance to be the lead on piano but never pushed himself. He told me it would interfere with his schedule. From what I observed he had no schedule. He had lots of activities but he alternated them because their schedules conflicted. His only constant was the street; he said the streets were where it's at.

I had come to appreciate the streets as a sanctuary because no one questioned what they knew or what they did not. I mainly stayed in the house reading, drawing and listening to music. My only true commitment was the promise I had made to Slick. I used sports as an outlet, a place to compete and challenge myself. The courts and fields were my domain, a place where people respected me enough that I could hide in plain sight. Since our football team sucked, the only coverage we got was the school paper so no one really pried into players' lives.

Basketball season was different. We were blowing teams out and I was a Freshman starting on an established varsity team. Our high school was known for developing top recruits for Division I colleges. Some reporter trying to make a name for himself did an unauthorized expose on me – Ern-Money. It appeared in one of those small neighborhood newspapers, *Flatbush Life*. But, the large city papers picked up the story.

Slick was the team captain and told coach how he wanted the press on me to be handled. Coach hadn't known about Lionel. Slick felt I should face it head on so by playoff time the story about my brother the murderer would fade out. By the start of the season's second half, each game was covered by the school paper, neighborhood papers, city and national press.

I got Girard to coach me. He was a natural with the standard form answers to provide, how I should stand, the facial expressions to make and when, and the proper vocal tones, pauses and inflections. After the third time I addressed Lionel killing Benny, the story died down. Girard had shown me how to quell the reporters' appetite by pretending Lionel's action needed to be studied on its own as an isolated incident, a moment of insanity, without using the word. There was no love within that context, with the streets becoming ever so violent, as the stick-up era having reached its apex plateaued and unexpectedly shattered into the brashness of a crack era that lit up the streets in neon.

Until then, our lives were like a foreign film shot in black and white even after the advent of color film. We had moved at a slow pace even though hip hop's BPM increased and less and less B-boys carried boom boxes, spray paint and cardboard boxes. As the year 1983 ended, I looked forward to spotting my sisters sitting in the stands. They maintained a low profile, only coming to away games. They would never speak to Girard or me. When the press intensified, they became paranoid, wearing hats, shades and other articles to disguise themselves.

On the Sundays Girard and I visited my mother's house, we would laugh about it. One Sunday, I caught a weird vibe. Marlene and Girard had a secret.

Marlene was the perfect blend of my mother and father. She possessed all their positive attributes divided evenly, the head turner to my mother's and Ghyslaine's stately beauty. They got their looks and whistles, but Marlene broke necks, stopped struts and caused a chain reaction of horns – the first to notice, the one who almost rear-ended, followed by the blare of stalled traffic. My mother schooled her early, at the same time she sat Ghyslaine down.

So, on the way home, I came out and asked him. "You fucking my sister?"

"No, that would be like incest." Girard gave me the type of answer he'd helped me rehearse for reporters. My silence meant he had to come clean. "OK. It started by accident. Some kid at her school was bothering her."

"What? Why didn't you tell me?"

"If you went and got into trouble, it could blow everything your parents set up, with them taking your mother's maiden name and all."

"OK, go on!"

"Nah, that's it! I am not telling you anything more." He was right. I definitely did not want to hear the details of him and my sister. "Why? You act like I ain't good enough for your sister."

I sized up Girard, thinking of how a growing boy, solid at his current five foot eight inch frame, could turn his voice from meek to threatening with not much effort. "I didn't say that. I just know how my mother can be and how my sisters are."

He rushed his words as if to calm my nerves. "Your mother doesn't know."

"Yeah right! If I could sense it, trust me she knows." I fired my words at the right pace, inserting the proper punctuations, speaking no more than two syllables before a pause. His left shoulder moved a little on the same downward motion of his left foot. I caught him off-balance, a little nervous, sensing the image playing over in his mind, of the day my mom smacked Eric. "Plus, Ghyslaine and Marlene treated boys real bad when I was younger. And whenever something went wrong, they blamed the boy. Lionel and Eric would…you know."

I left it at that.

A few weeks later, the day of the city championships, Marlene walked in with the guy she had Girard beat up. Had she been any other girl, he would have simply said something like the sex was horrible. Instead he held a jovial façade, swallowed the hurt as we chugged from the keg at the celebration being held at some rich student's home.

Slick had gotten his wish – a city championship.

Chapter 14

Sports had become a job. I kept playing so sports would pay for my college. I was on the varsity basketball team and also ran track to increase my speed and endurance. Freshman year, I played both JV and varsity football. The team had improved but not good enough to make the playoffs. This coming season I only had to focus on varsity. In August, I had to go to football team meetings and then sleep-away training camp for a week.

Eric and Manny came home in late May. They didn't do much roaming and stayed to themselves, mainly going to high-brow events dealing with music and the arts. They talked about joining the Society but never said what new information they'd learned and how it tied to Lionel.

They had a plan but only Manny got selected for the fall semester class. Eric didn't. His school didn't have a charter and he said the people, at the college nearest to him with a charter, were stand-offish.

We wanted to go visit Manny because his campus sounded like fun but he wasn't going to have free time. We visited Eric in early October. We arrived early Friday evening. There was so much going on around the small campus. It was part of the city, not its own different world as we'd imagined. The previous year Eric had maintained his aggressive persona. Now he was on a different vibe, more introspective. He had come to realize the less mess he got into the better his chances to join the Society. He gave us the keys to his apartment. "I need you two to stay out of trouble."

He left with a backpack filled with books. His roommate a bookish guy with glasses and unexpected swagger stemming from his being tops in his field - animation. He engaged us in conversation whenever he popped into the apartment.

We spent the weekend doing tourist stuff – Liberty Bell, the Mint, museums – and hanging out in the city at the other colleges. Eric finally came back late Sunday afternoon. We spent the time listening to music in his dorm room. We listened to his interpretations, as well as his attempts, of chamber music done on electronic keyboards and a drum machine.

During the trip back home, G and I didn't say much. I guess we had spent so much of the past few years emulating life through Eric's eyes, as one big chaotic party. To see Eric shift this way, his eyes so distant, a melancholic gaze had narrowed his outlook. We sensed for Eric the music had stopped.

Winter break.

Manny came back and he was hard. Even during his days as a stick-up kid, you could see tenderness, a hint of fear in his eyes. When he walked into the house in December 1984, his look had changed drastically. His setback eyes with bushy eyebrows no longer shied from eye contact. His mouth, with the now permanent downturn, flared - a puffiness, as if venom lined his gums.

Manny gave the house a different energy. We spoke without pitch and straight to the point. On one of the rare nights my father showed up early enough to join us in conversation, he quickly noticed he was the life of the party, the person with holiday glee in his voice. He carried Christmas gifts for everyone, bottles of booze and a sunny disposition.

We raised our glasses. Barbancout neat. Down in one gulp.

"My sons are home." He was not used to seeing us this mellow. "What's wrong?"

I was about to say, nothing, but Manny broke down crying, "They broke my rib. They broke my rib."

"What?" We stood except Eric. Manny also remained seated, his sobs threatening to choke him. We made to walk over to him, but my father stopped us. My father asked, "Did you get what they offered you in the beginning?"

"Yes."

"Then it's OK to cry. You are supposed to cry." Manny looked up at him. "Have you told anyone else?"

"No."

"OK, don't tell anyone else! You three, you know more than you knew before. But, don't let that affect you. We have to make this man president." He looked at Girard and opened another bottle of liquor, this time vodka, the Stoli he stored in the freezer. Girard and I remained standing, not sure whether to go to Manny and console him. My father poured another drink for each of us and gave a toast to Manny. "To the first one in!"

We spent the remaining weeks of their college winter break talking but never directly about what was going on with Manny. Eric and Manny had a plan but they couldn't share it. The four of us together made me realize the distance I felt between me and Girard dealt more with our inability to talk about Lionel, how he technically was the first one in, a sacrifice.

As Eric and Manny prepared to return to school after winter break, we went to a house party and I learned Slick got caught up on some trifling mess and was facing a three-year bid if he took the plea. I couldn't understand how one year he was living the dream, playing ball at a major program on a big campus, starting as a freshman, competing for a tournament bid, and the next year, in one instant, all of it gone.

I went by his house to hear it directly from his mom. She had been expecting my visit and told me not to repeat what he asked her to share. I thanked her and told her if Slick needed anything to call me.

Slick believed in love inasmuch as it is a dream, inconceivable, indecipherable, especially when focused on a narrow target.

With Slick gone, our team was nowhere near dominant. Everyone kept saying the weight fell on me, but I didn't see it that way, never planned to shoulder that responsibility. We made the playoffs but did not repeat as champs.

Chapter 15

When you have been in Love, it is hard to stop caring about people you no longer run with. You see the exits, the places you can jump off but it is harder than imagined. Girard and I went to visit Manny but to also get away from the city.

The city had gotten grimy, crummy. Every little dude had turned hard overnight, fancied himself a major player. Guns were cheap. Life was no longer free. The streets had a new code, "It's not a fair fight unless we win." Not sure who coined the phrase but people no longer shot you a fair one. Try to slap box someone, even a friend, and you were likely to end up in a box, if not mobbed by twenty. It wasn't just false bravado. Juice went from having back to never having to fight your own battles, which came to mean a never-ending war. Many coming up never learned to swallow their pride, to come back and fight another day. Every slight was magnified and gunplay became the norm.

We left the city right after school, rushing our way after seventh period, 1:35 p.m., to catch the 3 p.m. bus out of Port Authority. The bus ride was a bit over four hours. I boarded and went to a seat near the back. I put on my Walkman headphones and bopped to Run-D.M.C.'s King of Rock album. I took out a sketch pad and played with ideas of highways, divided roads and vanishing forests. Girard must have picked up something in the bus driver's eyes or the way he said hello, something that told him the driver was one of those white men who wanted to be loved by black people. Girard sat up front and chatted with him. G had this way of revealing his life to total strangers, sharing morsels to find commonality and instantly bonding. The driver had played varsity sports and opted for the military after high school. He enlisted after the Korean War and suffered an injury that eventually kept him off the battlefields of Viet Nam. He was there, but as a communications specialist; said he still had the bad dreams.

The small college town had a northeastern chic look, well-kept colonial homes recessed from the sidewalk, and two-way routes with single lanes on both sides. The town had two stops for the bus route - downtown and campus.

Girard exchanged phone numbers with the driver. I simply gave him a nod.

TGI was a secured campus, a former fort which became a military training facility, and eventually a private college. The sole front gate had barricades on the side and cones indicating where different types of motor vehicles entered. Pedestrians walked dead center, up to the guard in a booth. The brick enclosure had no plexiglass or a divider of any kind. On each side of the spiked gate, armed uniformed guards stood at attention, surveying each car and pedestrian. Guards seemed to know students upon sight, but still students slid an identification card for entering and exiting the campus. Once they finished, they circled back as their guests signed in or out of the campus.

We observed how students who had been on the campus waited for their guests. We noticed some guests, arriving alone, simply stated their name and the guard in the booth typed it into the computer.

That is how we entered the campus. Manny had left our names on general principle. Girard said his name and received a plastic card. I did the same and received one. We took turns inserting the card into the machine. The pass was valid for sixty hours. We did not ask any questions.

The campus was a short fifteen walk from the bus station and smaller than I imagined from Manny's descriptions. Not one to elaborate, he had said little of his first two years there so we were surprised just how known he was. We had gotten the impression he left his high visibility persona behind. We didn't mention we were there to see him, just listened in on conversations, each of us toting a backpack with the bare traveling necessities. We gathered as much information as we could but not much was being said. Even between us, when we decided to take this trip, we never determined why. In my heart, I thought of revenge and that is how I knew Eric and Girard to think. The fact no one spoke of striking back at whoever had battered Manny told me this was not an easy enemy to confront.

Students streamed aimlessly in all directions yet no one walked on the manicured grass. I took a moment and studied patterns, again knowing Girard would take in much the same. I respected that about him even though I found him lacking when it came to abstract thought. I looked around the quad and told Girard, "He's not here."

"I know, but he knows we're here."

The ID cards on ready served as a warning signal. His freshman year he said we were too young to visit and he needed to get his bearings. His sophomore year he had obligations and after our visit to Eric's campus, we weren't sure we wanted to go visit another campus, until Manny came home for winter break. I thought our first inclination would be to roll up deep to his campus, right away, but none of them brought it up as an option.

We hung around the cafeteria in the Student Union Building after finding out the party would be at Manny's house. No one spoke the address so we blended in with a group likely to be heading there. It was nearing 11pm. We walked to the security gate and inserted our temporary ID cards to exit the campus. Most people were driving and the group we trailed, separated into taxis. We hopped in with three people and the look on their faces indicated everyone on campus likely knew each other. We screwed our faces with ice-grill stares hoping to intimidate them into not asking. One of the two dudes asked, "Who y'all?"

Girard used his normal speaking voice. "Whoever you want us to be!"

The girl answered. "Brooklyn. Flatbush. Middle class boy trying to play hard."

I expected him to come back hard at her. Instead he said, "Junior. Mid-eastern United States. I can say more but I respect your standing."

She smiled as the two dudes' eyes gave way they did not understand the move Girard had made. Her opening line meant she knew the reason for the party and had told Girard how she either viewed Manny or her judgment of us based on how Manny had described us.

It was a tricky proposition and he didn't take the bait. Instead he determined she and Manny were friends who entered school the same year. As far as which part of the country she was from, he either picked up an accent or lack of one. Her standing? I really doubted she had any, particularly with Manny. She might have been some chick he kept on the rotation but nothing more. Girard gave her standing on the off-chance he needed a place to sleep or some ass for the night.

Girard was a hardcore tactician and his first move was always diplomacy, to befriend the person facing him. They kept speaking in this coded form. I picked up most of what was being said. Manny was throwing a party because we had come for a visit. It was an impromptu affair but only a select few knew why at the last minute he put his sound system together to mix some dope uptown music and hip hop beats.

Manny gave us big hugs and asked where we've been, that he'd been jamming since eight o'clock. We just laughed, relieved because we liked him this way. Though he was never one to show much outward excitement, Manny knew how to make people feel welcomed and free to party. I had never heard him dee-jay but he was on the tables, spinning hard core instrumentals fusing them into vocals from hip hop and reggae tracks. The house was not packed with people but there was a keg, lots of liquor and cess.

He told us to put our bags upstairs in the larger bedroom.

We partied all night. There was some dancing. For the most part, people lounged on the floor until close to seven in the morning. Girard got lost with who knows who. All I remembered him saying he was heading out with some chick. I spent most of the night checking out the beats, the people and the relaxed vibe. I dozed off in a corner against a cooled radiator around the time Manny stopped dee-jaying and let cassette tapes rock. He wound the party down with Sade's first album.

I woke early, around eleven, hopped in the shower and jogged to the campus. I felt comfortable enough to ask the security guard for the art building. He asked which one. TGI had several buildings showcasing different styles of art. I asked about the studios where upperclassmen worked. The three-story building leaned backward as if falling off the humongous manufactured rock behind the library. Scholastically, TGI was a leader in Architecture, Art, English, Fashion, Literature and Multimedia. It had maintained its traditional look with architecture that gave it a rigid yet harmonious feel. Newer buildings had been relegated to the outskirts. Wadsworth Hall housed the work of top students. Most of the classroom and studio doors were locked so I could not get the information I sought. The halls were lined with recent creations and one large exhibit room housed the work of alumni. Most of the pieces were behind glass or bolted, indicating their value. I spent a couple of hours studying the pieces.

Before heading back, I grabbed a bite to eat at the cafeteria, giving myself a chance to imagine myself mingling with the student body. The campus and its students did not have a creative vibe. It felt more like an institution than a place for creative freedom.

We spent the rest of Saturday at Manny's house. People came in and out but no one really interrupted our chill-out session. It almost felt like we were back at the house in Brooklyn. People would come with food, booze and weed. Some would focus on video games. Others would head to the basement or any of the bedrooms and no one asked questions. When it got late, Girard said he was heading back to the campus to stay with the girl from the taxi. "Give me a quick ride." Manny tossed him his car keys. "Nah, I've been drinking. Plus, Mr. LeGagneur said we're not supposed to have cars."

I said, "Word. Why do you have a car?"

Manny said, "You're going to have to break that rule real soon. Many of the rules have to be broken. No matter how much you avoid it, there's no other way not to go heads up with what's coming."

At that, Girard stared at him, pausing as if wanting to address it head on but he seemed to think better of it. "Thanks for the assist on Veronica. Too bad she really doesn't know how hard we ran."

Either Manny had gotten careless or he was trying to warn us without giving away his position. He simply laughed and said, "I don't tell people about us. It's nothing to brag about. We were sitting ducks."

Girard slipped his right hand into his jacket pocket. "What? You no longer believe in Love? You don't think we're hard?"

"You ain't gotta prove it to me, not us to each other." The phone rang and nobody moved to pick up. It had been like that all day. People came in and used any room they wanted. They opened the fridge without asking but no one ever picked up the phone until the answer machine started recording. Each message was for everyone to hear. It's like the phone was a central hub, a switchboard, some sort of proxy they all used for strangers. The level of privacy needed determined whether the answering machine got interrupted. Callers' messages made for good laughs throughout the day.

"Ayo Manny, pick up! Pick up!" I made to go to the phone and he waved for me to stop. "They stuck me with something and I need you to come up here."

Girard rushed to the phone but by the time he picked it up, Eric had hung up.

Manny rushed to speak. "Don't say anything!" He pointed to the other people in the room. "You didn't hear anything." He made to delete the message.

Girard stopped him, "Rewind that!"

"No, trust me! You can't go to him, especially you Ernest."

We pushed past him and cleared four messages before we got to Eric's message. We listened and Manny deleted it.

I called Eric's dorm room. His roommate said he had not seen him in a few weeks. Girard said, "Get your car and let's get down there fast." Manny was an odd mix of slow calm movements and anxiety, in how he evaded our eyes. Girard said, "We need to pack our bags and wash our faces."

As we left, no one in the house said anything, pretending to be or actually oblivious to any potential danger. The road was dark; rural, large patches of farmland, open fields. Manny drove with care, though you could tell he knew these roads intimately by how his left wrist instinctively bent with the curves even before the road shifted. He refused to answer our questions. "I know your first thought is to go save Eric, but it's like when your father said Lionel was dead but Eric went after him, and we went with him. You didn't go Ern so they have no reason to come after you. But, if you go after Eric and we come across them." He stopped and asked Girard for help. "G, say something!"

"Ernest should have come with us that day." Each time I played that day over in my head, I always saw it the way Girard just stated it. "I know your father said walking blindly into this is the best approach but I'm just not sure anymore."

An hour into the drive we hit the highway and Manny increased his speed. From there it was a straight drive with one more highway merge to get into Philly. We arrived at Eric's apartment. His roommate had left the door unlocked for us. As we sat in the small apartment, I ran the scenarios around my mind. I thought back to the sadness that had overtaken Eric. I really could not picture Eric living like this, a small apartment with his creative tools as the lone luxury items. We stayed in his room, waiting for him to show up or call. When none came, we went searching the campus and the nearby streets and other colleges, asking anyone if they knew him or had seen him. No one knew Eric, which was odd because Eric lived for fame, name recognition, the limelight.

We returned to his room and decided to make the call we dreaded. My father gave us the OK to call the police. It pained him to make such a choice. With it came instructions Girard be the one to call, to tell them Eric was last seen near the river. We couldn't tell them why we had rushed up to check in on him, only that no one had seen him for weeks. The police spent Sunday searching the river for a body. They found a body but could not identify him because of its deterioration. They found papers and clothes that belonged to Eric. It made it seem like Eric had committed suicide.

Even though that's what they inferred, I knew Eric would not have committed suicide. He tried to retaliate. I kept staring at Manny and Girard, expecting them to tell me something but they were crying. They could not tell me if they were involved in any retaliation. I never cried, at least not in front of them or anyone else.

Late Sunday night, Manny dropped us off at the bus station and he headed back to TGI.

Chapter 16

My father sat in the corner of the living room. He had carried a chair from the dining table and fitted it into the right angle of the wall. He leaned his right shoulder and head against the wall. He looked more relaxed than I anticipated, like he had rubbed away the hurt into the paint. Eric was his favorite. They looked so much alike and had the same personality and tendencies. They never fully mended the rift created when Eric went to Lionel's aid.

My father stood and opened his arms. Girard and I went to him. We stood in a circle, arms around shoulders, heads bowed. After a long moment of silence, he said, "When I got home last night there was a message on the machine. Eric said something about driving and a flood of headlights bearing down on him. I kept waiting to hear from any of you. I had no idea where you were. Did you try to go after someone, retaliate for what happened to Lionel?"

"No. We were visiting Manny and just partying."

Girard didn't say anything. My father asked him, "What did I tell you about not making a move unless you're following Ernest?" My father broke the circle and pressed play on the answering machine. Eric's message was identical to the one he left on Manny's machine, "They stuck me with something." Right after his message, a loud voice said, "What did we tell you about trying to retaliate? Turn around and walk toward the water. Keep walking! Keep walking until we tell you to stop!"

The complete silence, as the tape recorded for many more minutes. We heard the sounds of cars driving away. Drowning would make it look like Eric had committed suicide. They had to have had him at gunpoint.

I looked at Girard. The distant look in his eyes indicating the long game he was playing, the army he was building.

Girard finally spoke. "I didn't try to retaliate."

A pride swelled within me. Eric tried to retaliate. Knowing Eric, he had succeeded enough to garner a response.

I awoke, startled, a vivid dream whose images vanished quickly from memory. Our eyes met and he said, "Ernest, you're stronger than this. You're stronger than this." I sensed Girard had not slept. He held a pen and notebook. He always carried a notebook. As soon as he filled it, he started filling a new one with notes.

I had stretched out on the sofa, and Girard had moved the dining chair away from the corner, closer to the lamp tables so the soft light could illuminate his papers. The sound that had blended into my dream suddenly stopped. The running water from the bathroom at the top of the staircase highlighted my father's concerns. He'd hoped showering would erase the worry lines compressing his face, eyes swollen like a defeated boxer. He too had not slept. The way the light came into the room at odd angles allowed me to see he hadn't expected death, casualties on our side, even though he had killed, even though Lionel had killed. He had talked about his military life in opaque terms. I had only seen two photos of him in uniform. He'd expressed sorrow for things he had done, the way powerful men confessed their sins, belatedly coming to the realization their victims could not retaliate. As proxies of the State, the most he and his fellow soldiers could face, in a retaliatory act, would be the destruction of their property, like the setting of fire to an empty house. But, this was a direct hit. Someone had made one of his sons disappear, and he had to swallow it and accept Eric was dead – to him, to us.

My father walked out of the house without saying a word.

Girard closed his notebook. The frown on his face was a forced appendage to hide the vulnerability threatening to overtake him. I squeezed his left shoulder as he headed upstairs to shower. I didn't have a little brother until he came along. We were only a few months apart and though his knowledge base exceeded mine, he still heeded to age as the substitute for rank. When he returned downstairs, he said, "I'm heading to school. What are you doing?"

"Going to school too. Let me wash up real quick."

We walked in relative silence, uttering only slight greetings to fellow students. Some caught our stride and tried to initiate conversations. We would slow our pace and mix in jagged steps to give hint we wanted to be left alone.

Girard and I got to school and parted ways.

Love was over but I decided it was time to promote myself to Gun. I recalled the instructions of the defined situations in which a Gun could use his weapon. I gave the oath to myself. There were many scenes and personal interactions I avoided or limited even though I knew the people and could have easily linked up with them. Team sports provided more than the local fame and a potential for becoming rich. It was one of the spokes from where respect flowed. Teammates respected each other even when they weren't friends. I always carried myself as the ultimate team player. When the basketball coach coddled and pushed me out in front of other players, I fell back or brought the group forward with me. With the football coach, each year it was something different. This past August when we got to sleepaway camp, he wanted me to play Tight End. This would have cut into one of my teammates' chances of getting a scholarship. I went with the coach's decision but ended up injured during a scrimmage. It was a hip injury that really could not be diagnosed. My father took me to a doctor and he wrote a note and warned the coach I could reinjure myself if I got hit the same way again.

I focused on basketball as my sole avenue to a scholarship. My past play kept some schools interested and other top schools agreed to give me a look once I was fully healed.

The previous Friday's practice was the only one I'd missed all season. On days we didn't have a game, coach held practice during eighth and ninth periods, up to 3:30pm. I entered the locker room and approached a teammate I knew sold guns. He asked no questions as to why I needed a gun. We had been teammates for two years and that's what mattered. He told me to wait for him until after practice so we'd be the last to leave the locker room. We walked. Whereas Love had been out in the open, this gun crew was a secret. Everyone was in the hallway but not everyone knew why we walked together at the end of ninth period, when most juniors and seniors had already left the building. He offered me no names but I already knew everyone, including Girard, the freshmen and sophomores. Seeing us walk throughout the school, from basement to the top floor meant I was one of them. We were on the fourth floor. Having covered all the floors and corners of the school building, I had counted twenty-two students, mostly boys. The rules were simple. Each month I would give him fifty dollars. I would tell him what type of gun I wanted. He started me off with a small gun, a silver .32 I could easily fit in a pocket. He said to practice with it. He gave me the name of a place for target practice and a password to say at door. I was to go randomly, never on the same day and time in any month, no more than once a week. He pointed left, "I go out this way. If you're sure you want to buy in, you go down the center staircase and out the back door. If not, use the front door. Fifty for life. Price will go up but within reason. Someone will simply walk up and ask you for 'spare change' each month. You will get a new one only when you absolutely need one or it's your turn based on inventory. You let your contact know what type you need and when by. Peace."

He left and I let a few minutes pass.

Down the center staircase and out the back. As soon as I opened the door, I saw Girard. He was leaning against a parked car. He asked no questions and started walking with me, matching my stride.

Every day that week I kept thinking I would get a call to do something illegal but that request never came. At first, I carried every day, except when it was time to go to my mother's house. After a few weeks, I rarely carried, figuring the moment I feared would not come, at least not as a surprise.

Chapter 17

They were dressed in black, church clothes. We entered the house, not knowing what to expect, not knowing what, if anything, my father had told them. We wore designer jeans and Clarks Wallabees. On our way to the house, we practiced how to stay away from the topic but we could not get in-sync.

Her eyes, puffy and withdrawn, drained of all tears, my mother simply said, "We decided to attend the late service today."

There was no need to explain the somber mood that had stolen our voices and exuberance.

The way our lives had been set up, walking together presented a risk even though the church was only four blocks from the house. No one in this neighborhood knew of her sons. Girard had not spent much time in church, especially a Catholic one. He adapted quickly, as if he had served as an altar boy and had read and memorized the service. We stood as a family, somewhat giving way we were facing hard times, but not necessarily death. The police claimed to have continued searching for Eric, and his roommate said he hadn't shown up.

As parishioners my mother might have told the priests but she wasn't one to burden others with her troubles. When the priest called for prayers other family names were called but not ours, not even her maiden name.

The service lasted close to ninety minutes. Outside the church, to stave off anyone's need for introductions, we stood off to the side as my mother and sisters chatted with friends.

We spent most Sundays with my mother and sisters. We usually arrived close to one o'clock, timing our arrival for when they returned from the last of the early masses. My mother would be putting the finishing touches on Sunday dinner. I remember the first house in Queens. I was under seven and hearing her wake and make her way down the stairs. The best days were ones when there'd be a chill in the house. Outside, the gray of late fall still loomed. She would sit at the kitchen table and enjoy her black coffee and buttered roll. She would dip the roll into the coffee and savor each bite. Her face, calm with joy, caught in a reverie of the past and giving it a middle finger for not having allowed her to glean life's simple pleasures. By the time my father would make his way downstairs and give her a hug, she had four burners in operation and the backdoor open to offset the oven's heat. He would go get the newspaper and the week's groceries, and be back in time for church.

Nowadays, my father never attended church. He rarely visited with us on Sundays but at least once during the week, he would tell me my mother said hi and she'll see me on Sunday. I was not sure what he told them about Eric. I found it odd my father had not made the effort to come that Sunday. His album had shown me the loyalty to family amidst the complexity of his life. The twins became the only ones not to reach their thirteenth birthday with him living in the house. His life's work had not creased his face. At seventy-one, the smoothness of his skin fooled many into thinking he was only five or fewer years older than my mother.

My mother cleared the table of the serving plates and went into the kitchen. We each brought our plates and utensils to the kitchen and rinsed them before placing them in the dishwasher. We had sat for a long meal and neither my mother nor sisters asked questions. This evasiveness was the trait that had begun to alienate me from my family. I did my best to hide my feelings until Marlene asked Girard to walk with her. The unspecified destination jarred my senses. He seemed to still have a thing for her. Unlike his feelings for Cherise, there was no balance in his adoration of Marlene. She liked a type and Girard was not it. She envisioned herself living a jet set life, with a husband who was the progeny of old money. I took her invitation as a warning signal. Deep down I blamed Girard and Manny for the calamities that had befallen my family.

Right after they left the house, Ghyslaine asked the twins to leave us alone for a second. The twins were a mysterious pair. They gladly responded to being called "Twin". My mother never dressed them in identical clothes, but as soon as they turned ten and she gave them a say in their own outfits they started dressing alike. This past August, for back-to-school shopping, my mother gave Ghyslaine the money to take them shopping. My mother was not happy with their purchases, even though she was the only person who could tell them apart, the only one to call them by their real names. When they were babies, not yet walking, I tested her to see if she could really tell them apart. It got to the point, even the twins tested her. Eventually we all said the three of them were playing mind games on us. Ghyslaine never tried to make the distinction. She had been charged with watching them when they were months-old if my mother was not around. Her lone concern was the twins doing what she told them as soon as she commanded.

The twins left the room and headed upstairs. Ghyslaine gave me a conspiratorial smile and said, "Ernest, you have nothing to worry about. You don't know anything."

The way she said it caused me to run to the front door. The house had an unusual brightness to it – vivid – as if awaiting photographers to capture the décor. They lived as if their lives were an open book. Sheer white curtains adorned the living room's windows. The sun pierced through and illuminated the entire first floor. Marlene and Girard were almost at the corner. "Yo G, get back here!"

I didn't know if I was stopping him to protect him or my family. My sisters did not know just how connected Girard was. Girard stopped but did not walk toward me, and moved only when Marlene said, "We're going to the store. We'll be right back."

Girard moved but not in the direction I wanted. I went back to the dining room. "What are you up to?"

"Us? You're worrying about us, your sisters? You think we would do something to Girard?"

"I don't know. What did dad tell you?" I left it open-ended to see what she would admit to knowing.

She rolled her eyes and went to the bar cart, a fine piece of furniture, gold-plated with two glass shelves. She asked, "Do you want something to drink? To relax yourself?" She lit a cigarette and brought two scotch glasses. She sat across me.

Suddenly, Ghyslaine looked older, wise, much more than her twenty-one years. I had missed so much of my sisters' lives. I had attended the high school graduations and witnessed the disappointment in her voice when my mother refused to budge and insisted Ghyslaine could not go away for college and experience dorm life. She had to do college in the city and commute from home.

"Mom lets you smoke and drink?"

I never took stock on how what we boys were going through was affecting them. We never spoke openly about Lionel and living apart. "Ernest, I need a man who doesn't worry about the consequences of his actions. Manny had that when I first met him."

"I thought you only knew him from his visits to our house."

She was talking to me but not paying any attention to what I was saying. Her eyes were far away, sad. "Manny had that killer instinct until the night after your fight at The Center. It's like he just lost it."

"You knew about that?"

"Yes!" She pounded the table, her order for me to stop interrupting. "Manny told me."

I needed her to answer my questions or there would be no conversation. "You knew Manny before me?"

"How do you think Eric met him?" She walked away from the table.

My sisters were not to be underestimated and it's something I had clearly forgotten. Somehow I had blocked that knowledge from my mind. I used to watch the four of them carefully not knowing which one would strike at me, verbally or physically. Ghyslaine was the first grown girl I ever saw naked. I was eight and she was nearing fourteen. I had to pee and she was taking a real long time, and using our bathroom, instead of the large one designated for the girls. So I barged in to say, "I gotta pee." She punched me in the chest, hard, carrying on about telling me before about coming into the bathroom without permission. I started to cry and went to tell my mother. When Ghyslaine came out of the bathroom, I punched her back. The punch was nowhere near as hard as hers. She swung and I ducked and hit her again. Then someone hit me in the back of the head. Marlene had run out of their bedroom and they wrestled me to the ground. We all tumbled and even though they were getting the best of me, the twins jumped in. One started biting my right arm. The other my right leg. Little four year-old teeth hurt.

They didn't stop until my mother said, "OK, that's enough!"

I followed Ghyslaine into the living room. "What do you want me to do?"

Her height had long intimidated boys, except for certain short ones who saw her as a challenge. She grew to prefer their boldness. She could never bring them to the house so they exchanged secret glances to indicate safe places to meet. She moved from the window and paced the room. "Look out for Manny! Protect him the way he protected you that first night. That's what Marlene is asking Girard to do. It's like you guys have decided not to protect Manny. Lionel thought he was protecting Manny, but he only made things worse. Eric? Eric, who knows what he was thinking!"

I finally asked the question I had been holding in all week. "What happened to Eric?"

"He went off the deep end. I tried to reason with him but his mind, it started to unravel." She fought back a sob, the desire to tell me more. "Don't lose patience and try to go for it all at once. Pick a position and hold it, or else you're going to do like Eric and get yourself killed."

We went back to the table. My mother came into the room and took the drink out of my hand. She cut me a look that asked, how dare I drink alcohol in her house? My mother kept a watchful eye on my sisters but obviously the older ones enjoyed a freedom I had not earned. Unlike my father who let knowledge drip like water from a colander, leaving the thick stuff for us to figure out for ourselves, my mother spilled the beans. They were her priestesses and the house was her confessional.

My mother returned to the kitchen as Marlene and Girard came back from the store.

Ghyslaine continued telling me how, on the second day when we first moved to Brooklyn, Manny tried to stick her up. When she told stories, her body remained calm but her voice, with its dips and exaggerated exclamations, exposed the wit and humor she kept hidden from the outside world. She had grown tall too soon, adulthood bestowed upon her before puberty. She made Manny a deal: if he really needed the money, he could have it. If not, they would be hell to pay. So he took her to his home but did not agree to keep the money.

She didn't say it but I could see why Ghyslaine introduced him to Eric. She had looked into Manny's eyes and right then and there, they had made unspoken plans for a distant future, one that got ripped from them. She introduced him because Eric knew how to take things to the next level. Though he had never done crime, Eric was ruthless and loved to dole out revenge.

I visited Manny's apartment only one time. He lived in one of the tall buildings, down the main avenue, second from corner. I had been in the building and ran through its lobby during games of coco-leevio. I had scurried up its stairs to the roof and crossed over to the adjacent buildings, only to freeze when confronted by the steep drop to the first of the three shorter connected buildings. Manny's building had a musty odor to it. The front door was never locked so it was a favorite for the kids to access and ride the elevator for games of corners.

One summer day in 1983, at the last minute our crew decided to head to a block party. We were in a rush but Manny never went anywhere without looking fresh. He wanted to go change his clothes so I tagged along. I got the sense he didn't want me to go with him. He never said it but it dawned on me he was ashamed to let people in his home. Until then I never knew where he lived. As we approached the building, there were some burned out looking men sitting on the façade. I had seen those men and they'd never looked my way and I never really looked at them. I noticed Manny touch his left side, his ribs with his right palm. I asked him what that was and he said a signal to indicate clearance, whenever he entered the building. His father had set up a form of protection for the family. The unspoken word on the streets was Manny's father was on death row, charged and convicted of killing two policemen. He didn't use the elevator. We walked the three flights up to his apartment. His mother cut me a look as if she didn't trust me. She likely did not trust anyone who walked through her front door. His little brother and sister looked to be a year or two younger than me. I had seen them in passing. They walked the avenue in the quiet way bookworms who could fight did. They were playing with a white kid of about the same age. They all jumped up as we walked through the living room and followed us to one of the two bedrooms in the back. A bunk bed and a separate twin-size bed. They bombarded him with questions and requests. Manny gave them some loose bills. He grabbed some clothes from an armoire and headed to the bathroom. I sat on the edge of the bed and the three of them sized me up. They stood in a semi-circle and waited for me to speak. I grabbed a comic book from the desk and waited them out. Manny chuckled when he came back into the room. We headed out and they followed us toward the front door. I gave his mother a smile and slight head nod.

As we walked to the block party to catch up to the others, Manny filled in the blanks, of why there had been no introductions and such suspicion. Manny's family moved into the neighborhood a decade ago, before any of the other black families, except for Benny's and Girard's. His father's lawyer found them the place. The apartment belonged to the white kid's family. His father's lawyer had represented them in an earlier case. They agreed to let Manny's family live with them since they traveled a lot and Manny's mother agreed to look after their son. Initially it was to hide them out for a few weeks. It stretched out to some sort of amnesty situation when no one would hire Manny's mother and the government would not allow them to get financial assistance. The welfare system placed various hurdles. As his father's trial drew out, both of Manny's parents' families shied away from them. The white couple had their own complicated lives and one day never made it back from a trip to Florida. They sent instructions with the lawyer to have their son sent to his paternal grandparents. Manny's mother had raised the boy so he begged to stay. The plan, the promise was to eventually move Manny's family to Florida and out of the country with them. At first they sent money but it became dangerous for them to keep in touch even through intermediaries. Through it all, Manny and his mother knew, even though the landlord began to neglect the building and hired an absentee super, not having their name on a lease or bills left them vulnerable. Manny's father reassured her they were safe but she never bought into his faith.

Manny chuckled but I could sense his hurt because I thought he robbed and stole for sport. It hurt me hearing him admit, "I'm poor, man! That's why I do this shit, and to keep my mom from resorting to desperate measures. No other reason!"

I reached out my hand to ask for forgiveness and he shook it.

My sisters gave us a mandate to protect Manny. But deep down we all knew it really came down to protecting The Big Man from himself.

Chapter 18

For two years, we had a foolproof plan to protect Manny even though we were more than three hours away by car. The plan required me and Girard to team up on an effort. On the surface we had been each other's right hand men for six years, since the sixth grade, yet we had never lowered our guards and told each other how we processed life.

Girard clued me in on how he operated around other people but not why it worked. I explained I never led in anything. The year we won the city's basketball championship, Slick ran things even though I led the team in scoring.

So, to protect Manny from two hundred miles away, we decided to dominate in everything we did and give some or full credit to Manny Davenport. We swore a fierce loyalty to him, dropping his name whenever we could, stating he had paved the way for our success. This was partly true because during the summer of 1983, The Big Man had changed the game in ways we then did not understand.

Even though four years later the game had evolved to the point where crews were no longer eight men one gun, the mental sleight of hand Manny had mastered still worked.

My senior year the team lacked in so many areas. I carried us as much as I could and led in Points, Rebounds, Assists and Steals, as well as academics. When reporters asked which college I would attend, I committed to one line: the one that gave me the best chance of going to the NBA. When they asked about my outside interests, I said I had none.

Most times when not playing ball, I ventured into Manhattan for an art show, to a museum, the theater, any place where no one knew of me.

While we talked his name, Manny continued to work diligently on whatever mission he was on. We did not have to look for him. His movements got back to us. We had shone a spotlight so high on him, to the point he couldn't come to Brooklyn. Everyone felt they knew him, claimed to have run the streets with him, been to one of his college parties. We forced him to stay away because he had no reason to be in this part of Brooklyn since his family had moved out. During school breaks, he would drop by the house unexpectedly, kick it with us, ask us about our life, whether we needed money and stuff like that. We didn't because Girard was into things I didn't ask about. Just like he didn't ask why, in my senior year, I embraced the nickname Ern-Money.

We had Manny's profile so high he finally realized he had to get away. The word got to us he had joined with some counter-revolutionaries, had grown his hair out to dread locks and was sporting a full beard. He was never on his campus and no one knew where he was.

Until.

Girard and I came home from school on the second Friday in May and turned on the TV. We never turned on the TV but that day it was an instinctual move. I clicked the remote and started taking off my jacket. We saw the smoke. We saw the fire. We saw the location and knew we had to get to TGI ASAP.

Girard made a phone call and told me, "We can pick up a rental on East 23rd, near Baruch."

"We're not supposed to drive."

I recently had a chance to buy a used car, a nice '83 Maxima at a great price. It was the most spooked I had ever seen my father. "A car put limits on you that you are not ready for. You can't get drunk when you go out. You have to pay two types of insurance: your fault, and the other driver's. And then there's the police – you're basically giving them a free pass to harass you. The best thing to do is to take cabs."

Girard still questioned things when my father spoke. "Wouldn't cabs cost more in the long run?"

And, my father never really answered. "When you take a cab, never have it take you to your exact destination. Always get off a block or two away."

We had been chipping away at my father's rules. We packed two small bags and each grabbed a gun and as much money as we had put away.

We jogged to the subway down the block and caught up to the train's closing doors. My blood coursed through my body. It felt electric. My mind raced but unsure what exactly we planned on doing. We remained silent, realizing we had motioned a spotlight on to ourselves. The protection we set up for Manny was a double-edged sword. It asked for loyalty, and for love to be a substitute for power.

The attendant at the car rental place looked familiar and he knew both our names, but it was Girard who had cemented a bond through some random conversation. The guy was not from around the way, didn't carry himself like someone who would have dealt with the dark side of Love. Yet, here he was putting his job in jeopardy by assigning a car to unlicensed drivers who had not reached the company's required age to rent cars. He handed us keys and paperwork, and showed us where to hide our guns in case the state troopers pulled us over on the highway. I knew how to drive because my father had given us lessons. Each child learned as soon as feet could reach the pedals. He taught us so we could take charge in a medical emergency. Girard handled the wheel like he had been driving daily for years. I didn't bother ask how he had learned. The way Girard sped in and out of traffic, we should have been stopped. He seemed to have a rhythm, a method to stay within driving packs to not draw attention.

We arrived in Trafalgar and headed to the campus, wondering if there would be a security card for us at the gate. The gate was unattended. We drove through and turned left into the first parking lot. There were fire trucks, and hundreds, maybe a thousand people; just pure anarchy - topless students waving their shirts and bras in the air, open containers of alcohol, a bonfire, a burning building. Girard grabbed a guy running by, "Who's behind this?"

"Aman."

"What? How do you spell that?"

"A, E, I, O, U. It doesn't matter. He did it." The guy howled.

I processed Aman, Amen, Amin, Amon and Amun. Girard's focus was elsewhere. He did a three-sixty survey of the place. "Oh shit! That motherfucker Manny threw a coup. He toppled the Society. I'm gonna be president."

I gave him a push to the chest to get him back on my wavelength. "This is how you want to become president? If Manny's behind this, then that motherfucker is crazy and just signed all our death certificates." Girard kept walking forward. "Yo, G let's head back to the city. I am not sure what Manny is up to but we shouldn't be here."

"Now, I understand why Benny, Lionel and Eric were willing to die."

He had refocused my attention, as to why we placed Manny at the top of the hierarchy, lined up all our armies behind him in this real life game of Risk. "Why?"

"The Society is a monarchy." He pointed to the quad. I had taken my eyes off the fire, the burning building. It was the tallest one and only one of the top floors burned. "These motherfuckers threw a coup and went straight to the top. All these decades, people have been waging a ground war. But, the Society's numbers are too high, too many foot soldiers and levels to get through. How did he get up there?"

Manny had flipped our efforts to neutralize him and used the fame to propel himself on a much higher level. I looked around the quad and sensed something was not right. I still did not know the target. I followed Girard as he walked closer to the fire. I told him to stop. He kept walking so I yanked his left arm. "Stand the way you would if you wanted to be approached by the Society."

"Why? What do you see?"

The question was loaded. He knew we had come to the end but not far enough where I could see this game for what it was. "It's what I don't see. I don't recognize anyone from our last visit. I don't see The Big Man."

He stood still but the outward angle of his left shoulder meant he was studying his surroundings. "Trust me, this is the end of this level."

"OK, even if that's the case, is it your thinking we're on the same level as Manny?" Girard put his left hand in his pants pocket and closed his right fist, his right arm dangling near his body, swinging slightly forward and back. He told me to put my hands behind my back as if handcuffed, my left palm and fingers encircling my right wrist.

Students threw paper into the bonfire. They sprayed various liquids to stir the fire to greater heights. Campus police had erected barriers to keep people away from the burning building while the firemen hosed the flames. By the looks of it the entire wing of that floor would burn. The fire raged as if an accelerant had been used.

<0>

We held our position for about ten minutes and that's when we spotted you and Barbara.

As you approached, we tried to get a read on y'all but it was hard. Your styles were different from girls we'd been around, with your short afros, wearing no makeup and with curves for days. It quickly dawned on us. You were the two Manny had mentioned as his sisters, on campus. You quickly separated us. To this day I can't confirm what G discussed with Barbara but I know, at least, I think I understand what you wanted of me.

We had only spent a little over thirty minutes together. You said there was a contract on Manny. You felt he had to die. I figured it was a misunderstanding, a lover's quarrel.

You and Barbara were hard reads. You were hanging out with dudes like us, but their edges had been smoothed out, yet the fire burned.

When Manny appeared, it was the first time we heard someone call him Attitude. Between the three of you, there was love, a fluid manner of interaction I quickly read as unfinished transactions, an isosceles triangle.

I was stunned by Girard's interaction with you. I had never seen him nervous around a woman to the point he cut to the chase in order to hide his vulnerability. There was an uneasiness the way Barbara moved her left leg closer to her body, away from me. I glanced to my right and saw the stares of the three guys who had confronted me in the cafeteria. They had left Barbara out there with Girard, but they immediately came after you.

I thought it was because they doubted your loyalty.

Truth was they knew of me, and also that I was not of the Society and had no reason to respect its rules.

When you and Barbara walked away from us, to them; walked far away, the opposite direction from the fire, I wanted to put it all out there, right there, tell Manny there was a hit out on him and this was greater than the specter of violence that had loomed over his head for years.

You were in the Society, deep in it. I could tell you had no plans of leaving the Society, even if you could.

Before I got a chance to ask Girard what Barbara said.

Before I got a chance to ask Attitude about you and Barbara, Manny said, "I have to leave now. Follow my car but put some distance between us. Four cars are going to come right behind me; they're with me. Follow the fifth car but at a distance. Do not turn on your headlights!"

Attitude ran. Five guys followed him.

We moved through the crowd but didn't run a straight line behind him.

The five guys piled into one car. Attitude waited long enough for us to get into our car. He drove out through the main campus exit. The first four cars filled the gap and then came a fifth car. Its headlights came on. It was a black Lincoln Continental Town Car, windows with full tint and TLC license plates. It had been in the middle of the parking lot. I had not seen a person enter. The driver might not have been on the quad. A car turned left off a side street and got between the fifth car and us. It provided cover between the Town Car and us. We were now on the back roads of Trafalgar, a single lane on each side of double solid lines. The road headed northwest. Darkness overpowered us since we were not using headlights. Since it was a one lane route with fifteen mile per hour curves, there was no reason for the fifth car to think we were following it. But it knew!

Barely slowing down, it made an unexpected U-turn, and another one. The car ahead of us slowed down, separating us from Attitude and the other cars. Girard, being on the same wavelength, used his side view mirror to count three more cars behind what had been the fifth car. He said, "OK, I want to lose all of them except the Town Car."

I knew he could drive well but the moves he executed made no sense, yet we did not crash. He crossed over the dividing line as the road became two lanes on each side. He used his horn and headlights as a communication device. He alternated between high and low beams. He honked his horn and cars split to leave the middle of the road open. The car in front of us did not cross the yellow lines but the Town Car and the three others did.

We were doing about forty miles per hour. This part of the road was a flat straight away, which gave cars the opportunity to bail to either side as we approached. I glanced at the directional sign on the other side and told Girard the road would end. He could go east or west. He sped up. At the fork in the road, I fully expected him to go left and so did the car that had not crossed the yellow line. Girard made two hard rights and jammed traffic in all directions.

The car on the right side of the road bailed and hit an embankment. Only the Town Car was able to keep up with us. The other three had to take the left at the fork in the road or crash. With traffic jammed behind us, we reversed course. The Town Car followed us as Girard sped back, on the right side of the road, back toward TGI. I glanced at the speedometer and asked him to slow down as we reached eighty. He was driving on the dividing line. "Where are you racing to?"

Girard veered off to a side road, and another. He had lost the Town Car. He circled back but to the opposite side of the campus, only about five miles away, but on the other side of the mountains.

All the shops in the strip mall were closed. Girard pulled in.

I asked, "Yo, why are you stopping?"

"Don't you want to know who was following us?" The car pulled into a parking spot across us and one over to our left. We both reached under our seats, into the hidden compartment. We held our guns in our laps. We knew we could not approach a car with tinted windows. The driver side door flung open but the man came out the front passenger side, away from us. He left the doors open so we could see there was no one else in the car. Girard rolled down his window and asked, "Where's the driver?"

"When my safety is involved I drive myself." He waited for us to come out. We studied him for a moment. He had thinning sandy hair, a tanned yet pinkish tone to his skin, a bushy mustache, broad shoulders and a bit of a paunch.

We came out of the car, guns in hand. Girard started in on him. "Why are you following us?"

He laughed. "Somebody is giving you bad information."

"No. Someone's reading my mind!"

"No one's reading your mind! You're just playing on a level you're not yet ready for." Though we had taken a few steps toward him, he had not moved. I scanned his body and slight hand movements for where he would reach for a gun. "Who did you think was in the car?"

Girard didn't answer. The man had asked the question I wanted to ask, so I entered the conversation. "My brother. He's in the Society."

The man gave me a quizzical look. "He must be in the deep end!"

"It depends on how you look at things."

He forced a smile and said, "Imagine if everything was just black and white."

"How would you change that?"

"You would move closer and experience The Doppler Effect."

Girard caught on and raised his gun. "What? You're saying my father is fronting for the white man?"

"No, son." He pointed to his own chest. "This white man was fronting for your father." We pointed our guns downward and leaned back against our car. "Your father died..."

G interrupted him "My father's not dead. I spoke to him…"

"No. Your father's dead, happened in 1972."

Girard stepped to him like he was going to fight. "You're so sure he's dead. Maybe you killed him!"

"If he's alive then he must think that, and that would be a shame."

"OK, let's say he's dead. Then who killed him and why?"

"Not the man, who was on death row." It clicked. "I do not know who killed him. But now, since you are saying he's alive, I don't know what to think."

"It still doesn't explain why you're following us."

The man chuckled. "You're trying to reach a man whose protection got increased to a level that if you get to him, you basically sign your death certificate." He paused and added, "You know what? Since you were good enough to break through and get this far, go ahead, go to his house. When things get too thick, say you are looking for the wrong man. That will give you one free pass."

"OK." My voice was barely able to function. Girard didn't say anything.

Girard pointed his gun. "If my father's dead, who killed him?"

"Ask your mother!" Those words triggered the response I anticipated. Girard squeezed off two shots. I beat him to the spot and pushed his hand way up. The shots rang out in the air.

The man shook his head, mainly in sadness. He got in his car, closed the doors and drove away.

I heard sirens in the distance. Though they were on the other side of the mountain, heading toward the traffic jam, the shots might cause a police car to circle back this way. I asked G to let me drive. "We're heading back to the city."

"How?" He asked. "Ghyslaine gave us orders."

"After what we just learned, she'll understand."

"I have to get the answers about my father."

Those were answers he did not need. Seeing the sadness that overtook Girard when he realized Manny's father was wrongly convicted and executed, I drove toward Manny's house. He said it to me but more to himself, "My father faked his death?"

Our fathers led complicated lives.

I drove barely above the winding road's speed limit, blending with the traffic on this side of the town. We got to Manny's house and knocked a few times but no one answered. There were four cars in the driveway. Since the lights were on and the door unlocked, we walked in, still viewing it as the party house it had been during our previous visit.

The movements were quick. We were surrounded. Five guys, one black and four whites, real pale, the type you could never mistake for being of a different stock. One blocked the door with his back. Each of the others stood by windows. We had been in this room, lounging on the floor, on the sofa. This was a party room.

No one spoke for about a solid minute until one of the four asked, "What do you assholes want?"

Girard took two steps toward him. All five of them advanced the same number of paces toward us. All five had buzz cuts. Everyone stopped. They didn't say a word, only numbers. Up to this day, I do not recall the numbers. They took two steps back to their original positions. One of the white guys repeated the question. This time Girard responded with numbers of his own and the black one said, "Oh, sorry! We did not recognize that you were a brother."

"I'm not but my father..." Before he got the next word out, they were on us. We had been in many fights but these guys fought like they had received special training. Simply put we were getting our asses handed to us, and not because they outnumbered us. This was simple one on one with the other three surrounding the periphery. In junior high school, we once had a beef with some white kid one of our boys had robbed. To avoid a no-purpose fight, my homeboy had made the declaration no white boy around his size and weight could beat him. I had backed his statement as an undisputable fact, but not tonight. They should have knocked us out by now, but they were punching us only to inflict enough pain, dragging out the beating like Ali versus Ernie Terrell. My mind ran straight to shoot to kill. That last punch dropped G. I saw his eyes roll to the top of his head and his left hand reach. As I began to absorb the last punch and simultaneously reach with my right hand, there was a knock on the door.

They had locked the door.

One went to the door and opened it. "A Man, we have to go. We've been infiltrated."

Manny saw us on the floor. "What the fuck are y'all doing here?"

"You told us to follow you and these fucking white boys started illing." One punched me beneath my sternum and I fell to the floor. I pulled out my gun. "Yo Manny, drop!"

It's like he forgot his name. He stood still and the black guy, who had been by the door, turned out the lights. Manny said, "Ern, don't shoot! Nobody do anything!"

One of the white guys called out some numbers.

G called out some numbers. Manny shouted, "G, stop that shit! Nobody do or say anything! Relax!"

We stayed low on the ground, and in my mind, I kept praying Manny would get on the ground so I could shoot. He had divided his loyalties. In the dark, bursts of pain reverberated through my body. After about a two minute standstill, the front door opened and the lights came on. Everyone had a gun in hand except Manny and the four new black guys who had just walked in. The four of them said, "What the fuck?"

"Close the door!" Manny looked around the room, surveyed the tension and said, "Everyone put your guns down! Put your guns down! Peace always wins!"

The black guy who had been with the white boys, he nodded toward each of them. They put their guns away and stepped back toward the windows closest to the front door.

Girard stood up. "Manny..."

He interrupted Girard. "The name is A Man. But only call me that behind closed doors, only around a select few, and never around friends of mine from college."

One of the white guys said, "He's not a brother so how does he know our language?"

"That's Doppler's son!"

He fired back. "It still does not explain it." Girard had caught on, to keep his mouth shut. The same white guy asked, "How did you get through to get here?"

That question stumped us. We had not put away our guns and I could sense Girard and I were on the same wavelength. Manny was in way too deep. We said, "We're sorry, we're looking for the wrong man."

We had shown our loyalty, our love for him to get him this far. Would he return the gesture? Manny said, "Never tell anyone what happened here in this house. You have never seen these two. And, you have never seen any of these white guys. OK?"

At that, the white guys left the house, and the five black guys went upstairs.

Once they left the room, Girard asked, "What about my father? Was Lionel working for him?"

"You spoke to him on the phone and said he was your father. I have never spoken to or met Doppler."

Manny's answer was what I anticipated. I sensed he was dealing on the straight so I told Girard. "From now on, never mention your father. If anyone brings him up, simply say he's in the deep end."

Girard asked, "What's going on with these nine guys?"

"There are only five guys, five black ones, the ones upstairs. They're called The Outsiders. You don't know them yet." As Manny walked out of the room to head upstairs, Girard and I looked at each other.

We still had our guns out, and Manny had turned his back on us.

Part Three

BOW TO THE QUEEN

Chapter 19
IN NAME ONLY

We stepped out of the building, a three-story townhome in Crown Heights on St. John's Place. I turned around and surveyed the structure. It had the same color and facade but I was clear it was not the house Ernest took me into two hours ago. After all the walking we had done, the stops along the way so he could show me the places they lived and ran around, we had not entered this building. We had entered a building much like this one but the front windows faced south. He said his room was in the basement. Along the hallway toward the stairs, I heard voices in the adjacent rooms and upstairs. At that time, with sore feet and a belly recently filled with breakfast, I thought Ernest would make his play when he lied next to me on the bed. But, he rested there like we were siblings, 'cause we had bonded over his life story. I leaned in, on my left elbow and he shifted his head and sat up mid-chuckle. "Trust me Hope, you're G's. You will see."

I did not fight his proclamation because part of me understood why he felt that way, the historical links between mine and Girard's family. I also respected the fear Ernest lived under. Still it did not make sense Ernest was alive. Looking up Benny's family name in the Society's historical record will confirm what I have surmised. Benny's father's name would be redacted, just as Girard's father. These two families living on the same block as Manny's family was not an accident. It took a perverse mind to be so bold.

We reached Eastern Parkway and Utica Avenue at about ten-thirty. The streets bustled with activity like no morning I'd ever encountered. People talked as fast as they walked. Their movements zigging past slow ones jamming up the sidewalk. The lack of uniformity made our pace appear more rushed. Ernest wanted to make sure I had enough time to get back to the loft before the party's end. He had not calculated a part of me had no desire to return. No one had stopped us along the way. Yet for nearly fifteen hours no one had come to ask me whether my safety was at risk.

Why go in naked, with a gun but unarmed with knowledge, to protect Manny, a man who had yet to proclaim any allegiance to me?

My mind processed how best to steal a kiss, in this open space, to seal my allegiance. Unbeknownst to Ernest, the kiss would cover him with my protection, even if the mystery of the Society is never revealed to him. His height meant I would have to tiptoe or pull his neck down fast so his face would jerk down and our noses would touch. Even on this crowded street with passersby preoccupied with their own lives, whether a knight, man of honor or simply spoken for, no one would accept he did not kiss the girl. He could not have his manhood be in question. I took a sideward glance as we neared the steps to the subway. Ernest stopped to say goodbye and I yanked his oversized Fila polo shirt with my left hand and got on my toes. Though not needed, it had a clear effect. In that split second, all motion stopped. He hesitated. His eyes opened a little wider as I pushed my lips on to his. His mouth opened as my right hand squeezed his bulge. The hardness I felt made me realize the tremendous amount of self-control Ernest possessed. He slowly backed away from my kiss, a smile on his face, and shook his head. "Transfer at Atlantic Avenue for the D or R train."

As he walked away, the crowded avenue spun around me. I saw cars turn left as others in the opposite direction traveled forward. I waited for collisions as the clouds parted. In the August heat, a breath of fresh air had removed all doubt in my heart. For me, love existed.

I ran down the steps and hopped over the turnstile so I could catch the soon-departing train.

As I rode the subway, more aware what Attitude had done and why, I fought with myself. I sensed the eyes on me as I studied the flyer I had created, the hornets' nest I'd stepped into and subsequently gotten pulled out of by Ernest. Could love really be that simple, a matter of your word being your bond? Ernest had not said it but Girard used my name to flush Manny out. He said I put a hit out on Manny, which in effect put a hit out on me. Manny protected me by telling everyone I was his woman but he never closed the deal. I was his woman in name only. In his eyes, I could leave whenever I wanted. I could and I finally did but not because he or anyone gave me permission.

I got off the train and returned to the party instead of going to Grand Central for the Metro-North. I came back for Attitude thinking Girard would understand.

He had not.

<0>

This past May when they reached home after leaving Attitude's house, Ernest got a sense before reading the note his father had done something. The note taped over the keyhole showed him the side of his father he had known before Lionel went to prison. "I thought I told you NO CARS. Since you want to be a grown man, find somewhere else to live."

Though written in a simple legible script, in his father's way of looking at Ernest's disobedience, a rental for the weekend meant you bought a car. He calculated the number of times he had gone against his father, and there were few. For it to be so sudden, Ernest pondered the possible lesson his father aimed teach him.

His key could not access the lock. No shades on the windows. Through the darkness, he saw the first floor had been emptied, no furniture. They stepped off the porch and into the street to get a view of the second floor and attic. The street light shot enough of a glare for them to see the bareness of the rooms.

Girard laughed. Ernest was not sure whether the gravity of the situation had yet to hit him. They walked around the corner even though Girard told

Ernest he did not want to go home because he didn't want to confront his mother about his father. He didn't want her to learn too much of what he'd been up to. He needed time to figure out the truth on his own or to prepare his line of questioning.

The avenue was flushed with a low intensity of darkness even though the sun would not rise for another five or six hours. They had driven down slowly, in a silence marked by the beating doled out by Attitude's white boys. No visible marks but the pain and bruised egos and hurt feelings caused by the desertion of a childhood friend.

They walked in and spotted two large suitcases stacked in the corner of the living room corner. Girard's mother gave them a curfew and major restrictions. They had to be home by dark. She gave Ernest a rundown of the household chores, the new *no visitors* policy, and no loud music, ever. Church every Sunday with her, except when they went with Ernest's family. No drinking or any kind of smoking in or out of the house.

He didn't even ask her how his father knew where Girard lived and what had been stated.

Ernest liked living with Girard's mother. Space in the apartment was not an issue, not even with the two of them sharing a bedroom.

At first, she looked at him suspiciously. She barely knew him, except that his brother had killed another youth. The next thing she knew her only son had defied her and pretty much gone to live with Ernest's family, people she had never met. "Holding down the fort!" was how Girard said he had explained it to her. Then, unexpectedly years later, Ernest's father rang her bell and dropped off his belongings, simply stating they were hardheaded and asked her to give it a try.

Girard hated living under these new rules. Even though he never talked back to his mother, he really could not adjust. Their early weeks at Girard's, Ernest explained to him the benefits of such restrictions, but Girard constantly broke curfew. A few days after high school graduation, his mother played the final card she had: he either followed her rules or bounce.

They had finally reached the impasse that could permanently fracture the parent-child relationship. Balancing love and power from either end always proved tricky for them. She worried so much about Girard he made it a point to excel in all he did. As a trade-off, he basically parented himself while she worked long hours so they could live in one of the nicest buildings on the block.

She had to know Girard had no fear of leaving home. She told Ernest he could stay. He wanted to but didn't.

Girard had it all mapped out but Ernest preferred another plan: use some of the money they saved up and rent a room until the start of college.

Girard said, "We can't do that. We need to be visible until they catch up with Manny. It's the reason Eric made sure they knew where we were when he went after them. He gave us alibis."

"Isn't Manny still upstate?"

"No, we're the last ones to see him. No one's seen him since the fire. He didn't go to his graduation. I've been looking all over for him."

"When?"

"That's why I've been breaking curfew. I bought some time. I told them all I could make out is some chick named Hope put a hit out on Manny so he's hiding."

Barbara had given Girard her full name. The facts came back on her. She was cleared. The streets were connected. Her brother Lincoln had credibility in their world. Lincoln was upstate doing hard time for murder.

They spent June and the rest of the summer with a posse connected to a couple of dudes who had gone to their high school. According to Ernest, this group consisted of hardcore street kids, not in name only. With them, there was no blurring the line between regular b-boys and hard rocks. The crack epidemic had changed the pace of street life but they had been clocking dough for years, through weed sales, stick-ups and break-ins. Joining them wasn't hard because, on the first night, Girard walked up and started speaking their coded language – a combination of numbers and letters. At first Ernest thought it was not the best path to take because they would question how Girard learned, but they didn't. The older guys used terminology and sequences from previous decades and Girard also knew that version of the language. That gave them pause so Girard volunteered his father had taught him. They did the math of when Girard's father stepped out of his life and chose to ignore Girard's lie.

They looked at him. They looked at Ernest.

Two of the older guys ordered some people take their bags into a house. They walked Ernest and Girard through the neighborhood. Most of the people they came across were girls in their age group and younger kids. Technically these were the people who decided whether newcomers were accepted. Ernest recognized some and knew he had never crossed any of them, especially the kids. The same went for Girard even though it was clear he knew way too many of the girls - people's little sisters, girlfriends and so on.

Their crew did not use first names or last names, only initials, nicknames and numbers. As they met people, Girard vied to be the main one to be called G. After about an hour, they circled back to the starting point and he basically convinced them a person with a name like Gary was not really a G but a Gah. One of the two said we can call you "soft G". Girard laughed and others followed suit. From that point on he got called G and others were G1, G2, G-junior, GDB and so on.

Another reason they got accepted with no issue, Ernest saw the fifty dollar a month gun club contact. He and Girard simply nodded to him. For a place to stay in one of the buildings they controlled, Ernest coached basketball to a group of kids, ages eight to fifteen. It was not to build a team since all the kids played for their schools, AAU or church leagues. They wanted Ernest to keep them sharp over the summer. The kids played in major neighborhood parks. They traveled the five boroughs, Long Island, Westchester and New Jersey. Those same kids would then get school work tutoring from Girard.

Life was not always so easy. When you hang with hard rocks, you don't necessarily have to mimic their exact criminal intentions and overall rowdiness. What he and Girard learned was this crew, the guys and girls were constantly fighting, over anything, with anyone, for nothing. If they weren't fighting other crews, they were fighting each other. Most of the time, they were play fighting. That didn't mean you didn't hear, "Oh, he caught a bad one!"

Ernest and Girard caught their share and they also held their own, to the point where sometimes they would pick a fight just to sharpen their skills. On weekends, the crew would go into other neighborhoods just to start some shit. Go to a house party and crash, for the host to kick them out, so they could shoot up the party! Go to a club and if they couldn't get a gun or two into the spot, they would leave the guns in the trunk! Inside the club, they would act mad rowdy, bump into somebody, step on their toes or spill a drink on some girl's dress. Of course all this was so some Herb with a label on his clothes would bite and step up! Usually on that scene, no one rolled solo, so before all this went down, they would do reconnaissance. Even if they were outnumbered by that person's particular crew, they would start the beef! Normally a good old-fashioned saloon style brawl would be enough. But there were times when they found themselves real deep in enemy territory and none of the other combatants knew any of them, so gun play would come into the picture. Chances were in other people's neighborhoods, the bouncers were friends of the ones they planned on fighting, so the opposition would have guns inside the club and they wouldn't. So with no gun in the place, speed and smarts were important. Car key holders played pussy as an excuse to bounce, while the others held the front line by popping shit or knuckling up. Car key holders got to their cars, rolled up and popped the trunks. Time it right and as you made it outside, everybody's brandishing. The warner bucked two shots *blohp! blohp!* in the air to scatter the crowd. Those who didn't run were either on their side or got shot. From there the scenario could play out in many ways.

The key was that no one got left behind. It's one of many scripts so the best thing to do was be constantly on the alert.

Weekly hospital visits, prison visits and funerals filled the crew's schedule. On the hottest night of July 1987, after attending a wake for a cousin of a dude who hated how he had gone from G to Hard-G, Ernest roamed away from the avenue to a rooftop. He found G sitting on the barrier connecting two buildings. At first he thought G had a honey with him, but he was alone with a forty of Old Gold and a short fat blunt. He passed E the smoke and just started talking as if his brain was leaking. "Though we could aim to represent and fight like they do, would we be able to lead them? We have to prove the Society is on some elitist bull in saying poor people need leaders or they'll organize and tear everything down."

"You're trying to lead from the middle and it's not gonna work."

G nodded and said, "But that was basically our deal to protect The Big Man, right?"

"If that's the case, we've gone way above and beyond that. This ain't the life I want for myself."

"No one wants to be on the front line forever but some people don't have a choice." G passed E the bottle. "It's like this game has no rules."

E said, "The rules of the game are simple and the same for all people: assimilate and ignore the plight of the downtrodden."

G considered it for a brief moment and said, "I've been doing all kinds of research but making no new progress. The only way to get the information is to go into the Society."

E handed G the blunt. "Is that where you want to be? I ask because I think everyone else is where they want to be."

August came and the alert was particularly high. They got the word Lincoln was dead, and so were others connected to their posse. A suspicious prison fire. A couple of days later, one of the younger teenagers brought the flyer. Girard had basically turned the younger kids into his scouts, asking them to report anything coming from people they didn't know. The word had come through to gear up because it was a Black Love party.

They walked into the party and the scene was chaotic. Nearly a thousand people jammed into a loft in SoHo. Drinks flowed. All kind of flavors: Asians, blacks, Latinos, whites. They spread out to not be of a threatening nature. Their disguise broke when the DJ played the song they called the Flatbush anthem, *CD3's Get Tough!*

"Flatbush! Flatbush!"

As Girard made to walk over to the DJ, Ernest grabbed him by the arm and said, "Don't go over there! I know you don't want to believe me but that's just one more example of your eyelids opening up to a darker truth. It's just me and you. Our fathers and mothers are old. Our sisters are fighting on a different front. We're young black males. We fight for ourselves first."

"What about Manny?"

"That motherfucker's crazy! You saw that shit he pulled? You called it a coup! When's becoming president that way ever a good thing? I prefer the 'you' that fights for peace."

They blended away from the crowd. As they made to leave the loft, they bumped into me. They acted like they didn't recognize me and simply said, sorry. I followed them out into the hall.

"Hey, Ernest! Girard!"

The next morning, when I returned to the party, the security guard was not at the front door of the building. The lobby was empty. I hurried up the five flights of stairs. The hall was hot, steamy. One could sense the vapors. People were pressed against the walls, kissing and touching on each other. Inside the loft, incense burned. Powder had been tossed in the air and in front of powerful standing fans. The fragrances masked the smell of body heat, of people getting down to their core.

The song's lyrics...*feel the body heat, come on, go on, and get down*...blended into my dream and the reality that for days I had paced my house, a shell of myself, rummaging through my tapes and records, hoping the songs of the early eighties would keep me connected to them. *Bounce, Rock, Skate, Roll...*

They had found a way out but followed me back into a burning building.

Chapter 20

Girard and I stuck to the old script. He could not tell me anything that directly involved the Society. Still, I could sense the change in his eyes. I waited for him to tell me whether his college plans had changed. I had it in my mind to stay here in the city to attend one of the design-focused schools - Pratt Institute or Parsons. Girard's top choice was Harvard and he had committed. I was being pulled in all sorts of directions. My academics got me into most schools but basketball gave me a free ride to pretty much any school with a team.

The design schools would mean I would be in the city, close to the action and keep an eye on Manny now that we had found him. Hedging my bet, I had kept the three upstate schools on standby. Girard chimed in, "I didn't bother to apply to TGI or Semline 'cause I figured Manny would not be there by the time it was time for us to go to college."

"Well, he's not."

To hear Girard speak in a remorseful tone meant Hope had gotten to him. "We weren't supposed to be seen that day on TGI's campus. I misread the fire and thought it was a coup." I waited to hear his real concern but I filled in the blank. To make matters worse, we posed as members of the Society. G added, "We can't run away 'cause…" He paused. "We gotta fix it."

That last part worried me. I had no idea what we had to fix.

"Semline recruited you real hard, but the tuition and cost is too high for me. They don't accept outside scholarship money. Barrington does. After a year I should be able to get an academic scholarship to Semline and transfer."

"Why?"

"We have to be on the same campus."

"Barrington is actually the better school for me. Much better arts program than TGI, and Semline doesn't have an arts program."

Girard nodded. "Yeah but Semline has the better team and you need to be in the spotlight. The more visible you are, the safer you are."

I placed a phone call to Semline. The coach said it was late in the recruitment process but I could come up on Saturday for the open tryout being held for walk-ons. From there, he would decide whether to honor my scholarship offer. He used a disciplinary tone I didn't care for.

Girard said, "Once we drive up there, we can't come back to live here. We would be putting everyone in jeopardy." We spent our last few days saying farewell to pretty much everyone we'd ever run the streets with. Most understood we would cross paths again. They could come up to visit us but with the attention we were about to draw, we'd be like injured wildlife repopulated after being cared for by conservationists. We held a symbolic fear we'd be tagged for study or injected with something to contaminate the entire habitat.

We rode the subway to go pick up the rental car. The metal wheels squeaked along the subway tracks. The conductor's incoherent voice, muffled under an antiquated sound system, announced each stop. Other passengers confusedly studied us, as if trying to rectify our hard worn faces with our packed bags, seemingly heading off to college. The ones who didn't stare knew of us, not just that I starred in basketball. They knew we mobbed with a notorious Brooklyn posse, even though we had modified our looks, back to what it had been before linking with them. Gone were the parts in our eyebrows, the high top fades, the four-finger rings and gold ropes. Still we wore the faces of kids who had not smiled for months; for whom, laughter hid threats, and cadence and word play transmitted codes in plain sight.

Girard selected a black Ford Taurus because in his logic cops would take a pause before stopping this car model. I popped in a new house music mix tape. The tempo clearly bothered him. He drove fast but stayed longer in a lane than the last time we headed up the highway. It's not like he hated house music but he had a small case of hip hop cassettes he wanted to pop in. After my cassette had clicked over and finished Side B, G slid in the new album.

> *Even if it's jazz or the quiet storm*
> *I hook a beat up, convert it into hip-hop form.*

Eric B. and Rakim's *Paid in Full* album finished, and we still had close to two hours to drive. We played it again and again.

The Semline campus was steely, structures with steeples, the grounds circular, a labyrinth. The trees, lush, full of life but I could sense their true nature and envision their bareness during the cold wintry months, the dark, a sense of dread. The gym was smaller than I anticipated. For the most part it fitted with the college's population size of 2,500 students. Semline College attracted a limited group of students. The institution divided its academic offerings under two schools: Theology and Science. Their linkage was the sports program. The two schools shared recruiting duties. Some student athletes got in straight under the rigid science requirements with emphasis on SAT or ACT scores and core science and math grades throughout high school. The theology school with its sub-majors of philosophy, ethics and ancient civilizations funneled the students who were weak in math or science. I had a choice. In fact, the counselor encouraged me to select one of the sciences. I did not agree nor disagree. I needed to feel the vibe from the other players. If I was going to do four years here, attach my name to, and make money for the school, I needed to feel like this was the big leagues.

Girard held back a laugh as he could tell by my questions I was not buying the academic rigor the pudgy face counselor promoted as the reason to attend. G scoped the place and made a right turn and walked across the gym to sit up on the bleachers next to some girl. I went to the next set of registration tables and introduced myself. I received a jersey and pair of shorts and a locker assignment. Everything was formal, well-organized, a big league feel. I went to change. The empty locker room confirmed the other players had arrived early, a need to make a good impression. When I got back downstairs, Coach Overton had already split the twenty-three players into two groups – scholarship players and walk-on candidates. "We're going to run two games of 24 minutes, 12 minute halves. Current team and scholarship offerees on this bench. Walk-on candidates on that bench."

Coach further divided us – four teams of six – and partnered me with three returning frontcourt players. These three players were out-of-state starters who had been at the school for two to three years. The fourth was a walk-on from last year who had played his way into a scholarship offer. The last guy was an incoming Freshman Point Guard named Frank DeLoose. With a simple head nod, we acknowledged we knew each other. We were both New York City, public high school products out of Brooklyn. We had faced each other twice on the courts but ran in different circles and different neighborhoods, and played different positions on the court. So far, we could tell the mentality was the same – not much talk, b-boy code. One of the other players said, "We should run a high-low offense since they're likely not able to deal with our size. On defense, fall back into a 2-3 zone."

Frank and I agreed because on the surface what the other player had stated was logical but we knew he failed to realize what the other team lacked in size they would make up in speed. The question was whether they could shoot. We won the tip and scored on a simple dump down pass to the Center.

SPEED. Pure speed. Two hand claps. The ball had barely gone through the net and three of their players released. The one who had clapped was standing about seven feet to my left. He caught the ball and moved up court – two left-handed dribbles; bullet pass up court, into the lane for the Assist.

I glanced at Frank and he nodded. We stayed with the offense, letting the big men dominate on the inside. Their backcourt was the first guy who had scored – a six-foot one-inch pure jump shooter, a white kid with solid handles, mechanicals and court awareness, and a wiry, five-foot-nine speedster. The shooter scored most of their points whenever we were able to get back into the zone. Otherwise, their wiry Point Guard would run a speed game and find the open man. He rarely shot but showed good form on the one jump shot he took. I liked both their games and I could see them being our backups. Frank was in-sync with my thinking. We weren't necessarily throwing the game since we were not competing for spots on the team.

The real competition would be between the walk-ons.

The gym was abuzz, as if this had never happened before. But, the question everyone should have been asking was whether it really happened – that a group of walk-ons beat a team with four varsity players and two scholarship offerees. The game ended and we exchanged handshakes and names. When the Point Guard shook my hand, he held it firm, a little longer than I expected, and stared at me. As I started to say my name, he said, "I know your name. I'm Theodore Perkins. People call me Monk. Don't ever forget it!"

His voice had an old man's bass, to match his pronounced Adam's Apple. I couldn't quite figure why he'd said it that way. Still I gave it no more thought because he did the same with Frank DeLoose. I made my way to the water fountain and Girard came down from the bleachers. "What's up! Who's that kid?"

"I don't know. Why?"

"You didn't press him or try as hard as you could."

"It was a setup. Coach wants him and the white kid to make the team, and for good reason. He had the returning players instruct us to run schemes that played into their hands."

"Cool. I just wanted to make sure you didn't forget why we're up here."

"Relax, G! It's day one, and not even really that. This is a tryout, and not even for me."

"I got you. It's just that that girl, Bliss, I'm sitting next to says he's the best player on the court. She was saying it before the game and no one believed her but now...."

I chuckled and looked in her direction. Bliss was looking across the gym at Monk and Frank who were sitting together and analyzing the other game being played on the other side. By now there were a good one hundred or so people in the gym. Most had clipboards or notepads because they were here on some official capacity.

Game's end.

"Ok, let me get back to business."

"You can still show you're the best player while letting that dude get a spot on the team."

"I got you. Hopefully next game they'll put Monk on my team and we can put on a show."

His eyes reflexively shrunk. Girard grabbed my arm. "What did you call him?"

"Monk. He said that's his nickname. Real name is Theodore Perkins."

"WHAT! WHOA!" Girard staggered a bit. Turned around to look at Monk. "I gotta go introduce myself."

"Why? Who is he?"

"The reason you gotta go to school up here."

Girard had barely stepped on the court. "No fans on the court!" Girard took another step. "No fans on the court!" I kept thinking a team personnel was going to stop Girard from going toward Monk, who had taken steps to meet Girard in the middle of the court. They exchanged a few quick sentences and Girard turned to walk back towards me as Monk said, "No fans on the court!"

People who had heard were laughing. There were some players near the basket, shooting layups, jumpers or just talking. Girard said, "Yo! Ball!" One passed him the ball and all motioned in the gym stopped. Girard took two slow dribbles toward the basket, stopped about twenty feet out and shot the ball. *NET*

The player threw the ball back to him and he dribbled twice to his right but maintaining the twenty-feet distance. This time Girard elevated slightly and shot. *NET*

Girard did that three more times until he was pinned in the corner and shot one-handed, flat-footed, still from twenty feet out. *NET*...he then glanced, not at Monk, not at me, but at Bliss, who stood as if saluting or to get a better look, conveying she had missed something.

We walked toward each other. Girard had a sneer on his face. I had never seen him this angry. "He said he knew who I was and I should have done my homework."

"Well, did you?"

Girard avoided my question and simply said, "Monk thinks he's the best player out here. I put a question mark to that notion. The rest is up to you."

"What do you want me to do?"

"You figure it out. I'm driving out to Barrington to take care of my paperwork. I'll be back early evening."

Coach Overton proved to be no nonsense. After the first four games, he dismissed all but four of the walk-on players and put all positions up for grabs. We ran simultaneous two-on-two half courts, mixing various players but he never put me on the same team or up against Monk until the last game. Coach pointed at Monk and me, "Neither of you have lost a game. So you're on opposite sides. Frank DeLoose, with one loss, you are with Perkins. Terkel with LeGagneur."

Owen Terkel was the shooter I faced in the first full court game and later in a half court run. I respected his offensive game. It was not one I ever employed because on the court, I had no need to be cagey. We had similar defensive tactics where the approach was to give the opponent enough room to maneuver, study his tendencies and pounce.

In my mind, the starting backcourt would be Frank and me. I think Owen saw it that way. Not that I was expecting Monk or Owen to lay down. After all we're competitors and this was the game, in my mind, to show we could function as a unit, the team's four main guards because the two returning guards from last year had gotten outplayed. It was an odd pairing – technically, the two Point Guards against the two Shooting Guards. From a size perspective, I would match up against Frank. But I noticed Monk mainly defended me unless there was a rebound and a live play dictated he go up against Owen.

The game was straight Eleven on one half of the main court. Rebounds to Foul line or fifteen feet out to either side. I didn't like what I was seeing from Monk. A killer instinct that needed to be reined in. The game was pretty even, with each person able to exhibit his strengths but it was Monk's tenacity that electrified the crowd. Owen could not get a clean jumper off him and needed screens. I couldn't dribble pass Monk but my strength demanded he give me enough space to jab step and get a jumper off. On offense, his speed was too much for Owen – quick left dribble, right shoulder bump and pull up bank shot. Or, he would cross left-right-left, fake forward; watch Owen stumble back. If I closed in, he would hit an open Frank DeLoose.

The score was seven-up and I decided Monk could start in the backcourt with Frank, who could split duties at both Guard positions. I would go to Barrington, but first I would destroy Monk on the court. To do so, I had to expose the weakness I had seen in their games. I whispered to Owen what he had to do when he guarded Monk. I knew what I had to do when Frank guarded me.

Owen hedged more on Monk's left, forcing his first dribble to be with his right hand. I then angled my body so he could not pass to Frank and had to take a second dribble with his right. He now had to pick up the ball or dribble between his legs to the left hand or spin it back to his right hand.

Our right shoulders collided. I stole the ball as it came out behind his right knee. An exaggerated glance to my left at Owen froze Monk and caused him to fall back and guard Owen. With no delay I charged my dribble toward the basket, toward Frank - RIGHT-LEFT-RIGHT-LEFT-LEFT-LEFT...the last two inside-out dribbles crossed Frank to his ass, his right ankle slightly turning on itself. LAYUP.

8-7

Monk extended his hand to help Frank up and said something to him. Frank checked the ball to Owen so the pass to start the play would come to me. As soon as I made to put ball on the floor, Monk made an upward swipe at it and bumped me with his left shoulder. STRENGTH. I lowered my right shoulder into his and recovered the ball. He was up on me so I took two dribbles back and surveyed the floor and saw Frank was not going to let Owen get the ball. Monk was playing me straight up, waiting at the foul line. I could take a twenty-footer as if I didn't want to go against him or I could insert a cagey move into my repertoire. No, I told myself.

I took the twenty-footer. NET

9-7

Monk laughed and checked the ball to me.

We ended up winning 11-9 and the confusion of the coach, staff, other players and onlookers was clear. Coach said he would follow up during the week with each player about whether they made the team and their role.

The locker room was used for all varsity sports and had enough lockers so each sport had its own section and each player a personal locker. There were two set of showers on opposite ends of the room and two sitting areas before each. Ballplayers usually joke about the moves they put on people but I knew I had let Monk get into my head while Frank essentially kept his cool throughout. But, Monk was being an ass, "Yo Frank you let Ern-Money bust that ass. He made you a Maytag, son! You gonna be doing his laundry all next year."

Frank and Monk had forged a quick bond and joked with each other. I laughed but really stayed on the periphery. Monk cracked jokes on everybody, assuming a leadership role in the room, to the point where he said, "Owen, you know you ain't making the NBA so this is what I want you to do. Play here for two years then transfer to Harvard."

"I wish I could get Harvard grades." Owen quipped.

"Actually the Semline curriculum is stronger than Harvard's. Plus, I'm going to tutor you for the next two years."

"If you're so smart, why are you here trying out for an athletic scholarship?"

"I'm not. I got a full ride to Harvard but a change of plans forced me here. I also got offered a full scholarship to attend here." Suddenly there was a quiet in the room. The other players had left and only us four remained. "So, is it Harvard or what?"

"What's in it for you?"

"My name. Always remember it, especially when you become a U.S. Senator." At that, they shook hands.

Monk and I were the last ones to leave the locker room. He looked at me and said, "I respect what you did out there. Not sure I would have done the same."

"I'm curious. Why not?"

"Same reason your boy Girard shot those baskets."

When we got to the gym, Coach Overton called us over, stating some boosters wanted to speak with us. The players who participated in the last games were with a group of people. We joined them, shaking hands and answering basic questions. One by one, the boosters pulled us to the side for private chats, or an assistant coach would come by and introduce us to the boosters who had not join the fray. "Ernest, there's someone who would like to meet you."

The man had an air of importance to him, not 'cause of anything he said but how he and a select few were people the coach or members of the staff made a point to pull us toward for private introductions. "Ernest, this is Michael Henderson, a long-time supporter of the program and excellent evaluator of talent."

"Good to meet you Mr. Henderson..." I shook hands and Coach Overton simply faded away. I was a bit tongue-tied because I was familiar with reporters and street hustlers who preyed on athletes but this man with the navy blue sports jacket, thin dark mustache, well-maintained short coif, he represented something different.

As if sensing my discomfort, he said, "I'm curious as to why you chose Semline over all the other schools."

I needed to throw him off his comfort level so I could appear less nervous. "I haven't."

He looked over my shoulders to survey the room. "Perhaps we should talk outside." He turned without waiting for an answer. She stood and I saw her for real, for the first time. I had glanced at her while I played. She cheered, not exuberantly, my more difficult baskets and plays. I noticed her but not him. From afar Michael Henderson could blend into the crowd but up close, he smelled expensive, rich like cologne, leather, loafers underneath creased summer cotton, his right ringer occupied by gold, black onyx. My mind asked me to focus; for she was beautiful, radiant, with perky round lips under a red darker than any I had ever seen. I wanted to reach around him and pinch her. He looked at me and her. She smiled. "Oh, pardon my rudeness. This is my daughter, Diane Henderson." He opened the door, motioned for us to walk ahead of him. "She's the one who asked me to scout you."

All of a sudden, the Semline campus felt warm as if the green of the trees would stay year-round. A mixture of confusion kept me tongue-tied. "You're a scout or a booster?"

He opened the shotgun door for me. I got in as he walked in front of the car, the latest Mercedes sedan, the 560. He opened her door and his. "So, if not Semline, which school?"

"Barrington."

"What? The state school? That swamp?" I turned to look at her. She lowered her eyes in a sheepish manner but I could tell by what I'd just heard in her voice she stood firm when needed.

Michael Henderson laughed and said, "I tried to tell you. I tried to tell you for years." He shook his head. She folded her arms across her chest. "I'm going to be as straight as I am with everyone, especially her, so my words to you will only be the second straightest I'll ever shoot to you." He paused so I nodded. "Your NBA chances are slim to none as it is. Playing for Semline keeps you there, at that level. Barrington gives you no shot whatsoever."

"That's fine!" I expected her to jump in because I took her to be a gold digger but why would she need to be when this car, his smell, her look complete with hair highlights, Gucci bag and bangle earrings, indicated she didn't need me for money. "I'd love to make the NBA if that's my destiny but I'm more interested in pursuing my art, and Barrington gives me the best shot."

"No, it doesn't. There are top design schools in the city that give a better shot. Even up here, TGI has produced more famous, more top-selling…"

"I'm not doing it for either. I'm doing it for love." He shot me a confused yet conspiratorial look, as if asking whether that really came out of my mouth. I turned to look at her and she did not look impressed. I wanted to test whether whatever backing he planned to give me as a basketball player would transfer to my desire to be an artist. "Art is the first thing I chose to dedicate myself to. Everything else someone picked for me."

Michael Henderson turned to look at Diane but she kept extremely quiet. "Your freshman year of high school she came and told me you were going to be special. I didn't believe her but when your school won the city championships, I was curious. I reviewed all the game tapes, the numbers, the interviews and I really could not see it. I knew I was right because that team, after Slick graduated, never won the division with you leading. Your heart just isn't in it. But, she believes in you. So, spell it out. What is it you want? I cannot give you my daughter if you're just going to piss your life away."

"Give your daughter?"

"Oh no, it's not like that. It's her choice. Don't get me wrong, she's a high maintenance little brat but she's my first princess."

"Do I have a choice?"

"YES!" Her voice was strong as if insulted. I turned and smiled at her. Our eyes met and she stuck her tongue out at me.

"Let me tell you what I'm gonna do. Don't worry about basketball, art and all of that. Lift your legs out of the way." He pressed a button and a secret compartment pushed forward. "Grab that box." The wooden box was heavy. It had a clear fiberglass covering and I saw the gun. I did not look at him.

I could feel her edge up on her seat to look over my shoulder. "What is that?"

"Sit back. This is none of your business." He had raised his voice just a little, to push her back in her seat. He pressed the button to close the compartment. "I want to give you an opportunity to put all the skills you exhibited on the court to the best use possible. On the court you read the coach's intent right away and later on, he wanted you to destroy your opponent, you held back. You won but didn't…"

"Why do you say he wanted me to destroy Monk?"

"So he could rebuild him, in order to coach him. Right now, Monk is not coachable. That kind of kid will only listen to his dad. Sort of like her."

"Who do you think was the best player out there today?"

"Easy. Frank DeLoose." I looked away from the box with the gun in it. "He's the best because he stayed with the script and he plays strictly out of his love for the game. And, of course for the money it can bring."

I turned to look at Diane. She said, "None of that matters to me. I only want you for you."

I waited for them to ask me who was the best player out there but they didn't. "What's this box for?"

"That box is for people who make the best decision all the time. I am offering you the chance to become part of the secret police."

My voice went two octaves higher. "To protect the president?"

He laughed. "No that's the Secret Service." He leaned toward me. "The secret police protects information."

"And reports to you?"

"Oh no. Oh no." He put up his hands. You don't report to anyone. You're all alone. Don't get me wrong, you're part of a force, an army. The gun is for extreme cases, unlike the gun you already have." I shot him a hard glance. "I did my research, on not just your numbers, ON YOU. But I never guessed I would be making this offer."

"What's in it for me?"

He coughed. "Are you talking money?" I didn't answer. "Basketball is still the best way to get money to you. Everything else you earn on your effort, your talent. Listen. I'm a business man. I sell insurance, financial instruments. I invest in real estate, stocks and people. So I'm well connected in the business world, art world and wherever money moves. I've taught my daughter the same and you're the first person she's ever been so convinced has what it takes. Mind you, she was wrong about your basketball. But, she wasn't wrong about you."

"What if I don't want to?"

He sat back in his seat and simply said, "You would never forgive yourself."

I turned and asked her again. "Who was the best player out there today?"

"You were," she said without hesitation and took my extended left hand with her right. She felt cool to the touch, shaking a bit. I looked at Michael Henderson while holding her hand. "What are my duties?"

"Let go of her hand. After we finish our business, you can take her somewhere and do what you like, but don't touch my daughter in front of me." We let go of each other. "You don't have duties. You have a responsibility to protect yourself while living the freest life you can that does not impede on someone else. If you ever get in trouble with the cops or anything like that and you are alone, they will simply let you go with no problem. If you are with others or an accomplice in something, they will hold you until it's plausible to release you, even if that amount of time is years."

"How do I reach you in an absolute emergency?"

"If you see me, our conversations are regular ones. You don't reach me to talk about any of this. There's a card against the back of the box. Take it out." I opened the box for the first time. Except for the clear fiberglass cover, it was all wood. Against the back of vertical base, there was a slot with a business card: Mad Money Mike with a phone number followed by an extension. "Memorize the telephone number and code underneath. Once you commit to memory, rip it and discard it. Just like your gun, use the number only in emergencies. For other nonsense, use one of your other guns or have Diane call me."

"OK." I nodded, closed the box and stuffed it inside my small duffel bag, surrounding it with clothes so its bulge didn't show. I made to leave the car.

"Hey! Where are you going? You can't go back in there."

"I have to wait for my ride. He went to Barrington and won't be back for a couple of hours."

"OK, go walk around the campus, the town or something. I'll explain to Coach Overton you weren't a good fit." He stepped out and walked toward the gym.

I stepped out of the car and she did too. Diane stopped at the back. Her smile caused her to shift, bending one knee. "I guess I'll see you in Barrington next week."

"You're coming to Barrington?"

"Yes." She smiled again. I smiled. She looked into my eyes. I leaned down and closed my eyes. At first I thought there would be this rush, but our lips touched and we paused. The tip of our tongues met. We pulled tenderly, drawing our bodies closer, and we let go. She giggled and made her way toward the gym.

I walked to the front gate so Girard wouldn't have to come looking for me. I turned one last time to look at the car and its license plate: 3M.

The Society

established 1860

Strength Side	Pride Side
SBD (the brothers)	PMB (the MAX boys)
SUM (the sisters)	FLT (defunct sister organization)

Chapter 21

I was supposed to be the queen of the campus chapter.

As a fourth generation legacy of SUM and being from the oldest family for SUM on the campus, I earned the position two ways.

The vote came down during my absence over the summer. I hadn't attended any meetings. I was busy but the vote is a formality.

Unless I stuck to my decision to transfer schools, I was supposed to be queen.

No one knew I planned on not returning to TGI, except my parents and Attitude. Even if my decision was known, I would still be appointed queen. My name would be listed on the historical record. If I stuck to my decision and not return to school, then someone else would have been appointed.

A vote is not held unless I had done something morally reprehensible, where my face could not be the front for this sliver of Society life. In such a situation, to keep things running smoothly, the next person with standing, of a fourth generation family, would become queen.

So, they made Miranda queen.

I did not know the outcome until four days before returning to campus. It all made sense, why Girard had not bowed to me. My name meant nothing. After the fire, he had traced Manny's steps at TGI and researched the only last name he knew, Barbara's. Linking hers to The Conscious Daughters and my first name, he discovered my last name and saw it was not listed as a Queen.

Though the birth records had him as Girard Doppler, he was listed as his mother's legacy. She trained him, much the way my great-grandmother had schooled me about the Society. G's mother was a SUM woman. Except for birth records, her name appeared nowhere else in the historical record, likely redacted. All three families – Manny, Girard and Benny – had a hidden lineage, one that became linked in the summer of 1972.

The days after I returned home from the Black Love Party, I stayed to myself, mainly in my room or the basement, in my older brother's former bedroom. He had DJ equipment, lots of records and cassettes, including many of mine. My two brothers and I had spent many hours in the basement envisioning ourselves as rap pioneers. We listened to the records and fantasized ourselves in the stories being told. Leaving for my college freshman year, I did have dreams of one day cutting a record. Dreams I kept to myself because my family on my father's side believed in dreams only if they came from a direct line that was grounded in reality. My great-grandfather was lynched in the woods of Trafalgar. He was to have been deployed for World War I from the military training institute that became the college, TGI. My grandfather was a sailor and died in the attack on Pearl Harbor. Years later, my grandmother was a nurse who served overseas; she never returned. My father was drafted a year after I was born and served in Vietnam.

Neither of my brothers planned on joining the military but the eldest is studying criminal justice at John Jay College. The younger one is pre-med at Cheyney University. Me, I chose to follow in my great-grandmother's footsteps. She was new to Trafalgar when the white supremacists up there, in the town and region, murdered my great-grandfather. She stayed, raised my grandfather and expanded the Society. She poured so much of the ideals of the Society into me but was ambivalent about my opting to attend TGI. She felt it had become too much of a liberal arts institution. She thought I should become a great scientist so there was no way I could tell her or my father I wanted to be a rapper when I left for college. My plan was to take a major focused on words and just write and analyze literature, music and art for four years. I never expected TGI to be so cutthroat and radical. My great-grandmother never expected me to try to change the Society, back to how she'd left it when she was forced to step down as the national queen for SUM.

My mail had stacked up. The sealed envelopes were not the main concern. The digests and journals that highlighted, in coded fashion, Society life and our movements: they listed my name, only to say I had been initiated in the Fall of 1986. I retraced my steps since May. Everything I had done was within the auspices of the assigned mission. My father had gone cold on me, much more than the standard easing of the hold fathers used to shield their princesses. I came to expect the coldness and never bothered to ask how come when I asked to borrow his car to go to the bank, he pointed at the keys hanging on the hook where all the keys hung, instead of his usual answer that I should take my stepmother's car.

I made two turns into the strip mall's parking lot and headed to the bank.

She was standing left of the glass entrance doors, in front of the brick so those inside could not see her. She had a lit cigarette, polished nails and bangle earrings. She carried an air of certainty to her, letting on that six to eight years from now, when she's in her early thirties, she'll still be with the trends. Her body will not have lost the thick curves that would be less pronounced had she opted to order a size up in the bank's navy blue blazer, used to differentiate management trainees from regular tellers.

We'd made eye contact in the past but neither ever saw fit to say hello.

"Hello Hope." The rhythm was slow enough for me to gather my thoughts in case I had forgotten, four years ago, I gleamed her first name on her name tag her first week at the bank.

I matched her formality. "Hello Claudette."

She continued to lead. "You're here to check your safe deposit box?"

It was a question but it was not. So, I said, "Yes. How have you been?"

"Everything is fine. Can't wait for work to end and head down to One Hundred and Thirty Fifth Street to meet up with some friends." She pulled on the cigarette and blew out the smoke before it could reach her lungs.

"OK, have fun! See you soon!" It was the corner building, off the far end of the parking lot, to allow it enough space for a drive-through teller. Inside, there were two other tellers and no bulletproof barriers. The manager was on a first name basis with my parents. "Hi, Mrs. Hoffman. I think I left the key to my safe deposit box during my last visit."

"Yes. Someone from the staff found it. I didn't even know you had opened a box." She handed me a small pocket manila envelope. "Do you also need to access your account?"

"I will do that on my way out." I had never been through the doors leading to the stairs for the vault. The air conditioner and the plush carpet on the lower level denoted a different wealth class. She inserted her master key and I matched her movements and turned my key to open Box 135. I pulled out the closed metal box and she led me to a small room. Once she closed the door and left, I opened the box.

The bills were not crisp. Nor were they dirty. I counted eleven thousand dollars. There were two receipts on letterhead. Each thanked me for services rendered: art sales, and recruitment party. I earned Sixty-Three Hundred Dollars for the party. I didn't recognize the company's name but the address was the loft on Broadway.

Tears fought to come out but I held them back. Those would have been tears of joy.

My first thoughts were I would buy a car and live in the towers this school year. Until that moment, I was not one hundred percent committed to a return to TGI. I felt the campus would be a mess in the aftermath of the fire. They'd had the summer to recover, just as I had. But, now with the mission successfully completed, I had no reason to stay in the city.

I left the receipts and five thousand dollars in the box. Upstairs, I noticed the slight tilt of Claudette's head - to the left - when she saw me on line to see the tellers. She greeted customers as they entered the bank and helped those with privileged status. The next open teller was to my right so I casually let the lady behind me skip line. I waited for the next teller, one on the left. She brought up my account. My balance was thirty-seven hundred, enough to buy a reliable used car or pay for one year at the towers. I split the deposit in half for checking and savings. As I left the bank, I thanked Claudette and she said, "It's all Love."

I spent the last four days of summer break at home mapping out a plan.

They'd made Miranda Lopez the queen. I had not seen her in months. She left several messages over the summer months but I never called back because none of them sounded urgent. She simply asked that I call her back. When I finally read my mail, the historical record, the various digests, it was too late to call her back.

TGI and the neighboring colleges had strong influence on the state's political landscape. Many who governed during their school years went on to become politicians, lobbyists and other types of powerbrokers.

I drove up and before unloading my bags, I went to the Student Union Building to check my mailbox. Campus was bustling with activity as officers in various organizations checked their mailboxes and offices. This year I was slated to head the Women's General Assembly. I had been a member since freshman year and got seated in April as this year's president. In a few weeks, there would be a campus vote as to which organization's head would lead as the student council president.

I had to think of the most delicate way to handle myself when I saw Miranda. I cared about being queen but I loved Miranda. We were bonded as sisters. We met in Fall 1985, very early in our first semester at TGI and clicked instantly, a bond that solidified as we became Society initiates. Unlike me, whose family had been in the Society for four generations, Miranda was a first generation member. To vote her as queen, they relied on a loophole that allowed them to use the sponsor of her membership, a daughterless woman from a fourth generation family. But, even then, that placed Miranda's standing behind mine.

I had to be careful how I handled this because any rift between us had to get resolved amicably or else it will be marked on the historical record as a societal failing that two women who pledged together went to war against each other less than one year after their initiation.

When I saw Miranda, she started apologizing, reiterating she knew how much this meant to me. I told her I had a fallback position. I had enough leverage as the head of the Women's General Assembly to win the presidency of TGI's student's council. The fire and its aftermath, specifically the meeting with Trustee Trafalgar, had elevated my status with people I had rarely spoken to but who ran or belonged to prominent campus organizations. I came out of that meeting with concessions to be shared by all students and organizations.

The stage was set. All I had to do was run, until I heard the words, "Given, the chance I could love you."

Miranda simply laughed at him. It happened as we entered the gallery of TGI's Welcome Back Party. It was a cool September evening, the first Friday of the new school year. We had skipped the early part of the twelve-hour party. Our first two years we wouldn't have missed the outdoor afternoon session for the world. As much as we didn't want to go to the party, we had to make an appearance, even if only at the indoor portion. We met up with the SUM legacies from all three schools. We walked in four at a time. I was with the first group, a step behind Miranda, on her right. Though very few knew about the Society's customs, people would still talk of the bold guy who tried to grab Miranda Lopez as she walked with and ahead of three of her SUM sisters. She did not understand she could not laugh this off because she was used to men stopping her on the street. She now had to think of her standing and how her response would become the expected norm for all other women. We had debated this before, during our freshman year, when she argued lack of access to not just women but institutions of power led disenfranchised men to extreme acts to show their worth to women.

Beauty to her was an excuse used to oppress both women and men. To her, there was no beauty, only attraction. Miranda radiated with confidence and charm. I glared at him, with his self-congratulatory smile and daring gaze. I knocked his hand away. Had he grabbed her, it could mean his death. Miranda seemed flattered, turning her head to get another look at him. As the campus queen of SUM, Miranda needed to learn why we drew clear lines, and enforced and executed our power. Though she was not dating anyone on the campus, Ken was king of SBD. As such, he could make a power move, even if just to intimidate other men. Even though the Society was a secret organization, people knew where the power lied because of the proxy names, such as SBD and SUM.

People knew we believed in revenge and the never-ending fight.

Students posed by the walkway into the party. The guys at the door smiled and we walked in without paying.

The party was dead. The sound system blared but its noise echoed through a semi-empty room. Many were likely freshmen, some from the neighboring colleges, Barrington and Semline, who had yet to learn TGI on-campus parties were not worth the drive.

This would likely be the only on-campus party we SUM women attended this semester. We spoke to a few people and left in an hour.

I had a heavy load of classes and was focused on my run for student council president. We, SUM women, had nothing planned for the semester and things were going fine until I heard a rumor.

It was about two weeks after the Welcome Back Party. I was in the WGA office reading and answering phone calls when I overheard two people talking.

I telephoned and confronted Miranda.

She confirmed it. Yes, she was dating this freshman. Devon from Semline College. Yes, the boy from the party. She had tracked him down to explain protocol to him, and he bowed to the queen.

I too had to laugh.

"Do you want to ride out to Semline with me?"

"I'm working on my campaign. I need to make a major push because I don't have enough votes."

"Come on. I will come pick you up in ten minutes." When she could not get me to come just to ride along, she said, "I want you to come because I want to fix you up with Devon's roommate."

She sold me on his intelligence, his arrogance.

Had she told me his nickname, I would never have gone. She simply said his name was Theodore Perkins.

In the two years I'd known Miranda, she kept her business off the campus newswire. With this freshman, Devon, she had gotten sloppy. Miranda had a limited range of what type of men she found attractive. I only knew of three - all imports, no one from TGI or the other two schools. They were all model types with athletic builds, well-coiffed and well-dressed.

I figured Devon's roommate, this fix-up would be similar even though she never said so. Plus, that was not my type. She said there was no pressure and repeated he was highly intelligent like I preferred them. But, it would be up to me if all I wanted was a quick fling to take the stress off.

For barely one month of dormitory living, their suite was beyond lived in. They had video gaming systems, personal furniture to replace the standard dormitory furnishings, and empty bottles to show how much alcohol they'd consumed. Two guys played video games and two others sat on a sofa drinking beer. The typical freshman boys who thought independent living meant they had no responsibilities.

Miranda introduced them. Devon got up to hug her and me. He had a natural smoothness to his movements, the balanced way he took in my appearance, communicating his charm. The other three just waved. Theodore Perkins knew I was here for him, but he just sat there focused on his video game, heckling his opponent. His words overflowed in a staccato manner. The lack of effort in how he dressed and styled himself, though kempt, gave off a cavalier aura. I did not say anything to him, not even indirectly. I focused and participated in Miranda and Devon's conversation. The other two guys would throw a sentence here and there into our conversation but not him. I decided to disrupt them by putting forward my best treat me with the respect a junior deserves and you little boys should be blessed by my presence.

This type of playful banter and posturing was going on for about thirty minutes and Theodore didn't join until he asked without even turning around, away from the video game, "Hope, how come you're not the Sitting Queen? You're not even a Stand-In."

I looked at Miranda and her face tightened, indicating she was unaware he was somehow affiliated with the Society. I could not blame her because nothing about how he had spoken, gestured and carried himself indicated he was part of the Society. One of the Society's key protocols was to immediately and subtly identify yourself once aware of another Society person's presence. "What do you know about the SUM of our affairs?"

He ignored my cue that even talking in coded language, this was not a conversation to be had at this moment. "You don't seem like the type to not be able to rest on your morality. What exactly happened?"

At that point I was confused because he was talking around the margins yet had not identified himself as SBD. Before I could come up with a way to answer, Devon broke in. "Monk, leave Hope alone! That's why chicks don't dig you."

"Monk? What did he just call you?" My voice had raised on its own, pulling my body upward.

"What, now you're hard of hearing?"

I was on my feet, halfway wanting to kick him on the back of his head. "I didn't know there was a MAX pledge class on."

"Girl, recognize your elders and go sit over there if you want me to be your king!"

I was staring daggers into his back as my mind contemplated kicking the back of his head. "Who do you think you're talking to?"

He stood up fast and turned, and repeated what he had said. The anger in his voice took me back to the first time my father yelled at me. Anger was a function of my father's fate, a genius sentenced to a life of trivial pursuits, a mere paycheck to pay his family's way.

Standing there facing Monk, I quickly analyzed the situation. Miranda clearly had not put him up to anything. Why would she abdicate the crown and let me become Queen? Monk clearly got along with her or else she wouldn't have thought to introduce us. Perhaps he was as big on protocol and protecting legacies as I was? That was the space in which I could maneuver. I was set to ask Monk the question but she entered without knocking, like a whirlwind blowing away loose objects. With my back turned to the entrance, I mistook the inflection and the rhythm of her voice for that of a white girl.

Having spent my high school years in the suburbs, I learned early how to cut through all that black-girl-white-girl drama. I am a black girl, you're a white girl. That's it, end of story. Some people are real. Some people are fakes, and race wasn't necessarily a key determinant. The fakes, I knew how to spot them quickly. I turned to size her up.

"Oh, my god! Hope! What are you doing in this suite? How do you know these fellers?"

She spoke as if we had been introduced. I could have used her as my out by holding a genuine conversation with her, starting by asking her name. But, everything about her annoyed me, mostly the way her hair flipped as it neared her shoulder. In high school my clique used to write-off girls like her by simply joking, *"Don't mind her! She was raised by white people."* From there we were able to endure the nonsensical need some black girls had to diddy bop between two worlds, to be accepted. I never was one to simply shun people because of their race. In fact, there were some white students who were genuine and we had passing friendships. Though, through no fault of their own, their prejudices had been ingrained into their thinking, as not to allow them to see the benefits they got from teachers and school administrators. College was no different, and perhaps the prejudice even more blatant. It took me just one semester to realize when I walked into a class the professor started my grade at, let's say, a B; whereas a white classmate's grade started at an A. From that point, for us to be equals, it was up to me to work harder, or for that white student to prove she didn't deserve an A. So, this bouncy chick - introducing herself as Bliss and talking a mile a minute, talking of knowing me by simply having seen me, and on and on – irked me right away.

She made her way over to sit next to one of the guys. I could tell by Monk's reaction she also irked him. OK, so I knew I was right about Monk. He was young and needed some refinement, but I liked his aggressive approach. His eyes controlled his demeanor. They cut through the air, the space between people and drew you to him. Though Bliss had shifted the attention to herself, the next move was still mine. "Miranda, let's cut this visit short." I knew she would not want to leave because we had not been there long. My goal was to get her car keys. Whether I actually left her really depended on Monk's answer. "Monk, can you walk me to the car?"

"Why should I do what you say when you don't do what I say, and go sit over there?"

And, then there was Bliss.

She had this need to insert herself in matters that did not concern her. Bliss admired me. Since I didn't know her, I wasn't sure why. I learned instantly Bliss was a quick study, and realized this thing between Monk, me and her was an affair of the heart. "What, you let her sit in your special chair? This I gotta see. He doesn't let anyone sit in that recliner, not even me. It was his first personal gift to his grandfather, who in turn willed it to him."

It was too late. In fact it might have been the instant I had not sit when he first offered.

I will not know because this Bliss chick had cut into our dance and not allowed it to turn into romance. Sadly enough she thought she was helping, by feeding me information she likely did not earn on her own. She stared at me wide-eyed and with a tight, goofy smile, her head gesturing for me to go and sit there. "Miranda. Devon. You two walk me out. I don't have time for this game."

I hadn't really meant for them to walk me, but Monk was not easily moved. As I made to leave the room, he returned to playing the video game, instead of cutting in to offer to walk me to the car. Next, I heard Bliss say, "I'll walk with you. Come on Leroi, let's go walk Hope." Bliss got up and they both walked toward me. He gave Monk a hard look, and Bliss's words echoed Leroi's sentiment. "Monk, there's no hope for you."

Everyone laughed except for Monk and me. They didn't understand the ways of the Society: how a woman earns a Monk's love.

As I drove back to TGI, my thoughts ran wild. I wanted so much to hug Monk, to kiss him. Instead all I could do when I got to my apartment was telephone the first guy to bring those feelings out of me. I had promised myself to not call him unless he called but this was different.

Talking to Attitude would be hard because I could not mention any of what Ernest had told me and what I learned from Girard when I returned to the party. In calling him I had to lie to myself and say everything was fine, when they were barely tolerable. I still had strong feelings for him but now I had to call him about some other guy. There were other options but the quickest way to get this information I had to make this call. He picked up on the first ring and I dove right in. "Do you know there's a monk on the Semline campus?"

"Yes, Theodore Perkins. Monk for life! How do you know him?"

"Miranda is dating his suitemate. Are you behind this?"

He laughed. "Damn, sister, you give me way too much credit."

"Then, how do you know him?"

"I have never met nor talk to him. Only know him through a letter he sent stating he would like to know if the TGI chapter would welcome a MAX pledge class at Semline College under our charter." His voice sounded like he was playing with the telephone cord while lying in bed. I pictured him getting up, walking to the windows, the moonlight penetrating the room, landing on his cool bed sheets.

"Well, tonight he offered to reinstate me as Queen."

"Reinstate?" His voice lost its cool. "I don't think he means Queen on TGI's campus. He might mean in real life, like boyfriend-girlfriend, or maybe for you to transfer to Semline. What was the vibe like between the two of you?”

“Why? Are you jealous?”

“Nah! I would be honored if you ended up with a Max boy, especially a seventh generation.”

“What? One of his ancestors was a Founder?” I did a quick calculation. “I can’t deal with him.”

“Why not?”

“All that power but it can’t be switched to the Strength side until the next generation.” I switched the conversation. “If I need a date for coronation at TGI, would you be him?”

“Sure. Is there anything else?”

“Yes, I want to be queen by coronation. Make it happen!” I hung up without giving him a chance to answer.

History tells us that Max boys are dangerous
but until you deal with them on a one-on-one basis,
you really do not know how dangerous.

Chapter 22

Each campus held its own student government meetings throughout September. From October to the end of May, the three schools convened monthly meetings for all members of the student senates. The meetings took place on TGI's campus. Decades ago, the three schools formed an alliance in media and politics. Though each campus had its own apparatus, the three schools voted as one bloc when it came to the network of the state's colleges – private and public.

It took long debates to unanimously agree on the major issues. Prior to the bloc, we found ourselves strong-armed by the more conservative schools in the state. TGI tended to be the more radical, forward-thinking of the three schools, yet we found ourselves most likely to compromise. We had come to understand politics involved lots of people fighting for different things yet acquiescing to the group's strength in order to hold position or move in the same general direction. Politics was tug-of-war with your backs turned. Some say love is war. If true then can love be politics? What happens when love and politics are moving in the same direction?

This past May when I first saw Girard, he had imitated the brazen stance that conveyed SBD gunmen for hire. As the fire burned the building and students rallied around the bonfire, I rushed toward him and took Ernest away from the quad. His posture was less certain; through him, I could pass a message while Barbara talked with Girard. We walked to the cafeteria. It took just one sentence for me to realize Ernest was not SBD. I sensed he was investigating the Society. I had no idea why but I needed to use him to pass word Attitude was on the verge of being murdered.

We returned to the quad, more students had come out for the protest turned riot. The sun had not fully faded off the horizon. I figured Barbara had realized Girard was not SBD; she hadn't. Listening to the way he talked and carried himself, I picked up he was a SBD legacy. His words and eyes conveyed he had been well-schooled in the ways of the Strength side, much like I had before taking the oath.

Girard and Ernest were a team and they had spent considerable time investigating the Society's inner-workings, yet they had totally different aspirations.

Well, they had until they saw me at the Black Love party.

Something didn't sit right with Ernest. He fished openly for information about the Society.

Girard made it my call on what to tell Ernest. He walked away.

Ernest took me out of the party. He told me Manny's life story, how they grew up, the mystery surrounding Girard's father, Manny's father and his own.

Ernest made it my call, whether I would go home or go back to the party.

Girard no longer believed in love, for he had lost it at a young age. The first break with Cherise gave him his first palpitations, a totally different feeling from when his heart skipped from his first tongue kiss, from when he first put lips to it, hesitantly, unsure whether to simply lick up and down and around, or stick his tongue inside. He had nearly recovered but Marlene's beauty challenged him and made him keep secrets, made him an enforcer of her will, but then she made him swallow his hurt, taught him a paramour's arms is his main weapon. He carried those losses, along with the betrayal that made him refuse to claim his father's legacy.

I deduced he would enter the Society as a Max boy. To be SBD, male legacies enter the Society under their father's name and their mother must be a SUM woman. Girard would be a fourth generation SBD, a perfect union for me, as both of Girard's parents, like mine, were third-generation members.

His mother's name was mentioned only as a legacy member who had taken the oath, yet she knew enough to school him, to the point where his mind and body traveled the world like a veteran of many wars. In the historical record, his father's name disappeared for stretches but I followed the pattern of disappearances. With what Ernest told me, Girard's father had to be one of the two redacted names, one of the policemen in the Black Love underground killings.

Girard's refusal to claim the man must mean he had dug deep into his research. He knew what to look for, the words Black Love, something that should not exist.

He would not have known that. He needed to flush Manny out to get the story, how Manny's father must have relayed it. Girard did not know my last name when he said I put the hit out on Manny. Now that he did, now that he had enrolled up here at Barrington, Girard posed a threat to me unless I was willing to move in the direction he was heading.

I was amazed by how swiftly he moved. The talk coming out of Barrington, he had maneuvered to becoming Barrington's freshman class Senator.

Girard walked into the assembly hall with a group of Barrington students. The rotunda sat three hundred people in a circle broken into three equal arcs. Each arc had five rows. In the middle, the longest tenured school council president officiated the meeting. Above, in the balcony sat the reporters for the various school publications and student observers.

People running for committee chairs and other elected positions were allotted five minutes to address the body. I stuck to platitudes most organizations supported, not divulging my full platform.

Still I had no idea what the Max boys hoped to gain by helping me win TGI's presidential election and ousting Miranda as Queen.

After the meeting as people mingled, I slipped away from the crowd and headed toward my office. Girard followed me out the door. We didn't talk long. We were still sizing each other up. I had on kitten heels and he was not much taller than me. He had a slim yet rugged build as if he could easily put on weight. I was not sure if he had talked to Attitude but I didn't want to get into specifics.

I simply asked him for a name and he responded, "Trisha Hamilton."

The next day, during a conversation with a non-member, I mentioned her name in passing. Days passed and the name bounced around. I learned Trisha Hamilton was a sophomore on the Barrington campus. She was not a legacy and showed no aspirations of becoming a SUM woman.

That's all I knew and that's all I needed to know.

I waited impatiently as more days dragged. There had been no events that merited students to visit each other's school. I had no real reason to just show up on the Barrington campus. There were a few small parties or I could call Girard. I thought it best to wait to see him at the next Senate meeting. With TGI's elections six days away, the main newspaper, the one that linked the three schools, ran a pull-out section that handicapped all the races. Out of four candidates for president, I was dead last. There was a scathing column that tore my candidacy into shreds and wrote off my platform as being weak and outdated. It was written by none other than Theodore Perkins.

My first impulse was to call him and cuss him out. But I had to think like a Max boy. Monk's writing was beautiful, complex, forcing me to analyze what he was communicating and to whom.

Last month, after meeting Monk, I went to look at the historical record. Surely enough there was a Perkins listed in 1860 but no trace after that. Families fell out of the Society in the early days. This was before the Society implemented the Four Generation Rule that prohibited members from leaving unless they were not active for eighty years. Attitude said Theodore Perkins was a Monk for Life, a seventh generation legacy for the Perkins branch but I had never met any Perkins or their affiliates in the Society. I wondered what sacrifices his ancestors had made to hold up their part of the bargain for "120 years", what power they held by operating in the shadows while never asking for any financial benefits.

Now, with Monk being the Seventh Generation for the Perkins family and operating out in the open, I wondered how that power would manifest itself.

Sure enough, people started asking me about my platform, why I had such strong opposition from the Semline campus. The increased visibility brought forth by Monk's sideswipe had served its purpose.

With Max boys, you cannot worry about the layer, no matter how beautiful or ugly.

I was attacking on two fronts: campus politics and the Society.

The article appeared on a Wednesday. Afterward, for the next two days, I worked harder than ever to talk informally with students. Between the election, worrying about Trisha Hamilton and my studies, I needed to let off a little steam. I had barricaded myself to the point I hardly saw any of the SUM women. When I called Miranda, her answering machine picked up. I called Barbara and she was nowhere near recovered from her brother's death. I could still feel the vibration of her sobs and how the words had gurgled in her mouth when I arrived at her house this past August. "They killed my brother. They…"

I had heard it was a fire so I interrupted her. "They. Who's they?"

"Don't act like you don't fucking know! You think you can just storm the palace gates and face no retribution?"

She must have been studying hard. Our coded language had rolled off her tongue with no hesitancy. She'd only been a member eight months. It took the majority of new members roughly two years to become fluent. Legacies started learning the language at four years old, so I'm fluent to the point most members could barely differentiate between code and my regular communication. I could not entertain what she implied, that someone, many in the Society had done her brother harm. "No, no. Your brother's death has nothing to do with this."

She cried and cried. I stayed with her, comforted her until her mother unlocked herself from her bedroom. They held a vigil around the dining room table, trading stories of Lincoln's short life. I stayed with her for days. I had to leave but could not leave her like this. I asked her to come with me to the Black Love party and her face turned. "No, I'm going after them. They killed my brother."

Since coming back to school, she buried herself in her books and kept to herself unless our paths happened to cross, to share a meal, to allow me to squeeze her hands, her shoulders.

Unlike a TGI party, a Barrington party was packed. The place had lots of folks but it lacked a definitive pulse. The dee-jay struggled with what type of party he wanted it to be. The music mixed too fast within a genre and quickly skipped out to the next style; the pace uneven and the dancers doing extravagant moves to humor themselves. After about an hour, I decided to drive back to TGI.

I turned left toward the door and felt a hard stare. Girard stood about forty feet to my right, by the window. A girl leaned her back against him. The stare was hers. Using the light coming from the party's entrance, I figured out her identity. Neither of us made to walk toward the other or greet from afar. Nicole had attended TGI for two years then transferred to Barrington over the summer. There were various rumors as to why she transferred. I preferred to believe she was more into drama than her books. Our freshman year we had a class together and talked a few times but she was hostile about everyone and everything. Guys flocked to her and so did women. I eventually stayed clear of her because she was always into something. Now she was looking at me like she knew something about me. Girard's eyes were aimed past me, so I turned to my left.

Monk was leaning against the wall. I was the midpoint of the straight line to their eyes. Monk shifted his glance to me. In the semi-dark, I could not make out whether his was an inviting look. He was alone so the path was clear for me to approach him. All I had to do was go to Monk. I really was not sure what to make of the night in his dorm and the article in the paper. I wished he would come to me, at least halfway, but he didn't budge. He was wearing all black and had his hands in his pockets. Nothing moved him, not even the music. You had to know him to even guess what he was thinking. And, I did not know him. I turned away from the exit and searched the room for a friendly face.

Behind me was this group of black students from TGI who I was surprised to see partying with black folks, especially at Barrington. One waved so I waved back. He was TGI's sophomore class senator. I had seen Ted around but did not know him like that, to be waving from halfway across a space as large as a ballroom.

I turned back around and as I made my way out of the party, someone tugged my arm. "Ernest! How're you doing? I haven't seen you at all. What made you attend school here?"

He hugged me. "Long story, baby."

Though no real energy exchanged, I felt his presence complicated the situation with Monk and Girard. "You've got to tell it some time. See you around. Don't be a stranger!"

"Hey don't leave. Dance with me!" As soon as he said it, the party exploded from a mix into:

> Yes, the rhythm, the rebel
> Without a pause, I'm lowering my level

Girard and Monk were looking at me and Ernest. I really wanted to leave the party but there was this entourage behind him, a good fifteen feet away, sprinkled around the room like stars in a constellation. There were mainly girls and I recognized a few who attended TGI. I could tell they wanted to walk up to where we stood. The TGI girls knew who was who and by them walking away, the girls from the other schools realized I was not be trifled with.

The DJ got serious with it for a solid hour. I turned to see the place had lost half its population but clearly not due to boredom. People who'd wanted to approach one another had found the tempo and steps to do so. "Thanks for the dance, Ernest."

He bent his shoulders to whisper in my ear. "Don't go! At least not home alone." My slight chuckle caused him to say, "OK. I get it. I only got that one chance at bat."

"It's not that. You have way too much star power. I am not trying to fight off all your groupies."

"Can I call you some time?"

"Yes, but think about the times when I would want to call you. Will you be there?"

Ernest smiled. I reached on my tiptoes and kissed him on his cheek.

I left the party and did not see whether the other two had left. As I drove back to TGI, I had those three young boys on my mind. Ernest. Girard. Monk.

Max boys are dangerous.
They hide in the shadows.
You never really know their politics until you ask their help.

Chapter 23

The power had shifted drastically. My rough calculations showed I was set to get fifty-seven percent of TGI's senate vote. This meant I had the support of seventy percent of the student population. Monk's article had done its job. I continued to work around the clock. When I was not in class, I would grab some food and head to the office.

The Student Union Building administrative staff went home by five o'clock. They handled student life, everything from housing, campus-wide room reservations and interfacing with student organizations and student government. Once they left, the cafeterias on the second floor were the only open facilities and they closed at 10pm. The building's third floor consisted of meeting rooms with access until 10pm. After 10 p.m., the facilities and security team checked the building and only student leaders with key access were allowed, but only on the building's fourth floor.

I heard steps shortly after 11 p.m. but thought nothing of it until they stopped near my door. The knock was soft and I was a bit apprehensive because there had been two recent vandalism incidents in the building. "Yes. Come in."

He turned the knob and took only two steps across the threshold. "Hey. What's up! I went by your apartment."

"Girard, how've you been?" I thought to ask how he knew where I lived, how he got access into this building. "Come in. Come in." I stepped from behind my desk and went to him. He waited for my hug. His body felt tense. I leaned against him even after we let go of each other. His smell void of cologne but fresh, possibly a pomade used on his medium high fade. We let the low sounds of our breaths and rapid beats of our hearts do the talking.

He never came out and said it but I knew something had been done. The key was to not panic and enjoy his company, even though his detached steely mannerism made me nervous. I wanted him to kiss me because he believed in women. He was not a scavenger or a catch and release fisherman. I backed away, turned slowly, hinting for him to follow me. I walked between the office's two desks. The room was no more than ten by thirteen, filled with two desks, two swivel chairs, an old couch and three filing cabinets containing most of the Women's General Assembly's history. The walls had individual prints of great women in history, and bulletin boards with schedules, flyers and miscellaneous papers. I went to the window. It faced east, a bit to the north; a large tinted, wall-to-wall pane with two dividers that allowed the windows to open vertically but not enough space for a body to slip through.

I stared over the campus, and he wrapped his arm around my waist. He had a surprisingly tender touch. He did not rush. He held me and I leaned back. The center of my head rested against his chin. I felt him harden against me as his arms inched their way upward, folding across my breasts. First, I had to be clear on something. "You know I know your girlfriend, right?"

"Are you scared of her?" He kissed the back of my head and the exposed skin of my shoulders.

"Do I have reason to be?"

"Do you plan to keep me?" I turned to look into his eyes. I really did not know. I liked how he came for me and offered no deception he believed in obtaining power.

My eyes closed, my kiss was the answer. He unbuttoned my blouse. I unbuckled his belt and unbuttoned the waist of his jeans. He passed his right hand to the back and unhooked my bra with just one motion. We kissed slowly. My arms around his neck and he pulled my waist, tugging me closer. Caught up in the moment, I had not heard the footsteps. "Just one minute." I answered the knock because the door was not locked. We fixed our clothes and I went the door and peeped through a slight crack.

"Hi Hope. I am just dropping off the platform the multicultural bloc put together. Sign off on it, the election is pretty much yours and we'll go from there." After he handed me the document, he said, "What's up, Girard."

Girard was not standing in a position to be seen from the door. He did not turn around yet he said, "What's up, Ted."

"Sister, you should watch out before you catch a cold," Ted said as he walked away.

I locked the door and read the first page of the paper, the outline of the platform. I placed it face down on my desk, not sure whether to share this with Girard. He was seated on the heating vent beneath the window. I looked at the woods and the break in between where headlights coursed through the town. "How do you two know each other?"

"We met at the last senate meeting. You know he's seventh generation Max, right?"

"No. I didn't." That bastard, I thought. I didn't know who to be mad at. Attitude. Girard. Monk. Or Ted. "Are you fucking Max boys trying to run game on me?"

"Of course not."

"Then how come nobody told me Ted was a Max boy. He's been in this school since last year."

"Well, Max boys don't announce our presence. We run covert operations."

"Was he behind the fire at the quad?"

"I don't know. Why would he be?"

"Look, I gotta go." I grabbed the paper off my desk, and my bag and jacket.

"What? What about us? What we've started?"

"Look at this! This is the platform they want me to run on."

Girard looked at the document's overview. His demeanor changed to match mine. "What the…"

As he grabbed his jacket from the sofa, I noticed the extra weight. I reached for it to confirm what it was. "What's that for?"

"How some things get done?"

"What? You're going to go shoot a Max boy?"

"Not Ted! We've got your back. Us, Max boys. We're not the ones you should be worried about." Girard stormed out of the office.

My first thought was to run after him. Instead I browsed the student government directory to look for an address. Timothy Ely Duval – Ted.

I heard the door slam against the wall. Girard used the stairs.

I did not need to rush. I stepped out and locked my office door. These halls often gave me the jitters. They surrounded the elevator bank and had no sight lines or reflection point of what could be around the corner. I waited for the elevator. I processed the various angles as I made my way across campus. It had been hours since I was outside. The temperature had dropped to the forties. The night was clear and the quad was quiet, save for music and voices from dormitory windows. It didn't make sense that Ted lived in the regular dorms. He could have gotten a waiver and paid for an apartment in one of the towers or live off-campus. He was the other side of the Max legacy – beyond rich. I had seen him all of last year, in meetings, passing across the grounds. He was a boisterous freshman, with a crowd always around him; that got him elected sophomore class president. Even after hearing his last name at the student government meetings, I didn't make a connection because the family name is not unique to the Society and Ted never introduced himself.

I used my student ID to access the building lobby and walked up to the second floor.

I remained poised as I knocked on his door. Ted didn't open the door wide so I adopted a formal tone. I had to get inside and find out what this guy knew, and whether he was pulling these strings. "Hi. Though I have only browsed the document, I can tell you I cannot run on this platform."

"Now I know you did not come here to discuss politics, not at this hour."

I quickly caught on to what he was implying. Max boys only dealt in money and sex, the only forms of currency they accepted. "OK, if it were a booty call, would you open the door?"

"I would be flattered but I am celibate." He stared at me dead in the eye. I guess my eyes told him my displeasure of having been duped into asking him for sex. "Seriously, which part of the platform are you against?"

"Are you going to let me in or not?"

He hesitated as he made space for me to walk in. "This has to be quick. I am really not in the mood for your games."

"My games? How come no one knows you're Max? Why did you sneak this agenda as part of my platform for student council president?"

"Slow down. Slow down. Those who care know I'm Max." He waited for me to ask but I did not take the bait. "I did not sneak any agenda into your platform. In Max, we firmly believe politics is personal. If you do it in your private life, then that is the platform you should run."

"What? This voting bloc has alliances I have never made." He shot me this look of incredulity. I continued, "First of all, I am not a lesbian. Second, though I believe this country needs to abandon racial classifications, we are not there yet. Third, we do not need all these variations on black and white, mixed, etc. Fourth, I am not adverse to women-only schools and clubs, and the same should hold for men."

He interrupted me. "Where are you from the nineteenth century?"

"No I am from the explosion." My answer was reflexive.

He interrupted, "Yes. When God said let there be a light, out of that darkness came a light, a beacon to show the way, of the original path to our creator. From whence we move forward, it is really backward, when there was no division." He stopped as if no longer enjoying the sight, of my mouth hanging open. "Should I go on?"

"How do you know the Strength creed?"

"Sister, don't let the near-white skin fool you. I am blacker than you could ever wish to be." He put an arm on my shoulder. "This is a strong platform, and you will become TGI school president, the first woman and the first black."

"No I am not running on this platform. Being Queen will be enough for me."

"You're not Queen. Miranda is." I didn't say a word. Max boys often fight on different fronts. The look in my eyes and my nose must have expressed what my mouth held back. Ted backed away and grabbed his phone. He dialed and waited. "Miranda! This is Ted. What's up! What happened?"

Ted did not speak for the remainder of the call, only hummed to imply acceptance or shock. After he hung up, his relaxed expression changed. His blood rushed and veins pulsed, the translucency of his skin unable to hide his anger.

"Is everything OK with Miranda?" I had a feeling Girard's visit to my office meant something had happened but I hadn't gotten the facts.

Ted's room was about the size of my office. It had furniture for only one occupant. Ted stepped to the door and opened it to look down the hall. He closed it and turned the lock. He went to his desk and took out a gun from the drawer.

He cocked it but did not point it at me. My body tensed and I stood my ground, recalling my pledge program, my training, of no panic in the face of danger. He spoke slowly. "I have to make one phone call, and you have to tell me who to call. Think real clear, and think positive." Then he shouted. "Now give me a name!"

"Manny Davenport." It fell out my mouth. That was not the name he wanted because Max boys never turn on each other. I also could have gone with Girard or Monk. Any of these names ensured I did not remain in his crosshairs. My gut was telling me I had made one, if not, several bad moves.

"Don't say a word!" He made the call and put the phone between our two faces. It touched his left ear and my right. "Fly Max!"

"Max Beta!" I recognized Attitude's voice, in its half-sleep state, resting after a day of walking Manhattan.

"Do you really trust this woman with your life?"

"Yes, is there any reason I shouldn't?"

"That is something you have to ask her." Attitude didn't say anything else. Ted waited about ten seconds. He expected me to speak and Attitude kept waiting for a woman's voice. Ted hung up the phone. He stared at me, studying me but allowing me to look at him, the physique he hid under loose-fitting, preppy clothes, texturized hair and a fake falsetto. The gun was in his right so my eyes focused on his left bicep being choked by the white undershirt. I measured him. Without shoes, he was a solid six-foot three. The loose sweatpants masked his lower body's bulk. Still, I guessed him to be about two-twenty. His greenish-gray eyes did not twitch or look me over as he had obviously studied me for over a year. I needed to keep my cool. "What's up! You still want to have sex with me?"

"Can I leave now?"

"It's up to you."

He did not move to make a clear path to the door. As I squeezed by him, I inhaled and all I took in was the scent of soap.

I did not race down the stairs because his room faced the front of the building. If he looked out, I needed him to know I was not fazed. I had to call Attitude but I realized I couldn't go home. I had to go to Miranda's. She knew Ted was a Max boy and never told me.

Thoughts were overtaking me. I felt a pressure building up inside of me. As soon as I turned away from where Ted could see me, I ran. I accessed the building and walked to Miranda's room. I knocked hard. The sound must have panicked her out of her sleep. "What's up? Sis, you're OK?"

I knew better than to ask the same of her. Her pajamas and the depth of sleep she must have been in meant nothing had happened, not even Ted's phone call. I wondered if she was faking like everything was cool. I never asked her if Ted had called her, or if she knew he was a Max boy.

Perhaps I should have because the next day she went to Semline College to visit Devon.

Max boys are messy in their dealings.
They claim to operate in the shadows,
yet their every move is visible,
forcing everyone to wonder their true agenda.

Chapter 24

The word spread like wildfire.

It reached the library as I pored over chapters for my first mid-term. The library was not packed. What few students wafted in, all took a quick glance at me and instinctively went a half-step off stride. The study room to the right of the main entrance was for serious students, ones who did not need quietness to not be distracted. The room had many advantages, from computers, proximity to the snack machines, the pay phones and the reference desks. For these types of students to come in and notice me, not say hello meant something was being said.

A Saturday evening, the dinner crowd filing in, I spotted someone who would know and talk.

She said it was only a rumor.

I dashed back into the room and packed my books into my bag.

Barbara must have also heard. I spotted her, on my right, running toward Miranda's dorm. Her height and being unhampered by a bag of books gave her movements a fluidity mine lacked. The eyes of passersby, as I rushed through them, told me how unbalanced I looked. I slowed so I could match Barbara's strides. As I did so, I noticed the distance had obscured my vision. Her brow filled with pellets of sweat and her breath pushing out air like a locomotive, not slowing for a dangerous curve. She asked, "You heard too?"

We carried the same concerned pissed off look on our faces. We entered the building. "Open the door! I know you're in there. Miranda, open the door!"

The urgency of our knocks and loud voices caused the girl next door to fling open her door. Our cold stare saved us the need for words. She quickly closed the door. After a few more knocks, Miranda opened the door. She left only enough room to show half her body. I asked, "Are you OK?"

"Look! I don't want to talk to anyone right now."

"Well, you need to come up with something better than that because you're the top story on the campus newswire."

Barbara cut to the heart of the matter in such a slick way that Miranda had to go on the defensive. "Were you really in bed with Devon and some other girl?"

I had not heard that.

"No, I went to visit him and we were in his room. The girl was in the other room." Miranda moved from the door so we could enter. She had paid the extra fee to have a single occupancy room but had not chosen a queen size bed. One half of the room had the standard dormitory desk and a twin-sized bed raised, as if on stilts, so crates, boxes and a small fridge could fit underneath. The other side had a sewing machine, a chair and fabrics. Both closets overflowed with clothes, packaged food and assorted items.

"Oh! So you were OK with him going back and forth between the two of you?" Barbara seemed to have heard a more complete version of the story.

"No. He would leave the room, always with some good excuse. At one point, I heard noise in the room next door. When he came back, I asked him about it. He said it was Monk."

Barbara sat on Miranda's bed. "They were both having sex with the girl?"

"No, Monk was not there. He's his suitemate. He returned early from a trip and found the naked girl in his bed. She screamed and the commotion woke me and Devon up."

Barbara interrupted. "That story's not going to wash. We have to figure out a way to take you out of the whole scene, to say you were never there."

"How? Why? This is just gossip gone out of hand. The facts will sort themselves out."

"By then, the brothers are bound to hear about this."

It was then I realized I was missing a key part of the story. I asked, "Why would this impact the brothers?"

It was then Miranda realized Barbara knew something she shouldn't have known. "Sister, I'm sorry."

"There's no need to say sorry to me. Men are men. They're going to do what they can get away with. Our goal is to make sure we contain this story and you remain Queen."

I said, "Wait, I'm missing something here."

Barbara looked at my face. Miranda's face was flushed with embarrassment. Hard knocks on the door. Ken entering without waiting for an answer gave me another piece of the puzzle. The room seemed to collapse around him and he froze. He tried to retrace his steps by saying hello to us. He made to hug Barbara. She slithered out of his embrace, as he placed a kiss on her left cheek. She said, "I guess we'll leave so the King and Queen can work out whatever needs to be discussed."

"There's nothing private to talk about. I just stopped by..." Ken was in the middle of the three of us. All he needed to do was take one step back, to not be an arc in our completed a circle. I could have given him a hint to help him but this situation was working out to my advantage.

"She knows," said Miranda.

"So, it's true about you in a threesome over at Semline?" He asked it but none of us were buying he didn't know what Miranda meant.

"No!" Miranda over-emphasized the word. "She knows about you and me."

"About what? Me and you?" He put up his hands. "Don't try to change the story. You weren't at Semline last night?"

"No."

"You have not been sleeping with this freshman named Devon?"

"No."

All Ken had to do was step back. Instead, he volunteered, "I was at Semline last night, in the parking lot outside his dorm and saw you leaving around one in the morning."

This was the perfect place for Barbara to jump in. I thought she would since she convinced Miranda to lie about ever being there. Instead her words were, "Hope, are you still going to help me with that?"

"Sure!" I was leaving with Barbara because she knew Ken was in that parking lot and I needed to know how. She obviously had all the angles worked out. "Miranda, I will call you later."

"Barb, I will see you in a few. I have to discuss some court business with Miranda," said Ken.

She smiled. "Sure, baby! I will be up waiting." With Ken's back turned, as we exited, Barbara mouthed to Miranda, "You were visiting Bliss."

We walked down the hall and Barbara placed her left index finger over her lips and said, "The walls have ears." We left out the main door and turned left, toward the Student Union Building. She curtsied in exaggerated manner and said, "I bow to you, my Queen."

"Did Attitude put you up to this?"

"Attitude? You give that boy way too much credit. This is SBD family politics. He doesn't know how we SUM women roll."

"You mentioned Bliss. How do you know her?"

"I don't. I did my homework and learned she lives in that dorm and hangs out with Devon's crew."

"She's dating Frank DeLoose."

"Is he cute?"

"He's Semline's star basketball player."

"Hope, who cares about the details! You wanted to be Queen, and it's going to happen."

"You claim to be behind this operation. Give me a name!"

"Listen to you! You're looking for this big conspiracy. There is none." We did not enter the building. Instead we looped to its western side to walk behind the administration building. Barbara had also come to college with music goals. Through our friendship we soon realized how contrived our dreams were. Like Miranda, short hair accentuated her beauty, to the point where Barbara continued to cut her hair close to the scalp, continued an exercise regimen that caused the curves and bumps of her body to stun people. Men froze. Women rolled their eyes away and down to her toes and worked their way back up. "There are rumors Ken and Miranda have been doing their thing behind my back for months."

"I've never heard those rumors."

"But Miranda has heard them and it restricted how she could live her private life. She saw this as the opportunity to dethrone the king."

"At a major loss to herself? Why?"

Barbara's voice remained normal. "Her name was already out there, so she might as well make it seem like the incident with Devon was a power play."

"Do you know what type of harm you've put Devon in?"

"The jerk is screwing everything that moves. He deserves it."

"What's in it for you? Do you want to be queen?"

"No, I want to be president of the student council."

I had lost my ability to hide my emotions. "How come you never ran for an office?"

"You get a voting bloc I can never get and I delivered one you could never get on your own."

"The multicultural platform? So, I'm your puppet?"

"No, you are my sister."

I stepped away from her, the way Ken should have. "So is Miranda!"

"The roommate was not supposed to show up. Ken was supposed to tire of waiting and go upstairs and confront them."

"Do you know Monk?"

"No. That's Devon's roommate, right?"

"Yes, but there's more to him than that. He's seventh generation Max. You just used his name."

The shocked look on her face lasted less than five seconds. "If anything, I will give him some pussy, and it will all be straight."

"No, stupid! You just told Miranda to use Bliss as an alibi."

"Yes, and?"

"Miranda's not going to do it. She's going to tell Ken the truth of what happened at Semline, and everything you said when we came to the room."

"She's not. It doesn't benefit her. Plus she senses, to protect his own name from the rumors alone, Ken will get the family to vote her out as Queen, under The Morality Clause. Once that's done, by Tuesday, you will have both positions."

"Earlier today, I dropped out of the race for president because of the multicultural platform. They'll announce my decision on Monday."

"What? Why?" Her voice finally moved.

"I thought the Max boys were behind the multicultural platform."

"You give them fools too much credit."

"But, what about Trisha Hamilton?"

"Isn't that the girl who was in the other room?"

"Yes, but how did she get there?"

"Ask Bliss!" She laughed.

"Are you serious?"

Barbara's voice went back to normal. "No, I'm not. I don't know Bliss. You're looking at this as this great big conspiracy. It wasn't. It was about love. With Ken and Miranda as campus king and queen, even if it is only duty to title and offices, they were seen as a couple." She took hold of my shoulders. "I listened to what was going on. Ken and some of the SBD brothers warned Miranda about Devon when they first heard of his interest. She thought she could keep the affair low-key but I knew eventually Devon would slip up. His name is all over the place. All I had to do was leak the word so Ken would hear. All the other stuff just happened."

"And, that's not a conspiracy?"

"No, it's about knowing the timing of men, the ones who think they can operate with impunity. Can you believe this Devon character had the nerve to pull off some mess like that? Having sex with two women in adjacent rooms?"

"What about Miranda?"

"I have no problem with Miranda. If this doesn't teach her about men, I don't know what will."

"You told Ken to come by later."

"No, he said he'll come by later. I don't need him. He needs me."

"Got it!" I had forgotten this side of Barbara. I still had no foundation as to why she thought like this, that every confrontation had to come to extremes.

We reached my apartment building. The campus had two towers built in 1975. Though much shorter and narrower, the buildings were on par with a modern Manhattan high-rise, complete with concierge services, fitness room and security in the lobby. I opted for a furnished one bedroom apartment. Other residents included a few of the younger and visiting faculty members, funded graduate students and wealthy upperclassmen. I turned and said, "Sorry I dropped out of the presidential race."

"It's OK. I will wait and see who the winner is and proceed from there."

We parted ways and I entered the building lobby, the bright lights, clean linoleum, black and white diamond tiles patterns done in such a way to avoid a checkerboard style when standing at any angle. I gave a quick hello to the security guard. He understood my rhythm and could tell this was one of those days I couldn't stay and chat. I needed to get upstairs in a hurry. I pressed the button and the elevator doors opened.

I needed an answer to the question: Could it be that simple? I thought of eating and composing myself before making the call. Instead I put down my bag and sat on the sofa to dial his number. I came at him in a straight line, leaving no wiggle room. "Attitude, it didn't have to be that messy."

"What?"

"The stuff you and the Max boys pulled to oust Miranda."

"What are you talking about? I'm mad cool with Miranda. Why would I want her ousted?"

"We discussed this."

"You never gave me a chance to answer."

"But the Max boys ran some sort of operation…?"

"What Max boys? The Outsiders don't deal with other people's politics."

"No, Ted, Girard and Monk."

"None of them are Max boys. Ted and Monk are legacies but they have not taken the oath. Girard's family is SBD."

"He plans to switch sides." I listened to the white noise of his silence.

"Even if that's the case, the three of them have no allegiance to the queen unless they choose to, when they get initiated."

"Then how come Ted can call you on the phone…"

His voice hinted of worry. "Ted? Did you give him my name?"

"You didn't know it was me?"

"No! I never gave you protection."

"Who did you think it was?"

"Barbara!"

"So, it's like that?"

"Yes, as it should be! You don't need my protection. You're fourth generation on both parents' sides. Why would you need me?"

"I don't." I slammed the phone, only to call him back and say, "By the way, I have a date for the coronation."

"Are you taking away my invitation?"

"You can still come but I could never have you stand by my side." I was hurt but I should have never said those words.

Things unfolded quickly. Miranda could barely walk the campus without someone snickering behind her back. She was asked to resign as queen for violating The Morality Clause. I was appointed queen. To everyone's surprise, I selected Miranda to be my Stand-In Queen. She wanted no parts of it. She even said she would not come to the coronation.

Weeks of quiet and simple friendship showed her I was not trying to show her up. I felt bad for my role, if any, that led to her reputation being sullied. She had no reason to think I was involved. The way the story got recorded in the historical record, my name never came up.

Trisha Hamilton withdrew from school.

Girard and Ted stopped speaking to me. For Girard, there was an excuse: I had not seen him. Ted actually walked by me two, three times a day, and never even looked my way. My running for student council president had a grander meaning for the Max boys. I asked Barbara what it meant for her. She said it meant a Black woman was willing to stick her head out, live and die for what she believes in: equality.

"Are you mad I backed out?"

We were sitting at a secluded table in one of the two smaller cafeterias. She seemed a bit less on edge, as if the mourning of her brother's death had fallen off like the stitches of a wound. "You asked me that before and no, I am not mad at you."

"The Max boys are."

"Well you got Attitude to threaten to burn down the school if there weren't changes made in the grading policy."

"Is that how the other voting bloc got together?"

"No, that got done by sleeping with the enemy."

She let it hang out there so I tried to hit it out the park. "Is that why you sleep with men?"

She only laughed. It was not a small laugh. Her coughs stifled it; food had gone down the wrong tract.

Max boys are loyal.

Chapter 25

Ken came to see me.

From the moment he walked into my apartment, I knew protocol would hold for the coronation. He bowed, crown down with chin touching his torso. I had not asked for the vote to oust him. As such, I could keep silent. He preempted the vote by stating he would remain King in name only. He made the choice out of love, stating Barbara was his woman in real life, in or out of the Society. He accepted he would have no say in how I would rule. "You have not called for an explanation."

His attempt to draw me in meant my request had been fulfilled. Not sure if this was his attempt to take credit after the fact. It did bother me why he would sit hours in a parking lot, worrying about Miranda. "We both got what we wanted."

"The word is you are not satisfied and will not be seating a King next to you at the coronation."

"Only because these coming years will involve victories or defeats history would automatically credit to a king, much like you are trying to do at this moment."

"No. The historical record shows protocol did not hold and that is why Miranda was replaced by you."

"Whose signature is on the call?" Ken did not answer. "Did you make the call? Did you answer the call?"

"The man who answered the call should be sitting next to you."

"He thought I was someone else. He didn't even know who the call was for."

"But Girard knew. He gave you Trisha Hamilton's name. He came to my apartment threatening to shoot me over some dumb shit, the platform he thought I was forcing you to run under."

"I didn't send him." Ken paused. I could tell the confusion. I said, "I have no war with you. We all had the same information. We just processed it differently."

This new knowledge took his last resolve. In moments of anger, he would blush a red that approached maroon. Instead he sat as the blood thinned from his face and he paled at the alternate conclusion he was unwilling to face, if I indeed was not behind dethroning him.

I offered him a drink and he agreed to something strong. He sat on the edge of the sofa, the brown leather, hard under his weight. I waited for him to finally settle in after faking that his eyes were taking in the artwork on the wall. I eased my way to the back, closing the bedroom door. I didn't know whether I had the stomach to sit there and thereby share my culpability on how various people's self-interest had caused them to go to war against Miranda Lopez for no reason.

Ken was now another person whose ability for love or falling in love would forever be slowed.

I took a swallow of Grand Marnier and dialed Girard's number.

She answered on the first ring as if my call was expected. I asked, "Hi, may I speak with Girard?"

"This is Nicole, his girlfriend. Do you have my number?"

"No."

"Well, I have yours." Nicole was a hard chick. In a fair fight we would draw each other out. "Do you want me to call you later?"

Nicole was always into drama, knew everyone, their business. She was one of those chicks who had no aspirations to become a SUM woman. So even though she heard the rumors of who we were and how we operated, there was still a sphere in which a person deserved a fair one. She gave me a fair one, a shot to take her man. She gave a name to him, most likely her own enemy she wanted vanquished. "No, just tell Girard, I said sorry."

She did not move the telephone far from her face nor cover its mouthpiece with her palm as she shouted, "That chick Hope says she's sorry." A short pause. "He says OK."

She waited. I waited, thinking of a way to be in their presence, see them together, the way a young power couple moved; perhaps sit at their feet, paint her nails, feed him grapes, listen to the rain cascade on the lonely semi-bare branches as autumn leaves something else to ponder; the beauty yet the hopelessness of a man sipping the strong liquor leaving the bitter taste he had stirred through either the inability to be satisfied or the fear of understanding all of the game's levels need not be climbed.

Miranda finally agreed to be my stand-in queen. As my stand-in queen, I was responsible for buying her dress and jewelry. She, in turn, helped me organize the event. We went with lavender with touches of white for décor, invitations and menu. The food catered through the campus but ordered from the region's finest services. The Society covered the cost of all non-personal items. A campus coronation is one of the most important events in the Society. It's sort of like a debutante ball. It is also the night where a new member's rank is formally entered in the historical record.

Amidst the festive mood of men in tuxedos and women in formal gowns, a live band, a quintet, there was a tension. It resided closest to Ken, who stayed by Barbara's side like a dog on a leash. The maneuvers had left him with title but no authority. With protocol holding during the coronation, his title, in effect, made Barbara a stand-in queen.

Each time I glanced in their direction, I sensed the wonderment in Barbara's eyes. She loved pageantry but I kept looking for any glint indicating she wanted to be queen. Technically, though a first generation SUM woman, she could have called for a vote to be crowned the campus queen for this charter since she too came into the Society under a fourth generation legacy's sponsorship.

While helping me put together the event, Miranda started to understand the scope of the history I was trying to protect. She asked, "Why did they elect me and pass you over?"

"The man I love turned me down…" I stopped there and said no more.

My family alone had eighty people in attendance from the Strength side: SBD and SUM. The lone person invited directly under my family name, who was not part of this side, was Attitude.

Since the campus had no initiated, recognized MAX legacies, I technically did not have to invite anyone from the Pride side, any MAX boys. But I did out of respect for and the need to maintain the peace that existed. Ted replied NO, and The Outsiders never replied.

When Attitude walked into the room to be the lone occupant of the sole Max table, I introduced him to my immediate family and others at our table. Had it not been a formal event and I not used his full, given name, they would not have known him. My date for the evening, my cousin, Richard said, "So, you're Davenport?"

It was clear Attitude did not know him in any capacity. "Yes, the one and only."

Richard extended his hand. "Thank you for covering my queen's back."

Attitude shook his hand. "That's what the queen's army is for." The men gave a hearty laugh. And the women, even my great-grandmother exhaled like he had wooed them with just one line. After shaking hands with everyone, he said, "Good meeting you all! Enjoy the festivities."

"Hey, where are you going?"

He pointed to the empty Max table. "I have to represent the family."

Richard put his arm around his shoulder. "Do it here, and let the word go out that there's no animosity between our two sides."

The first chance I got, I whispered to Richard. "What do you think you're doing? You're here as a proxy, not to make decisions."

He whispered, "Have you looked at the wall and the paintings?"

Not having been in the ballroom these past two weeks, after we gave the decorating scheme, layout and table arrangements, I had not seen the paintings on the wall.

Earlier tonight, I had entered as part of the formal march. The head, center table was too far from the walls for me to clearly see the paintings. From where I sat, the canvases I saw depicted hardcore street life. Throughout the rest of the ceremony, my focus was elsewhere. Plus, I could not see what was on the walls.

I had not seen him in months, not since the party at Barrington. I followed his movements by reading his weekly column in Semline's school newspaper. He had a carefree bounce to his steps and was not dressed for the occasion. The carpeted walkway guided him on how to make a beeline to the center table. He approached the table like a gate crasher even though he was invited, with a plus-one, as part of the Pride side.

Richard, my father and my two brothers stood quickly as he approached. Everyone could see the anger in Monk's face and body language. The band stopped playing and everyone in the room turned to look. I tried to make eye contact with him to say, this was not the time nor place. I stood and said, "Hi Monk."

The word monk caused everyone to look at Attitude. He shrugged his shoulders and kept eating.

As the eldest, my great-grandmother stood and spoke, "What is your name, son?"

He showed her respect, even though, due to lineage, he did not have to. "Theodore Alan Perkins."

My great-grandmother nearly fell back in her seat. "Perkins? Whoa! The Perkins?"

"Yes, Ma'am!"

"Then why did your family not come for the coronation?"

"War was declared and no one has proclaimed victory nor called for a truce."

Everyone looked at me. I looked at Richard, who then extended his hand to Monk. Monk did not take his hand so my father stepped in. "This is a peaceful gathering…"

Monk showed his rudeness, interrupting him mid-sentence. "It's not for me. Why would I need to take your hand for cover?"

By now my family was confused and looked at me again. My father asked, "None of ours stood up to protect you?" When I did not answer, he said, "OK, Monk! It's clear now."

At that, Monk extended his hand to Richard, who gave Monk a real firm handshake. Monk smiled, really more of a smirk as if to say, *You punk, I ain't scared of you.* After the handshake, Monk turned to Attitude. "I had a chance to view your artwork and would love the opportunity to interview you for an article in the paper."

They excused themselves and headed toward the exit. Richard followed them. They kept walking toward the stairs. Richard stopped just outside the ballroom, over to Devon and extended his hand out to him. I turned to the eyes that mattered. Ken did his best to hide his anger. Miranda had her head slightly turned away, feigning focus on her date.

My eyes turned to Barbara but she gave no hint of interest. The band started up again, as I counted the missing pieces of what happened. My stepmother broke my concentration. "Two Max boys fighting for you? What are you up here doing?"

I corrected her, "Actually four and there could be one more joining them."

My great-grandmother added, "And, I always thought you were a good girl."

My sister laughed and everyone at the table, including my father, laughed.

My thoughts went elsewhere.

We spent the rest of the night at the various small parties being held throughout the town for our guests. I did my best to enjoy the crowning achievement of my life, something I dreamed of for nearly a decade. Still that night I slept uncomfortably with Monk's words that someone had declared war.

The next morning before the farewell luncheon, I rushed to the ballroom to go look at the paintings. They were not there. I asked the building's facilities manager. He said they were taken down last night after the ball and packed to ship out.

The paintings had been there for two weeks and Richard said Manny Davenport had covered my back. With final exams around the corner, I really needed to study. Even though I had attended my classes, my mind's been elsewhere.

Whatever the Max boys were up to would have to wait.

Max boys don't see
What we go through
To become SUM women.

Part Four

RISK – PLAY AT YOUR OWN

Chapter 26
REBEL WITHOUT A BOSS

I got to work right away. As soon as the luncheon ended I asked the women to join me for an emergency closed door meeting. The meeting was to clear the concern of initiated SUM women and uninitiated legacies matriculating at the three local colleges. I had drafted a letter to grant any SUM legacy permission to apply for initiation and membership at any school not under TGI's charter. This allowed uninitiated legacies to not have to go through a process and to gain membership rights without having to transfer schools. They could matriculate at one of the three colleges but they would have no vote in internal matters even if they opted to attend meetings. They could opt to pay dues as an affiliate chapter member and to pay tribute to the queen.

Bowing to the queen in public and private was optional until we convened the next formal meeting and voted on protocols.

For any woman seeking initiation and membership under TGI's charter, whether a legacy admission or a blind candidate, there would be a pledge program.

The SUM alumnae women were not pleased. A few had daughters currently matriculating at one of the three schools. No matter their questions and concerns, I clarified their daughters would not be viewed as cowards. I reassured them the short-term loss of revenue would be made up by bigger gains because I and the other two conscious daughters and any other future members who come through this chapter would focus only on the big ticket items, which in turn would bring riches, powers and freedoms they never imagined.

The meeting ended with obscenities and wishes that harm come to me.

My great-grandmother did not say a word.

The pleasantries of the previous night had come to an abrupt end. What I saw as a compromise on my previous stance - requiring all legacies matriculating at any of the three colleges to have a pledge process - was not well-received.

The next two weeks as we headed toward Thanksgiving break, no matter where I went in public, no SUM woman bowed. In fact, no SBD brother bowed. SBD brothers were known to let SUM women handle our own affairs, but this particular executive action cut across matrilineal lines. Some of them, their mothers had attended school here and they too wanted their potential future daughters to benefit from the TGI lineage. The money flowed upward to chapters and got disbursed to families who then distributed downward to their kin based on age, standing and activity.

Before pledging, I had pulled myself away from my GG Celeste's legacy and it really was her option whether I would receive any family money and, in this case, what amount.

For now, my money would only come from chapter members initiated after me.

Out of the six uninitiated legacies on the three campuses, only one submitted an application. Only one blind candidate submitted an acceptable package. Between the three schools, we normally got twenty-five to fifty applications per initiation class. We held one class every three semesters. Sometimes more time would pass in between classes because we rejected most applicants.

Both accepted applications came from Barrington.

I had not been to the Barrington campus since the party in September and didn't bother to check whether Barbara or Miranda wanted to go.

I walked in before tip-off. A split amount of SBD brothers bowed. The bow was sly and indiscernible to those not in the know. I scanned the room looking for Girard before remembering Barrington's legislative sessions were being held from six to ten. Ten women bowed. I knew their faces from the photos in their application packets. I gave them each a smile.

I searched the room for the two women I had come to meet.

They had spotted me and as our eyes met, they bowed and smiled. I returned both gestures. They were seated on the short bleachers facing the players' bench. Lauren, the blind candidate, was with a group of people. Diane was by herself but with no clear consecutive empty seats next to her. I didn't want to squeeze in so I went to the other side of the gym.

I climbed the steps to a nice corner where I could keep a low profile and spotted her to my right, a good fifty feet down. Nicole sat with a group of women and as our eyes met, without hesitation on either of our parts, we waved and smiled.

Within the same motion, she returned to jostling and giggling with her friends. I went up a few more rows. For Ernest to find me way up here would mean he had been looking for me during home games. He never called, had yet to come to TGI for any type of visit, as far as I knew. The game started with Barrington winning the tip-off. They scored on the first possession and the game's competitiveness gave me a chance to see the source of the hoopla being reported by the papers, radio, television and students, even those who did not follow basketball. This early in the season, predictions were being thrown out the window. Barrington, once picked to finish last in the conference, was on pace to have its best season ever, with Ernest LeGagneur leading the way.

Strength and Speed. His form on the jumper was not the most technical or fluid, but still he netted most of his shots. After his third straight made jumper, I opened the event's program. For the season: Ernest's Field Goal percentage was 52% while averaging 28 Points, 12 Rebounds and 4 Assists.

This past summer, he did say he was great but with such nonchalance he, in effect, had downplayed his ability, to the point he was playing for

Barrington, in this conference. Fouled on his way to the basket, a fan, not seated too far from me and rooting for the visiting team, heckled Ernest. Since the arena was quiet in anticipation of these two free throws to put the game out of reach, Ernest heard, made to turn his head but then changed his mind. He would have clearly seen me and for some reason I was preparing to cover my face with the program. I wondered what that was about.

He made both shots and the other team called a timeout. Knowing people would soon make to leave, I looked across the bleachers and used my eyes and head to signal to Diane and Lauren I needed to speak with them after the game.

I stepped outside the gym and waited on the side. People moved quickly, their steps staggered since our positioning forced them to maneuver around us. "Hello. Nice to meet you two. Diane. Lauren."

They had the smiles of sweet girls hurrying to push their teen years behind them. Lauren was the shorter, her curves more pronounced below her waistline. Diane was a pinup in any era, a starlet with the amplified accoutrements. "Queen Kendall..." These two appreciated and respected protocol.

I interrupted them. "In public or private, please call me Hope. Do you know each other?"

"No."

"OK, get to know each other. I looked over your application packets, and I am quite impressed. Final exams are in a few weeks so we are not going to meet until next semester. In the meantime, do you know Miranda Lopez and Barbara Wilson?"

"Not personally."

"That's fine. Get their numbers. Call them to introduce yourselves. I've given them each a copy of your application packets. Next semester, I will contact you and we will proceed from there."

"OK."

"You both have my number. Tonight is Thursday and I will be around until, at least Tuesday, before leaving for Thanksgiving. If you need any help with anything, let me know."

"Thank you."

I left the building. I rushed to my car but to nowhere specific. The parties would be at Barrington. The road to Trafalgar had more hills and dips than curves. What curves it did have forced one to slow to under twenty. Frosted roads with no divider. Woods and ravines. Miranda rarely came out to see me. Barbara was always with Ken. We mostly ran across each other in the cafeteria, sat for lunch and scheduled our study hours to talk some more.

Most nights to stay in rhythm, I would head to the WGA office, hangout with the officers, share ideas, do paperwork and get into my own studies. But, tonight I had skipped all that and went to Barrington, so I needed to go by the office and check for my mail. Not much in the box except for one seemingly important envelope from my advisor's office. The note read: Please come by to see me tomorrow, Friday at 3 p.m. in my office regarding your article in FIRST IMPRESSIONS, that interview of Manny Davenport.

He hadn't signed the note and it was typed. I had had Dr. Moore as an advisor since my first semester when I declared my major. This type of letter in such an impersonal tone and style was unlike him. Something was wrong; perhaps multiple wrongs. I had not submitted an article for publication. He'd encouraged me to write for one of the school's newspapers or to work as a research assistant for one of the school's professors. No matter how much prodding, I never heeded his advice.

I'd never heard of this publication and wondered why he would be so concerned with this interview to request my presence. My mind went into overdrive. The MAX boys had made their move. I recalled Monk asking to interview Attitude and the painting on the walls at my coronation.

They had attacked under my name but without my permission. To get a copy of FIRST IMPRESSIONS, I would go to the library. I thought of my car so I wouldn't have to circle back to the Student Union. But then realized I needed to walk, some cold air to keep me calm, composed.

The night air failed to calm me. The November chill, the slow but persistent wind, the flurry of activity in the library, the glare of fluorescent lights, bright white walls with large plated framed artwork amplified the dreadful sound bleating into my subconscious. I glanced into the main reading room at the usual suspects arched over their books.

At the Reference Desk, a student, a face I couldn't place, looked quite sure of herself, much like the daytime staffers with their silver hair, square frames and wool sweaters. She looked up upon hearing my voice. "May I help you?"

"Yes, do you have a copy of First Impressions?"

"We do not carry it. It's not publicly circulated." My raised eyebrows questioned her. She typed on the keyboard and turned the monitor toward me. Before bending down, I looked into her eyes and realized I was one or more steps behind in this game. The information on the screen stated FIRST IMPRESSIONS was a monthly publication in private circulation for 100,000 subscribers at $500 per year. I let her look into my eyes and she answered, "No. I don't know where you can get a copy."

"Thank you." I walked away knowing the letter had been placed in my mailbox after classes and business hours so my only choice would be to come to the library and see her. My advisor now knew I had not submitted the article to FIRST IMPRESSIONS. What exactly was in this interview? I thought of calling Great-Granny Celeste because she might know of the publication, or even be a subscriber.

I went back to the parking lot behind the Student Union to pick up my car. TGI had strict parking rules and most times it made no sense to drive, especially with the campus being so small.

My apartment began to feel like the place I selected and decorated so company didn't feel too comfortable. Yet, still from the living room, at this time of night, of year, the moon tilted upwards enough where its light crafted a romantic ambience. My great-grandmother had misspoke, contradicted herself from years of warnings during my adolescent years. She said I had two MAX boys fighting over me, forgetting she had said, "MAX boys don't fight over women. They fight because of women."

What order, what directive had Monk and Attitude thought I had given? Could they be as in love with me as I felt when I first saw them? If so, why not a telephone call? Perhaps they were as stuck as I. I had found a way out this past summer. I had found freedom. Not once had Attitude mentioned the Society. He just went about his work, his art. The fire had burned and he had been out there. He never mentioned it. I hinted at it and he waited for me to say more, until I called to say there was a monk on the Semline College campus. Attitude knew and did not feel intimidated by it. He even said he would be honored if I ended up with Monk, a seventh generation MAX boy, one who did not want to be known, who did not follow protocol. Yet, for some reason, my name had replaced his name as the interviewer of an underground artist who thought fame was nothing but a protection racket.

I woke without an alarm. My first class was 11 a.m. but it was 7 a.m. and I had yesterday's clothes on and its worries on my shoulders, on my head. "Uneasy lies the head that wears a crown," Shakespeare had written. Looking in the mirror, seeing bags under droopy eyes, I did not question whether it was worth it but whether I would let Ernest down. By as early as the start of next semester, just two months from now, he could be walking into the Society.

The shower hadn't done as much as I wished, to make me look less drawn. I didn't press my clothes since they were no more than a long tee, jeans and a sweatshirt. With a spray of Obsession perfume, I masked my uncertainty so that while Dr. Moore or I read the interview out loud, my scent could push his mind toward a seductive place, a place he likely never thought I would lead him.

Afterward, alone, I would process what the interview meant.

I got to campus at precisely 8:40 a.m. so that both 8 a.m. and 8:30 a.m. classes had seated and campus grounds and the Student Union Building lobby would be pretty much empty. I headed to the cafeteria and grabbed breakfast to go, toward my office to eat and see if anything needed my attention. I glanced over at my mail slot and the filled sign indicated I had a package to pick up at the campus post office. Odd that mail would have been delivered this early.

There were two notices for packages that did not fit into this small box designed for envelopes. I wanted to eat my breakfast and the heat and aroma coming through the bags made me doubt whether these packages and their timing mattered more than my hunger. The post office was in the basement of the administration building, two buildings over in the quad. I jogged there in case anyone saw me and wanted to talk, my run would confirm I could not stop.

The two boxes asked me to choose which was the more important. The one from the SUM national organizational Queen weighed nearly fifteen pounds, and the package from FIRST IMPRESSIONS weighed about five pounds. Instinctively I knew what was in the Queen's package and knew the contents of the interview tied into why she sent me the Ring & Scepter. This conundrum led to a moment of enlightenment, an answer to the age old question of which came first, the chicken or the egg.

The rooster came first. Men always fed their hunger first and all these movements were no more than tests to see who I would put first. I walked to the first isolated corner I could find, a place away from stares, potential foot traffic, surveillance cameras, and I ate my breakfast. The fried eggs with bacon between an English muffin; in fact, the two of them were so tasty and filling I really felt like taking a nap but first I gulped down the small carton of chocolate milk.

I opened the Queen's mailing and didn't allow my attention to be drawn to the Ring & Scepter. Her letter was terse: *I know it is rare for a SUM Queen to go down without a fight but in truth, I am proud of you. You have set a new standard for the Society. Rather than lead a war in which I have no stakes or belief, I hand you the throne. Wish you well my sister, my queen...Queen Ames.*

War? Of this magnitude? I hesitated, quite apprehensive in opening the other package. I now realized after the rooster came, he must have fallen asleep or abandoned the chicken and the egg. If he fell asleep, the hen must have killed the rooster. If he abandoned them, then the egg's content, society would eventually kill him. What war did these MAX boys start? I opened the package and read the interview. At first, I said that makes sense, and then I said "not really" because Attitude would not give those answers. He would deflect, reframe. Why would Monk come from that angle? He's a seventh generation MAX boy. He had nothing to prove when it came to being down for the race. His family's allegiance to the struggle could not be questioned. So, why go on record with those words?

But, the interview was not under Monk's name. It was under mine.

What? My allegiance to the struggle was being questioned?

What the fuck!! The Queen handed over the crown because I spent a summer partying with some white people, and now I have to fight an old war. She could not stand for me, and now I had to confirm my oath, to a brazen magazine cover image-

> *The signature inscribed on the left bottom corner: Davenport. The background paint is yellow. A man floats atop a blood red ocean. A flag pole is planted on the back of his head; a man wearing knee high boots stands and holds the flag; in his huge palms he is holding a number of people; far off in the distance to the right of him a woman is trying to keep from drowning, her hand is stretched out towards him. The title- "Bloody land. On the strength..."- is printed neatly on the top right corner.*

My first impulse was to walk up to my advisor's office and demand why Dr. Moore needed an explanation of this interview. Let's suppose I felt a Black artist had to address race whenever his work rested on either extremes of black life, what concern of it was his, especially when it had nothing to do with my school work?

But, I could not storm into my advisor's office with such a tone because we had a cordial relationship. He taught me which professors to avoid and always provided encouragement when I told him what I planned to do with my degree. So, what worried him and the Queen so much about this interview? I reread it and saw other angles by removing myself from the picture. "*Are You an Artist or a Racist?*"

Art, from any Black artist, that does not address race has a lesser value.

Why would anyone take such an unpopular position in 1987? That question allowed me to give the Queen some slack. I got up from my corner and found the nearest bathroom.

My breakfast left me but not this new burden I carried in two boxes. The note in the second box said: *Thank you for your contribution. Attached is an initial payment of $5,000 for the first of our syndicators willing to distribute your interview. Each time one of our syndicators publishes your article in full or a piece based on its premise, you will receive an additional $5,000. Along with this you will receive a complimentary one year subscription of FIRST IMPRESSIONS, which you can renew annually.*

The check reminded me to look into the Queen's package. Yes, there it was, the bank account that now belonged to me. The beginning balance was zero, but it also showed the last withdrawal was for $700,000. She was not a popular queen; in fact, a mousy one who gave away much of the strongholds fought and won by my GG and the queen who overthrew my GG. Each month after the accountants distributed the money to the Society's families, there would be a balance left over, that balance got transferred into the reigning queen's account. It was hers to keep until she relinquished the crown, along with whatever was in her personal account. When my GG Celeste was asked to step down from the throne, she bragged her balance was two and half million. Carried over into 1987 money, that would be over six and half million dollars.

My class would start in twenty minutes but my mind said to go to my apartment to put away the Ring & Scepter, and both packages.

I arrived and reread the interview and saw another interpretation. I thought of calling Attitude or even Monk, but I had to keep a clear mind for my meeting.

I decided to skip both of the day's early classes. I masturbated and took a nap. To make sure I didn't miss the meeting, I set my alarm for 2:30 p.m.

I fell asleep right away. Whatever worries I had dissipated because when pressed with the information in the interview and knowing no one above me in SUM could pass rules I had to obey, I didn't have to say anything.

I wondered who would be the first caller to congratulate me, to worry about my safety.

I washed my face, brushed my teeth. I sized myself up in the mirror, noticing my clothes were wrinkled. I didn't fret because the disheveled look afforded me a bit of the nonchalance I needed to act as if this were truly my doing, my aim.

Friday afternoon, just minutes away from three o'clock, the official start of the weekend, happy hour at the various bars in town. Students strolled from various quads, heading toward the main gate. The administration building had very little foot traffic and most office doors were closed, secluded workers simply counting down the last two hours. Above the fourth floor were the offices for senior faculty who often had to interact with the campus professional staff and executive administrators. These offices had one receptionist responsible for the affairs of a specific department or cluster of related academic subjects. Still I expected the Interdisciplinary Studies Department's receptionist to be at the spoke for the offices arranged in a circular fashion. I knocked twice and entered to see an empty room. Dr. Moore's door was wide open so I walked in, looked around and took a seat. Less than ten seconds later, a panel I never knew to be a door opened. It startled me. It was Trustee Winston Trafalgar the Fourth.

"What are you doing here?"

He motioned for me to be quiet by placing his right index finger across his lips and motioned for me to close the door. As I returned near the desk and not sure whether I would take a seat, until he asked, "Are you pregnant? Are you in love?"

In love? My mental preparation did not include seeing Trustee Trafalgar and knew I could not disguise my eyes enough to withstand his questions. I decided to play it straight until I got my bearings. "No. What are you doing here?"

"Did you really think that Dr. Moore would be here? He's on sabbatical until next fall. You didn't even know that, so your GG Celeste was right."

"Right about what? You called her?"

"No, she called me. We had breakfast when she was up here for your coronation." He noticed my confusion. "Yes, she too didn't understand why I was not present. She thought I was playing you like my dirty little secret."

"Your what?" I raised my voice.

He spoke lower, secretively. "Exactly. I explained to her I reached out to you back in May but after our initial meeting I hadn't heard from you."

"I didn't know I was to be reporting to you?"

"You're not but she's worried about you. She told me you're mixed up with two MAX boys but that you said there might be four or more on these three campuses." I got my bearings, steeled my eyes and did not answer. "We had done an excellent job of keeping MAX boys far away from this school and the neighboring colleges, ever, ever since your great-grandfather's lynching. But, she told me Manny Davenport is one, which now makes sense, as to why you went to Manhattan and spent the entire summer there."

"You're spying on me?"

"NO! Of course not. It is an exchange of information. I was worried about you when I hadn't heard from you so I called your father. Of course, I did so under the auspices of my work here with the college. He told me you were hardly home and spending your time with some artist named Davenport who just graduated from here. I looked it up and I was impressed by what professors had to say about him. But, then I connected the dots. He's Aman." I did not say a word. "I kept waiting for you to call to say he was behind the fire, the theft..."

I interrupted. "Theft?"

"Yes. Once we cleaned up the debris, we realized all the art and jewelry we thought burned were actually stolen. We lost forty million and a white girl…"

"A what?"

"No. We really did lose a white girl." He sat down. "The fire was a ruse. We realized it many days after. Well, this student had come to us months prior claiming she was receiving anonymous death threats. We let her stay here in one of the upstairs guest apartments. She came and went as she pleased. Two days after the fire, her parents called campus police to say she had been calling them every day but they had not heard from her since the fire."

My eyes were steel. "I still don't get what that has to do with me, Manny Davenport…"

He interrupted, not with words but an exasperated sound, like he was surprised I couldn't make the connection. He stared at me, clearly indicating I needed to say something. I sat knowing he knew much more than I anticipated. "Lena was your SUM sister Barbara Wilson's roommate. You were seen warning her to get lost before she showed up on my steps asking for protection."

Right then I knew he was bluffing. Someone was feeding him information. I'm not saying he was lying about the missing girl and the stolen art and jewelry but the reasoning was shaky. That was what an outsider would see. I simply said, "I still don't know what that has to do with me. So, when we talked in May, did you think I worked for you because you gave me a gun and said to go find Aman?"

"Really? Wow! Manny Davenport really is Aman?" We locked eyes, neither giving way. He softened his stare but kept the contact. "So, this interview? I called you in here thinking you had nothing to do with it. But you are fine to go out there and let members of the Society gamble their lives away for forty million and a white girl?"

I didn't answer because I really did not know who was behind the fire, the theft. But, let's say it was someone from the Society, whether SUM, SBD or PMB better known as the MAX boys. Or, under ideal conditions, it was a job pulled off by all of us together. A forty million dollar job coupled with what seems to be Trustee Trafalgar's prized possession. He probably valued her at or more than forty million dollars; that, that is a war I would want my name on. "If that is the war the queen must sign off on, then I will."

I could feel and see his heart sink, as his Adam's apple jutted downward and he squinted to hold back the tears. I wanted to reach out, to let him know I remember the past, the link between our families, our previous kiss and that I did not see him as my enemy. He looked away to ask, "Be honest with me, did Manny Davenport have anything to do with the fire?"

"No." My reply came out at the correct speed, volume and tone, to mask the possible lie, my uncertainty.

"Are you pregnant? Are you in love?"

"No. Yes."

He swiveled, turning sideways, left, to the computer terminal and started typing. After what seemed to be his answers to a series of access points, he got up from behind the desk and walked back behind the panel from which he had entered. The amount of minutes he took told me he had gone upstairs to his own office. Trustee Trafalgar came back carrying a bunch of cabinet hanging folders filled with files in them. He motioned for me to take them and I did so. We both sat down. "These are the files of all Fine Arts majors, graduates and those who left without a degree, from TGI and Barrington. You are now a member of COSA, the Council for Oversight of Student Arts. All your work is private and independent. I've also given you access to the mainframe and the FIRST IMPRESSIONS library so you can see images of their work, their writings from since they enrolled at either school and all past issues of the publication."

I hit him with the shot he thought I would not take. "Can you pull up Manny Davenport?"

"Yours is his only mention in FIRST IMPRESSIONS. Accessing the mainframe, you will see he got great grades in his classes and annual student competitions. The highest compliment he ever received, "The black Kandinsky"."

I chuckled. "Let's say it is the case. He's that highly regarded. Why has only one publication syndicated my interview?"

"Well that is easy! The work he did here dealt with…well the abstract truth; if we are just riffing or speaking metaphorically."

"No other interviews or reviews? Are you saying there's a lesser value in an artist's work when the subject matter or images are of black people? Is that what I will learn from these files?"

"We got a call about three weeks ago Davenport wanted to exhibit his collection now as opposed to next semester. We said fine. I had no idea your coronation was scheduled. We rushed out and invited the press, all the normal people who attend our premieres. Mind you, it was a rush job, the event I mean. People, hundreds, came the first night for the opening. Manny came, shook hands with the patrons and answered all the reporters' questions."

I interrupted him. "Manny was here? And you didn't confront him but expected me to…"

He interrupted me. "I had no idea he was Aman." He continued, "People came throughout the two weeks. Why did they not write reviews? No interviews? How come no one put bids on the pieces? I don't know. But I will say these paintings were not what we expected."

"The Black Kandinsky!" I chortled at that one professor's critique and then asked, "You did say, forty million and a white girl, right?"

I stood up and all he could say, "I am not your enemy."

"Of course not, never said you were. We are almost family but you must always remember I do not work for you."

He stood and bowed from crown to chin touching chest.

I left the office thinking whatever the Max boys were up to would have to wait. I went to my office and put the files away so I could head to the library. I locked them in my file cabinet. The plan was to retrieve them after my library visit. The quad was empty with most students at happy hour. Still there were a few milling around. They had yet to vacate campus for the weekend and take a trip downstate into the city or further north to other colleges. Some had already abandoned campus for the Thanksgiving break. The wind broke westward, its crack against the flag. Hawks circled above; the clouds failing to mask their eagerness. The feel of flanking movements but it was only one person, the rush with his left arm thrown around my shoulders startled me, warning of a paranoia I had never felt. My math was quick: six-three about two-twenty with his weight concentrated in the trunk; arms muscular, and legs looked to be sturdy but not bulky. I would have to elbow him in his rib cage and do a quick jab step to his fibula. From there, I could decide the exact threat level to use to excuse my actions. "Get your fucking hands off me!" He started to say something as he matched my strides, marching on the same feet. I interrupted, "NOW! And don't you ever touch me in public!"

Ted stopped walking and asked, "I thought you were not holding protocol."

I turned but didn't stop, only slowed my steps, giving him a chance to catch up. Of course there was no way he could know about the Ring & Scepter. And, even though he was a seventh generation legacy, my new ranking put me on a respect level where he should not touch me in public without permission. "Protocol or not, do not ever touch me without permission!"

"Is it that we got off on the wrong foot or you simply not wanting my assistance?"

I veered towards the woods and said, "I think you have me confused with someone else, like I can't hold my own."

We came off the sidewalk, into the narrow road that encircled the inner campus. To the right of the road, on a diagonal were the dormitories, a few service buildings and an exit to the campus. We went left, where students discreetly entered the woods. About a tenth of a mile down, there was a clearing but if one looped right, off the path, the woods went on and led to a creek and a secret passage to the town. We stood surrounded by bare branches, with dusk staring far on the horizon like a vulture. He'd had about seven minutes to refute the notion I needed him, and another ninety seconds as I undressed.

I looked in his direction but not at him, as I removed my sweathood and tee-shirt. I took off my pants in one fast motion and removed my panties. I laid down my panties on the backpack and unzipped the front pouch. His reaction was not to my naked body but to my steady hand, stiff forearm and slightly bent elbow. His steel hazel eyes told me not so much that he'd had a gun pointed at him before but he'd known horrors and traumas worth dying for. "I can give you a story by simply running out these woods yelling."

He described the gun by its history. "Glock 17. Given to first daughters of the Trafalgar family. My third cousins through marriage, back in the late nineteen-twenties, a fourth generation SBD union."

"Makes no difference to me. A bullet to the face or give your word you will never sneak up on me or touch me without permission!"

"Even if it is known I bowed to the Queen?"

"On what terms?"

"In the Student Assembly, the WGA votes the same as the Sophomore Class. You hold fifteen percent of the vote from all the women organizations. I can guarantee the ten percent from the TGI Senate and Girard's ten percent from the Barrington Senate. Our united front will make sure any legislation needs our backing because no way the Radical Student Association puts their fifteen percent with the Conservative Assembly's fifteen percent."

"What about the other student alliances?"

"Well, we could have had you as the Assembly president to influence their vote as a bloc but chances are their votes will be scattered."

I lowered the gun and waited for him to mention the ten percent from the Semline Senate, to see if he knew about Monk. Just like I hadn't known about the two of them because Max boys don't announce their presence, he and Monk might not know about each other. Yet, Girard knew about both of them. "My legislative vote means that much to you?"

"Yes. I also hope once I am initiated into the Society that in Matters of

Matrimony." His voice slowed to confer a humility I hadn't expected. My body shivered for the first time from the cold air. "In Matters of Matrimony, if approached from the Pride, PMB side, you will allow SUM women to carry the male legacy to either side of the Society, even if the father is not present."

"So, you know about the Ring & Scepter?"

"Yes, and I will bow to the Queen in private and public."

I looked around, the trees and the total darkness soon to cover us, thinking someone was pranking me. "On the Quad at 6 p.m. today!" Ted went down on his knees, first right followed by left. I took a step forward and said, "You may touch the Queen."

An hour later, the chimes from the clock tower serenaded the campus. I went to the cafeteria's tall windows. Ted casually walked to the center of the tiled mosaic. He went down on both knees, with arms spread out in supplication. His forehead touched the ground on the sixth chime. He held it for five seconds. Passing students giggled or ignored the spectacle, thinking he'd had a few too many. Most in their drunken stupor, returning early from happy hour, only worried about catching dinner at the main cafeteria before its closing. Those in the know would spread the word the Duval family had thrown its weight behind the SUM Queen.

Nationally, the balance of power in the Society had shifted. Not only was the Queen in charge and all credit and duties would be attributed appropriately, the Kendall and Duval families had strength in numbers. I went to my office to gather the files.

I reached my apartment and was surprised at having no messages, no blinking light on the answering machine. I picked up the telephone for the call I should have made months ago. This call was not about power but love. Perhaps, in reality, love was the only real power. "Hello, may I speak with Monk?" The person who answered covered the mouthpiece and came back to ask. "Tell him that it's Hope. Hope Kendall from TGI." This time I could hear muffled voices and noise in the background – Monk wanting to know what I wanted. I wanted the vulgar, the sensitive, the tongue, the dick. I know if I said that Monk would have no choice but to come to the phone because of the clowning he would face if he did not get himself to TGI ASAP. "Tell him I just called to say Thank You."

It would be a matter of hours before Ted found out the MAX boys in play were not only Girard and Manny, men he outranked. He would have to contend with Theodore "Monk" Perkins, an equally powerful rival in the Society for the Queen's loyalty. Depending on how he played his hand, Ted could have the Semline Senate as another ally in the Student Assembly.

The day's stress, the emptiness of living, perched like a bird, in this nest, a tower amidst shorter campus buildings; it all bubbled up in my chest. I rolled a joint and fixed myself a solid drink as I read the interview again.

"Are You an Artist or a Racist?"

Within months after graduating Trafalgar Garrison Institute, Manny Davenport has garnered critical praise for his work as a painter. This coming semester, he will become the first African-American TGI alumni ever invited to exhibit his work on the walls of Garrison ballroom. I caught up with Mr. Davenport to ask him some questions as to why some praise his work while others demonize it.

Hope Kendall: I have seen your exhibit, your graduating thesis, many times and I do not know what to make of it.

Manny Davenport: In what sense?

HK: First, the title of the collection.

MD: Return of the Angry Black Man? I chose that title because there clearly is an effort to show some Black people as nonexistent, simply because all of us do not busy ourselves with confronting the dire straits our race face.

HK: Well, upon this return, do angry Blacks rectify this? In your paintings you show them in the exact environments which others use to depict them, for lack of a better phrase, as less than human. You have boys on the corner shooting dice. Women prostituting in alleyways. Drug peddlers. Stick-up kids, and so on.

MD: In essence, the series is to show that through their travels and travails, angry Blacks have found peace with their past, the whole of it, including the negative aspects. So, within that framework, we are willing to celebrate our faults.

HK: How does seemingly bringing down the race help further its growth?

MD: All of our battles have always been to quote-end-quote fight the good fight. But, how do you go about raising the people on the bottom? How do you get them involved?

HK: Your work shows them in a noble light but in a negative environment? Is it your goal to give their experience credibility?

MD: That's a different proposition. I am not trying to replace street credibility with street nobility. I am speaking specifically about people with nothing to lose. You cannot involve them in the good fight. You have to allow them to set their own agenda because they are able to get into places that, for lack of better term, "society people" cannot.

HK: No. I did not get that from your work. My primary question deals with how you represent the race. If a white person or any person of a different nationality was to depict the images you show, he or she would be considered racist and ignorant of Black culture.

MD: If it was a true artistic representation then what is the problem?

HK: Well then, are you an artist or a racist?

MD: I am an artist who uses race as my primary mode of communication. If in an artist's work, he or she is categorizing the work as a study of race, then yes, the artist is free to explore the underbelly as well as the glory of our race, no matter the creator's nationality. But if you are an artist who has a limited viewpoint of what constitutes Black life, whether it is high society or street life, and uses that limited viewpoint while not specifically addressing the race issue and pointing out the victims as well as the culprits, then you are simply a racist hiding behind art to push your agenda.

HK: Does that include a Black artist?

MD: Especially a Black artist!

HK: Does that extend into other spheres of life?

MD: Most definitely!

HK: What is next for you, in regards to your art?

MD: I have already started putting together the theme.

HK: I would welcome the opportunity to view it before you exhibit.

MD: I doubt I will exhibit this one. Most of the pieces you saw in the 'Return of the Angry Black Man' series were painted as gifts for friends. At the end of the exhibit, I will give each painting to the person who inspired the particular piece.

HK: You don't sell your work?

MD: Yes, but this collection was not for sell. It was for my people.

HK: I'm impressed.

MD: Thank you sister. I appreciate your admiration and respect.

I put the magazine on top of the files and locked them away in the cabinet in my bedroom closet.

Chapter 27
DOUBLE JEOPARDY

The way things unfold most years my family didn't get to see GG Celeste unless we made a trip during the holidays. We've been ensured, long ago, she's not alone or lonely, that friends come by, pretty much daily. It was not like her not to call. She'd always let us know she received the gifts, the cards and we, in return, would let her know we received what she'd sent. She was one for sending targeted gifts, nudges on what we should be focused on in the coming year. For Thanksgiving, I went home. Both my brothers visited. I came back for finals and just buried myself in the books, at the library, at the office, in my apartment. I would meet with Miranda and Barbara to partner up on studies, to have that feeling of sisterhood.

Still I felt out of sorts - the intense workload, always in a rush, always wearing sweats and faded jeans; heavy eyes. I went home Christmas and spent lots of time in my room. I limited my socializing to touching base with some high school friends who called. I reached out to Richard but he was hesitant to make plans and mentioned having a real girlfriend, for the first time in his life. I returned to school the week after New Year's, weeks before the start of the spring semester and got to work right away. I buried myself in the files Trustee Trafalgar had given, as well as the subsequent correspondence from the chair of the arts council. COSA met once a semester to determine which current students and alumni will be given an exhibit, film screening or reading. Students were presented in November, and Alumni in late April, with a notation that flexibility for an artist's schedule is allowed.

Our job was to observe by attending various workshops, reading critiques by students and professors and evaluate grades given. It was pretty much the same for alumni, except the stakes were much higher even though students had a more limited window. All in all I knew Trustee Trafalgar did not give me these files to simply monitor grades. I knew little to nothing of these students or the contemporary alumni artists, so I focused on the professors, their patterns, whom they recommended, any ties to the artists, their area of research, travel, etc...When I got to one who spent every Summer in Washington DC, his research rooted at the Smithsonian, focused on anthropology, my mind took an abrupt turn to my great-grandmother and my summers outside the capitol. At first it was a drop-off for a month, and then at twelve, I became a solo traveler – the train ride, looking at the inner breaches of the country. I would arrive and get the biggest hug, followed by hours of conversations. She would want the ins and outs of my entire school year, even if she had seen me for Christmas break. She wanted to know how items we previously discussed got resolved. Why grades were what they were, but never passing judgment if I hadn't earned an "A" in a class. Her big talks always came at the very end of our dialogue, after hours of back and forth, it would be my turn to listen; with a full belly, fatigue giving way to the sleep that had been drawing me in, GG Celeste would suggest my next moves for the coming school year.

After this first night of talk, the remainder of my summer visit would be about my next step into womanhood. One year it was about learning to hold my liquor. She gave me my first drink when I was nine during a Christmas visit. At fourteen, she looked at me and asked, "Do you like boys?" I was caught between two worlds: yes I liked boys but I wasn't planning to do anything about it. She just nodded her head and each day after lunch she would have me join her for drinks – beer, wine, and spirits of all kinds. We would drink while gardening, while playing cards, shopping at the mall by discreetly pouring drinks in Styrofoam or plastic cups. GG Celeste would laugh, making fun of people while we sat in food courts. She mentioned boys again a couple of days before my return trip. She took my hand and with a smile and nod, she said, "When it comes to boys, learn your limit."

During the summer, I had thrown up in the dahlias, and on the living room rug; had stumbled, fell against a garbage can at the mall, but not once had I forgotten she was my great-grandmother, which in turn meant I knew myself, my position.

My junior and senior year in high school, I found myself challenging my dad a bit more, his notion of behavior suitable for a girl, his daughter. I appreciated the lessons on how to shoot a gun, the way he had integrated me into the household after I decided to no longer live with my mother and older sister, and the countless lessons on sports. I think he, likely through my own miscommunication as a pubescent opting to come into his household and live with him; he did not realize I planned on being the type of daughter who wanted makeup, sexy dresses, heels, the latest hairstyles and expensive jewelry. The first year, coming into my teens, my dad took me along with whatever he and my brothers were doing. For the other things, I still traveled to my mom when she had time. But as the years passed, I grew closer to my stepmother who often acted like she wished she could have traded one of her two sons for a daughter. Even within that growing bond, there was a part of me only GG Celeste understood. I carried this doubt I could really mess things up if I didn't push myself to the very edge, to learning my limit.

The phone rang until the answering machine clicked in. I had reached my limit and was not going to simply say I had called the way I had done for over a month. "Hi GG Celeste. I really don't get this. All these years, these talks about being my own woman..."

She picked up the phone and I could hear the background, half-laughter mixed with the shock conveying the thought whether I had lost my sensibilities. I knew the house well enough to know she had stepped out of the parlor and closed the pocket doors behind her. Though a dramatic personality, GG Celeste did not do melodrama. "Have you lost your mind? What are you doing leaving me that type of message? I have people here..."

I interrupted her. "I've called you for over a month and I know you got my messages."

"Did you just talk over me?" She waited for an answer. I gave her my silence. "I just got back today and your messages didn't convey any urgency. How are you?"

"I'm fine. I miss you. We didn't see you this Christmas."

"Well, that's because of what you did." She didn't understand my silence. GG's pacing had no fixed pattern to reveal her mood. She spoke freely, quick bursts followed by long pauses in the middle of short sentences. "You freed me. I can go as I please without a security detail, to random places…"

"How did I do that?"

"What do you mean? The Ring & Scepter made people leery but even then I wasn't sure I would venture randomly because some people still harbor resentment for many decisions I made during my reign as the national queen. But this truce you brokered with the Duval family. It reunited the Society. There are so many families on both sides that are linked to them. Most people are focused on the money that is now flowing and you're going to have many pledging allegiance to you because of the money and power. But for me it's the freedom. Do you know where I have been since Thanksgiving?"

"Where?"

"In Florida, Arizona, Las Vegas. And, I get back today and I am entertaining friends who have not been able to visit me for decades." Her voice went flat—sorrowful. "A lot of that. Most of it was my fault. My reign was a different period of our history. There is so much I didn't have a chance to teach you, to tell you. Things that are not explained properly in the Historical Record. I thought I had ten, fifteen years to teach you these things. But, then you started making trouble, even before your initiation. You had me worried. You still got me worried. But it seems like you have a plan."

I interrupted. "I don't have a plan." She was quiet. "I don't know why

Queen Ames gave up the crown."

"She knows something I and no previous queen understood. There is a time to let go. I'm still learning that, and that's partly why you don't hear much from me."

"But..."

"No buts. Old ideas have to die. There are many challenges ahead."

"Do you miss me?"

"Oh, of course. But I feel rejuvenated. So much pride in what you are accomplishing."

"What about the MAX boys? You always told me to stay away from them but you seem happy they're backing me."

"Again, old ideas. A grudge I held for your great-grandfather's murder." She paused as if composing herself, to hold back tears. "Some real bad judgments on my part when it was time to rely on them, when it was time to step down for new leadership. But, that is not to say you have to be out there giving them MAX boys all of what they want."

"What is it that the MAX boys want?"

Her laughter pulled me from across the miles into her living room. "Let me sit down and simply tell you. MAX boys are called that because they always want the maximum, the most out of any situation and the only way to get that is through war."

"War?"

"Yes, war and if you don't give them the war they want, they consider you their enemy."

We both stopped talking, as if we were contemplating whether that was an old idea.

My great-grandmother was a teacher, a warrior who lived through some of the roughest times in American history, born at the onset on the twentieth century, thirty-seven years after Emancipation. She wore the battle scars of ancestors, not given a proper accounting, who had been stricken off history's page. The Society existed in small numbers the years before she joined. She quickly rose through the ranks. After WWII, she was elected to lead SUM as its national queen. At the end of 1972, she was forced to step down and has since been under protection. As a child I didn't understand her movements, her inability to travel freely, but Queen Ames knew she did not want such a fate so she abdicated her throne.

No one my age, this young had ever run the Society. The experience and connections needed. The complex alignment of seven generations of families, including those who had splintered away but still knew enough of the Society's secrets and methods that they kept their mouths shut. There was so much infighting that caused new alliances to form, groups to splinter, direct family members to turn on each other.

The historical record was contained in a series of publications, initially pamphlets followed by newspapers and journals. Of most importance were announcements of births, marriages and deaths. Knowing who was in the Society and wrote for which publication allowed members to follow current news events – local, national and international – and learn of the going-ons of the Society, its national stances, as well as where families stood on issues. I knew my own family's history, as well as the notices filed indicating the start my own legacy, apart from what had existed since the 1920s when my great-grandparents joined.

Knowing there was too much to learn and not enough time, I focused on the prominent journals and digests, where the top level issues were aggregated. These journals were in circulation at nearly all major branches of public libraries and college and university libraries. At TGI's library they were available for loan to upperclassmen and graduates students who were majoring in certain fields, and for use by lowerclassmen and others only at the library. I bore into the publications, mapping out decades, actually more than a century, to be exact one-hundred and twenty-eight years of history that started with just seven families. And, in this the start of its seventh generation, the Society now had one twenty-one families. Most families only traced back to the post-war era, after 1945. But, the Vietnam War era, particularly the years of 1963 to 1968, the generation of my birth, the one preceding my initiation, this one clearly showed the range of ideas and division within the Society. The Society had reached a certain stature in the public, it started to focus on enemies within, and it really was not prepared.

On February 1, I returned the final journals and digests to the library. The semester started the previous week and it was time to finalize the steps for the chapter's first meeting, clearly noting on the historical record the meeting's scope was only for campus members and the two new initiates. As expected, even though matriculating students had garnered their membership from other colleges, they all sent petitions for affiliate chapter membership along with their dues.

When the time came, I did not invite them to this first meeting. I replied their bids would be discussed at the meeting, where we would also decide whether campus meetings would form the basis of national policy, allowing chapter affiliates and other visitors to serve as proxy for theirs and other families.

We met at the home GG Celeste purchased in the 1920s and allowed SUM to use. The four attendees thought they were coming to a courtship session because I scheduled this as the lone meeting of semester.

From this point out, protocol would hold and the approach would be formal and unless specifically itemized, all matters would be logged in the historical record.

The first challenge came from Lauren Hathaway. "In Matters of Membership, the historical record notes that all first generation members must follow the standard membership sequence of court, pledge period, ceremony and membership; and Semline College on January 15, 1987 under your leadership and rule extended that provision as standard for all members including legacies."

I had gone through all the "Matters" and replied, "Statement accepted but not as challenged. Please note in 1917, Irene Cooke gave birth to a child, a daughter who would be raised outside of the Society, mainly as a result of the split between a PMB and FLT family. The FLT arm though now defunct in the Society is still acknowledged in Matters of Legacy. This confers fourth generation status to Lauren Hathaway. The second part of the Statement notes that there is no formalized sequence or process as to when membership can be offered to a person whose petition has been approved; therefore membership for Lauren Hathaway and Diane Henderson has been finalized, with recommended sequence for membership being Membership, Pledge Period, Ceremony and Courtship. Please note acceptance of the Statement by a vote of Aye, and dissent by a vote of Naye."

All four stared at me, as if I had lost my mind, but also in pure adulation. I could see Lauren's ambition level rise by the calculating smile on her face. She knew what entering as a fourth generation member would mean.

On paper Lauren and Diane were thorough, straight 'A' students since high school. With the strong push of affiliate members following my ascension to national queen, I needed the minimum membership level of five for campus voting and autonomy. In a perfect world the two of them plus Miranda and Barbara would always vote the same once I put a Statement to vote. This would have all Matters leaving this campus with the backing of five families, which in turn meant nationally five families backed this stance. This would cause a wave, a ripple effect to carry my platform forward since most families were linked by marriage.

Unfortunately ours was not a perfect world, not much different than the world in which my GG entered the Society in 1921. They read through the agenda and I studied their body language, already anticipating when each person's eyes reached the Matter that would bring the next challenge. The raised eyebrows followed by the disbelieving stare into my eyes came from the two I thought would need less convincing. Lauren waited for Barbara to speak but no words came out, as if Barbara did not want her name in the historical record as putting forth a challenge. Lauren waited and I waited for them to simply check the box so we could continue with the agenda. My goal was to have full acceptance of my platform. I crossed my arms and leaned back into my chair. Miranda and Diane did the same and the three of us chuckled.

"Well?" I asked.

Lauren shifted in her seat, an effort to suppress a twinge, as if a spring had pushed through the cushion. It took a lot for her to maintain her composure, a twist near her mouth to sound diplomatic. "In Matters of Matrimony, you state a new provision wherein, I quote: Legacy Status into SUM can be conferred to first generation petitioners where either parent is a duly noted member of any of the four arms of the Society; end quote. Please note this goes entirely against the division set forth in the founding of the organization, what differentiates the two sides."

This was my chance to show the four of them an explanation, a provision to sway any dissenting vote. "Challenge accepted. Please put the Matter to a vote."

"No." Lauren applied a more forceful tone and quickly lowered her voice. "Judging by our body language, it is clear the vote is split and your vote will come into play as the deciding vote. As such, I request that the historical record show the origins for such a thought. It has been previously noted, in the historical record, the Duval family supported your ascension to campus queen, after-the-fact, but the support was simultaneous to your ascension as national queen."

She stopped but I wanted her to keep going. She waited so I noted. "Rumors and innuendos are not listed in the historical record. Dates of all events you mentioned are already listed in the historical record. Do you have a Matter of Fact you would like added to the historical record?"

"I do so in the form of a question to which your answer will be the fact."

OK, this chick was beginning to be a headache. "No. Just as you have your vote, I have my moves to make. But, in the interest of sisterhood, what I am advancing in Matters of Matrimony has long been my position." I motioned toward Barbara and her. "The three of us come from family units that were non-traditional."

Lauren interrupted me again. "Rules of Engagement, Section 5-120: Votes on Society Matters should never rely solely on personal testimony or anecdotal evidence. Voters should always keep in mind the long-term ramifications on the Society's membership and more importantly the Society's ability to function."

"Are you changing your vote?" I asked her.

She looked to Diane and Miranda. "Have either of you looked at the next item on the agenda?"

"Excuse me, Ms. Hathaway, you are out of line. There is a discussion and vote on the table that has not been quantified. Are you changing your vote?"

I cast the deciding vote on a Matter I now knew would die on pretty much all campuses and family level. What surprised and hurt me was the realization I would not have the full support of my campus court on policy matters that could transform the Society into the full democracy it needed to be in order to advance the next generation.

The next item dealt with Matters of Inheritance. I expected at least one dissenting vote but was curious as to how it would play out, and whether in the future there would be any grudges or blowback. Surprisingly, Diane was the first to check the box to proceed, but there was Lauren who said to her, "I'm sorry but you're not going to challenge this. I mean have you not read the historical record, Rules of Engagement, Court Platforms and what responsibilities a member has to the Society?"

The unexpected outburst from Lauren, directed at Diane, caused us – Miranda, Barbara and me – to glance at each other. We had observed them and done our research, and found them to have no evidence of conflict. So this surprised us. We all looked at Diane and she just smiled. "Oh I see, just because I'm pretty…"

Barbara spoke up, "Who said you were pretty?

We all laughed including Diane.

Miranda also asked, "Yeah, who said you were pretty? We want names because you know how rumors get started."

After we all got our laughs in, Diane said, "In Matters of Voting, a member need not state her defense of an item on the agenda. Rules of

Engagement, Section 6-75."

Lauren took another turn. "In Matters of Policy when an item is entered which can negatively impact a new member's family, such person can be required to state why she supports the item."

Diane looked at me. "Are you requiring?"

The two of them were giving me a headache. I now had two new members who obviously had spent considerable time in learning the Society's parliamentary procedures. If I sided with Diane, which technically was the correct move, I would likely lose Lauren's support throughout court hearings and possibly throughout her membership.

"Yes."

The word popped Diane back, away from the self-righteous perch she had taken. She straightened up in her seat, to note everyone's shock, including Lauren's. "Can I go off the record?"

"No..." I cut Lauren a stern look. She immediately backtracked. "I'm sorry Queen Kendall. As noted..."

I interrupted her. "Ms. Hathaway, though I'm sure you can find a notation to support your stance, I will likely find one that counters yours. So, let's proceed by letting Ms. Henderson go off the record."

Diane wrung her hands. Even though her position, her moves would not be on the record, she was exposing herself, her strategy to four families with whom hers had no alliance. "I vote in support of the queen on all matters because we are on the verge of war, and she needs all other campus families and the membership in general to know she has our backing."

"War? We're going to war?" asked Barbara. I wondered whether her voice would have sounded so high if we were on the record.

"Yes, what war?" asked Lauren.

"War for what?" asked Miranda.

Diane looked at me like she was totally confused. "Well, the floor is yours, Ms. Henderson."

"Really? Really? We have a seventh generation MAX boy attending TGI. We have a seventh generation MAX boy attending Semline. We have a fourth generation SBD legacy transferring his allegiance to the Pride side as soon as the next pledge class starts. We also have Ken, a former SBD king whose family heritage was MAX until his transfer to SBD. You three know Ken right? Intimately, right?"

Lauren raised her hands. "I have questions. Lots of them."

"Go ahead!"

"None of what you just stated is on the historical record. I know of Timothy E. Duval but not personally. Who are the others and what are their stories?"

I stepped in. "In short, when protocol held during the courtship period of my pledge class, I formed an alliance, an allegiance with Ken. Something went terribly wrong toward the end of our pledge period and to save our sisterly bond, he had to break the connection to me. He was courted to Miranda, but she did not want anything to do with him."

"Not true!" Barbara said. "He was in love with me from day one. The glances, the smiles, etc…it was inevitable."

Diane and Lauren looked at each other and then us. "Y'all are scandalous. The Conscious Daughters are scandalous."

We all laughed. "No, we've learned not to let a man come between us."

We, all five, groaned in in agreement.

Diane answered the second part of Lauren's question. "To continue: Timothy E. Duval simply known as Ted. Theodore Perkins known as Monk, and Girard XYZ at Barrington cannot simply be up here by accident. I don't know the reason but..."

Lauren laughed. "Monk and Girard? Girl, please! State your reason for siding with the queen on Matters of Inheritance. Don't hide behind the MAX boys for cover."

"What?"

Lauren ignored Diane. "Can we go back on the record? On Matters of Inheritance, can we call for a vote, Queen Kendall?"

I was stumped because this was one vote even if I now won with all four of their votes, it would technically be a loss. "Please let the records show that I have withdrawn my petition that states: On Matters of Inheritance, in events where broken trust exists, with fault not a factor, SUM women are not entitled to all legacy amounts if certainty is proven by paternity records not existing within the union. This policy breaks with all previous rulings on the Matter and enters a new challenge to current policy."

"Thank you Queen Kendall." I detected a smirk in Lauren's voice. "Final item on the agenda, in Matters of War..."

I interrupted her. "Let me guess. You have a challenge."

"No, totally not! I only oppose the queen when she takes policy positions that would allow members of the Society to operate at their weakest level."

They expected me to take offense or counter her statement. I just smiled since I already had her vote in Matters of War. "If there are no challenges, all please check the box so we can adjourn the meeting."

Barbara moved her pen over the paper but the tip did not touch. She wanted Miranda or Diane to make a challenge. They did not say anything but neither had checked the box. "I am voting The Old Guard, and require a vote on the matter."

I gave Lauren the opportunity to tell Barbara this was not the manner in which a vote is taken.

No one said anything. We waited about fifteen seconds and realizing the stalemate, Barbara said, "Rules of Engagement, Section 4-17 states that the Queen's army functions as a protectorate of, as well as a point of attack, for SUM. In Matters of War, you have added an addendum: the Queen's army owes no loyalty to the Society. I need a point of clarification: Does the addendum not supersede the initial provision?"

"Do you need clarification for your vote or for your conscience?"

"My vote remains the same but having just learned that Girard XYZ will not be joining the Society as SBD, I feel..."

I stopped her. "Ms. Wilson, we are still on the record."

"I understand that Queen Kendall and as such, there are points on the historical record where redacted names eventually will be revealed and point to a conspiracy that does not exist against the former campus King and former campus Queen." Barbara was shaking. I knew her enough to know she was acting, attacking.

"That has always been the case for the historical record, Ms. Wilson, and that is why as members of the Society, we know enough to keep our mouths shut."

Miranda looked at Barbara and at me. As tears welled in her eyes, to rectify the stalemate, she said, "In Matters of War, SUM women are required to back the queen in Matters of War. Please put to a vote."

I told Lauren, "Let the historical record show that your previous statement backing the queen has been retracted and you can vote as you please. Please note acceptance of the Statement in regards to In Matters of War by a vote of Aye, and dissent by a vote of Naye."

Miranda and Barbara voted Naye.

Lauren and Diane voted Aye.

I voted Naye.

I summarized the meeting:

- *In Matters of Membership: sequence can be altered;*
- *In Matters of Legacy: SUM acceptance of the FLT arm though it is defunct;*
- *In Matters of Matrimony: Strength now recognizes sons from the Pride side for membership;*
- *In Matters of Inheritance: withdrawn; children born outside of matrimony still not recognized*
- *In Matters of War: the queen's army owes no loyalty to the Society and SUM women are not required to back the queen.*

I barely had the words, "This meeting is adjourned" out of my mouth when Miranda stormed out of the house. I cut Barbara a look to say, you did that shit on purpose. Lauren and Diane stole a quick glance at each other.

That night I knew right after the meeting Lauren would pour into the historical record, make phone calls to affiliates to build bridges, and hit the rumor mill. From there, she will learn of a name who could set the historical record straight.

As for me, I had trouble brewing on both sides of the Society, and on both levels: campus and national.

Chapter 28
HEARTACHE

After previous gatherings and the informal meetings we would hang out at the house. Diane and Lauren would be responsible for the food and drinks, as well as the entertainment, which would be mainly them performing skits for us. It was an infinite loop. We laughed at their performances more out of the spirits catching up with us. They were not funny. They were way too analytical to simply let go and have fun with it. Part of that stemmed from our inability to find an appropriate moniker for them. We focused on successful female entertainment duos and that proved harder than we imagined. Female duos were hard to find, even in SUM. SUM had had a lot of pledge classes with three members, and quite a few solos. Solos existed because a legacy would enroll at a school with no SUM history on the campus and petition for a charter. As long as she was able to add four more members by her senior year, the charter was granted. TGI's charter has been in existence since the nineteen-twenties. Legacies came to school in the region because of the chapter's history. Other women with no knowledge of the Society enrolled at Barrington as a fallback school due to low admission standards and rolling admission. Once they learned of the Society and what it took to enter, they worked hard academically, socially and morally.

I still could not place why Diane ended up at Barrington. For Lauren, it was a financial decision and her knowing she could make SUM rather quickly. On paper, the assumption would be the two of them would not get along. Stark differences separated them physically, in family structure, aspirations and taste – actually preferences. They were not a total contrast of one another, the situation that normally caused a breaking point and led the Society to have many solos and very few duos. Duos that got along rattled chapters because if they took extreme positions, it was hard to find common ground and sides taken led to acrimony, thus splintering entire chapters.

When it came to three women bonded together, with enough flexibility and level-headedness, they formed a circle when they were at their best and a right triangle at their worst. Miranda opened the house's door, stepping right into the living room. Her eyes, red with anger, the aftermath of a storm of sobs; readied for a confrontation. I stood. "Where is everyone?" Her voice cracked, "How could you do this to me?"

I was remorseful. "I already apologized, made amends. What more do you want?"

"You did for the outcome but you never told me why, that you were in on it. All this time I thought those events unfolded naturally. I listened to all the rumors and still did not make the connection between the fire, what happened with Devon, and Girard threatening the King's life."

"Well that's the point! It does not connect to me. I went into the cafeteria. Ken knows that. He knows I wasn't the one talking alone with Girard."

"But I am the one who left from the cafeteria before all this unfolded. I am the one who lost my crown after Girard threatened to kill Ken. I'm the one Ken came to, drunk out of his mind after he left your apartment."

"What? You?"

"Yes. My absence makes me a suspect." I laughed, falling down on the sofa, holding my stomach, unable to keep it all in. "What's so funny?"

I said, "That fool is in denial. I guess love does make you stupid." Miranda clearly did not get it so I continued, "Ken came to my apartment, thinking I put a hit out on him. So, instead of going to the next obvious person, he went to you."

"What? Are you serious? Barbara?" She stopped talking and sat next to me. She grabbed the drink out of my hand. She finished it with one gulp.

"Love is blind after all."

"So, you took the blame?"

"No. I know enough to keep my mouth shut."

We both said, so true.

I added, "Fuck around and implicate the wrong person."

I got up and fixed us drinks and sat back down. She asked, "Are you OK, though?"

"I'm fine, just been buried in the historical record, paperwork."

"Thank you for taking the crown away from me." We both laughed. "Why did you want to run this entire organization?"

"I didn't, at least not yet, but somebody wanted me to."

"Had I read the entire history, the regulations, protocols, the dot dot dot." We laughed again. The drinks already had us giggling silly. Miranda continued, "After coronation, I read much more of the historical record. From having read and learned the basic requirements, it became easy to want to join the Society for just the pageantry and money. But parts of the historical record scared me something awful. Do you think Barbara has read enough of it?"

"Yes, she started reading it when she got out of the hospital."

"It still doesn't explain why she put a hit out on Ken."

I looked at Miranda, making sure she knew this conversation, especially the next part, did not leave this room. "Lena. The white girl who disappeared. Her old roommate."

"Is she dead?" I did not answer. "Barbara and her were that tight?"

"Yes. They had become best of friends. It's like she lost a part of herself when that girl died."

"But is she really dead?"

I raised my voice. "The historical record says she's dead. And, one of the biggest mistakes you can make in this Society is to go looking for dead people, or fighting wars to avenge their deaths."

"But Barbara! They killed her brother. Is her brother dead?"

"Oh my god, what the fuck is wrong with you? We're freedom fighters, not fucking Ghostbusters!"

"They killed her brother."

"There is no "they". It is US. We are SPADES: the Society to Protect Africans from Doers of Evil and Sin."

"We are also the Society to Protect Africans Doing Evil and Sin."

"No, that's the MAX boys."

"On our behalf to protect US, They, or whoever, whatever the fuck this Society is."

"Well, why did you vote against me in Matters of War?"

"It would have passed if you had not voted against yourself."

"And, what, go to war without you two, essentially against you two?"

It finally dawned on Miranda the strength of my loyalty to her and Barbara. "What about Double Jeopardy: Pepsi & Shirley?"

I laughed. "They like the Double Jeopardy part, but not the heartache part."

"That's going to be their name whether they like it or not." We got up to fix ourselves a plate from the food Lauren and Diane brought. While preparing our food, we revisited their rendition of, Pepsi & Shirley's hit, "Heartache."

> *Life is so hard*
> *needlessly*
> *no fairy tales*
>
> *Tell me am I history?*
> *A broken heart if you say good-bye.*
> *I never knew you could leave this way*

We started eating and Miranda asked, "If Barbara thinks Ken had something to do with Lena's disappearance and her brother's death, why is she with him?"

I was beside myself she asked that question but did my best not to yell at her. She knew the answer but still I said it out loud. "The king gets no vote unless there's a tie."

We drank some more, verbally veering off the topic but I could sense the processing going through her mind. We had not spent the night at the house since our days as pledges. The front door opened into the living room and was the first floor's socializing point. Three sofas and an entertainment center with a television, stereo and books formed a square. To the right, a pass-through, led to a den, two bedrooms, a full bathroom and two staircases. Left of the living room was the dining area, sectioned off with a table and six chairs, a cabinet with dishes, glasses and silverware and stocked with liquor. Adjacent the dining area was the kitchen closed off by the wall behind the entertainment system and separating the den.

We slept on the two sofas closest to the dining section. Sleep had come late in the night after hours of talk. We awoke and washed our faces and rinsed with the mouthwash and toothpaste in the medicine cabinet. Most years two or more SUM women lived in the house. When the school year started, since the three of us, The Conscious Daughters, were the only full members at TGI and opted not to, the house was empty.

We enjoyed spending time alone without the pressure of books or the affairs of SUM being the center of our conversation. We sat at the dining table, across each other but not at the head of the table. My back was closest to the window, to the wall. Miranda revisited what I hoped was a dead issue. "Can I ask you a question?" I nodded, knowing truth would only do. "Who is Girard XYZ?"

"You don't know him? Do you remember rowdy Nicole from our Freshman class who got kicked out after Sophomore year? He's her boyfriend."

"Who was with him that day on the quad, at the fire?" I didn't say anything because she should know this since Ken told her about Girard months ago. "I don't want to guess. I want you to tell me because there's a rumor going around."

I got up from the table and went to my book bag and handed her the

FIRST IMPRESSIONS magazine with the interview of Manny Davenport. She studied the cover for about thirty seconds and turned to the pages with the interview and his artwork. "Is it true you put a hit out on him?" I did not answer because that was not the current rumor going around. That rumor was the past. "If true, you and Barbara gotta teach me this spell that allows men to let you in their beds after you try to get them killed."

She wanted me to laugh and I needed her to focus. "What is the rumor?"

"The person with Girard is not represented in any of the artwork."

"Exactly! Not in the historical record past or future."

She asked, "Who set his protection?"

"I didn't realize he had it before I met him. I'm more interested in who is trying to remove it."

She calmly got up from the table and put her dish in the sink and made no effort to wash it, like this wasn't her house. "I'm leaving here in a few minutes and once I walk out that door, I am waging war on Girard XYZ. If the person who's his right hand man means anything to you…"

I stopped her by going to her and softly grabbing her hands. "Girl, you need to stop. There is something major going on. Do you know anything about this publication I just showed you?" She shook her head, no. "These motherfuckers declared war on the very top levels of the power structure we've been fighting since 1860 and didn't hide their identity. They're not the motherfuckers you want to go to war against because of some minor campus scandal."

"My name is associated with that Semline dorm scandal. Barbara's name is associated with that motel room scandal."

"Yes, and my fucking name is on the record as backing this war."

"Well, you put it out there!"

"No I didn't. One or more of the MAX boys and, or Ken did."

"My name, Hope! My name! It's associated with adultery - behind the king's back, in a dorm room, on some back and forth sexcapade with Devon and some no-name chick." She started sobbing. "And to top it off, the implication is I tried to kill the king over that mess."

I held her tightly and cried with her. "His name is Ernest LeGagneur. The star basketball player for Barrington."

"The rumor is about him. If it's true then Ernest's protection will get removed. From there, I'm gunning for Girard."

"What is the rumor?"

"Call an emergency session! It's pretty bad."

<0>

"I call this emergency session because there is a rumor floating around that Barrington's star basketball player tried to rape a fellow Barrington student by the name of Lucille Patterson. If true, this is a matter we, as SUM women, must account for and force the school's administration to take action against him, starting with him losing his scholarship."

Lauren interrupted. "No one believes that rumor. It's such a minor ripple I'm not sure why it is even being brought to us."

"Minor ripples become big waves especially when we are dealing with an athlete who has a chance to become a SBD member."

She scoffed. "He's not. If he does join the Society, it will be as a MAX boy. Plus, I don't think he will join."

I turned to Diane. "Do you know Ernest?"

"Yes, we're friends. He didn't do this."

"So you heard the rumor and as his friend, did you ask him about it?"

"God, no! That would be insulting."

"What about you Lauren?"

"No! I know that girl and she's a cornball."

"Is it your position to blame the victim?"

Lauren shot me a hard look like she wanted to smack me. "There is no victim because there is nothing to the rumor. I don't know how it started."

"So you asked about it?"

"I asked who told me."

"And, who was that?"

Her face asked the question before her mouth. "Are you serious?"

"Yes, we can go off the record..."

Miranda jumped in. "Man, just order Pepsi & Shirley to find out..."

Lauren and Diane stood up as if ready for a physical confrontation. Miranda stood. I stood up. Barbara remained seated and asked, "Are y'all serious? We're back to fighting over a man?"

"I'm not fighting over Ernest." Lauren sat down. Miranda sat down. "I need to know what happened." I sat down.

Diane sat down. "I don't care what happened."

"So you're fine with a potential member of this Society forcing his way on women?"

"No, of course not. But the question I'm asking is why is some minor league chick who doesn't put out going out on a date with a pro prospect who is heading to a life worth at least forty million dollars?"

Diane's question silenced the room for more than a brief moment until Lauren asked, "Can we go on the record?"

"Why?"

"I will take the mission with utmost objectivity and in return you authorize separate monarchies at Barrington and Semline."

"Heartache..." Miranda chimed in with some more lyrics...

> *And now you're giving me a heartache -*
> *Fool's game - It's a shame shame -*
> *It's a heartache and I feel the pain.*

I turned to Diane. "Is this what you want?"

"I don't care. LOOK this whole thing, with you making us members on paper only, putting out legislation that will pass at so few other collegiate chapters, let alone on the national family level; it is getting out of hand. We need to do a pledge program to become official, even if it is during summer session."

"Yes, let's take it to the basement," added Lauren.

I folded my arms, leaned back into my chair and looked at the two of them. Miranda and Barbara looked at them, looked at me, and leaned back into their chairs. The three of us said it in unison. "Let's go on the record. Ms. Hathaway, could you restate your proposal?"

"Rules of Engagement, In Matters of Alignment: I, Ms. Lauren Hathaway, propose a realignment of the TGI Charter to make a slight distinction so that Semline College, and Barrington Graphics and Art Institute are able to host Matters of Ceremony."

"Could you clarify whether you would like to make a slight or a clear distinction, being that the clear distinction would provide each of the sub-chartering schools the potential to conduct all matters and not just a ceremonial undertaking?"

"I am only seeking a slight distinction."

She either had backed off her initial charge or I had taken more offense than merited. "Ms. Henderson, do you support such a proposal? If so, in what manner, clear or slight?"

"Any which suits Ms. Hathaway!"

"In the Matter tabled, please state your votes." All four voted Aye. "Meeting adjourned."

We went off the record and I made to leave the room. Diane spoke up, "Queen Kendall, when do we go to the basement?"

"No time soon!" I looked around the room. "I am so disappointed and disgusted in all of you. There's a war on the horizon. I'm doing everything I can to cover your backs, and all I keep hearing are your individual agendas."

"Can I speak freely?"

I was exasperated with the constant chatter. "Yes, Diane, what is it?"

"Fuck the MAX boys!" The others murmured their agreement. "Can we have a vote on that?"

"How about this? Get to know them. Talk to them, and stop believing the hype that they're these boogeymen."

Lauren looked at Barbara and asked, "Is she still in love with Manny Davenport?"

They all laughed because she was genuine in her asking.

I too laughed. "You need to stop asking silly questions and go find out about that rumor."

Chapter 29
RUMORS

When I got to Barrington, there was a lot of hoopla. I purposely did not visit the school or sign a letter of intent until the deadline to avoid the write-ups in the school newspaper, and all other media crush. Once I got to the campus, I dealt with it. In all my interviews, I continually repeated I selected Barrington, not for Basketball but its Fine Arts department. No one really listened, except the coach. Though I was on a full basketball scholarship and he recognized me as the team's top player by building the system around me, he never coddled me. Barrington was only a Division I school because of the neighboring colleges and the conference requirements. The school was a mid-sized public college with limited resources, and neighbored two very wealthy private universities, TGI and Semline College.

Between classes and basketball, I had very little time for anything else, until one day in early October. A schedule conflict caused us to share the gym with the women's volleyball team. Guys being guys, our focus was on their uniform, the little form-fitting shorts. They had a game later that day so I came back, not for the game, but her.

Lucille Patterson. She had heard about me and, in her mind, likely had a picture that was pretty much correct. I had groupies on a rotation, but even that I limited to just four women. I could have had a fifth but she told me she had a plan so she couldn't get caught up in any scandals.

Our season was grueling, especially when I realized why the team had a bunch of scrubs. The coach grinded players to the point veterans quit the team or transferred to another school by the end of their sophomore year. I was killing players on the floor, at practice and real games. Guys with hoop dreams started taking advantage of the free education they were getting 'cause they started realizing what NBA level really was. My stat lines made me conference MVP and Freshman of the Year. The team made the NCAA national tournament as fodder for a team seeded number one in its region. When we returned to campus, though I celebrated and partied with the campus as they all hailed a great season, later that night, I cried alone in my room.

Around two in the morning, I made a power move and telephoned and asked Lucille for a date. This chick had minor league game but she was great at it. She pretended to not know who I was. When I reminded her she had been on the quad with the other students celebrating, she said that was for school spirit.

"Whose spirit do you think that was?"

"God's!" She waited for me to say something but I was speechless. "And, you're calling me this late for...?"

Her pause meant there were many options. For me there were only two: minor or major. I chose major league game. "I am calling because I need love. And I think you're the one!"

She hung up on me. I didn't call back because I could not tell why she had hung up. The next day I saw her as I entered the freshman cafeteria. I waved and she returned my greeting. Then all her friends started laughing. She joined in. After I got my food, she called me, using a come hither motion, to come sit with her and her friends. I acted like I hadn't seen her summoning me like she was some queen on a throne. I went and sat with one of the chicks on my rotation and could feel Lucille staring daggers into my back. It was now a waiting game as to who would finish eating first and leave the room.

Too long. Thirty minutes passed. I finished eating so I left.

A few weeks passed and it was clear we were avoiding each other. The semester would soon end and I would not see her until after summer, unless

I made a move. Nothing major just waited for her near the cafeteria and asked her to a movie. This girl was a beauty and so was her answer. "I hear so many positive things about you, brother. Let's not ruin it by getting too close to each other."

"How will getting to know me ruin your impression of me?"

"You are looking for something, but it is the wrong thing. Brother Ernest, you need Jesus."

One thing I do not do is take the Lord's name in vain. I was not sure what her story or game was but at this point, I really was not interested; better yet, not that interested. I mean I still thought she had the purest face I'd ever laid eyes on. I got silly and proper on her, a game I call Cooperative Calvin. "You know something Sister Lucille. You are so correct. Let's not ruin our impression of each other."

As I made to walk away, she said, "You know where I live. Pick me up at eight. Do not be late!"

Believe it or not, I was giddy. I could not keep it to myself. Girard was the only one who knew how much I really liked her. Back when I first saw Lucille, he tried to tell his girlfriend, who was part of Lucille's crew, to talk me up and that did not work. But that night, he told me to cancel going to the movies and catch her next year. To me, dude was bugging. There was no way I would cancel a date with my dream girl.

The date was nothing special. Normal first date banter. Politeness hiding lust. I was on my best behavior, even when she thought I wasn't. All I wanted was a kiss good night. We had clicked. We were going up the staircase that led to her dorm room. I knew how dorm politics worked in her particular suite. There was always someone home, and most likely they were all sitting in the living room portion. I was not going to blow the chance. At least I had to ask, by making a move. Nothing aggressive. Only slowed her step by gently tugging on her left hand as she reached the floor's landing. I stepped toward her, just one step, my feet not even firmly planted. She stepped back against the wall. It was like her body went cold. Her words threw me for a major loop, "Back away from me or I will scream. And, I will press charges!"

I was embarrassed for her and me. She slid sideways, using the space I made for her. The stairwell door leading to the hallway closed behind her. I figured this door to Lucille that had opened was temporarily closed. That this sort of thing would stay between us, and we would soon talk about it, clear any misunderstanding she may have had. Deep down, I hoped what happened could become the type of funny story we would tell our grandkids.

The very next day, Lucille's version of the staircase incident was campus gossip, hanging on the grapevine like rotting fruit. I heard of it, as I headed to brunch after coming from playing pickup games in the gym. The word rape was mentioned, as in she thought I was going to. Though I never believed that is how she originally told the story to her friends. Even with her minor league game, she was skilled enough to know messages get filtered and repackaged. That she no longer controlled the message once it left her mouth. I didn't see her for two days and was truly avoiding her. She idled not too far from the gym's entrance. I was walking out with some teammates. We were coming from our last team meeting for the year and I was in a group of men who had my back and wanted to retaliate, in the worst way. I stopped any ideas cold with a basic command, "Leave that girl alone!"

As if very little had changed, she called my name. I ignored her. She called again. I told my teammates to wait for me. I needed witnesses. I walked over and her eyes showed a sorrow, the mortified look of a child who had broken a pricy vase. "Ernest, I am sorry. None of what you are hearing is true. I simply said you went for a kiss while we were in the staircase and I panicked."

I stared into her eyes, at the solid stance amidst the uneasiness of not knowing my thoughts. "You obviously got enemies. I hope you can save yourself."

"Jesus will save me!"

I smiled and nodded. "Have a great summer!"

"You too."

"Call me if you ever need me!"

"I will."

We said bye and walked away. My teammates asked what that was about. "Nothing."

<0>

Lauren left the write-up in a sealed envelope in my office's mailbox. All I needed was a phone call of two sentences. She could have even written a couple of paragraphs but to type it and not sign the paper? Still, she signed the sealed envelope so she could get the credit to make official the Matters of Alignment agreement?

Lauren drove an hour from Barrington and did not come to my apartment or wait to see me on campus for a simple hello. I sensed rumors were not her thing but obviously there was a component of this she left out.

I needed this rumor squashed but could not have my name attached to its counterattack.

It was time for a much needed ally down an avenue I'd been hesitant to stroll.

Nicole picked up on the second ring. Her voice sounded rushed from the stress of the coming finals week. "Hi, who's this?"

"It's me, Hope."

"HEY!" The switch to sheer delight warmed me and loosened my apprehensions. "What's going on! How come I haven't heard from you?"

"I've been swamped with work. You could have always called me."

"I wanted to but Girard said not to because any phone call I made, even to just say hi, could open up a whole lotta mess."

"Why is that?"

She paused. "I know I can trust you but you're one of the few names out here that as soon as it is mentioned, Girard gives me that hard look. My other friends have picked up on it."

"Why would my name come up among your friends?"

"Come on this is college! There's this pecking order. I knew you to be up there since our freshman year, but now, it's like no one can reach you. People are scared to talk about you, talk to you."

"OK, so what is the rumor?"

"Well, the main one is that you be having guys come over, get on their knees, take care of you and leave, with no…you know, no reciprocity."

I let out a hysterical laugh. She joined me, mirroring my laugh, perhaps to lower my guard. I laughed some more. "It's nothing like that, but let them go on with their rumors." I paused to get the correct pacing for the segue. "Speaking of rumors. There's one out about one of your friends, Lucille Patterson."

"That's not about her. It's about Ernest. So, you're calling to help him?"

"How so?"

"You're going to act like I don't know." I didn't say a word because that was just a ploy for me to give her more information than she already knew. "I am at Girard's a lot. In their suite, the guys are always there drinking, shooting dice…"

"Shooting dice? On a college campus?"

"Yes, gambling is how they resolve conflicts. Instead of fighting or letting it get out of hand to weapons, like hurting each other for real, with guns and shit, they play cards, throw darts, shoot dice. Whenever they have a heated debate, they shoot for it. They have a major beef, they shoot for it."

"What do they shoot for?"

She got quiet, as if confirming she could trust me. "Sneakers. Silence. Money. Women."

"Women?"

"Yes, as in if I win I can fuck your girl." She waited for me to speak but my blood was boiling. "It's more like you have X number of tries to fuck the loser's woman. But I have heard it go as far as the loser having to convince his woman."

I sat down wanting to brace myself. "Is that why Ernest went after Lucille?"

"No, not her. When he first saw Lucille, Girard told him she was in my crew. He didn't know I knew her 'cause he's always busy with basketball. Girard came to me, talking about how Ernest's in love…"

"Maybe he is!"

"Fuck he know about love, being in love!" She paused. I didn't say anything. "That fool up here slinging dick like there's no tomorrow."

"So?"

"I know what you're thinking. The rumors you hear about Girard? Well, he asks me for permission like he did when he wanted to get with you." She meant for it to sound like that. I stayed quiet. "They had a contest last semester. A bunch of them. Their crew and others. Ernest put up what they're calling major numbers.—twenty-five."

"Twenty-five what?"

"Twenty-five different women. They count points for the four bases, hitting for the cycle…"

"The cycle?"

"Girl, you don't want to know."

"Girard told you all this?"

"No, of course not! I fake like I'm asleep when they're in the suite. Sometimes I leave a tape recorder running when I leave the room."

"What? You can get killed doing shit like that." I paused for her to say something. "What do they say about me?"

"They never ever say anything about you."

"Yes, they do. You just don't know the code they're using." I can hear her gulp, her choking back on her gullibility. "Twenty-five women. The cycle, all that stuff stands for something else."

"Even if it does, Ernest is out here putting up major numbers, at this school, on the road, and I ain't squashing no rumors to help him and his basketball career."

"Then do it for your girl, Lucille. This is coming full speed at her."

"So! She's not my ace."

She left it hanging there and this time I had to ask, with the implication being real clear I have to cover her best friend. "Your ace?"

"They shot for her and lost her."

"Why do you say they when you clearly know who it is?" Nicole didn't say anything. "Was this before or after Lucille?"

"Before. No one has shot for Lucille."

"What is your ace's name?"

"Smiley."

"OK. Now I need you to do me a favor. Stop eavesdropping!"

"If I hadn't, you wouldn't know all of this."

"I didn't need to know any of this. Now I might have to go to war over something that has nothing to do with me."

"Let me know and I'm there."

"No you can't help but like I said freshman year, you would be great as one of us."

"One of y'all?" She lost all composure as if I triggered a memory and brought her to a place she'd fought to escape. "All my life I've been trying to get away from women like y'all - spreading rumors…"

I was quiet, knowing the pain, having witnessed other girls, but Nicole had bottled her words. "I'm sorry you had to go through that. Can I ask you one more thing?" She waited. "When they shoot dice, who usually wins? Better yet, who do they say is the biggest gambler?"

"He's not at school here. He was at TGI with us. The Big Man!"

Another part of me sunk but I still had the resolve to complete the mission. "Please stop eavesdropping, and squash that rumor on both ends."

"OK, only if I can get your word on something."

I shouted, "What?"

"If I kill someone, would you cover for me or at least make sure I don't end up dead or in jail?"

I hated to ask this because of its sexist implication. "Are you asking for you or Girard?"

"You're trying to say I'm not my own person?"

"Exactly. Why would you need my permission?"

"The victim might be one of your sisters."

"You would have to join us to get that type of coverage." She was silent. "I love you Nicole but this Society is not what you think it is. The things you hear, you're being allowed to hear to make a terrible move. Call me before doing anything drastic."

She was quiet, and so was I. "I love you too Hope and I will take care of that rumor, but only for you."

How do you stop being in love with someone when he hasn't left your life using the door that only locks from the inside. So many entry points where we meet, even when I didn't call him, long for him, a thought of him would cross my mind in the most inopportune time. "How have you been?"

"Hope!"

His excitement had not quelled my anger but I was able to keep it below the surface until needed. "How come you haven't called me?"

He shot straight and gave me an answer I didn't expect. "Calls to you are not on a secured line unless the person has that type of clearance. But, the calls you make are secured and we can talk freely."

"Did you win me in a dice game?"

"You? No." He stalled, to do the mental math. I waited. "I won Barbara."

I waited but he didn't say anything. "I thought you loved me?"

"I do but from the beginning it was always both of you as sisters, best friends of mine."

"What then? You lost me?"

He laughed. "You? You've always been too high level to be gambled on."

"But you came after me!"

"Yes, after you made it clear you wanted me, and then you turned around and deserted me. Not once but twice." I didn't say anything because he was opening up to me again. "Last summer you told me you were going to transfer to a school in the city, come live with me…but then you throw a Black Love party and opened up a door to the past."

"You should not be selling art in the street. You should be in galleries…"

He interrupted me. "I know but some games you lose. When you do, you just have to get up and try again. But it doesn't mean it has to happen overnight, that you get to start at the same point, same high level you were on when you lost."

"You wanted me to leave the Society. I cannot do that and then you got my name into some shit that it wasn't supposed to be in." He did not say anything, indicating he was not the one who gave my name. "Are the MAX boys and their crew of friends really shooting dice to determine who's going to sleep with women?"

"No. Someone gave you some great information but you're too smart not to know that's only half of it."

"I'm listening." He laughed at the thought of me pulling rank on him. "Do you really want to go to war over this? It's minor information."

"I need to know."

I expected him to ask for something in return but he didn't. "It's the same concept as the duels men have done with swords, guns and other lethal weapons. We shoot dice and gamble in general for women in order to pick up the protection on their family. Everyone wants these jobs because there's lots of money to be made but sometimes people do it because they truly love the woman."

"But still!"

"It's a code, Hope! Get over yourself! You SUM women spread real nasty rumors to get men and other things you need. We all have our nefarious M.O's."

I sniped back. "Well you failed in your protection. Her brother still got killed in jail."

He was quiet. I too remained quiet. He spoke. "Our ancestors set a fire, many fires for their escape. That is how the Society came to be."

"Oh my God! You MAX boys. Her brother, he's not dead? Ken was behind this?" He was quiet, real quiet. Some things should not be spoken. "I'm sorry. I'm sorry. Oh my God!"

"So, are we good?"

"Yes. Yes." I paused. "So, Smiley. What's her story?"

"I don't know who that is."

"Ok, you know but you can't say. What about Girard? What's his story?"

He laughed. "A minute ago it was about our love. Now you're ready to move on."

"I will always love you. But, you're scared to touch me. You are so worried about my family. I need a man who can stand next to me in the Society."

"Theodore Perkins."

"You say Monk. Ernest says Girard."

"I'm sure that was before Ernest met Monk."

"What? Did Monk win me in a dice game?"

He laughed. "Nah, he a church boy, a choir boy, a boy scout. He wants nothing to do with the bullshit we're on."

"Is that why his name didn't appear on the FIRST IMPRESSIONS interview?"

"Oh, that!" I waited. "Monk cleared it for me and provided the contact. But the rest was my doing. I interviewed myself. It was my big F.U. to the local establishment. I submitted it to the local Trafalgar town paper and next thing I know it's syndicated in FIRST IMPRESSIONS, like someone major accepted my challenge."

"But, why even put that out there?"

"Because we got infiltrated and I needed to tell all our backers to not side with us in this war."

"That would be suicide. Just your thirty-one against hundreds, thousands?

"That is how our ancestors did it. Odds will always be against us. Plus, we're slowly picking up new backers. Haven't you checked the bank account FIRST IMPRESSIONS set up for you?"

"No, but why my name?" He got quiet. "Your army already knew I was now on your side."

"Not just by my side. On their side. We will fight whatever war you choose."

"I would rather fight yours. Just let me know when."

"You will know. As soon as this pissing contest between Ted and Monk is over." I waited. He continued, "The next MAX pledge class. I told Monk he can have it at Semline but he's waiting for Ted and Girard to do theirs on their own and get out of the way. He wants nothing to do with them."

"What? He doesn't want to fight my war?"

He laughed. "You really need to go talk to Monk."

"Why can't he come talk to me?"

"See, you're doing it again. You did the same thing with me. You keep forgetting your status. Whose great-granddaughter you are."

"Yes, but Monk is a seventh generation, just like Ted."

"Monk is looking to marry you..."

"Marry me? I haven't even had a long conversation with the guy."

"In the Society, the way we did things back in the day, one step away from arranged marriages."

"Like Deirdre and Ernest."

"What? What did you say?"

"You heard what I said." He did. "Now back to your war. Trustee Winston Trafalgar the Fourth placed me on the Council for Oversight of Student Arts and gave me a bunch of files and access to a database. I have made some progress..."

He interrupted me. "How long have you had this?"

"Since November. Days after the interview got published."

"Wow! He just gave it to you? No fight, no nothing?"

"In May, he sent me after A Man, not realizing that was your code name." Manny was really silent. "When he found out it was you, he seemed heartbroken like we had double-crossed him."

"He had a chance to walk through what we did."

"But his family. Have you not read the historical record? His family has always been on our side."

"That's where PMB, us MAX boys, differ from SUM and SBD. We are not out here trying to set the historical record straight. We only want revenge."

"Well that's how people get labeled traitors!" I knew I should not have said that the moment it came out. "I'm sorry I shouldn't have said that. Your father…"

"Did I make a mistake saying you were on our side?"

I did not answer. "Are you around next week? Once grades are in, I can come down with the files."

"If you have them with you, go to my house on Noble Street and put them in the second garbage can on the side of the house."

"You own that house up here? I thought you were a renter. Why can't I just bring them to you?"

"Your security detail. Too many people will know you came to see me, whereas your movements in town are not monitored."

"Does that mean I can't come see you this summer?"

"I'm not around this summer. I'm doing lots of traveling to hit the streets in various cities." I waited for an invitation but I now knew I had an invisible security detail and it would take too long to clear that type of plan. "I can leave the keys and you can drop by whenever you are in Manhattan."

"I would like that."

"Can you tell me the COSA notes on me and Ernest?" I went to the files and read him each of his evaluations and the lone one from Ernest's first semester. He was happy to know his. "You take it as a compliment to be labeled the black Kandinsky."

"I know what you're saying but that's how they grade stuff. But the money makes it worth it. The fame I can do without. But, I'm worried about Ernest."

"What's wrong with his being original?" He was quiet. "OK, I will leave the files for you. But, promise me as you break the codes and whatever you find, you will let me know."

"Definitely!" He paused and we said it at the same time. "I love you."

I will always love you with all my heart, that I held back.

I hung up and called Ken. He wasn't home so I called Barbara's dorm.

"Hey Hope! What's going on! You missed library hours again."

"I'm fine. Is Ken there?"

"Yes."

"Tell him I love him."

She shouted away from the phone and I heard his voice in the background. "He says he loves you too. Do you want to talk to him?"

"Yes, put him on the phone for a second." As soon as he said hi, I shouted, "4-5-6, motherfucker! C-Lo!"

Caught off-guard, he chuckled and recovered with, "Oh OK! I'm glad you got a copy of that exam and the answers."

"Yes. It will stay between us."

He handed the telephone back to Barbara and we discussed our studies.

Part Five

FORTY MILLION AND A WHITE GIRL

Chapter 30
INTERVIEW WITH BLISS

I took the summer off, stayed mentally away from Society business as much as possible. I spent my days exercising, a cross-section of running, lifting weights and picking up on my martial arts training. Though I didn't dedicate myself the way my father planned when he enrolled me when I was younger, I still enjoyed taking an occasional class. When not improving my physical strength, I volunteered nearly full-time hours at a series of nonprofits that provided services to kids. My days started at seven in Westchester. From there I travelled mid-day into The Bronx. Most days I ended up in Manhattan, to catch happy hours with brothers and sisters after work. I lined up my schedule and called anyone I had a personal relationship with, even if it was from a casual one-time conversation. Each thought the call would deal with the politics of the Society, but I immediately put them at ease, to know I just wanted to meet to go shopping, have a drink or grab a bite to eat. The men, the brothers of SBD had no obligation as my rule was not over them even though it impacted the women of their families, particularly ones in my age group or younger. Still I made it clear I just wanted to get to know them better. The first brothers who agreed to meet me did so for lunch or a casual shopping trip. Most were married and assured me they, in no, way would place me as the second to their wives, even though I was trying to put forth legislation to give 'second women' greater rights within the Society.

Next, they were the single men who were courted to another SUM sister, either through their choice or the advances of the woman or either of their families. These brothers were a bit more apprehensive to meet, especially when it was clear they had no inkling of marrying that woman outside of the ties established in the Society. My mother was such a SUM woman. Talking to these men, I came to understand the politics that led to my older brothers being born to my stepmother in wedlock, and my older sister, squeezed in between them and born out of wedlock to my mother. I technically was the child that didn't need to be born.

These men clearly loved and respected their courted woman but did not want much, if anything, to do with the Society, except for the money and the connections. Their acceptance of my call and meetup sat on top of their left eyebrow, not wanting to outright ask, "What do you want?" I kissed a couple and rested my forehead on their shoulders or chests, waiting for them to make the next move, letting it be just that, a need, a desire, an itch. But, they wanted something, something I was not in the business of giving, a way out of their commitments to the Society.

The single, uncommitted brothers were the brashest. They would blow off my call or ask to meet at crowded places with loud music, smokes and drinks. To some, I was a trophy, even though unless we were with other Society members, no one really saw me that way. I was your everyday cute girl, average in height-weight, pretty face, medium frame, dead center in skin tone. I was pretty but not a showstopper. I wore the latest fashion unless it was overly sexy. I sort of blended in until someone held eye contact or asked my opinion.

With these brothers, when the hours got late and they had a place or if during the day in between volunteer hours, we would mix it up, no commitment extended, so secrecy withstanding, it was just that, a roll in the sack. None ever left me wanting more, to lock elbows and smile, and plant a wet kiss on his cheek. Even the ones who spoke of passion and grand plans in the Society once they became initiated members, they never asked for my hand. Deep down they knew they could not accomplish their chosen mission, so why take my hand only to whimper when blindfolded in a dark room.

The boldest, brashest man I knew lived in Brooklyn and his woman lived in Colorado. I had each of their allegiance, and they had mine. The question was, do I call Nicole or Girard?

The summer packed itself into short days, and long weekend afternoons when sisters showed their shopping acumen. Most requested fashion and jewelry as the trip we should take. I learned so much about them, no longer judging them as SUM legacies who dared not put their name on the pledge line, for various reasons, but were now affiliate members for a campus charter at schools they attended. We avoided that conversation. Instead we talked around the margins. We drank and smoked, gossiped but stayed away from rumors. We talked about our childhoods and some confided they felt the Society had outgrown its purpose; that we were free.

I semi-agreed with them but reiterated the Society was never solely about our individual freedoms. Our task was to help those who weren't. Most of them felt at this stage if someone, in America, was not free, that person just did not want it bad enough. I asked them about the freedom only revenge could bring. A few agreed. Most laughed and disagreed. The biggest laugh and disagreement came from Diane.

Her shopping was different. We met on Sunday, August twenty-eight, way toward the end of summer. She felt slighted I had put her so far back in my calendar. I reminded her of the group meetings she had blown off. She said she wanted her own time. I technically owed her two meetings because Lauren bequeathed her slot since she was in Houston for the summer. Diane and I entered the world she was accustomed to, places with doormen wearing white gloves, visitor sign-in sheets; a mix of high-rise buildings, Harlem brownstones and upper east side townhomes. With each entrance and introductions, she would hand her business card. Diane didn't believe in revenge after so many years, decades, etc… "Most of those people are dead and their families want nothing to do with us or any war we're bringing to them, so why make more enemies? The ones who are still after us, we just need to trap them, lure them into a dark alley and BANG!" She said it so loud two older women, Golden Girl types, the younger ones, who still could drop a decade with a dye job, nearly jumped out of their slips and garters. She smiled at them in an apologetic manner and whispered to me, "They don't want anything to do with us."

Second Avenue was busy. I felt comfortable because I had walked it when selling art. The sun bleated pale streaks from in between buildings. I asked if she wanted to grab dinner. It was going on six hours and we had never spent so much time alone. Diane had a buoyant nature most SUM legacies learned to carry by age nine. By high school, we pushed most of the facade to a pragmatic level much like she had always shown me. Today she seemed to be floating. I liked this bubbly side of her. It helped me to reconnect to last summer in the city when I walked the streets peddling art. "Have you ever been in love?"

She held the fork close to her mouth, hesitating before stuffing in the food. She replied, "I would rather not answer that. It could come back to haunt me."

"No, no this is off the record. Two girlfriends enjoying dinner."

"I know. I know that, but again. It's just one of those things. You saw my file." She riffled through her bio. "Grew up in a brownstone in Sugar Hill not far from the Polo Grounds. Went to private school. What my file did not mention was that I spent lots of time in the projects, the various neighborhood playgrounds, even in Rucker Park watching rising ballers."

"Was it your way to gain protection?"

She laughed, real heartily. "You know, we had a good laugh, after you told us to go visit the hood this summer. Where do you think the four of us grew up? You're the one who grew up in Westchester, the nice part."

I laughed too. "I know I came off a bit self-righteous."

She balanced it out. "Oh, I know your history. I looked you up when I realized I was going to be attending Barrington. You're originally from The Boogie Down. Lived there until you were twelve. Baychester, not far from Co-op City. The word on you is that you pack a mean punch."

"Where were you planning to attend?" She didn't answer. "Is that where your first love went and you changed your mind because you broke up?"

She blinked and said, "Do you know Lauren's transfer to Semline got approved?"

"Yes." I replied. Diane nodded. I nodded.

Diane insisted on picking up the tab and as we parted ways, with her hailing a cab for uptown, and me one for SoHo to Attitude's loft. She hugged me and as we let go, she held my hand and said, "Love hurts, always."

The loft was quiet and empty most times I visited during the summer. Once in a blue one of the roommates would be home. People filtered in and out but the vibe was different than last year. Not once did I get the sense they still sat around the circle. The place had a stronger commercial feel to it. The large prints on the walls were in frames with metallic edges and glass screen. I mainly came when I didn't feel like taking the Metro-North back home. Most days, I left my car at home and jogged to the station. Others, I drove and left it at the park and ride.

School was less than a week away and all the tallies - campuses and national family level - were in. I had little support for my agenda. It was clear the expectation would be that I make promises and build alliances to get the votes needed. The stand still was good because I needed to study and really think about what was happening at Semline College. In the past, TGI controlled pretty much what happened in the region. Semline would be a force in academics, with Barrington never becoming a factor except as a place where men went to pick up women. Barrington threw the best parties simply because they had a male-female ratio that forced women to compete for men. At Semline, it was the opposite.

I had pegged Monk to apply to the Society by sophomore year to have enough time to establish the Semline chapter for the MAX boys. My stepmother came in as I was deep in thought. "Hey, look who's home!" I laughed. "I thought last year since you were hardly home, we could pretend you were away doing summer school. This year is worse in that you actually came home most nights only to disappear for the entire next day."

We used to have great times together my last two years of high school. "Oh, don't make me feel bad. There's so much going on."

"I know. The Society does not move swiftly." Rhonda was a second generation SUM legacy.

"Oh, that's not the foremost thing on my mind."

"Is it a new boy?" She rubbed her palms and sat next to me on the bed. "Give me the juicy details."

"You met him. Theodore Perkins." Reflexively her eyes widened and she forced a grin. "Oh yeah, there's a war going on. Or there's going to be a war. Keep your ears open because your eyes can fool you."

"What do you mean by war? People keep saying that."

"Just that sweetie! People draw a line in the sand, and if someone crosses it, they die!" She hesitated yet did not switch gears. "That Monk fella, what's his political leanings?"

"It's hard to say. He is extremely low-key. I used to have an in to his thoughts but he stopped writing for the school paper to focus on running for a senate seat this coming year.

"He's a Perkins so it's easy to peg him as a race man. You see how dark he is. I mean you can't look at a person and judge him by skin color, but his entire family tilts in that black-blue part of the spectrum." She paused to gather her thoughts. "For a seventh generation Max, that's pretty odd. Don't you think?"

"I never thought about it but both sides of the Society have a whole range of hues."

"Yeah, but a seventh generation Max? The point was to meet in the middle."

Her words forced me to question why Ted was damn near white and Monk so dark. "Have you ever dated a Max boy?"

"Oh no! I've never even thought about it. Most women I know who have been with a Max boy say they're good for a quick ride, and nothing more."

She reached for my hand. "I am not saying you shouldn't give the young man a shot if you can't stop thinking about him. Just don't get caught up in what he's fighting for!"

"Even if I believe in it?"

"There is no it! They're fighting for nothing. Why do you think Fly Lambda Tau ceased to exist? Women, we fight for something! Them, the MAX boys fight because it's their nature. The only good you can do them is to get the women around them to leave during their pledge process. When that happens, Max boys can actually see the error of their ways."

She surprised me by how much she knew. "I didn't realize you were this deep into the Society."

"I'm not. I mainly focus on the family trees."

The remaining summer days I researched two family trees. Though Monk's people were not poor - solid middle class with some holding more assets here and there - they had stayed below the radar when it came to the Society's affairs while paying their money, their dues and contributions. They always voted against change. I now realized when people said they were voting The Old Guard, they meant the way The Perkins family voted.

From their family sprung countless families, with most members switching to the Strength side - SBD or SUM when allowed at the fourth generation of being in the Society. The first switches happened shortly after World War I. There was a large exodus of PMB and FLT – branches from Ted's and Monk's family trees. My heart pounded as I searched deeper to make sure I was not related to either of them. I breathed a sigh of relief, recalling that my great-grandmother was our matriarch and she joined during the fourth generation, in the 1920s.

The Perkins last name was the lone branch of that family tree that has never moved – Pride side, PMB from the very beginning.

On the other side of Pride were the Duval who had the same starting history as the Perkins but they were wealthy beyond imagination. Nowhere in the history did I see a clash with the Perkins. In fact in the fifth generation, a few marriages occurred that linked them on the SBD side. But neither Perkins nor Duval families had an original SUM woman, from a fourth generation or earlier, as a direct link.

I felt like walking up and punching both of them square on the nose. But it was my fault for not looking at this part of the historical record. Many, younger members, make the error of neglecting to look at the Society's birth records, the family trees.

Those two fools never loved me like that. I'm just a way for their families to get more power.

The Duval voting history was messy, with no pattern that showed a political leaning, except they always backed the Queen. On the most recent votes, all their votes followed me, much like I had done in Student Council for Ted. We were a team and as long as I kept my crown and continued to push "In Matters of Matrimony" even though he knew it could take a generation or two to pass.

Thursday, September 8, 1988: SUM Meeting

I allowed all affiliate members to participate but without a vote. I tabled no new propositions but from the gallery came a challenge for us to consider extending membership for the next pledge class to qualified first generation members and other FLT legacies.

Without discussion, I put the challenge to a vote. Both Lauren and Diane quickly said no.

Before Miranda and Barbara got to vote, the sister making the proposal interjected, "Are you willing to consider each individual on her own merit, as we have one young woman who's a seventh generation FLT? Her name is Bliss Dubianson. She currently attends Semline College."

The room was in a state of shock, astounded by the request and the generational level. I spoke. "How are you able to track a seventh generation for an organization that went defunct at the start of the fifth generation?"

"Her grandmother has been confirmed and…"

"No, we cannot extend anything past fourth generation rights to FLT legacies. Additionally, the next SUM class is on record as consisting of only two members."

"We would make the exception," said Lauren. Diane nodded in agreement.

I did the math in my head, knowing Miranda would vote yes. "Permission to strike the previous conversation off the historical record, as it stated a factual error listing a person as a seventh generation of FLT. With that said, I will conduct the interview of Bliss Dubianson and if she's able to meet the qualifications, and as agreed by Ms. Hathaway and Ms. Henderson, she can join the next SUM class.

The sister walked over and handed me a folder.

After the meeting, during the social hour, I pulled Lauren to the side, conspiratorially whispering, "What are you up to?"

"What do you mean?"

"You asked for recognition of Semline and now you're putting someone who could be considered on equal or higher footing on your pledge class. What if she decides she wants to head the campus as Queen?"

"I'm not worried about that. Are you concerned for me or you've got something against Bliss?"

"I've only met her one time and she just didn't strike me as SUM woman material."

A few minutes later, I eased myself out of the house and went home to look over Bliss's file. She had top grades and the physical regimen - ballet, martial arts, dance and sports. On the bottom, under her bio, the recommendation simply said, "Bliss is a well-rounded chick, with an edge, a jagged one like a hunter's knife."

The sister who had made the recommendation knew her way around the Society, so I couldn't simply say no that I had met Bliss and hated her ways.

For the next two days, as I walked the campus, I listened to people talk, looking out for Bliss's name, to see if it reached this far from her campus. No gossip. No rumors. So I made the call and immediately Bliss was the same as the first time we spoke, that one time in Monk's dormitory. She had the voice inflection of a white girl down so solid, she could fool anyone over the phone.

"Hi. This is Hope Kendall. I am actually calling because you have been recommended to join SUM as a woman with a past FLT affiliation."

Bliss laughed and got Black-girl serious on me. This voice transformation caught me by surprise. "Girl, I truly appreciate the offer but let's be for real. Why would I want to go from freedom, love and truth to strength, unity and morality?"

Her response meant she wanted to establish her family was indeed around from the very beginning, and she was not about to joke around with me about her legacy. If not for FLT's cessation, her legacy would be equal to Monk's and Ted's. I maintained my formal manner. "Is this Bliss Dubianson whom I met last year?"

"Yeah, it's me! I am not interested in SUM. I have too many activities on my plate."

"You just spoke of something you should have no knowledge of."

"Like what, how strength, brotherhood and determination and was linked to pride, morality and brotherhood?"

"Do you know you can get killed for speaking out of turn?" I stood as if her words had pulled me up.

"Is that what you think of me? That I'm some ditzy chick talking out of turn?"

"I am not sure. I am just asking."

"Sister, I have been hearing some bad things about you. I don't want to believe them…"

"What have you heard about me?" Though I knew this would be an awkward interview, I didn't expect this level of head games.

"I'm not going to go there. Instead tell me something you'd like to know more about."

I got right to the point. "Is there a Max class on?"

"No, but when there is I plan on helping them."

The boldness of her statement dropped my guards. "You don't want to do that. If they succeed, there's going to be a war."

"That's why I'm helping. If there's a war, we get to establish the Free Love Society."

"What? Why would you want a war?"

"We've got to free love, 'cause love's in jail." Right there, Bliss had transformed back to the girl I met in the suite. Everything about her voice reverted except there was no giddiness. "The Free Love Society is an offshoot of FLT. It deals with the possibility of women ruling the world. On the Semline Campus, there are about forty of us. Nationwide, there are so many of us, you would not believe it. To not scare people, it's not always called the Free Love Society, but all the organizations embody the same principles."

I am not sure what made her stop but I was listening. "Who's part of the new Max class?"

"I can't tell you that."

"Is the Free Love Society the women helping the Max class?"

"Oh, no! I am the only one involved, just to help my boy, Devon."

"What about Monk? I would think Monk was also part of the MAX class."

Her voice switched again and there was anger. "He is but I can't stand Monk. He's gotten worse. Freshman year, he had sex with my friend LaKeisha, and just 'cause she told me about it, he cut her off. He hasn't spoken to her since."

"Monk had sex…"

"I know, right? That's why I don't do community service." She laughed as if she'd said something hilarious.

"Is that the only reason you hate Monk?"

Her voice transformed again. This time sadness carried the words. "Remember Frank DeLoose? He was my boyfriend. Monk caused us to break up."

I threw her a curve. "Was it payback for Trisha Hamilton?"

"I knew nothing about her being there. I only called Monk because I saw those three SBD brothers in the car, and knew Miranda was upstairs with Devon."

"That's not what I heard."

Her voice flipped again, filled with a bass. "Look, sister! Don't try to run some minor league game on me! I am being straight up with you."

"Then how can you support what Devon did, and be mad at Monk?"

"It's easier to coerce a morally corrupt man than a Monk!" Unlike her normal pronouncements, she paused for feedback. I had nothing to say. "So, are you in? Or, are you going to drop out of this race too?"

I hung up on her.

Bliss had talked herself into a bad corner, but I was willing to let her slide because we had connected, though awkwardly, from day one. I logged I had the interview with Bliss in the historical record but did not write a report. I did not even convene a meeting. I simply told the sponsoring sister Bliss was not interested in becoming a SUM woman. When she asked why, I said, "I think she is scared to go through the process."

In calling Bliss, I got information about Monk and Devon, and a potential Max class. I got the word to all the SUM women, telling them to find out the identity of the women helping the Max boys.

I also put any plans of starting Lauren's and Diane's pledge period on hold until the start of the next MAX class. No meeting. No vote. Lauren and Diane came to see me together. I called Miranda and Barbara. "This is between us and only us. We have a traitor among us. That interview with Bliss was a setup. It wasn't Ms. Stewart because she wouldn't have put her name on it as Bliss's sponsor."

"What do we do about Bliss?" asked Lauren.

"Nothing. Bliss knew nothing about the setup. What she's after has nothing to do with us."

Chapter 31
PICKING SIDES

The new semester had just begun and I could sense how antsy Ted was compared to Girard, and definitely to Monk. The longer they waited, the more it played into Monk's hand that the next MAX class would be at Semline. We had just left a student council meeting, focused on preparation for the year's elections. I was one of the last to leave and Ted was standing outside the assembly hall. As usual he was with a group of people. He slyly raised his right hand to request permission to speak with me. Those with him did not pick up the gesture. If I continued walking, they would not have seen the slight.

I looked at his direction and stopped for two seconds, indicating now was a good time. As I headed out of the building, he excused himself from his group and we met in stride. He opened the building's door. The night chill at 10 p.m. was the last corner before temperatures dropped. "Hey Hope!" He went for the informal and direct route. "You know I'm a junior this year, right? And you're a graduating senior."

"I was thinking of staying for grad school."

"OK, so you think this is funny?"

"I'm not sure why you're acting like I'm the one stopping you from doing your pledge class."

"Only because I think you're reading the history wrong." I gave him a quick, hard glance. "You have this idea we MAX boys are your enemies."

"You guys are the only ones telling me I need your protection."

"It's how it is set up. We are the queen's army."

"Then why are you worried about Girard and Monk?"

"Not Monk. Only Girard." I continued toward my building. His right foot angled, turned right, heading to his dorm building. "I live in King Hall this year."

"Don't tell me you're scared to come up to my place!"

"No, only apprehensive." I didn't offer a defense and turned toward his dorm. Ted continued, "Girard is a SBD legacy. The historical record shows you thought him a member at the bonfire. Until he takes the oath and signs his name to change his affiliated side in the Society, I see him as SBD, not as a MAX boy."

"Fair enough. That is how it is always done."

"He's at Barrington with Diane Henderson, Mike Henderson's daughter. You allowed Lauren Hathaway to transfer to Semline College where Theodore Perkins is."

"Oh no! Really? You're scared?" I laughed as he opened the building's front door. I had not visited King Hall since I moved out two years ago. The hallways were empty but not quiet. Conversations made their way from under door room doors and the various lounges. We didn't talk until we reached the third floor and entered his room. Ted's room was neat with all furniture flushed to one side of the room. On the empty side, was a workout bench, jump ropes and lifting weights. "You have the pairings wrong."

"If I was assured those were not the pairings, I would start a pledge class tomorrow. What you've set up is a challenge to yourself at those two schools, much like what happened with you and Miranda."

"And, your family always backs the Queen! I didn't ask you to stop backing Miranda." He didn't say anything. "It's you, isn't it? You want me to commit to you but you're scared to stand next to me in public."

I stepped closer to him and he backed up and moved to his right. "What are you doing? You're not looking at this correctly." His back was against the wall and I stood on my tip-toes, my lips reached to his chin. Ted looked into my eyes to do quick study of my thoughts but he realized the longer he held my stare, it would give me a chance to study his eyes, his thoughts. He closed his eyes and we kissed. I pushed my tongue deep into his mouth. He gently pushed me away and clapped his hands two times. "Stop! You need to focus on two years 1964 and 1968."

"The assassinations of Malcolm X and Martin Luther King?"

"No, Malcolm was 1965." He hesitated before adding. "But, it is very much a choice between the Ballot or the Bullet. Me or Girard – that's your only real choice."

"So, you really believe Girard pulled a gun on a SBD Sitting King and no one did anything about it?" Ted didn't say anything. "I am quite sure Miranda told you that's what happened, and I think it's quite noble she is fine letting you be my protection but I don't need it."

He coughed as he nearly choked on my words. "You don't need it? Your great-grandmother felt the same way and you saw how she basically lived under house arrest until you became Queen and got my family's backing."

His comment hit me hard and I hid my emotions enough not to lose all composure. "You think it's safe to mention my great-grandparents to me?" He didn't answer. "You know what? Have your pledge class and you have my word I will not take sides with any of the MAX boys against you."

"You really don't get it. MAX boys never turn their backs on each other, so I'm not worrying about Monk or whoever takes the oath. You have this idea the Society's two sides are equally divided with us MAX boys being on just one side… "

"OK then, spell it out for me!"

It was a weird request – so against the secretive ways of the Society. Ted hedged. "You have Manny Davenport who no one sponsored to be a MAX boy and you have Mike Henderson's daughter…"

"Her father is an insurance agent. He's wealthy but…" Ted slammed his palms against his thighs and gave me this look like I was the dumbest fuck in the world. "You know what? Drop your protection! That's a request. I will put it in the historical record that it was my choice and you can keep voting with me so your family's loyalty doesn't get questioned."

Ted reached for my hand as I made to leave the room. I knocked away his hand but not too hard for him to think I would hold a grudge.

Outside the building, the air felt different, rustier, as if I had been living in a purified bubble. I went to the library for books and straight to my apartment where I poured myself into a deep study of the Civil Rights Movement from its unofficial start date of 1954, the end of "separate but equal" up to its technical end in 1968, King's assassination. Yes, much work went on after but by then the Movement had incorporated the ideas of or morphed into the Black Power Movement. As the Society had done with previous outsider movements, we ran intelligence and counterintelligence operations within and outside those movements. I had read the historical record and there was nothing the Society did in years 1964 and 1968 where Michael Henderson was a factor. Born in 1944, he was from a fourth generation SBD family that joined the Society at George Mason University. Michael was one of six children but the only to continue active affiliation with the Society. He attended many balls, invested in various financial instruments. Any notation of Michael Henderson disappeared in 1964, and reappeared in 1968 on the birth records for Diane and later her two younger siblings. He had been courted to a Mary Danforth in 1966. The family's affiliation was inactive at the time of the courtship.

The next constant notations appear only as footnotes for mentions in mainstream publications in 1973. The mentions are about his being a socialite, husband and father of three, his work as an insurance agent. I called the company and learned he started working for the firm in 1963 and has been with them ever since. It all sounded a bit too squeaky clean. But, even if Mike Henderson is the Society's preferred insurance agent, in that he sets up all the types of protections afforded to members, why does that worry Ted?

Diane was born on February 20, 1968.

Now who was born in 1964 that fits this puzzle?

Ken, due to graduate with a Master's in Accounting; a fourth generation MAX who switched affiliation to SBD in 1985. I checked the birth records.

Though their families are not linked by marriage, Ken's great-grandfather was sponsored by Ted's cousin. They have no links to the Henderson family and no real commonalities in voting.

The other 1964 birth was Manny Davenport. Birth records: Derek Davenport and Brenda Curry, not a SUM woman. Davenport is a fourth generation SBD family. Derek's name appears nowhere until the 1972 shooting that left the four policemen dead, as listed in the historical record. Two names are redacted in the historical record and the other two names match those of two people not affiliated with the Society.

Why would there not be a war on the Davenport family if Manny's father killed two Society members? Shouldn't Manny be dead? That is the way: you kill a Society member without permission, you lose a generation of the gender killed.

What if, LeGagneur, Eric who was born in 1964? But no, he was born in Haiti, and they're paying the price for Lionel killing Benny, whose father was SBD. Benny's family name is in the historical record but no notations except in the birth records. But, then why is Ernest still alive? What if Eric, like Lincoln, Barbara's brother, is not dead?

We know Benny is dead but who ordered the murder?

Is Ernest's protection with Michael Henderson's organization?

If so, then we know who tried to get it removed. But why?

I thought on this for months, and my grades continued to slip. Now it was a certainty I would stay to complete my master's here at TGI since there's no way I could gain regular admission elsewhere for a master's degree. In continuing a master's in a related field, a TGI student was allowed automatic entry as long as there were no breaks in matriculation.

It was less than a week before Finals. I needed to make a trip to Barrington but I could not announce myself nor draw attention. The visit had to look like a social affair. Who was I fooling? This was the moment I had worked up for since August 1987 – *set me free.*

But this was not the revelation I anticipated. Going to war against Diane Henderson was not over a man, but treachery, beyond what is permitted within the Society. I threw on a dark gray sweathood, knit winter ski hat, dark jeans, loose fitting so I could conceal a gun and knife.

I took the highway and not the smaller routes that could get me there faster. Though the highway allowed me to drive faster, it looped around the back hills and added seventeen more miles. I arrived on the campus and parked in the lot closest to the woods. Barrington's woods encircled the entire campus except its main entrance, its eastern side. There were two less-traveled paths that led to the campus but only up to the parking lot. I put my car between two parked cars in a middle row so it was not visible from a leveled field. There was another hour or so of daylight. I walked from behind the library, a muddy path where three students snuck puffs on a joint. One said, "What's up sweetie do you want hang with us?" I quickly wondered how being bundled up, he could discern whether I was his type or was this banter extended to all women who stepped on Barrington's campus. I turned and removed my hood and hat to give them a good look of my face and eyes. He swiftly backtracked with, "Oh hi. Didn't realize it was you."

I smiled and replied, "See there I was, beginning to feel special." I left it wide open for him to say something to make me remember him, to maybe think he could be worth a late night sneak trip, or a bullet to the face. I replaced hat and hood and went to sit on the left side of the library's steps.

Barrington bustled with activity from all directions, including the driving path on the outer edge that connected the various quads. The state poured lots of money for its construction but had not done much to the grounds and buildings since. The architecture was from the same mold as most of the other state schools. The few trees and green space to lounge were near the driving path, adjacent each quad's furthermost building. Within ten minutes of my arrival, I saw the figure running toward the library, the light spring air causing her breath to rush out her mouth. She ran faster than I pictured she could. Diane did not try to pretend to be the type of woman whose first instinct was to put up her hands to strike you. I measured her steps, where her running outfit left room for weapons. Her steps were too quick, her body off, as if not anticipating what I would be doing on her campus in war gear. She came to an abrupt stop. Her breath crushed through her diaphragm, rupturing the words out of her mouth. Her first question shattered any misgiving. "Who're we going to war against?"

Her diction never this garbled, I processed her innocence, namely her measure of guilt, her lack of it. "No one. I came by after my run because I had some stuff on my mind."

"Oh, OK." Her measured words meant she now thought of the possibility.

I got the question off with the quickness. "How do you know Manny Davenport?"

"What? You think I'm after your man?" She turned to walk away from the library. I was still thinking woods but she headed toward the dormitories. "Going to school up here is so annoying. Every chick thinks someone wants her man."

"Isn't that why you spread that rumor about Lucille Patterson and Ernest?"

She thought about her next words for a second, forcing her eyes to not blink and her lips to not part. "I met Manny Davenport in 1972. He came to the house with his mother and two younger siblings. It was cold, during the holiday season and they had no place to live. My father was the insurance agent for Derek Davenport, who had not died during the ambush. But, he was supposed to. The way the policy was set up, the family would get money to carry them for a long time. With him alive, they were not going to get any money, even if the state executed him. They had nowhere to go, and really nowhere to hide. It took my father about two weeks to find them a place to live, people to watch over them and he had to pay off enough people so their lives would be spared. I was only four years old at the time, but over the years my father often talks about that case, so I know it inside out. Plus, I saw it play itself out over the years. While at my house, Manny and I formed a friendship. We were little so at first it didn't mean much, but every two weeks or so, he'd come by the house. When he didn't come upstairs, I would go down and see him. He would come by to get a little money to go visit his father, help cover bills for his family, etc...and then one day, he came by and he was fly as hell. His gear was on point. Haircut, cologne, the works. It was easy to take it as nothing more than a teenage boy finally knowing what it took to get the flyest girls. But it wasn't that so I asked him and he told me the truth. His neighborhood had organized itself. She chuckled. He asked if I wanted in, and whether I could get my father to bank them. I asked how much he needed. It was an amount I could afford on my own so I covered it. Our first major gamble was for the city basketball championships in the Cross-Borough League for the 1983-1984 school year. The event was about three years away so we had enough time to build a reputation - win a lot but lose enough to keep people gambling. We took out insurance on the major players by contacting their families and letting them know the odds of them going pro or even getting to play at the college level. Everything was going fine until we got a policy opened through a third party on an Ernest LeGagneur. A life policy. With me running the bank in the background and my father being the front person for the insurance because he had all the licenses and had been doing similar business for a long time, the person, who took out the policy on Ernest, had no idea Manny was connected to us."

Diane stopped talking as we passed a group of students in front of her building. "You live in an apartment? I thought these were for upperclassmen only?" She laughed as if I had not been listening. "When did you meet Ernest?"

"It was going on three years and I had not met nor seen Ernest so I decided to catch him the first time his high school played in Manhattan. I had no idea how built, stoic, fine and powerful he was. At the game, he kept glancing into the stands, real subtly. There were his four sisters split into two pairs, seated apart. It was like that most games I went. I could never build the nerve to just walk up to him and introduce myself so I watched from afar. His stats were not doing him justice. He was the best player I had ever seen. He played within the team concept with this other guy Slick being the leader. To me, Ernest was the truth! And just as I thought, one day, the media started tilting toward his school winning the championship. Our money was already in from three years ago with some crazy odds. Whoever was coming in would have to give up so much to go with us. We cleared about one hundred thousand dollars on a high school game. Unheard of in street level gambling circles. My father had become not just a place to put a little money on some action, but he had truly become Mad Money Mike, street legend. For the next two years, I lost money on Ernest but it was OK because I didn't put too much on the line. I really didn't care about his basketball. I just wanted the man. I basically followed him to this school. And, out of nowhere, here comes this chick, not only turning him down but bragging about it to her friends, right after doing it."

Diane paused to look at me and all I could say was, "But why try to drop his protection? You could have gotten him killed."

"No, you misread it. Lauren and I hinted it to you but you weren't catching on. He doesn't need the protection and I don't want Ernest in the Society. That rape rumor would have barred him from getting the vote."

"Yes, but you put that girl in harm's way."

"She stays in harm's way." I indicated to her I was drawing a blank on anything else. "Guess who Lucille Patterson is dating? Gave him her virginity this past Valentine's Day!"

"Ernest?"

"NO! Devon Jefferson. Miranda's Devon!"

She just stated something that made no sense to me. "I thought Miranda was through with that boy."

"Are you through with Manny Davenport?"

I ignored her. "But why did Lionel kill Benny?" She groaned, exasperated. "With no retaliation from his family?"

Her downstairs buzzer sounded. "Oh! I had called Lauren, thinking we were going to war." She pressed the buzzer. She rushed her words so the conversation would end before Lauren arrived. "That's the choice Benny's family made. They collected the insurance money on his life and to leave to never be seen again. And in return, the LeGagneur family got to buy in and enter the Society in the deep end, except for Ernest who doesn't have to enter because he didn't come to the meeting where my father and Benny's family negotiated the terms."

Diane opened the apartment door before the staircase's door opened. Lauren entered the apartment. "I went by the library, the woods, thinking we were into something."

Diane handed each of us a drink and went to a drawer for her stash. We rolled joints with Lauren abstaining.

Lauren did not smoke but she was not too good of a girl – to be carrying such a heavy gun. I could see the outline. She saw the focus of my eyes and smiled. She took her gun out of the inside lining of her jacket. "My family believes in big guns, mainly Colt .45."

She placed it on the table.

I took out my silver .25-caliber semi-automatic, my first, and placed it on the table. "A gift from my father."

Diane reached her right hand inside her sweats, her inner thigh. The sound of Velcro, a holster for a long barreled gun, a luger. She offered no sentence on its origin but I knew this model to be military grade, foreign wars. She placed it on the table and said, "One of many."

We raised our glasses in the air. "Did I tell y'all I'm staying up here for my master's? It's a two-year program."

They said it simultaneously, "Renegades for life!"

I reassured them. "No. I just wish the MAX boys would hurry up!"

Lauren said, "They don't want none of this."

Chapter 32
THE ABSENCE OF COLOR

I spent the past summer at museums, book readings, art galleries and the theater, mainly Off-Broadway and a few Off-Off-Broadway productions. When not immersed in politics, MAX boys excelled in the arts. Attitude had followed through and shared his research on the names. He was still at the beginning of whatever plan he had in mind but told me what to look for when it came to the TGI alumni and the COSA's notes. The code was which critic mentioned color in their evaluation of the artist's work. He grouped them by color. From there, he planned to do a genealogical trace back to 1860, the start of the Society.

We were outnumbered then and now. The forty original members killed over two hundred people, whites and blacks. In planning the uprising, they never accounted for slaves who would refuse to run. They made the hard call and killed those blacks.

They divided themselves into seven families and scattered during their escape. Their point of contacts led them to the northeast and mid-eastern states, where they received help from unsuspecting people. People who gave them shelter, new names and all types of cover.

In the art reviews, people who descended from the lineage of the whites who were killed, they were not assigned colors. I was concerned about the comments on Ernest's work and the consensus that he "lacked the ability to fully blend color into his work. Whether utilizing tones that suggest sharp contrast or blended mattes, the absence of color is stark as if he had used a pencil on a clean state and used the brush to fill in the blanks."

I researched other artists who had received similar reviews and the outcome was rather interesting. No black artist who could not be assigned a color ever became rich or famous. At the same time, a white artist's career path was akin to throwing paint against a wall. Some were called brilliant and became rich and famous, while at the other end of the spectrum, some continued to mire in obscurity or simply quit.

Ernest presented a problem and an opportunity. He was famous because of sports and if he continued doing both, his art would gain recognition. I kept playing that scenario in my head. Using Ernest as the baseline, the anchor, I ran through thousands of probabilities and the names began to make sense and so did the colors.

I could look at pretty much any artwork, even ones with no ties to TGI and estimate an artist's career trajectory. The majority of black artists fell under black just because it was a simple classification. Did most belong there? Not really, because white artists who copied black aesthetics succeeded under many colors.

Most interesting were these white artists not labeled black but whose work clearly fell under the color black. These people stood out because their work, to be this dark, this rooted in the same clash, this same war and not asked their take on race, the central national problem. This fact, this omission gave away their position.

I had a choice to make. Had I known all of this when being initiated into the Society, I still would not have gone in under my GG Celeste's legacy, even though half the benefits derived from my success still flowed up to her.

No one ever asked me if I wanted to go under my mother's legacy. She was of a lesser numbered generation but the fact I went in under The Legacy Exception, it would have not mattered. I never understood the choice my mother had to make as a woman courted by my father in the Society, but who never loved each other outside of it.

Even as I built my platform, I did so under the belief I would never be impacted by the things I championed.

I had a choice to make. Should I run back to my apartment, take another shower, get gussied up, or simply run over there? Friday afternoon before Thanksgiving, the library was beginning to swell with people who normally spent these hours reveling in possibilities. For the master's program I had to rededicate myself to stay in the books and participate in all the ancillary activities related to the coursework.

I packed my books into my bag and stored them in one of the guest lockers in the Student Union Building's lower level. I went to the bathroom to wash my face and rinse my mouth, giggling at myself, at the audacity to presume anything would happen, particularly this soon. By the time I left the building, the quad was empty. Workers had left for home. The students confident in their studies and those who didn't care headed to catch happy hour. The Administration Building housed administrative offices in the lower floors while the top floors hosted choice academic departments, and the offices for deans and trustees. I took the elevator and walked down the hall and exited to the secret entrance that led to his office.

His secretary greeted me with a pinched smile. "Hi. Can I help you?"

"Yes, I am here to see Trustee Winston Trafalgar the Fourth."

"I'm sorry but he's left for the day."

I tilted my head just a little to put her on the defensive. "Can you call him and tell him I really need to see him?"

"No, that is not possible. If you leave your name…"

I interrupted. "My name? You don't know who I am?"

"Should I?"

"He's never mentioned me?" I waited for her to process it and added some more. "I would think as his secretary you knew so you could intercept calls, clear his calendar."

Her eyes gave the answer I needed. "What did you say your name was?"

I smiled at her and backed away to take a seat in one of the lounge chairs. I read her nameplate. "Stephanie, he knows who I am."

She turned her chair to the side to dial him. She whispered. I could not make out the conversation. She turned to me. "Trustee Trafalgar asked whether this can wait until Monday."

I picked up a magazine from the coffee table. She eyed me as I read. She had questions but she dared not ask them. Her uneasiness provided me the same information I would get from a conversation. She wanted to know my age and I placed her at about twenty-eight. She wanted me to be his illegitimate daughter but I was not that young. She figured I was a student but how did I have access to this floor from the elevator. Why did campus police allow me to access this elevator bank?

An hour later, Trustee Trafalgar entered the room with a strong push of the door. I stood and beamed in his direction with the kind of smile that worried married men. I hoped to push his memory to two of the questions he asked last time we met, "Are you pregnant? Are you in love?" I sensed his pulse in his eyes, the confusion, the number of extrapolations running through his mind as he rushed here, wondering why I came unannounced to his office. I ambushed him with a question, refocusing him on the cover I had established in Stephanie's mind. "Winston, how come she doesn't know about me? How come she doesn't know my name?"

He almost said something to reject the obvious cover but then thought better of it. "Stephanie, sorry to keep you so late on a Friday."

"It's OK. I'm in no rush."

We made eye contact. I smiled. "It was nice meeting you."

I turned and walked toward the double doors, twisted the brass door knob and entered his office. I waited by the door to hear her leave and then scurried to a seat on the leather sofa, sinking into its comfort. Trustee Trafalgar didn't come to sit next to me on the sofa. He turned the chair at the head of the table. He sat and looked at me for five seconds. "You got me. I have no idea why you would want my secretary to think we are having an affair."

"You need an edge, a dark side." I gave him a chance to ask a question but he didn't. "I'm thinking I misread what happened between us when we first met in May 1987." I paused for him to tense up a bit, unsure of the angle I would take. "You wanted me."

"I was wrong for that. You are a student."

"Yes, but I'm fully grown now, first semester in grad school. The rules that applied to me as an undergrad no longer come into play."

"Yes, but I'm a married man."

"It's your choice. She's not in the Society. You can dump her and marry me. Or, we can have an open affair."

I looked at his shoulders for any slumping; his forehead for any furrowing; his hair, the stiffness of an expensive cut where the peak curved, each strand starched to submission. He walked to the cabinet near the bookshelf and poured two drinks. He sat on the sofa but left enough distance between us. I swirled the drink and sipped as he spoke. "I'm trying to process this. Are you in love with me?"

The question pulled a smile out of me. "It feels more like infatuation. Remember the kiss we shared. No matter how deep I pushed it into my memory, it resurfaces quite often."

"Is this strictly a political alliance or do you see us…you know?"

"Do you want to smell me?" He nearly choked on his drink. He coughed, turning a dark red. "You are asking the wrong questions. Did I misread your feelings for me?"

He stared into my eyes. I searched his for anger but only saw hints of fear. "Our children, they'll be…"

I finished his sentence. "Members of the Society."

He shook his head. "I see." He squeezed his hands. "You are drawing me into a fight I never thought you would enter."

"You gave me a gun!"

"Only to use as an escape because you were already deep into it by then."

"As deep as you?" He didn't answer. "You talk of your grandfather and my great-grandmother, their friendship, their alliance. On the surface it made sense, but how could that be if your family is not in the Society?"

He sat back and crossed his legs, as if daring me to continue. I didn't give him a hard stare but did let him know he had to say something. "Have you selected a foreign language for your master's? I am fluent in French and German, and know some Italian."

"I'm leaning toward German. It goes best with my thesis, The Absence of Color." These coughs were more pronounced. He got up to shake it off. Once he composed himself, I stood to face him. "Is your contention that your family, you are neutral?"

"Did you know I play in a jazz band?" He paused and I waited. "A quintet. We do it out of love."

"We could provide each other cover."

He chuckled and grabbed my hands. "I'm flattered you even considered us together. Unfortunately I play an under-appreciated position in this war and would put you in grave danger."

"What is your instrument and favorite song to play?"

"Bass. On Green Dolphin Street."

Chapter 33
WHAT'S YOUR NUMBER?

I buckled down this past year and was back to being the type of student I had been before investigating A Man for Trustee Trafalgar. No longer dealing with student government really freed my time and kept me away from lots of distractions. What in the past would be major gossip barely registered as no more than the cycle of college life. The SUM chapter pretty much ran on automatic. Each year my national platform gained a few new campus votes and backing from families.

Miranda and Barbara had graduated the previous year and opted not to do a master's at TGI. So, for this SUM charter, only my vote counted when it came to In Matters of Membership as it related to start date, type of process and end date for the pledge class. On all other issues, the votes would be up to Lauren and Diane. They never voted against each other so I never had to break a tie. Most times whatever I put on the table got their stamp of approval.

Ted had drawn this out long enough, to the point even though he could have graduated this past spring, he picked up a second major and enrolled as a full-time student, to give himself one more year to become MAX as an undergraduate. There was an outside chance he could wait until the spring semester but I got the clue I needed when I learned Ernest would not play basketball this semester. No injury reported; simply he was focused on his art. I took another look at the file the Council kept on him. It now included digital images of works he had submitted. He rarely painted in color; charcoal, oils of black, white and various shades of grey. The grades and comments were consistent but now a few students sang high praise of his work. I focused on these outliers because these students were likely the unconnected ones, the ones not part of the charade the only standing value to Ernest's art was its originality, its stark difference.

He passed all classes with no less than a B-minus and an occasional grade of "A" popped up but never in classes where art was created or critiqued. Other students were afforded the beauty and benefit of operating at a master's level or an understanding the fundamentals of; but all Ernest got was that he brought a different perspective to the discussion.

I took a step back and let myself accept that Ernest brought a different view of the same problem. My current problem was I had made part of my platform that legacies would undergo the same pledge program as first-time sponsored aspirants. *The Basement.*

There was a time when the Society used a different measurement as to what type of sponsored members, males and females, it would accept into SUM and SBD. Unfortunately the system got rigged in that first-time members knew all they had to do was be chaste or scandal free until initiation, likely freshman or sophomore year. No modification worked. The Society even tried installing a minimum number of three and an unstated maximum number to bar promiscuous women. Those same standards boomeranged and began to impact legacy members in that they started getting negatively compared to sponsored members. The push to end the old membership process came to a head in the 1960s around the time of the second wave of the Free Love movement, communism's final push and integration.

"The Basement" became the new process to replace "What's Your Number?" yet small pockets, non-cooperating chapters still used the 'Number' method. I personally didn't like 'Number' when I learned what it consisted of, with its requirement a person had to list on paper all persons he or she had had a sexual encounter. From there, the person would pick a person from the list as their 'courted spouse' into the Society. Even though we still courted before the process, it became more ceremonial, being that by coronation or graduation, either person could move on.

This happened to me. I was courted to Ken based on legacy and standing interest, but we were not a good fit. Plus, he loved Barbara. I accepted that, knowing the man I loved didn't want to live the Society as I did. I hoped we could be together, find a compromise. But things moved so quickly, and the next thing I knew Trustee Trafalgar pointed to him as the enemy. And, it turned out to be true.

But he was not my enemy, once I heard how he grew up, why he put his personal revenge above the Society. My GG Celeste, upon hearing his name, didn't hold it against him. She had followed her heart in the same manner, but at the time, the Society believed in revenge. But, then in 1973, she was forced to step down. She never spoke of the details of her reign. She just kept waiting for the tides to shift back to her way of thinking.

I too waited to see how the MAX boys would play this. This was the start of the fourth year and unless Monk planned on doing what Ted did, they had to make a move.

These four years, while reversing the membership process, having Lauren and Diane on the books but not receiving any monetary or social benefit of being SUM women, I had afforded Lauren and Diane the opportunity to include as part of their court any SBD members initiated at any school since they entered college, and I now added the option of courting these upcoming MAX boys.

Court was in session.

We convened the meeting on Thursday, September 6, 1990. The session was crowded. "In Matters of Membership, I make two initiatives. The first, for all non-courted women, please be advised there is a MAX pledge class in operation as such you are free to detract by offering SUM pledge invitations to all women who are serving as auxiliaries. Whether or not they accept, the goal is to lure the MAX pledge class to surface so they are required to be courted to SUM women. Along with the current pledge class, there is still the matter of the previous MAX class known as The Outsiders.

They are still eligible as they did not court.

"The second initiative, the SUM court process will begin on November 3, 1990. From then until May 31, 1991, weeks after the last of the graduation ceremonies for the three affiliated schools, any un-courted SUM woman and the SUM candidates, Ms. Hathaway and Ms. Henderson can petition for the right to court. We will use the "What's Your Number?" rules of Engagement."

The gallery murmured then rumbled. "Hell no! We're going to The Basement. We didn't wait over three years for this. We didn't pass up our votes on these campuses for this. We're going to The Basement."

"Silence! Affiliate members have no say in such matters!"

They replied, "We will not recognize them if we don't go to The Basement."

I stood up and faced them. "So what! I put my life on the table for these two women."

"The Strength of your Loyalty is noted."

"Exactly, which of you went to The Basement?"

The silence was deafening and as I put pen to paper, Lauren and Diane cleared their throats. Lauren spoke, "It is our wish to mend fences and bring harmony to our three schools, this chapter."

"Yes. We're willing to go to The Basement," added Diane.

They always talked of The Basement, through this romanticized lens of what goes on down there, never thinking of what could go wrong. Looking into their eyes, I saw more fear of "What's Your Number?" than for "The Basement".

Now they had me worried. I had not heard their names in any gossip or rumor that could impact them when it came to their number but I never went digging.

But, numbers bubble up like a growling stomach exposed to undercooked food. "I will take a recess for private session and will return with my judgment." I asked Lauren and Diane to follow me upstairs to the master bedroom for the utmost privacy. "OK, stop playing around. What are your numbers?"

They sat across me – one in front of the boudoir, the other on the sitting chair near the window where the sunlight should have been, instead of the gray cascading above these fallen leaves. Lauren said, "Mine is zero."

Diane quickly followed with "23" as if trying to blend her number with Lauren's.

"He does not count so it's only 22."

"What? What the HELL? What have you been up here doing?"

Diane got defensive. "Why does the higher number get the scrutiny? Plus, you don't believe she's on zero, do you? Ask her how she rationalizes that number?"

I sat on the bed and palmed my face with both hands. "You two are trying to kill me."

"We didn't ask you to put your life on the line for us."

"Not that. That's the simple part." I paused and looked at each of them. "How are you on zero?"

"No penetration of any orifice by a penis."

Even though that made sense, it forced me to ask a different question. "Are you two walking around telling people on your campuses you are Queens?"

"Yes, ever since you agreed to a realignment of the TGI charter."

"Oh, wow! Those rumors people think are about me, they are about you – how you have men coming over, bowing to the Queen with no reciprocating."

"I give hand jobs."

Diane added, "Don't forget fingers up their asses!"

Lauren gave Diane a curt stare. "That's only like two guys who…"

I interrupted her. "How many have they been?"

"Zero."

"What do you mean zero? You just said…"

"No one's penis has ever penetrated my mouth, my vagina, my…"

Diane offered mediation. "It's seven. By my method of whether the man ejaculated on or used his fingers on her."

"You're bending the rules to suit your needs to qualify Ernest."

I looked at Diane. "Please tell me you really have not been with 22, 23 men!"

"Yep. I get busy and none of that kiddie stuff either."

"It's not kiddie stuff. It's preserving my temple, saving myself for my husband."

"Stop! Both of you. We have a dilemma on our hands." I forced them to focus. "Why can't you just court one of the other men? You can always move on to Ernest after the process."

"I am not selecting a man for the process but Ernest has to be recorded on my list for our legacy, if we go with, "What's your Number?"."

I turned to Lauren, "What's your objection to Ernest?"

"It's not about Ernest. I plan to be courted to a legacy out of Maryland, and her method of counting will complicate my standing with his family."

"What you two don't get is that The Basement brings the worst out of everyone. Your true nature comes out front and center, especially the darkness that dwells within you."

"None of the other men I've been with are available. I've basically been pining for Ernest all these years. These men have other women in their lives, and some of those guys still check in on me to see if I've changed my mind about being with them."

I did not want to get in between the two of them by making a wrong decision. "Does Lauren know how long you've wanted to be with Ernest?"

"Yes. She knew I first saw him playing basketball my freshman year in high school."

I got the answer I needed. Even though I had my mind made up, I needed to know what it was about her time with Ernest she felt counted. "OK, what exactly happened between you and Ernest?"

"About a week or so before coming to Barrington, I finally met Ernest and we exchanged a warm kiss. The semester started and I waited days for him to come looking for me. We did not have any classes in common and I wasn't living in the quad where freshmen lived so I figured he didn't know how to find me. I went looking for him at the gym but he wasn't there. He wasn't at the outdoor courts, cafeteria, etc…Just as I was about to give up, I asked someone who said he was likely in the School of Arts. He was painting. Focused, his back slightly hunched, paint on his clothes, a drained, inspired look on his face. The scene took my breath away. Words couldn't come out. He turned and said, 'I thought I smelled perfume. Hi beautiful. How are you?' I said I was fine and I'd been thinking about him. He said, 'Really? You're the talk of the town.' I told him I've always been. As much as he has. He smiled and I walked over to him. He had paint on his hands, a yellow t-shirt. We smiled again, and I waited as I looked deeply into his eyes. I waited for that kiss. But then he said, I would kiss you but I wouldn't want to get you dirty. I stepped closer to him and looked into his eyes, at the sadness. I wrapped my arms around him so he could feel my heartbeat. We were one. At that moment, we were forever. I would have stood like that, in front of a firing squad, for him, with him. As we held each other, I saw the canvas, the squiggly brush strokes, what seemed like hundreds of them, detached but combining to illustrate a feminine form and a man with no eyes. I asked him to come see me tonight, that I'll fix us dinner. I ran home to get my car, went to the market and came back to cook, prep myself. I let my hair down and I could tell when he walked in that my beauty stunned him. I was fresh-faced with but a sliver of peach lipstick. I wore a loose pink silk shirt, crème slacks and slingback, peep-toe pumps. He was pleased and his words hugged me, with a look that said 'you remind me of my sisters'. He kissed me. I tried so hard to just consume all of him. I could feel my body's heat rising. The oven's timer sounded. We ate Cornish hens, vegetables and rice pilaf. We drank Chablis chilled to forty-eight Fahrenheit. The background music was some dope ass konpa he'd never heard. He asked about me. I told him what I was studying, about my family, my little brother and sister. He kissed my forehead, and I sucked on his Adam's Apple. I squeezed him, his arms, pects, neck and pulled him closer to kiss him. As we exchanged murmurs, I unbuckled his pants and pulled it out. He stopped kissing me to say he wanted to move slowly. I mumbled OK as I stroked down, up, down and though he'd stated he wanted to go slow, he exploded on my shirt, down my sleeve and hand. I could tell he was a bit embarrassed but I reassured him that it was OK. I kissed his face as I unbuttoned my shirt. He took it off and unhooked my bra. His mouth was large enough to fully take one into his mouth. He sucked my breasts so well, so long and so passionately that bursts of energy shot out my body and when he stopped I could see the red hickie marks against my skin. He stopped to take a breath and I was panting heavily. I asked him not to stop as I took off my pants and panties. I kissed him again and looked down, as I put my knees to my shoulders. He rubbed me and then put his middle finger in. The sound slushed into puddles. He moved around a bit, circling to touch the walls and an occasional come-here finger motion. He had excellent technique but I needed him to put his mouth on it, tongue in it. I then thought perhaps he had never tasted love before so I gently took hold of his balls, moving my hands up his shaft. The girth I expected was there. I slid my hand up and down and just as I was about to plunge my head downward and swing my right knee over his head and shoulders, he repeated, 'I want to move slow'. Fucking total buzz kill. I couldn't even look at him. My heat had turned to anger. I didn't face him as I put on my panties and shirt. He pulled me down to him, and kissed the top of my head and said, 'We have four good years ahead of us'. I turned and looked into his eyes and gone was the sadness and fear. I kissed him again and we tickled each other. He left a little bit after midnight, after helping me clean the kitchen and put away the food. I put some in Tupperware and he went home with it. Days went by and we didn't see each other. As I came out of class one day, about five days later, he was standing there and we walked back to his dorm room. We closed the door and kissed a little and listened to music. In the following weeks, I heard rumors he was having sex with other women. So I made sure he heard rumors about me. He never asked and we didn't see each other as much. And, that's pretty much how it has been these past few years."

Diane had barely finished when Lauren blurted, "See it doesn't count, even Ernest knows that. That's the point he's making – no penetration means no sex."

"Love always counts," I said and turned to leave the room. They both rushed and each grabbed an arm with force.

"What's your decision?" They asked in unison.

They let go of my arms when they saw my eyes had gone cold, flipped into a persona neither ever witnessed but heard rumors of. I rushed down the hall and down the stairs. They followed quickly behind but likely resisting the urge to tackle me, unsure of what my count was for their numbers, unsure what I would scream to the gallery. The sisters heard my steps and all talk stopped. Everyone, including Lauren and Diane, held their breaths until I shouted, "To The Basement!"

They all cheered for five seconds and finally it dawned on them: Lauren and Diane were technically no longer SUM women.

I grabbed my bag and notes off the conference table and made a mad dash to my car. Lauren and Diane were running behind me. "Big Sister Queen Kendall, what now, what do we do?"

"Go back to your campuses, talk to no one and wait for my call." They got into their cars, headed down the street, and parted ways at the fork in the road. I looked at the house, seeing shadows move behind the shades, the jubilee of those inside. The profound remorse of what I was feeling inside forced me to my knees in a convulsing pain. I managed to get into my car and headed in the opposite direction from the direct road to the TGI campus. I drove alongside the backwoods and followed the sounds of the creek. I looked down the creek's edge, where parents took children for their first fishing experience, where if one crossed to the other side and followed the North Star, there was a direct path to Canada. Hours away lied a freedom, one he had promised me, one I had hesitated to take, but I came running after him for reasons, confounded and confused, yet he still took me in.

I sobbed under the fall night where the moonlight hit the water and the waves rippled like pop lockers; the inviting darkness, of a plunge, with head, neck first and no attempt to use one's hands to slice through the water and tread the currents to the other side. If I could call him now, I still would not be able to get the words out. I needed to go see him, first chance I got, to tell him how I stood on the overpass, and heard him whisper to me and all I could say was, Love hurts, always.

Chapter 34
THE LOFT

It was one of those bright autumn days, the kind that used to surprised me my freshman year at TGI back in 1985. I decided to attend TGI without a campus visit. I hid my application from everyone including GG Celeste. My family history linked to this place and I felt no other campus and town would suffice when I entered the Society. I wanted to be connected to the place my great-grandfather was lynched. To learn how GG Celeste built up this chapter of the Society, while balancing her distrust of the MAX boys.

Over the years, through GG Celeste's actions and their own doing, the MAX boys had ceased operations in the region.

Their resurgence came in Fall 1984 when Manny Davenport switched allegiance from SBD to PMB, something that was rarely, if ever, done. Using his life and art coupled with Ted's lineage, I was able to determine the identity of TGI's other MAX boys, The Outsiders. Since they do not follow the Society's strict reporting of birth records, it was hard to trace their organization unless one stayed plugged into all of the Society's families and the gossip. MAX boys use their work, mainly the arts and politics, to transmit messages to one another, and other members of the Society.

There were MAX boys in many other industries but the arts and politics allowed them to operate in a very public sphere, and are two arenas in which people double-crossed each other with no hesitation.

Weeks ago, I phoned Attitude to find out his progress on the COSA research. He filled me in on the recent parts of the code he had broken. From there he planned on creating some sort of database, a project he said would take years to pull off. He farmed out tasks to other people and asked me if I had any interest in helping. The answer was yes and no.

The files Trustee Trafalgar had given me and all the other stuff I'd learned about the Max boys gave me a clearer picture of how the money was being moved. Still I was missing a crucial part and the only way to get it was face to face. So, I called Attitude and asked him if I could interview him for my master's thesis. He laughed when I told him the title, *The Absence of Color*.

He told me I knew the place, to come whenever.

I wanted to go down the very next day but I could not because later that night the SUM meeting had gone wrong. Things had taken a drastic turn and my anger, my hurt feelings, caused me to agree to send Lauren and Diane to The Basement. This threw off my timeline by two weeks because I had to put together the necessary steps and submit the paperwork.

Once that was out the way and the pledge period had become routine, on a Friday, sunny with no leaves blocking the glare; still a perfect day, I decided to drive down. I figured I wouldn't be missed because Semline was set to host Barrington, whose basketball team had been depleted of all its talent. With everyone's focus on the game and SUM sisters occupying their energy on the pledge class at TGI, I threw on my shades, packed my bags and grabbed two cassettes filled with house music to help make the time fly. The drive from TGI to Manhattan was a straight shot if one's willing to pay all the tolls. One simply connected to I-90 and I-87, a solid four hour drive that can be done in a little over three hours when not worried about a speeding ticket from the state troopers.

I was in a hurry but time was on my side. I left after my lone Friday class and was on the road at eleven. Traffic moved; a few bottlenecks but very little delay at the toll booths. I hit a bit of congestion on 87 near the exit for the George Washington Bridge. Once I got off the FDR Drive, the pace threw me off a bit. Unlike the steady high of the highway, on the local streets the city drivers' vigor was more of a response to the herky-jerky motions of taxis and the mass of transit buses. Each movement caused me to pull, turn a slight angle signaling my inability to anticipate their moves. I'd only driven in Manhattan two times, each with my father, at my request. His nervousness had overshadowed my own, thereby forcing me to keep a steady hand and having the other drivers react to me.

I circled Bowery and eventually found a parking spot that could serve me overnight if need be. I made sure to leave nothing that would attract attention in the body of the car. Broadway had a pulse of its own. Tourists blended with students, shoppers with hawkers. People stopped in the middle of the sidewalk to hold conversations, oblivious to those who had to circle around them. The high sun, the cool breeze, the fashion forward, the torn jeans, the blended wool three-quarter length coats unbuttoned to display the colorful sweaters, the patterned scarfs, it all brought me back to Summer '87.

Ever since that summer, no security guard monitored the front of the building. I pressed the buzzer and entered. I looked down to the back and heard chatter but no one looked out of the booth so I pressed for the elevator. I rang the loft's bell and it was obvious Attitude was expecting someone else. "You said to come whenever."

"That, I did." He motioned for me to come in. "Don't you still have your key?"

"Oh I'm supposed to just open the door not knowing what you got going on in here?" I turned to fully take in the changes he'd made to the loft. Gone were all the bedroom separations. Attitude took a step closer. His lips covered mine, the momentary loss of breath, closing the gap of years since we had last seen each other. He pulled on my left earlobe and brushed his open palm across my neck. The welcome kiss I had imagined but not expected. I took a slow step back with my left foot, unsure whether we should be kissing. He tugged on my overcoat to pull me closer. We hadn't kissed in years and had only seen each other once in three years. Two weeks ago I was certain this was what I most wanted in life. Being "just friends" when it was not your idea was worse than being the water boy on a team. The water boy did not expect to play.

I yearned for this way too long for it to happen now, so soon into my visit. I needed to clear the air, ask some important questions. Part of the reason I chose today as the day for the interview, we, SUM women, had convinced all of the Max little sisters to stop helping the pledge class. I didn't want things to progress from here, and for him to find out what we did to the Max pledge class. I pulled away from him and whispered, "Stop!"

He still held my jacket. "I thought you wanted this. And, that's why you stayed away, and surprised me today."

"I stayed away because I did some more research based on what you'd given me." He looked weathered but not beaten down. The strands of his locks, thick, sunburned, causing some to fade away from a deep black. He shook his head and walked away, to his desk. Attitude faced the computer screen and started typing away. "I don't want to be in your life that way anymore…"

"That's cool!"

"No, it's not cool!" I sat on the swivel chair behind a high table used for reviewing prints and other art. "…anymore unless you can be dead honest with me. I looked into your father's crime. So you've known all along or for a long time?" The loft's former living section no longer had its airy creative feel now that it had been divided with short separations, cubicles though each partition contained, not chair and desk, but piles of canvases and rolled-up prints. "I read all the newspaper clippings, the legal briefs and even contacted some of the people involved. Everyone says your father was guilty. He never filed an appeal."

"Guilty? Maybe, but guilt is not a verdict. It is an emotion. He never expressed guilt. I went to see him every other weekend up until they put him in the chair. Eight straight years." He looked at me, the steel in his eyes, burnished amber earned from years of sleepless nights. "I saw them put him to death."

The doorbell rang. "If you are expecting someone, I can come back later."

"It's not what you think." He yelled out, "Who is it?"

The voice sounded familiar. "One Two. One Two."

He whispered to me before walking towards the door. "A conversation is going to take place. You can use contents from the conversation as part of your interview. You must change their names and you are never to say you saw these two alone together, especially never here."

Manny opened the door. Bliss was a dramatic chick. The moment she saw me, she headed straight to me. I didn't stand up. That didn't stop her! She approached like we were best friends, bent over and hugged me. "I didn't know you were going to be here."

Monk didn't say a word to me. His haggard look confirmed what I knew about his being part of the Max pledge class.

Attitude asked him. "You two don't know each other?"

I smiled as Monk said, "I'm just wondering why she didn't run over and hug me the way Bliss did her."

Something was going to go down and I didn't want to be a hindrance, so I stood to make my way over to hug Monk. "Hi Monk…"

He cut me off. "Sit your ass down! I don't want a hug."

Bliss stepped toward him and hit him on the left pect with the heel of her right hand. "Watch how you speak to the queen!"

Monk laughed and pulled me to him. He made as if he was going to kiss me on the lips. I turned my head and he smelled me, my cheek, behind my ears, and my neck. "You smell good. You should let me hit that."

Attitude and Bliss laughed and she said, "Oh yeah, I'd like to see that. We should have a mini-orgy."

I couldn't get a sense of them and their humor, especially after they all said, "I'm in."

I backed up and sat down. They looked at me, as if waiting for an answer. "I guess I'll leave y'all to your business."

Bliss took off her coat and her sweater. She was not wearing a bra. I looked away from her to the men. They were still looking at me until Bliss said, "Man, you are such a sucker."

I stood up. "Check yourself, chick! You don't know me like that!"

She turned her head to them, not realizing she was the wrong word away from a busted eardrum. Her next words stunned me. "Do you know she called me two years ago, bribing me with SUM membership if I helped her stop the next MAX pledge class?"

They laughed and Monk said, "You two kiss and make up."

"Yeah, some girl-on-girl action," Attitude encouraged.

"OK. I'm game." Bliss looked at me. "Free Love, baby. Are you in?"

All three of them laughed.

I made to leave. "I came here to interview you about your art, not all this other bull."

"Who's an artist?" Bliss laughed when I pointed at Attitude. "I heard he was a gambler, a low-level criminal…"

Monk laughed hysterically. Attitude was looking at Bliss like what the fuck! "A, can I crash the fridge?"

She put her sweater back on.

"Sure, man. Bring me a beer! I need one to hear this chick explain to me how I am a low-level anything."

I too wanted to hear Bliss's zaniness aimed at someone else. Monk brought over a beer for everyone, but neither Bliss nor I wanted one. "First, let's start with your art. I did my research. I have seen zilch of your stuff referenced in collections, galleries or publications of any note, except for FIRST IMPRESSIONS and that was only because she interviewed you, and her name carries weight."

"That's 'cause I'm underground."

"Let me guess: you're keeping it real!"

"I don't have to keep it real. I am real."

"From what you say: it's one of two things. You are either a criminal or a crossover artist pampered and patronized by white people."

"First, how can I be a crossover artist when my work is about my hate for white people?"

Though my job was to chronicle what was being said, I had to jump in. "You? You hate white people?"

"Yeah. What did you think?"

"I've seen you in action since my freshman year."

Bliss interjected. "You're confusing hate with fear."

"That summer I was here, you were rooming with three of them. And, you looked really chummy with them to me."

Bliss stepped in. "Think of it as his deep cover. Let's get back to my point."

"Look, chick! Don't interrupt me when I'm talking!" Bliss had this confused look on her face like she couldn't believe my confrontational stance. She looked to Attitude for confirmation. He turned away to the computer and started to type. Seeing this, I remembered I was here to listen to the discussion. "You know what: finish your point because I did interrupt you first."

Attitude turned back to us and Bliss continued, "So, you say you're not a crossover artist, then why are most of your customers white people?"

"They get my art because the Middle Passage really happened."

"And what, Black people don't get that?

"I wouldn't say that. We get it but we can't see out of the maze because we're reliving the passage daily." He paused with a ta-da. When no one agreed, he added, "But, if one is able to stop moving and look at the structure, the world from a different vantage point, they would get it and see the maze itself travel away. The maze moves."

Bliss said, "I made a special trip to TGI to see your first collection, *Return of the Angry Black Man*, and all it had were images of black pathology."

"See, you! You for example, you're curious. But you are looking at it strictly on the surface, and applying standards you have been taught. If you had been raised in the environment you consider pathological and were exposed to my art, without preconceived notions, you wouldn't look for hidden meanings. The meanings would reveal themselves."

"So, expose me to something!" Her jerky body movements expressed contempt but in a jokey manner.

Attitude walked to the southeastern section of the loft. In the open space, the canvases faced the wall like students on time-out. He brought back three and handed the first to Bliss. "This is from my new collection."

I was as curious as Bliss to see his new collection. His first collection had images of people, a departure from every piece he had done at TGI. This collection was of objects yet still a departure from the pieces that had garnered the high praise and grades from his time at TGI. Through these lenses, I now had a thorough understanding of his work.

Bliss was a quick study. She rubbed her hand across the canvas. Afterward, she stared at the image and handed me the canvas. Bliss said, "In this one you are using vertical lines. You have created what I approximate to be twelve compartments. There are no horizontal lines. As you reach the center the paint color lightens. The brushstrokes are away from the center."

Attitude gave a slight nod. "So? You are close, but what is the message?"

"I don't know. It should be love."

I chimed in. "Hammer, they put me in the mix."

Attitude turned to Monk, who also said, "Hammer. Hammer. They put me in the mix."

The three of us started singing the chorus of the song, *They Put Me in the Mix.*

Bliss grabbed the next canvas from Attitude. She rubbed her right palm against it. "In this one, you use the corners of the canvas to form two sides of a square. All together there are four squares. Although the whole canvas is red, if you count the space occupied by the squares, the unused portions should technically form a white cross. That could be the flag of a country; perhaps Switzerland."

"No, focus on the image!"

She extended her arms to look, to magnify the image. "A cocktail glass? How does that fit in?"

She made to hand me the canvas.

I waved her off, not to discount what she was seeing. But, no matter how valid her viewing of Attitude's work, I said, "Bloody Mary."

"I'll have a Bloody Mary." Monk laughed at his own joke.

"You're right. I mistook the crack down the center of the glass for a cross."

Attitude laughed and this fueled Bliss's wrath. "You can't tell me I am wrong. If you touch the canvas, you can tell by the preparation that went into it."

"What if I told you all three of you were right because your environment determines what you see? I could show you a blank canvas and you wouldn't see it as the same."

I smiled at Bliss for the first time in my life, my way of signaling a truce. She balked. "We cannot all be right! What is the name of series?"

"Voices from the Margin."

"Then you need something to connect the two extremes. Otherwise, it's too abstract and left to interpretation."

"That's how I stay alive!"

"Then you are a criminal!"

"No, I am a gambler."

Bliss stood firm on her convictions. "Look at it this way! Gambling – shows you have no loyalties. Artists are criminals who gamble with their lives. What you're selling is an idea, something that does not really exist. It's like you're conning people. When they discover the scam, you either end up homeless or dead."

Attitude turned to Monk. "You really picked a winner."

"I can show you how to hedge your bet and win real big."

"I have already won big."

Bliss walked a small circle around him, sizing him up. "Something is missing from your work, and I can help you put it in there."

"You want to be my muse?"

"If you need to give it a label, that's fine by me."

Attitude laughed. "Thanks but no thanks! My work has all that it needs."

"It's missing the gray"

Bliss stumped us into a stone silence. She remained quiet until Monk figured it out. "She means love!"

As if relieved someone got it, Bliss exclaimed like a magician saying ta-da, "It needs love."

Attitude was not interested. "Love doesn't sell unless someone dies! *Romeo and Juliet. Love Story.* I can go on."

"People can live forever if there is love." Bliss spliced her sentences into two tones. The first came out as a statement of fact; the second like a plea. "If you show love, you must be willing to share love."

I crossed my arms to hold myself, a way to not engage Bliss. She had made a startling error. I wanted to tell her: Hold up! My family has been in this Society for a long time. Love is Black, and we keep it a secret because if you expose Love to the world, everyone will want to use it, yet no one will give credit to its origins. No one will allow love to serve its primary purpose – to unify and uplift the world. They would distort it.

Bliss turned to look at me and Monk, who held the best poker face I had ever encountered. He shared no body movements, no hint he knew she had erred – Society people did not think like this. She blasted the words in Attitude's direction. "Don't talk to me about race, about your hate unless there's love involved! You don't think we were able to last centuries in this land without love existing on both sides, do you? Love is gray."

She had silenced everyone. Attitude picked up the last canvas and showed us the image. There was a brown ladder in the middle of the canvas. A white circle served as the spotlight. The rest of the canvas was black. He pointed at Bliss first. "What do you see?"

"I have to touch the canvas to tell you."

He bypassed her. "Hope!"

"When it's all said and done, no one will know our roles."

Monk said, "It wasn't me."

But Bliss went there, "Can there be love if there's no public recognition?"

Attitude was miffed at her stubbornness. "Are you serious?"

"Yes! I want you to have an exhibit at a gallery of my choosing. If you sell for a certain amount, then I will buy in."

Attitude pointed at me. "What about you Hope?"

"In what?" I played dumb.

The phone rang and after speaking for about thirty seconds, Attitude put it on speaker mode. The voice sounded real panicky. It sounded familiar but I could not tell for sure. As soon as he finished speaking, Attitude told him to hold up and put the phone on mute. The three of them looked at me. All I could do was smile. Bliss smiled back and said to them, "I told you so."

Attitude shook his head. "You SUM women are too much. Is that why you came here today?"

"Partly! I also came for the interview."

Bliss spoke up. "Tell Devon, all the women didn't leave. I am still in and have a group of women who would be more than willing to stand publicly with the Max boys."

Attitude said, "No, you are now part of the Black Love underground. Max life is too tricky to navigate. It's too soon and too dangerous to try to play two roles."

"I said I can do it."

"Monk, what do you think?"

"Only if you make Devon the rock of the line!"

Attitude asked her, "Do you trust Devon?"

"Oh yeah, especially if he is able to stand tall after the pledge process!"

Attitude clicked the phone back on. "Do your research! You have one woman left: Bliss. She'll get you pledges enough women to stand by you. So y'all can still surface tonight without any help from SUM women."

Devon said, "Thank you."

Attitude hung up the phone.

I did my best to hide my hurt that he had recruited Bliss into Black Love, to essentially replace me. I did not know tonight was the night the Max line planned to surface. The pressure was on and my voice betrayed me. My breathing was off and my words were rushed. What I had heard and seen made me have to change plans. "Attitude, I am pressed for time and need to head back to TGI. Can we reschedule the interview?"

He asked, "If you're heading back upstate, can you give Bliss a lift back to Semline?"

"No. That's an hour out of my way. She can get back the way she came."

Monk spoke up. "What's up with you and all this hostility?"

"You're talking about hostility? How about how you never returned my…" I stopped myself, realizing more than my breathing was off. This gathering? Why were Monk and Bliss together, when Monk should be pledging at Semline? I needed answers so I said, "OK, Bliss can ride with me."

Chapter 35
A TWO-WAY STREET

Bliss, at dusk, light fading as we walked northeast, surprised me with her silence. Her eyes focused on the people walking by, those coming toward us and the ones overtaking us. For a person whose mouth and mannerism always put her on a collision course, Bliss walked slowly as if she feared being bumped into. Walking in New York City is a contact sport; that's what my father taught me during my first trip alone with him into the city. You had to know who to hit hard, who to avoid, and how to brush up casually against people, to simply recognize them as one of yours.

I purposely hurried to see her reaction. Once I got three full strides ahead of her, I turned to hint for her to catch up. She maintained her same pace. Her lithe body angling away from the sidewalk's center toward store entrances, only to tilt back as customers exited on to the sidewalk. Seeing Bliss move gave me an appreciation for a cachet not visible in small quarters, a worldliness about her, an understanding of incidental forces at play. I slowed to match her steps, to measure our shoulders, to see which of us passersby gazed as they approached.

A quiet Bliss was not as alluring. She blended into the crowd as if the nearly two-inch difference was not to her advantage, that her shoulder-length hair, full and crowning her angular visage did not highlight the glamour understood only by those who never had a need to flaunt their wealth. Eyes fell on my eyes and cheeks and headed straight to my waistline and below. The looks Bliss had not dodged held her face, wondering, taking in the four senses held above the shoulders. Bliss had the type of beauty that made one realize the fifth sense, that of touch, also resided above the shoulders. People touched her with their eyes, noses and ears. Their mouths flirted via groans, whispers or sudden mid-sentence pauses.

This moment did not last. Once locked inside the car, barely having maneuvered out of the parking spot, Bliss started talking. "You've known Attitude longer than I have, and you couldn't tell he was a criminal?"

"I tend not get involved in other people's politics."

"Why were you there then?"

"To interview him about his work for my thesis."

"Your thesis is about him?" I glanced in time to catch the way her face scrunched up at the thought.

She really did not respect his art. "No, I need an artist's point of view on color, specifically color gradient in producing abstract art. Your arrival ruined what I planned to ask..."

"Oh, I thought you had gotten enough information based on our discussion." I let her statement fly by as I turned on to the ramp for the FDR Drive. She continued, "You can ask me whatever you didn't get from what he was saying."

"How long have you known Attitude?"

"That was my second time talking to him."

"And, that makes you an expert?" I asked it as a brushback pitch.

"No, but I know more about him than you do. And, you've known him, how long?"

To her my silence meant she could just blab. Bliss was the typical loose lips sink ships person. Even though she sounded like she was making things up as she went along, I must admit she had me wondering with Max boys being masters of deception, whether Bliss and the knowledge she would pass to me was a ploy. They could have pumped her with false information to veer me off my course. Something about Derek Davenport's conviction didn't sit right; for everyone to agree on the official story, for him to have no allies, yet his son walks freely in the Society. As I ran the scenarios through my mind, she asked, "How many underground artists do you know with that kind of lifestyle? What was his last job?"

So I decided to toy with her, "Maybe he's a communist? He did say he gives his art for free to friends."

"That wouldn't be so bad. He also said he sells his stuff on the street or has someone who handles that for him." She shook her head. "Actually I think he's more of an anarchist."

My mind went back to our student protest days and I recalled some of the platforms Attitude represented. The one thing he said today that threw me for a loop and I wondered where Monk and Bliss fitted in this change or if that was the ploy. So, I asked Bliss, "Do you hate white people?"

"Why would I hate white people? They freed pussy." Bliss was weird like that and I was getting used to her way of thinking. She added, "Think of any society not run by whites, and you'll see what I mean!"

"Is pussy meant to be free?"

"Yes, but for love there's a fee."

"Yes, as MAX boys their loyalty is supposed to be to the queen but I don't get that sense from these MAX boys."

"It's a fine line they walk. They're covert operatives, just like me."

"You?" I was not able to hide my surprise.

Her "Yeah!" sounded like "Duh!" She broke it down for me. "My loyalty is to the MAX boys. Yours is to SUM and therefore SBD. But, let's not forget we are women, so our war is to make sure male domination is ended." She knew the roads enough to see I had decided to take the slightly longer distance, the toll roads toward Semline or TGI. Bliss reached in her purse for a twenty dollar bill to help with tolls. I stuffed it into the ashtray. She'd extended herself to me from the first moment we met yet taking this road was my way of letting her know I could either continue straight to TGI or veer off halfway up the interstate for the local road that leads to Semline. Our conversation stalled in between the miles even though traffic was somewhat light. After a few minutes of silence, she picked up the conversation. "You and I would make a good team. I can attack all the men who pose a real threat to us free women as we try to liberate the bound ones, you know, the women who act like they can't live without a man."

"How do we go about freeing them?"

"You come in and seduce them, make them feel comfortable in the arms of another woman, and show them how to properly deal with men."

"Why would I be seducing women? I am not a lesbian."

Bliss didn't believe me. "You're not? I heard…"

I interrupted. "Forget what you heard and know what you're being told!"

"OK, I will seduce the women. And, you sleep with all the men!"

"You are not making any sense."

She got angry. "Yes, I am! Right now we're operating on extremes. We need to come to a consensus. Withholding sex would cause men to become more violent, and that's a battle we can't win. At least not yet! So we have to establish a society where love is free."

"How so?"

"Tell a man he can have sex any time he chooses without any hassle, and he'll join us."

"I think you are confusing sex with love."

"You know what, you're scared of pussy power. You don't know what pussy is, do you?" I paid the toll and gave Bliss a hard look to let her know just how weird she was acting. I merged on to Route 28. She grabbed my right hand. "Here! Touch my breasts!"

I pulled my hand away. "Chick, I ain't touching you!"

"OK, then I will touch you." Bliss ran her right hand across my breasts causing me to lose control.

The car swerved left. "You put your hand on me again, not only will I kick your ass, I will leave your ass on the side of the road."

She laughed. "You can't do the first. The second you would not do because you know I'm right."

"I can kick your ass! Really I can."

Her hysterical laugh silenced me. "You really can't but the fact you're willing to stand up and fight, I don't need to bust open your face."

I recalled the dossier on Bliss stating she started martial arts at eight years old, about the same age I took my first class. We remained quiet. She likely was doing the same permutations and by now realized I likely would win the fight. I decided to stand down by switching the topic. "You mentioned you'd heard things about me. What did you hear?"

"That you were a coward, and needed your brothers to fight your battles."

"What?"

"Is it true SUM ran an operation that exposed unfair grading practices and you asked the SBD brothers to confront the school administration? When they refused, you had the Max boys take up the fight?"

I kept being honest with her. "I mentioned the situation to Attitude and he took it upon himself to take action."

"Next time, you're in a situation that requires some sort of protest, don't call the men! They have their own agenda and battles to fight."

"We needed to address that situation and didn't have an in with the administration."

"Next time, do a naked women protest! And, trust me all other women organizations on the campus would have joined you. Naked women make the authorities nervous! We personally have never felt the need to use it, but it's coming."

"Who is this we you keep talking about?"

"It's an organized body linked under a loose structure. Women like me act a certain way to help other women accept this freedom as the most natural form of womanhood."

"What does all of this have to do with me?"

"Our women do not get accepted as SUM pledges. Y'all have this strict morality code, and it is the broken link with the Max boys."

"So, this is about the Max boys!"

"Yes, they're the easiest point of attacking the Society, if SUM would stop equating sex with morality."

I veered off the highway, on to a parkway that led to routes direct to

Semline, and corrected her. "Sex is not our point of contention with them. It's that they think they're free to not marry into the Society." Bliss didn't take the bait. I now took it as fact Bliss was indeed a seventh generation FLT. "You know the history. As written, when the Society divided into four organizations, freedom was not the first word for their side, your ancestor's side. Truth was the destination. Do you know the first word?"

"It was Pride. For what our side had to do, we needed the Freedom to operate. Do you think it was and is easy to live the type of life these women had to live?" I didn't answer because my only knowledge of FLT was from what my GG told me. Bliss challenged me. "If you think it was easy, join us. Help us take down the Max boys."

Though I wanted to stop the Max boys in their quest to start this war, I had to cement to Bliss I had no interest in her plan. "I am a Society Girl until I die. I fight for Black Liberation. I don't have time for your plan to divide us from the men."

"What exactly does that mean?" She ridiculed me with her laughter. "Let's say Black people were to become the rulers of this new world you envision, what would change for women, for the better?"

"It's not about being rulers of the world. Our goal is to establish…"

She interrupted me. "Girl, what is your major? Rhetoric?"

"Yes, it was for my Bachelor's and my upcoming Master's."

I sensed the wheels turning but she could not ask the most direct question linking to TGI's history as a military institution. Bliss circled back. "What happens when a SUM woman marries a Max boy or any man who has no historical link to SBD or SUM?"

"Her sons cannot enter the Society as a SBD. That's one of the items my platform aims to change."

"When FLT ceased to exist, it actually went dormant in order to join with other organizations. The first women were FLT legacies who no longer wanted to be linked to PMB. They linked with women who had had the opportunity to express their freedom more than we had."

"You mean white girls, right? I'll pass."

"Are you in or not?"

"In what? If you can't tell me the name, then how do I know what to look for?"

"I like to call it Free Love, but it's much more than that."

I needed her to divulge more information. "How do I know you're not making all this up?"

Bliss looked at me with a seriousness I had never seen in her eyes even in her fits of anger. "Don't try this on your own!" This portion of the parkway ran through small towns that had not funded and approved an overpass or exit off the roadway. As such, the highway transformed into a road with cross-streets every mile or so. The main road's stop lights stayed green as to not create traffic jams, and the cross-streets had flashing red lights. I followed her instructions. "Put your car exactly in the middle, over the yellow dividing lines. Do not swerve! Turn off your headlights. Turn them back on. Hit your high beam twice. Turn off your headlights. Turn them back on. Maintain a speed of forty miles per hour."

The road had bends and dips. In the distance ahead, I could see approaching cars a little under a mile away. I drove for about ten seconds, and noticed one car's lights ahead of me, mirroring the on and off routine I had just completed. "What do I do now?"

Cars coming toward me honked their horns, but moved to their right, avoiding my car. Bliss spoke slowly as if trying to put me in a trance. "Life is not a conspiracy or about uncovering one. The goal is to learn life's rhythm. If we can accomplish that then we can establish that true love, one love. Every time we get close, we get infiltrated, better yet discovered by our enemies. They do something drastic, some sort of violent act to drive a wedge between our constituencies. We have learned whenever something happens and we cannot discover its rhythm, that is to say it has no rhyme or reason, step away because if it continues it will lead to much destruction."

"Bliss, this car is coming dead at me. What am I supposed to do next?"

I was not sure if she were hypnotized or trying to hypnotize me. "Repeat after me! Life is a game of chicken. It is not a conspiracy or about uncovering one. The goal is to learn life's rhythm…"

I turned to look at her. She was clutching the shoulder strap of the seatbelt and bracing herself for impact. I shouted, "Bliss, what next?"

"Life is a game of chicken." One minute the lights were bright and bearing down on me. I looked through the windshield and saw an old lady. She looked about my great-grandmother's age. There was this sort of wicked grin on her face, yet she looked scared. I guess she was chicken, the sacrifice. The next minute I saw darkness and heard the crash. The sound had a delay, as if the car had traveled dozens of feet through air. The severity of what I had done hit me on the stomach. It felt as if everything I had consumed my entire life wanted to gush out my mouth. Bliss was full of glee, like she was high on something. She kept saying, "Let's do it again!" By now I was veering back to the right side of the road. If I did not stop, I would not only throw up on myself, I would lose control of the vehicle. As soon as I stopped the car, I saw where the old lady's car had hit mine. My side view mirror was shattered, the frame, facing downward, barely hanging by its screws. My door had wrinkles, where the cars' bodies had rubbed. "Sister, we can't stay here much longer. The police will be here any minute." I was throwing up my guts and Bliss's voice sounded far, a squeal, that little white girl quality when I first heard it and what I hated about it. She continued, "Let me drive! We have to get out of here."

I composed myself enough to look up. What I saw frightened me. The other side of the road, about a mile down, there was a traffic jam, a pile up and a burst of flame, possibly a car on fire. Ahead of us, on the other side, cars were making way for an ambulance to get through. Its siren blared intermittently, its lights spinning red and white. "Let's get out of here!"

Bliss said, "Let me drive!"

"No, you're not driving my car. I would leave your ass out here, but I need some answers."

I rushed into the car. My anger sobered me and turned me toward her. Before I was able to speak, she asked, "What's wrong? We're now sisters."

"No we're not, stupid! I am pissed off."

"You're not. You're just scared."

This chick was still trying to run game on me. "Stop with the nonsense!"

"It's not nonsense. You cannot drive this car. With the left side view mirror down and a sister possibly dead, I have to drive so I can signal clearance for us."

"Tell me how to do it!"

"I can't. You're not on this level."

"Check it out! The Max line is surfacing tonight, right? Whose legacy is on the line? And, what is the wager?"

Bliss's surprise registered and she made no move to hide. "So, you do know about the secret messages in Attitude's canvases?"

"Yes, but how stupid were you to decipher them in front of him?"

"I need him to run."

"Why?"

"You're the queen, right?" Bliss was panicky. "You gotta let me drive. If not, turn off your headlights."

"I thought you said it's not a conspiracy."

"It's not, but we're the only ones still going up towards the highway."

I glanced at my rearview. There were no cars moving, behind us or in front of us. Traffic on both sides of the road had come to a stand-still. The road was no longer a two-way street. A concrete divider between the two sides – one lane each. I turned off my headlights and drove slower, "Who gave you orders to kill me?"

"What? No one wants to kill you. The Max boys would protect you at any cost."

"Bliss, do you consider yourself a black woman?"

"Yes, of course."

"This is the most honest I will ever be with you. Somebody's got you hanging on a string. I don't know who it is, and I am sure you don't know who to trust. So, I am offering you a way out. You have to trust me! You are playing yourself cheap. I am a SUM woman, a sister of Stay Black and Die! I am not afraid of you or whatever the fuck you think you are representing."

"No, you bought in. You are no longer a SUM woman. You are now part of The Sisterhood, the Free Love Society."

"OK, little girl, keep believing that! We are less than twenty minutes away from the Semline campus. You will be entering a war zone. I will do my best to keep you cleared and protected. Trust me, I speak the truth. I mean you no harm. OK?"

"OK!" She reached out her left hand to me, and I squeezed it. "And, know that I mean no harm to you."

I nodded and for some reason I believed her.

We arrived on the Semline campus. The main quad was deserted, with students likely packing the gym for the basketball game. The place had a spooky feel to it, and not because of the decorations put up in preparation for Halloween. "By the way, who funneled you the information about Attitude's art?"

"My mother is an art professor. I grew up around this stuff." She was lying because there was no way to pick it up so quickly. "I am going to be acting totally out of character, to do my best to protect you. But when the time comes, you have to protect me."

I tried to knock some sense into her. "NO! Leave them Max boys alone. Those fools are dangerous."

"Not from them! From your sisters! Don't forget you must drop the morality trap!" I just shook my head in pity for the poor girl. "You still do not look well. Do you want to come upstairs to rest?"

"I can't be seen with you. Where can I drop you off so no one sees us together?" She pointed to a parking lot, off the main circle of Semline's open campus. I drove around the next circle which led to the dormitories.

"Park in this spot here!"

"Where can I use a phone?"

"Every dorm has a phone in the lobby. Lauren lives in the dorm over there." I didn't say anything. "No, she's not part of The Sisterhood. She's a fucking virgin!"

Bliss slipped out and walked in the opposite direction.

This was only my second time on the Semline campus. Though only the middle of October, the wind and low temperature made it feel like the dead of winter. The minute I hit the cold air, I felt like vomiting. I hid behind a dumpster and afterward walked around to the front entrance. I hadn't eaten anything, but it's like I had been poisoned. Bliss was a poison. I am not sure if she had always been like that, or was it her interaction with the Max boys. For now, it really did not matter. The Max pledge class was due to surface, and Great-Granny Celeste said the best way to defeat Max boys when they surfaced without SUM women was to ignore them. "I am here to visit Lauren Hathaway."

The hall proctor telephoned her room and asked me to sign the visitor's log. Though I only had to walk up to the second floor, my energy was sapped. My face must have shown my weakness. Lauren ran to me and supported me by putting my right arm around her shoulders. We got to her room and she walked me to the bed so I could lie down. "Big Sister Hope, did Bliss do this to you?"

"Bliss, what does she have to do with this?"

"Well, she called here and told me you were coming and not to let you drive. I know she was upset you and the sisters did not want her to join SUM."

"Who told you that?"

"No one. We just assumed since she didn't pass the interview."

"On your application, we had major concerns your great-grandmother was a FLT woman. Are you part of any organization that's in any manner affiliated with FLT or support any of their objectives?"

Her face, teary-eyed. "No, Big Sister Hope! I already answered those questions."

"I know but I need a sister who I can trust with my life."

"You can trust me."

"OK! Put the call out that the women of SUM are boycotting the Max pledge class."

"We can't do that. They're surfacing tonight. That would be considered an act of war."

"Didn't you just say I can trust you?"

"Big Sister Hope, if Bliss did something to you, I will kill her for you. But to make that phone call and boycott the Max boys only plays into their hand. Other organizations will join the boycott. These new MAX boys will have no loyalty to SUM." I looked at her, my face showing the ultimate disgust in her sudden timidity when it came to the MAX boys. I made to leave. "Maybe Bliss is right and you should not drive. Why don't you take off your clothes and take a nap? Maybe a bath?"

"No! I need you to make the phone calls and boycott the Max line. We are going to war."

"Over what? Against who? What should I tell them the war is about?"

I had connected the dots. "We're fighting for Forty Million and a White Girl. And, whoever tries to stop us is our enemy."

I sat up on the bed, feeling spent and watched her dial the two numbers.

When she finished, she sat at her desk and just stared at me. I asked her, "If you were queen of the Society, what type of ruler would you be?"

"I would be a benevolent leader like you are."

"Keep that in mind when you become queen!" As I dozed off, I asked, "What do you have against Bliss?"

"Nothing! I just thought she did something to you."

"What type of girl is she? Is she loose?"

"Bliss? Loose? No! She's like everyone's little sister. Everyone loves her!"

"What about you?"

She took a moment to answer then mumbled sheepishly, "Yes. Bliss brings joy to everyone. She exudes love."

I sat up, totally confused. "Then why would you kill her for me?"

"To protect your legacy!"

"What? What do you consider my legacy?"

"It's on the line, still in the making. Diane and I are doing our best to extend it. So far by highlighting the sisters' gripes, you've given everyone else a voice. That's your legacy. And, I will kill to protect it."

"There's no need to kill!" Sleep began to overtake me. "I called the boycott because Max boys operate in the shadows because no one has ever given them a voice. If we take away their ability to operate in the shadows, we will truly get to find out what they stand for."

Chapter 36
THE BASEMENT

I awoke with a splitting headache, from a moment of sheer panic. There were blinding lights, a horn and a deafening sound, a BOOM, an explosion. Our creed materialized in my thoughts: *When God said let there be a light, out of that darkness came a light, a beacon to show the way, of the original path to our creator. From whence we move forward, it is really backward, when there was no division.*

Followed by the words, "We killed that old lady." This time, unlike in my sleep, the words were coherent. They came out of my mouth. I looked at the shadowy figure across the room. The standing lamp, its bulb's wattage no more than twenty-five, illuminated only this portion of the room. Since all other lights were off, I only saw a silhouette. "Who's that?"

"It's me Lauren."

"Oh, I'm still here? It feels like days, weeks have gone by."

"It's Sunday, 5:45pm. It's been nearly forty-eight hours."

"You! What are you doing here? You should be in The Basement."

"I requested that we observe no weekends or holidays until you have returned. We are utilizing a 7 p.m. start time on Saturdays and Sundays."

"Even so, you need to get going. TGI is a solid one hour drive. You've gone both nights since I've been here, right?"

"Yes. I can make it to TGI in forty minutes when pressed." That didn't seem possible, with the miles, traffic and bend in the roads. "Big Sister Queen Kendall, there are questions. Questions I have not been able to answer. Everyone wants to know why we are at war, presumably against the Max boys."

"No, no. There's an operation. It took place in the sixties and ended in 1972. The Society's historical record states four policemen died. The mainstream publications only report the death of two policemen with the shooter arrested and sentenced to death row."

"Wait up! We're at war because of Manny Davenport and his father?"

Her knowledge surprised me and made me wonder why she would be reading this section of the historical record, particularly about this small operation. "I'm sharing this with you because I might not make it out alive. Someone's going through extreme means to protect that operation, what really happened. Someone's gonna try to stop me again, from finding out the truth." I got up from the bed, my clothes the same from Friday, the underlayer drenched from sweat, a smell. Lauren stepped forward to help me balance myself. "Thanks, I'm fine."

"No, you're not. Each time I return to the room, you're on the floor after a fall off the bed. You're jumpy when you are able to stay awake. But, that's only for minutes, thirty at most. You fall asleep only to wake within two hours after mumbling and shaking throughout."

"I'm fine. I'm fine. I just need to shower and borrow a change of clothes to head back to TGI."

She pointed to them on the floor by the desk chair. "On Friday, you brought up those two bags from your car."

"OK, you get going to arrive by seven. I will see you at TGI later tonight."

"You really should rest, Big Sister Queen Kendall! Take a bath instead of a shower so you do not slip in the tub."

"It's a slam lock, right?"

"The panel makes it optional. I will unlock it so you can reenter after bathing. There's food in the fridge."

"Don't mention the details of this operation to anyone! We need to see who responds." She gave me a worried look and hugged me.

This dorm room was a single occupancy. It had one queen-size bed, one desk, a double-paneled wall closet, a miniature fridge and microwave. I had my own bathing and beauty supplies but needed a towel from Lauren's closet. I had planned to spend no more than one night away in Manhattan. It was never wise to be absent from pledge class activities for more than a night when you were the person in charge. I needed to return tonight or this would be my third night away. Lauren had not looked wearier, not on day one, not from day one to today, day forty. She and Diane had a resolve that made me comfortable to leave them for a night or two.

I showered and warmed something to eat.

Lauren had not searched through my bags. Items placed to alert me whether someone had looked through my knapsack had not been disturbed. I saw myself in her except Lauren possessed an ability to be both decisive and trusting of her decisions. One bag had clothes while the other contained my supplies, my nearly-completed thesis, the lone notebook I brought with me to Attitude's loft, my tape recorder, my camera and my gun. With his advance blessing, I had secretly taped the conversation. My conversation in the car with Bliss had not been taped because it would have been against protocol unless she agreed.

Trust? Could I trust the three of them? Attitude and Bliss, yes - even though they were always moving the conversation and target beyond my scope.

Monk was steady but unreachable. I could think of no reason for him to be in Manhattan during - what is - the pledge process to charter PMB on his campus, under his legacy. His family had no recorded dealings with any of the Society's operations. Their only focus was to forever be the steady hand, the old guard.

I dressed in layers, putting the sweathood on top of my dress shirt and short-sleeve t-shirt, a ski hat and gloves.

Any signs of sunlight, even its purple haze when blended with a clear early night sky had disappeared. The collision had distorted my internal compass. The Semline campus had the feel of a maze, its circular layout with the library serving as the endpoint of the diameter on the mid-western side. My walking path from Lauren's dorm hit the roundabout and I had to walk clockwise to head toward the parking lot. From the distance I noticed no student bothered to observe the sign indicating the direction to walk. They simply walked across the divider, stepped up on the border, on to the dirt, by the trees.

I kept a slight gaze to my right shoulder where the first path led to the main gate. I got my bearings, recalling that once past the gate, I veered right and this second path, if traversed, would lead to a quad, where the Founder's statue kept guard over a lake; frozen but only recently; a few ice skaters cheerfully making rounds, their laughter blending with distant soundwaves, the jumbled notes of music from dorm windows, alternating with the swoosh of speeding cars from the highway below. The lake ran north toward TGI. From the third path, I could walk to reach the various parking lots. Small sedans, rarely one with a dent; most cars looked relatively new, an affluence a step or two above TGI with its old-money legacies. The various faces, nonintrusive, all kept a moderate pace. Modern buildings, and with the older ones having gone through gut renovations, Semline was a college whose place in history was not etched in only how long it had been around, but in how it had led the times.

I arrived at the spot where my car should have been but it was not. There was no broken glass or any sign that something in the empty spot had been tampered with. I scoped my surroundings to see if I could have been spotted by anyone when I parked. The visitors' lot was packed with cars, including those with the Semline student parking permit decal. The lot's proximity to the next path which housed the library, computer labs and gymnasium likely made it a favorite. To the right of the lot there were a range of buildings. I walked toward them to read the signs. Health Center and two sets of campus housing: dormitories and apartments; both for students. My first instinct was to go ask someone where Bliss lived. I thought better of it and considered whether she took my car, it was perhaps to go run an errand or for my safety. On the off-chance, she did not and someone stole my car, it could be to expose me to the kindness of strangers. I could not go back to Lauren's dorm, not only because I had locked the door, but to also not place one more burden on her shoulders. She had enough to deal with.

As I returned to the parking lot, I spotted the first black faces I had seen since leaving Lauren's dorm. "Hi, do you know how I can catch a bus to TGI?"

"One leaves daily from town square at noon."

I replied, "I'm always thankful for the kindness of strangers."

The young couple simply said, "OK" and walked away.

I went to sit in front of the library to see if any SBD brothers had not made the trip to TGI. But then I recalled not only was there a SUM pledge class, SBD were also running at all three schools and using Barrington as the base. It was as if they had conceded Semline and possibly TGI to the Max class.

The temperature dipped to the low thirties so I walked to the nearest cafeteria, the building between Lauren's dorm and the library. I sat within earshot of a few black students and listened to the various conversations they held and looped it with those of the white students behind me. Neither group of students was connected to the Society though I did hear mention about the Max pledge class and about two girls putting on freak show at TGI. I had never heard anyone refer to a SUM woman pledge class in such derogatory terms. I raised my head and looked in her direction. We made eye contact and the nonchalance of how she turned her head confirmed she did not know of me or recognize me. She continued with the gossip as my right ear heard a woman at a table of three say, "I will bring the booze. You bring food and you restock on condoms. Free love for everyone."

They giggled and bused their trays as they left the cafeteria. My first impulse was to follow them. They would lead me to Bliss. What would I tell her? What would she tell me? I'm not supposed to be here. What if my car's disappearance was to leave me stranded, either to be in harm's way or to spy on the Max boys!

Could my GG Celeste have been right? I recall how I always looked down on The Outsiders. As SUM women, our tradition called for us to convince women not to help Max boys during their pledge process. At the start of our pledge class, we got word that Manny was running a process. We rid of their little sisters in less than a week. We never heard of the Max pledge class from then and since no Max legacy was thought to exist on any of the campuses, The Outsiders should not have been allowed to get initiated. We thought Manny made them as renegades but we had no way of knowing Ted was on the campus. Max boys never make their presence known unless they needed something or were in full blown attack mode. And, then on the quad, at the bonfire, we heard gunfire as the administration building burned. The Outsiders stood there with the bravado and moxie of gun slingers, mercenaries. They made no effort to introduce themselves to any Society members then or days later. At graduation, they took their papers and left. We barely knew their names, whether their families were indeed of the Society and, if not, who sponsored them.

It was. It is a dangerous game that Max boys play, to let you in with no cover, no protection from the Society and run operations that oft-times counter the Society's core beliefs. With this Max class, from the women who left we could not get the names of all the men who started and left, and all those still part of the pledge class. We, in fact, respected the women for not telling. It told us they would keep our secrets. But with the surfacing of this Max class, we now had the names to put into our historical record. People will search birth records, match their parents to previous operations, previous votes, and so on.

My task was different. I was on the Semline Campus to find out the identity of the women who were trying to help the Max boys free love.

Semline was a twenty-four hour campus for all support services and facilities. Only staff and administrative functions operated on a traditional or business schedule. Bliss mentioned these women were part of a club so their names would be listed and I could get it tomorrow. For now I had to look for signs of the pledge class. So few people, if any, knew me on this campus.

Moving freely was no problem yet not the best situation. I truly did not understand how in four years up here Monk had set no protocols for safety, to alleviate duress for any visiting member of the Society in distress, or any who just wanted to come visit him.

I went to the gym for a quick stretch and to hit the punching bag. I had tons of energy flowing through my body, signs the jitters were evaporating. Security at the door was no more than a formality. I walked in without an ID card and did a workout.

At 10 p.m. as I made to leave the gym, I saw them coming toward the main entrance. I steeled myself to not panic, to not alert the security guard that I did not belong. I slid into a side room, a racquetball court where I listened for their steps to fully pass the door. I stepped out and listened for murmurs of those who could not contain their curiosity. Once I located their whereabouts, I had to figure the best vantage to get a sense of what was going on. To my surprise, there was a crowd of people looking into a room. There were seven on the Max pledge class. I recognized four of them so I did not need photos of them. The other three I clicked several shots the way others were doing. They were going through a fighting exercise. They were dressed in thermal garment up top, gym shorts and bare feet. The drill was full contact and each man for himself. They wore blindfolds and head gear. Shots to the face or crotch area were not permitted.

They fought for two hours.

At the end, it seemed no one won because, at no time, did the group allow any one member to get ganged up on. They packed up. I retreated into another room and saw them line up and march out of the building. I followed with a few others but as we got to the parking lot, I was the only one still following. Luckily I had kept a good enough distance from the front of the crowd. I turned left and entered the woods in a different section. I spotted them a football field or so away. They were in a clearing. I crept up as close as I could. I stayed behind a brush of woods, making certain I did not step on a branch or slip and give away my position. I could not make out who was who but sequential patterns gave an indication.

They were doing a firearms training drill where a person stood blindfolded in a circle. He held the gun downward. The other six would fake as if running toward him. He would stay still and accept a flying kick that would land him to the ground. After the kick the person who had kicked him would scramble to another point of the circle. The blindfolded man inside the circle would get up firing, but never low, at the reentry point he estimated the kicker had reached. Shots were shoulder length and higher. The ones outside the circle would by then be flat on the ground. This was an exercise but the point was clear – know your enemy and his movements.

They each took a turn and what left me stumped was they were using a silencer and live rounds. They stayed out there for two hours. When it was time to leave, they ran back toward the parking lot. Each jumped into a different car and as a passenger. These seven cars and several other cars left the campus using various paths. I ran back to the library – cold and hungry. I reviewed maps of the campus and town, and made printed copies. I studied the various roads, how even though there was one main exit, one could leave campus via four other exits. Those secondary exits required a student ID shown to a campus police officer for entering and exiting.

I had to think about the main entrance and my missing car. Lauren would not return until eight a.m. Still I would not bother her. I needed a place to sleep. The Max boys had left for the night but it was not sleep time for them. It was still training time. They were likely learning what needed to be learned in order to survive between the hours of two a.m. to seven a.m. I would await their return.

Libraries were a good place to sleep. I would find a corner in one of the stacks, either under a table or behind a ladder.

In my dreams…

Lauren said I was waking from nightmares. I was not one to remember my dreams the morning after. If by chance I woke during the night, only bits and pieces remained with me, and not in color or in stark contrast of black and white. There would be this fuzziness, a haze, dark violet dots interspersed with bright specks. Images would collide with thoughts, as if drawn from a collective and not just my memories and experiences. That night I felt a hand touch me. The dream was clear, lucid. The hand slid through, separating my knees. Its knuckles rubbing against the side of my right knee bone. It pushed upward as if it wanted to snatch. I woke in a panic, my chest burning. I looked around for a garbage pail. A cold sweat had formed on my forehead. My body convulsed in small heaves as I held the rim of the can.

I took the can to the nearest bathroom and tied the bag and put it into the large can against the wall. I washed my face and mouth and brushed my teeth. I put the garbage pail back in its place so the janitorial staff would replace the plastic bag.

I left the library and headed to the cafeteria. I needed coffee, OJ, cranberry, something to remove the feel, the taste from my mouth. I sat two tables away from the only black students in the place. Two girls and a boy rambled on about classes. Patience would win out in this one. I needed a clue on the average black Semline student's allegiance. Did they feel the Max boys had the right to lead the Society? They were not saying much until out of the eastern window, I heard the words—

> *Old pirates, yes they rob I*
> *Sold I to the merchant ship*

The boy shouted, "They're here! Let's go!"

"I told you I ain't going out there. I'm supporting the boycott."

"Man, the queen called the boycott on her deathbed as some sort of Hail Mary pass. She didn't know who killed her."

"It doesn't matter. I want to become a SUM woman next year so I'm not crossing the picket line."

The other girl got up and said, "Fuck the queen!"

The boy and the girl panicked, and surveyed the room. My hat was on. My hood was on. Still, I dropped my head, to look at my drink. I needed them to keep talking. "Chill with that! Max boys are still loyal to the queen. You don't want me to come after you in the future."

She laughed. I glanced up to get a good look at her. The other girl sat as they left the room. I checked my watch. It was almost 7 a.m. I left out of a different exit, one closest to the window. In the distance I saw them running single file. They stopped in front of a building near the campus's main entrance but the building had no access points from the main road. Since one could not drive a car into this portion of the campus, a car would have to circle all the way around and park close to Lauren's dorm. They must have reappeared from the same points they left from last night.

The Max pledge class was nearly finished singing-

Wouldn't you help me sing?
These songs of freedom
'cause all I ever had
was Redemption Songs

The crowd of about seventy students joined them in finishing the song. The Max class entered the building. They went to the very front. Some knelt. Some stood. Some sat. All had open arms. The students followed after them and took places all around the chapel's open area. The chapel reminded me of a cathedral but there were no statues or symbols denoting denomination. Two sections of pews, roughly thirty rows where each row could sit ten worshippers. The room was silent. It remained this way for the duration. Some people left after just a few minutes, including Ernest and Girard who likely had to drive back to Barrington for a morning class. Ted and three others left shortly after.

I left the chapel, processing the different angles this had gone down and what needed to be done. I needed a place to position myself to follow Devon when he left the building. As I stepped outside, I spotted Lauren. Devon's back was turned so I pointed in her direction. There were a couple of students near me and I needed them to tell me the latest gossip without them even thinking. "Oh that's the girl trying to be the SUM of our fears. I feel bad for her. She's trying to stay strong but the other girl is just offering sex to anyone willing to protect her. Her price for protection is way up there too yet no one is willing to take the risk."

I turned in the other direction, trying to process what the girl had said. The Society, SUM women, leaked information as a counter measure. No matter how one broke down the code being put out there, this was a no-win position. The word was out that I was dead, basically asked for war knowing I would not have to fight it. Diane was asking for protection from any man willing to pay. But, Lauren? This was her campus. She would have to deal with this. She had to know, even and especially, in glory, a queen is an easy target.

It was time. Devon jogged along a path leading to the apartments. I followed from a distance. My inkling was they had not slept. This was bed time for those who did not have class until later.

It was too early to go into their student government offices for the names of Free Love Society members. That would raise suspicion. I needed to find a place to blend in and just wait until Devon came out of his apartment building. I walked along the back edge of the campus, behind the core buildings, through the parking lots. I passed the spot where I left my car. No one had parked there. Pretty much all other spots were taken, except that one, as if no one wanted my place or no replacement had been found.

I circled all the way around in the opposite direction from Lauren's dorm. The Student Administration Building was near the lake and another set of dormitories. I sat in such a way that anyone entering the building would be noticed by the people facing me. Their eyes would tell me the person's ranking on the campus's hierarchy. I only cared about a few and needed to see what business, if any, they had in this building. Devon made the call to Attitude's loft. Monk and Bliss were there, and Lauren is letting rumors of my death spread. When I reappear, there will be a notation on my record that I hid during the early days of this war. The only way to fix that would be to produce the identities of the women in the Free Love Society and the person who tried to kill me.

Semline campus, for all its tranquility, was seething underneath due to regimentation, an unstated order. You could be free but only under specific rules. The openness, lack of security checkpoints were all a façade. To walk up and ask the names of those women would send out an alert – that I did not trust Bliss. Lauren vouched for her, and up until an hour or so ago I had no reason to not trust Lauren.

So I stood down and refocused on the Max pledge class, on Devon. I went out into the cold and just walked the campus. Across the lake, people sliding, gliding; the geese under the bare branches, on the edge as if thinking the water froze early this year. I spotted Devon running toward one of the academic buildings. I was certain I could beat him to it or at worst come in behind him. I took off as a strong breeze smacked me in the face. I was a decent runner in both sprint and long distance but at my moderate pace I was gaining on him, I knew something was off, something I could not spot last night. He was favoring his right side, languishing. I stopped cold, turned my back knowing this sort of movement would alert him to look to his right, for the ambush. Two students walked toward me, two white boys wearing school paraphernalia. I asked, "Who's that guy running across the campus?"

They both said, "Oh, that's Devon, the rock of that pledge class."

"Thank you. I'm always thankful for the kindness of strangers."

They smiled and moved on. I walked away, focusing my eyes to the ground as tears streamed down, thinking of Miranda. A part of me wanted to go find Monk. I didn't know what I would say or do, in this moment of anger, sadness and vulnerability. It really would depend on why, how could he leave this campus so open, so unprotected, for a king to lose his crown?

I went to the cafeteria building and found a corner booth to eat my meal. The corner was so I would be visible, if they knew what to look for. The room was packed and loud, a constant stream of people sitting, rising, only to be replaced by a next set.

At 6 p.m., I left the cafeteria and found a spot where I could view Lauren's dorm. I was not there five minutes when she came out and headed to the parking lot behind her building. Roughly 6:30 p.m., each group from the three campuses of the Max class entered the library. I stayed out of there, finding a place in a nearby building that allowed me to monitor the front and back exits, as well as the mid-eastern exit. But there really was no need to monitor exits, for I knew after library hours they would head to the gym for some sort of physical training, be it, weights, sports or fighting. The next step would be the woods to train on how to evade and anticipate your enemy's movements.

The mystery was what happened from 2 a.m. to 7 a.m. chapel time. It was a mystery that no matter how many days I stayed, not showering, only taking birdbaths in public restrooms, rinsing out and rotating my three underwear. On the Semline Campus I had no way of finding out. And to be sure of that, someone took my car. I accepted I was either dead, a prisoner of war or simply stranded at Semline. The only option was to take the bus but to not be able to explain my car's disappearance would force me to have to say we killed that old lady.

I waited. Each day I walked by the empty parking spot, until one day my car reappeared, right after the gym regimen. Someone had given me a new door and a new side view mirror. I dropped my two bags into the back seat and left campus using the main gate, the only one visitors could use.

When I arrived at the SUM house, the first sister who saw me fainted. The second one screamed, "She's alive. She's ALIVE!" People came running from all directions of the house, hugging me. Tears flowed down cheeks. Their words toppled over each other's words.

I asked, "Where are they?"

"In the basement."

I reached the basement and decorations had transformed it. A neon glow, silver streamers, the feel of a gentlemen's club, smoky, dark with red light, a disco ball rotating overhead; it was a skit that had etched itself as an identity...

> *There once was a girl named Nikki.*
> *I guess you can say she was a sex fiend*

"What the hell is going on here?"

"She broke that Friday night you disappeared. We figured someone got to her."

"What about her? Why is she standing there frozen?"

"She's barely moved since that next day. She's refused to leave the basement."

I ordered, "Turn off the lights." I spoke into the microphone. "Put on your clothes and come out of the room. It's over." The sisters were relieved.

Lauren and Diane came out of the room. I hugged them and said, "I'm so sorry for leaving you so open, so unprotected."

Lauren was crying. "I thought you were dead."

"Why? I told you I was leaving and would see you…"

"Yes, but you never showed up and your car was not there. There was no word anywhere."

"I'm fine." I hugged her. I looked at Diane. Her eyes were cold but she was going to hold her tongue about whatever it was. "Are you OK?"

"Are we finished?" Everyone felt the iciness in Diane's voice.

"Yes, but I'm sure all the sisters would love to do the ceremony again since they did not witness it the first time."

"Are you going to say who tried to kill you?"

"No one tried to kill me. I told Lauren this."

Diane looked at Lauren. "So you knew?"

"Look, she denied it. What did you expect me to do?"

"I expect you to tell me the truth, to be truthful. The way we've always been with each other."

I grabbed the two of them and put our heads together. I whispered as low as I could so only they could hear me. "Shut the fuck up, the two of you! No one tried to kill me. OK?"

Neither said a word.

We performed the ceremony.

Chapter 37
BLIND MAN AND THE QUEEN

Barrington's campus had a different energy than the subdued tone at TGI. With Finals Week not yet completed and graduation taking place next weekend at Barrington, it felt like the first week of a new semester. There were so many people milling about the open spaces, many of them carrying beer and liquor from one place to another. Others rode on skateboards and tossed Frisbees. Instead of going to the library steps, I asked the first student who looked to be in the know if she'd seen her. "She's at the playground near the Fine Arts Building."

Diane had more name recognition than she ever wanted.

The sun hung behind them, slightly above the mountains, jagged brown peaks seemingly etched across a flat blue sky. Ernest stood behind her, pushing the swing. Her legs held straight out. Each push elevated her to higher ground. Her laughter swished through the air. He saw me and waved. Even from twenty yards, his wide smile felt warm. The tip of physical fitness, his friendly hug encircled me, pulled me into his rock hard chest. We exchanged a friendly sentence to congratulate each other on our upcoming graduations. He excused himself. "It's time I head to the studio. See you later?"

"Of course." Diane puckered up and he leaned down. She wore a yellow shorts set with patterned suspenders, giving her an innocent, fairy tale look. Her hair was just beginning to grow back to the point where she could spike it up or gel it down. Today she looked as if she rushed out the house after rubbing only a bit of grease on it. "Hi," was all she said.

"Hey sister, I've been trying to reach you."

"I'm usually at Ernest's." I waited, not sure why she was avoiding me. "He lives by himself in an apartment and he says it's more comfortable than mine."

I matched her short laugh and small talk. "So, it's been seven months as a couple?"

"Yep, if we count the month while he was still pledging." She stopped to emphasize the conditional or perhaps the risk he took. "The night of the ceremony, I'd barely reached home and the word was out. The campus was abuzz with people wanting to congratulate me. But I wanted nothing to do with anyone. There was this knock at my door. I felt it." She clutched her hands in front of her heart. "I opened the door to the strongest, most comforting hug."

"Are you avoiding me because of the basement? I told you that..."

"Basement, my number, all that shit was nothing for me to walk through. Nothing, except your death mattered at that point." I made to interrupt her. "If you say what I think you're going to say, I will never speak to you again."

"What is it you want me to say?" I paused. "I have no idea who wants me dead. If that is what happened, then that's fine. It keeps me sharp, though. It keeps me sharp!"

"Forget who ordered it! I'm talking about who called and left the message on my voicemail that they executed the mission." She held back tears. "I remember the first time I heard your name: Hope Kendall. Manny had come by the house. It was Christmas 1985. He told me he was in love and behind the word 'with' was your name. The next time I heard your name, it was May 1987. I got a call from Girard saying some girl named Hope just put out a hit on Manny."

"You have to understand."

Diane's voice was void of emotion, which made her anger more pronounced. "No, I really didn't have to understand. I'm a woman. I know love hurts and that whatever he did to make you make that type of choice, he deserved. Only because he said that he loved you, to me, to me." She paused to look at me, fully, to make me see her full face, the tears welling up in her eyes. "When he found out I took the contract and put it on the board, he promised to never speak to me again. Again, I was fine with that because deep down I knew you would take the hit off, and also no one in Love would take the shot at Manny. That's the trust I share with people."

"The basement changes people. Love changes people. From what I understand she hasn't been the same since she broke up with Frank DeLoose."

"So? She should not be meddling in the SUM of our affairs." I waited for Diane to continue. "First time I saw her. It was at this open tryout for Semline Basketball. Girard walks into the gym but acts like he doesn't know me. I'm not sure why until I see who he goes to sit next to. They weren't too far away. We were in the bleachers. She was a few rows up, sitting there like some queen on a throne, talking about each player's game. My father was impressed, especially when she said Theodore Perkins was the best player on the court. I turned and asked her how much did she want to bet?" Diane left that hanging but I didn't dare ask. She continued, "When I spread the rumor about Lucille Patterson, do you know Bliss had the nerve to call me, to say 'if you can't say his name in public, that he is your man, then you got to let him go to see if he will return'."

"If you had beaten her and still had this rivalry with her, why did you backdoor an application for her to become a SUM woman?"

Diane laughed and gave me the look Ted had, like I was the dumbest person they knew. "Ask anyone at these three schools who's the baddest chick out here, and see what they say." Now it was my turn to laugh. The look on her face made me question and wonder what the obvious answer should be. She continued, "It was the Friday night the MAX class surfaced. Only one person had called the bank to claim the markers on your head. I didn't call back since there was no hardcore evidence you were dead. I got to the basement and Lauren got there a little late. She said you were in her room. I was relieved and told her she had to bring you back to TGI right away. The next day she stalled. She kept stalling. I stayed in the basement because it was not safe for me to leave that house. Someone was trying to find out who was behind the bank." Tears rolled down to her cheeks yet she was emotionless. "I got home from the initiation ceremony and finally got to check my messages. You would not believe how many more people called claiming that money on your head. The rules are the rules. After three days, if a player does not return, the bets must be paid. They took down the house, emptied the bank."

I hugged her, realizing the damage that had been done to Diane. "Bliss did not try to kill me. She didn't call you."

Diane, at first, did not answer but between clenched teeth, she said, "You had a chance to stop her by telling people what she said during the interview. You still have a chance to stop her but you refuse to tell people what happened to you that night."

"Why don't you stop her?"

"I tried but she beats me every time."

"Was Monk the best player that day?"

She raised her voice. "Ernest did not take the correct final shot, so we will never know."

"But, you're with Ernest now. He returned."

She sucked her teeth and wiped away the tears. "I am filled with joy to be with him but I know it's not going to last. I keep asking him for us to move away after graduation, to leave the Society behind. He keeps asking me why I didn't have a coronation like Lauren."

"Yeah, that! You boycotted her coronation. You know how that looked?"

"I ain't bowing to her in public. Chick ain't even make me a Stand-In Queen for her campus."

"Protocol holds. Some people value that. That people who pledge together..."

She interrupted me. "She even wants me to call before coming to visit her at Semline and, of course, to clear my agenda with her for any Semline visit to someone else. Would you do that?"

"Yes. I stopped by here and afterward I'm heading over to Semline."

"You bow to her in public?"

"Yes, it's protocol." I paused and waited for her to agree but she didn't. "What's this about leaving the Society? What's really wrong?"

"Nothing is wrong. I only came to this school to be with Ernest. Your court had certain policies for membership, so I agreed. I had no qualms about just signing my name as a legacy. In fact, it would have been better. My father tried to disown me the moment he realized I wasn't just going to sign my name. I have lost both my father's and brother's backing because of you."

BOOM! It hit me dead in the head, precisely on my forehead. She looked at my eyes and all I could say was, "No, I didn't know."

"It's OK. No one knows."

"Does Manny know?"

"If he does he never lets on. He's still claiming he's Derek Davenport's son."

"But…"

"It wasn't until you came here ready to kill me over Manny and asking questions that I looked into my father's history in the Society's ledger, the years he disappeared. The only way the dots connected was for the two younger children to be Derek Davenport's and the oldest son to be my father's with Manny's mother."

"That explains how Manny came into MAX as a fourth generation legacy from the SBD side."

"Aren't you going to ask me if Manny called to collect the marker on your head?"

I laughed and got up to leave. She rushed up as if to try and stop me. I hugged her and backed away and held her hands. "This thing we're in. It's about family, not just blood relatives. Family has secrets. Family has fights. Most of all family has love. And you know what Diane? I love you sister. I never meant to hurt you."

"I love you too, Hope. I will always love you. Remember I got the names of those who called so when things start rolling downhill…"

"Stop, Diane! Stop!" I started walking toward my car and Diane strolled alongside me. "We all live in this Society with a rumor that stays with us – ruins our reputation even to those outside the Society. Yours is you offered sex for protection. Lauren's is that she tried to kill the Queen. Mine is that I put out a hit on Manny, your brother. None of those are true."

"I got that call from Girard. He said you put out a hit on Manny."

I said it with such force, enough to force her to believe me. "It was a misinterpretation of a message, but I carry that badge of shame. I have to, to protect the Society. Until today, I always thought Manny knew I would never do such a thing." An overpowering sadness flushed over my face. It came and moved so quickly, I had no time to suppress it, to lessen its visibility. "But it's fine. We're fine. Take some time to yourself. Don't dare tell anyone you want to leave the Society!"

"I wouldn't tell anyone. My grandmother taught me well."

"I always wondered why you went under your father's name and not under her legacy."

She told it to me with much hesitation. "My grandmother…Last of the white women…before The Exclusion of 1950…My mother was not allowed to become a SUM woman even though she was a legacy. Her wish was to let this side of our legacy die out. But my grandmother, she is overjoyed I went in, and through The Basement at that."

I nodded and squeezed her hand to acknowledge the delicate nature of the information she'd shared. As I turned to leave, I was surprised to see Nicole standing with a group of people. She must have come for Smiley's graduation. I waved and motioned for her to come over. She made a motion she would call me. Diane laughed. "Let me guess, she's a friend of yours?"

"Yes. She's…"

Diane's laughter gave me doubt. "She and I got into it first month of school…but anyway, as long as you say she's a friend of yours and she remains Girard's woman."

I looked at Diane quizzically, worried that by not asking to have protocol hold on her campus, not formally crowning herself as the queen at Barrington, she was operating from a different power base: invisibility, and requesting a different sort of loyalty and respect. She stopped walking before the turnoff to the parking lot. The straightest distance between her and the closest student could only be walked on a worn-out path, patches of grass and dirt, of what a nasty rumor had done to her name. Only two people knew her number and she never asked if I had told, simply because I had no reason to.

I got in my car. Distance-wise the same number of miles separated the schools, with Barrington to Semline having more backcountry roads, squiggly patterns on a downward mountainous ridge when heading to Semline. The directional signs stated suggested speeds, deer crossings, signal lights ahead, merge and more. On this triangle of roads between the three schools, to cut down in time required not just a steady pace but the willingness to overtake slow drivers whether the roads were one or two lanes on each side with no physical divider. There was also a way to communicate with oncoming cars. For the past few months I had gotten into the habit of going on the road, at first, being the slow driver, listening to how other drivers told me to get out of the way, move left, move right. Sound of the horn and flashing of the lights. A distinct, secret but not hidden communication. I had never driven from Barrington to Semline. The start of this semester was my first solo drive from TGI to Semline.

My first time to Semline, Miranda drove. Returning from Semline that night after I met Monk, I battled the roads, sloped straight, a vortex of fog, the lights of oncoming cars demanding I flush right as much as possible because the other side had no shoulder.

Heading to Semline from TGI for Lauren's coronation gala, I drove slowly, studying the flashing light patterns on both sides of the road, and listening for the length and rapidness of horns. She wore a velvet brown gown and a tiara. I bowed when I came upon her table and handed her a jewelry box. She formally introduced me to Sterling, her king, SBD brother, second generation. I smiled and bowed.

I sat at one of the tables TGI purchased. Many tables filled with family members, octogenarians down to teens, her preferred cut-off age of sixteen. I sat with Miranda, Barbara and Ken and a few others. We marveled at the number of attendees, awed by how Lauren had convinced three years of Semline SBD men to hold off being courted until she made SUM. On the surface, the campus looked to be under SBD control but no one spoke of how no MAX boys were invited to attest to this fact, not even Ernest whose name Diane Henderson had written on her induction papers as her court king. No one spoke of why Diane was not in attendance. Most would think it was due to the MAX boycott which I had yet to officially lift. But, it was well-noted in Matters of Ceremony, Lauren could have invited the Max boys even with the boycott in effect. This was after all her queendom.

People were whispering, prior to but not during Lauren's coronation that Diane had basically crossed the picket line in Matters of Matrimony. I made no fuss about it because I had no problems with any individual MAX boy, especially Ernest. Even then from a policy standpoint, I would have to stand down because just as I had come to accept being queen meant people would try to kill me; putting a hit out on a MAX boy meant the same.

<0>

I listened to the door and heard many voices in the apartment. I could not fess and not knock. With Semline graduation only two days away, a week before the other two schools, the truce would have to happen in this upstate region, the milieu the Society's civil war first started when a MAX boy's carelessness led to my great-grandfather's lynching. Even though she had built up a strong army at Semline, this was not a war I wanted Lauren to have to deal with next semester now that she opted to matriculate an extra year, for graduate school, to build up SUM at Semline. I knocked on the door and multiple voices said, "Come in."

I opened the door and the entire room froze, except for Devon. He rose quickly, still sharp from his Max training; his right arm reflexively dropping as if reaching for a weapon. I smiled and took two steps into the room. I gestured with the customary slight bow used in public amongst strangers as to not give away his identity, that of the king of the Max pledge class. "Congratulations! I didn't get a chance to see you last time I was on campus."

"Thank you." He smiled and reached out to me for a hug.

I introduced myself to the two women in the room: Lucille and Simone. They attended Barrington. We exchanged simple handshakes. I leaned down to hug Frank. Leroi stood to hug me while Monk remained seated on the couch. Out of all them, he seemed the most shocked to see me. I bent down and planted a kiss on his right cheek, leaving my mouth slightly open so the wetness of my tongue could leave a clue.

The silence in the room was loud, air being suppressed. I turned and sat in Monk's grandfather's chair and you could hear at least two of them gasp and swallow their words, inhaling deeply to stifle the coughing spasm dying to escape. They all looked at me, not at Monk, because they could not believe his silence. I took in the living room's décor, the semi-open kitchen with the chef's window. I took out a large bag of weed from my bag. "Can someone fix me a drink?"

Devon was still standing in the same spot.

Leroi and Frank were staring at me like I was the boldest chick they'd ever seen - to have the nerve to walk in, to a finish a four-year old conversation.

Lucille finally spoke up. "I will check what's available. What do you drink?"

"Pour me whatever is the finest. No ice and the best beer they have." She got up and went to the kitchen. "What are y'all watching?"

Devon answered, "House Party but we're talking over it."

"Oh OK. I really just came by to congratulate you all on graduating. In four years at that."

Lucille walked over. "This is Hennessy and here's a Heineken."

I looked at Monk. "So, aren't you going to ask me?" I finished rolling the first joint and handed it to Leroi who was on my left. "What about you Frank?"

"How would you know?" asked Frank.

"I heard the question was out there. So, I put my nose in it." I got up and handed Simone the second joint, skipping Devon and Lucille, indicating I knew a little about their politics. "The tournament game was not fixed. The money shifted away from Barrington when Ernest decided not to play his last season. Even though Semline was the favorite to win the conference, the money split evenly throughout the conference. The TGI odds I can't explain because I don't bet on sports."

As I made to hand the next joint to Frank, Devon spoke up. "I got this one." He asked a question that could be interpreted two ways: the actual way he asked, and the coded way Society members spoke to each other. "What were the markers?"

"From what I understand forty thousand at one thousand a piece over a four-year period."

"You don't think that shit was fixed? How the hell do you bet from four years out on who's gonna make what shots and win the game?" Leroi answered but he didn't fully understand what I had just told Devon and presumably Monk.

I looked at Frank and then turned to Monk and said, "You should have been on the team from day one."

Frank answered, "Yeah, the fucking coach is a buster, said Monk was not coachable and that's why he didn't pick him for the squad." Monk was seething with anger. Frank continued, "So, Hope, are you saying the coach wrecked our chances on purpose?"

By now I had rolled a joint for each person including myself, except Lucille.

I had to frame my answer so that it addressed both Frank's and Monk's concerns. "I'm saying the game is not over. You didn't lose anything. I know there will be some lingering bitterness for how things played out, but

Monk did the right thing."

Frank got up to go to the kitchen and gave Monk a hard five, hand-slap-shake combination. Monk finally spoke. "Nah, had I shook Girard's hands, Ernest would have ended up going to school here at Semline and y'all would have won all four years."

The room fell silent. Frank turned. "What do you mean?"

Monk continually tapped his chin with his right index finger. "The game was rigged but in our favor. I blew it for you. I blew it."

I wanted to say something but it would have blown the room to pieces so I stayed quiet as Frank said, "Nah man, life's not like that. Things happen the way they do. Plus, I told you that scout offered me ten G's to throw the game."

Everyone was quiet like this was a road they had been traveling for months. Frank stopped himself and Monk said, "I didn't shake Girard's hand because of Bliss."

Coming from Monk the words didn't have the velocity, the ferocity they would have had had they come out of my mouth. They all laughed and Leroi said, "Not this again!" He looked over to me. "This Bliss versus Monk saga has been going on for years."

I tested the waters. "I heard she's the baddest chick in the region."

Simone was the first to balk. "The fuck outta here!"

Others simply laughed to show agreement with her. I pried further. "So, who's the baddest?"

You could tell Simone had herself in the running by how she couched her words with a caveat. "It depends on what we're playing for and measuring by."

"Love."

"Oh, that's easy. Diane Henderson. That chick pined for Ernest for four years of college and throughout high school, and has threatened or tried to kill any chick who's come near him."

Devon tried to stop her. "Yo, hold up! That's my brother's woman."

I didn't let Devon stop the conversation's flow because Simone had said something foreign. At the same time, I had to be careful how I got a SUM sister's record out in the open without it looking like I started the gossip. "I'm sure she gave someone else some play in between."

"Nope! White as the virgin snow!"

I looked at Lucille Patterson who was nursing a glass of white wine to see if she would throw her name in the running against Diane. I turned to Monk who quickly said, "Nah, Diane, she good, at least to me!"

Frank quickly boxed him in. "Come on Monk, that chick was there that day. She was fine as hell and on that light-bright spectrum you prefer. And you never went for yours."

"See that's the kind of dude I am." Monk stood, took a pull on the joint as he walked toward the kitchen. "It was clear Diane came for Ernest. Girard picked Bliss the minute he walked in. My game was on the court."

Fuck it, I decided to roll the dice. "I heard Bliss thought you were the best player on the court."

"I was."

"No you weren't." Frank jumped in real quickly. "Coach wanted you and Owen to make the squad so he gave me, Ernest and the other varsity players the hint to not play our hardest."

Monk laughed. "Then I guess the tournament game wasn't fixed."

That low blow silenced the room. The politics within this circle perhaps was more ruthless than I assumed. I looked at Simone and Lucille but my question was for Monk who was about to take a seat. "So, you got everyone paired up so I'm curious…"

He interrupted me because I was the wrong person to ask the question and he knew the women in the room would feel slighted. "Nah, I don't have everyone paired up as if love's not a gamble. I'm just saying Society has rules, laws, a flow to which we must abide, and on that day, I let Pride get in the way of the Strength we could have had as one team."

I took a quick glance at Devon who shifted just a little bit, giving hint he had never heard Monk utter those words together, never heard Monk use the Society's code. I remained quiet, knowing the others had no idea what

Monk had just said.

Frank tried again. "Monk, tell them what Diane Henderson said to you that day."

Monk had everyone's attention. "It was way after the tryouts. I was sitting on the bottom bleachers, boosters ignoring me and shit. People who had been in the stands were on the court mingling, getting to know the players. You and Bliss were joking around on the other side of the gym. Diane's father returned from outside without Ernest. He walked by without looking in my direction and went straight to Coach Overton. A few minutes later Diane walked back into the gym and stopped in front of me, wearing these tight-ass jeans, crotch all in my face. She said, bet your life savings on TGI in four years."

"Well, did you?" All of them looked at me except Simone, who was looking at Monk.

The guys waved their hands at me, to dismiss me, as if not believing Diane Henderson could have predicted the future.

We all left the conversation at that.

It was nearing 10 p.m. and I had been there for seven hours. I really liked hanging with them. They were the college crew I never cultivated. I'd made the Society my entire life. We were encouraged to mingle, make best friends outside the Society and Monk had done that. The other three guys had different ways about them. The two women were hard reads especially Lucille. Simone had that don't give a fuck attitude as if she didn't know, didn't care of my link to Diane. It was her way of letting me know Diane had made plenty of enemies and all of them over Ernest.

It was weird like everyone was waiting for me to leave, until they realized why I had come.

They had to leave, even Frank who lived in the apartment with Monk. "Come on Simone, let's head out."

"I'm in no condition to drive."

"We'll go hang over at Devon's."

She caught on but Leroi hadn't unless I missed some signal Monk had thrown him. "Come on Hope, you can crash by me so you don't have to drive back tonight."

I smiled. "That's so sweet but I'm fine."

"Is that a forever no or a raincheck?"

"Put it this way, I will leave you something in my will." They all laughed. He extended his hand to give me five. I grabbed it to pull myself up and gave him a big hug and a kiss on the cheek. "Congratulations on graduation!"

I walked to each person and did pretty much the same thing. There was a mix of confusion, kudos on my being so bold, etc…going on. "Bye Hope!"

As soon as they all left, I walked up to Monk. He was still seated. "I need to take a shower. Do you have washcloth and towel?"

He stood and looked questioningly at me. I lifted my crew neck long sleeve t-shirt over my head and unhooked my bra. Monk looked into my eyes, still curious as to what I wanted. I undid my jeans and came out of my underwear. I stood with hands behind my back and even though my face was leveled and forward, he lifted my chin to kiss me.

I picked my clothes off the floor along with my large pocketbook. Monk handed me towels from the linen closet in the hall and I shut the bathroom door to shower.

I came out to hear him cleaning up the living room and kitchen. He heard my footsteps and came down the hall. He looked at my face, playfully inspecting my eyes, nose, ears and mouth. "You're scrubbed so clean I guess I have to wash up."

I nodded and went into his bedroom. It was larger than I anticipated and looked larger because his bed was pushed right near the window. I got on the bed, relaxed as if I had spent dozens of nights with him. Still, my heart raced with anticipation. The night lamps were on their lowest setting. Monk entered the room and the hall light had only given me a glimpse of what I thought I saw on his left rib cage. Once he closed the door, I could see the forming muscles as if he had let his slim muscular build go flabby when he hadn't made the team, and now set to enter life after college, he was preparing to undress in front of strangers. He got on the bed on my left side. With his right elbow supporting him, he kissed tenderly. I grabbed his face to mine because I wanted all of him in me. In my mouth, his tongue…but I could not help myself. I touched his rib to confirm. He stopped and asked, "What? Do I need protection from you?"

"No. No of course not. It's just that." I stopped myself and rolled him on to his back. Monk was strong, forceful and exploded inside me with force each time he came. There was a trust he was showing me that I wanted, that I was certain I would not have been ready for years ago.

We woke in the morning and neither made any motions of awkwardness, no hint that it was time to part ways. The morning was different. We made love; the rhythm was precise, caring. I nestled my forehead in the crook of his neck, nibbled on his shoulder blades. He squeezed me his tightest, making jazzy circles as I held his back, his side. After the last go around, after we had spent all energy, when it was clear time it was Saturday 4 p.m. and preparations needed to be made for our separate graduations, I lowered my face into my right palm and shouted, "What are you doing with the SBD brand on your body?"

He was standing in his boxer briefs near the window. "Perkins men always wear this brand."

"Not possible! Fourth generation and Eighth generation. Every four generations, those are the only times a legacy's side can be changed."

"Who said anything about changing sides? I'm PMB forever."

"Then you should not have the SBD brand."

"Really? Your family just reached its fourth generation. Observe for a generation and get back to me." I remained quiet because Monk pulled no punches, the reason I'd stayed clear all these years. He made light of the stand still. "Plus, no one has dared tell us Perkins any differently."

"Do you love me Monk?"

"Yes."

"No! I mean really, really love me, like you can't live without me?"

"You never gave me a chance."

"You know what? My fault. You're right." I got up to dress. "Did you give up your legacy because of me?"

He was quiet like this was the real moment of trust. "No, we left the king, Devon in this case, unprotected, as part of a bigger mission."

I said, "And, they broke his rib!"

"Had they not done so, I heard you would have shot him dead in the quad in broad daylight. Right?" His words stunned me to silence. "Don't worry! He accepted the risks."

"But, Miranda! People will think that's her work."

"What does it matter? Devon knows it's not her. Plus, she seemed proud of her reputation as a king-killer when Ken lost his crown."

The moment cemented how dangerous Monk, Manny and the Max boys were. Their idea of protection was, in basketball terms, a speed offense; in football, a run and shoot. To them, the best defense was a powerful offense. "The difference is Ken is SBD. He has an army and Barbara, a SUM queen."

Monk pulled my card. "What they did to Devon, they did the same to Manny Davenport and then he met you and he thought he had a SUM queen. He needed a woman he could trust with his life. He needed a wife for the mission."

"Oh, what? You think Bliss is my substitute? You think Bliss is the baddest chick out here?"

"I don't get into these games. All the little games you and the rest of them were into these last four years."

"Little games?" I couldn't hide my shock. "You think my putting my life on the line was a small matter? I gambled all of you would stay loyal to each other and to me, and not try to kill me."

"Yes, it's quite simple. Make a phone call. Make a dozen! Ask any of these motherfuckers who the baddest dude up here is. Go ahead!"

"And what, I ain't the baddest chick up here?"

"Of course you are. But each time you get into one of these little tiffs, all you're doing is making your opponent stronger, unless you kill them off, which you haven't done."

I approached him. "Are you picking me?"

"I picked you four years ago."

"Based on what?"

"The party when Devon met Miranda. You knocked his hands off. I was in awe that you would take a backseat to and protect a sister of lesser rank. I asked Devon to have Miranda introduce us." He shook his head and sat on the bed, next to me, faced me. "The first time I met you, breathed the same air as you in a closed room, misconceptions be gone, preferences out the window. I saw my grandmother, the kind of woman I could grow old with. But then you went against her, your line sister."

"You sat out four years of my life and now what?"

"You came here. You tell me."

"To say congratulations. Have sex! Nothing more."

"That's fine. It really is." He looked at me with no acrimony. He grabbed me to him and kissed my forehead. "It's fine. We list our names together as a royal courtship but there are no expectations, except that Strength and Pride are united. A truce."

"But you are not in the Historical Record as having taken the MAX oath!"

"Didn't you do the same with Lauren and Diane for three years?" He laughed at my shock that he knew this. "Put my name as XYZ, a redacted entry if it makes you more comfortable, until the day I'm official."

I nodded to agree, gave him a soft kiss on the lips and held him just a little longer. "Again, congratulations on your graduation."

"And you on achieving your Master's."

I turned to leave and he rushed to put on pants and a t-shirt. "You don't have to walk me to my car."

He laughed. "You're a funny chick."

"I mean, being that I have all these enemies, I wouldn't want you to get caught in the crossfire." Monk walked outside and without prodding turned in the direction I was parked, the same direction and space I parked when I was stranded. "Answer me one thing. Did you bet on TGI this past season?"

"Yes really big, four years ago, on TGI to win this past season. I also won big on Barrington my freshman year."

"You really can't see what's going on out here, can you?"

"No, and I don't really care to."

"It doesn't bother you that people are gambling their life away for love? To prove love is stronger than pride?"

Monk hesitated and put his hands in his pants pockets. I needed him to confide in me, that he would live by the oath. "I'm a seventh generation MAX boy by birth. That's my legacy. I am blind to the ways of the queen. If that's not good enough for you, then I don't know what to tell you."

We got to my car and he stopped before I did. I looked at my car and at him. I waited for him to know how he slipped up. But then again, I thought maybe it wasn't a slip up; just our little secret. "I love you Monk."

"I love you too Hope."

We squeezed hands, my left, his right. I got in my car to return to TGI. This time I decided to not use the visitor's exit to leave the Semline campus.

THE END

About The Author

G. Dan Buford grew up in New York City and has spent many years residing in other parts of the country. Though he hopes this new novel is well-received, he is still weighing the differences between writing in obscurity versus infamy.

Please visit www.thebufordnovels.com for information.

www.ingramcontent.com/pod-product-compliance
Lightning Source LLC
Chambersburg PA
CBHW032136270626
47172CB00008B/67